A DEATH IN MAYFAIR

MARK ELLIS

ACCENT

First published in 2019 by Headline Accent
An imprint of HEADLINE PUBLISHING GROUP

1

Cataloguing in Publication Data is available from the British Library

ISBN 978 1 7861 5 6723

Typeset in 10.5/13pt Bembo Std by Jouve (UK), Milton Keynes

Printed and bound in Great Britain by Clays Ltd, Elcograf S.p.A.

HEADLINE PUBLISHING GROUP
An Hachette UK Company
Carmelite House
50 Victoria Embankment
London EC4Y 0DZ

www.headline.co.uk
www.hachette.co.uk

To Ivor and Alice Maud Morgan

A pound, of course, went a good deal further in 1941 than it does today. There are different ways of analysing equivalent vales but, as a rule of thumb, a 1941 pound would be worth 40 times more today. The 1941 exchange rate for dollars to sterling was roughly four to one. Thus £1,000 in 1941 would be worth approximately £40,000 or $160,000 in today's money.

Chapter One

Friday December 5th 1941
London

It was an hour before dawn when the officers gathered at the street corner. Their target was ten doors down the terrace. Clouds of frozen breath trailed off into the darkness above them. Across the way a parked cart stank of the horse manure stored under its tarpaulin covers. A cat wailed in the distance.

They were seven. Merlin and his men, Johnson and Cole, and four uniformed constables from the local East End station. Merlin examined faces with his torch. Everyone was tensed for action. He raised his right hand. They all knew the drill and moved silently down the road towards the house.

The two stockiest constables carried a compact battering ram, a heavy iron tube with a large rounded end. They waited for a whispered 'Yes' from Merlin before smashing it into the front door. After four blows the policemen were able to clamber into the unlit hallway. There they were met by panicked screams, shouts, and the sound of frantic footsteps. In the midst of this came the unmistakable noise of gunfire. One of the constables fell to the ground, and the other policemen took cover. More shots lit up the air but none hit home. When the firing stopped, Merlin's torch picked out several shadowy figures racing up the stairs.

'Inspector Johnson, take Cole and one of the constables and follow. You two others search the ground floor. For Christ's sake

1

be careful. I'll check on the lad here.' Merlin knelt down to the stricken constable who was conscious but clearly in pain.

'It's my arm, sir.'

Merlin found the wound a couple of inches above the elbow. 'It looks like it's just a flesh wound, lad. I'll tie something around it. We'll call the medics as soon as we can.'

Merlin made a makeshift tourniquet with his handkerchief, squeezed the man's hand then headed up the stairs. The first and second floors were clear. On the third and final floor the stairs opened onto a large space, unfurnished save for a heavy metal bed frame in the middle of the room. Two unhappy-looking men were standing handcuffed to the bed under the gaze of a constable.

'That was quick work, officer.'

'They tripped over each other, sir, and fell flat on their faces. We were right on them so it was easy, really. Two others got out onto the roof, though.' There was a noise from behind and Merlin turned to see Cole climbing out of a window with Johnson about to do the same.

Merlin followed his men out onto the roof and found them with his torch scrambling along the gables to his right. The terrace was a long one with interconnected roofs. They were not steeply cambered but the surface was icy and treacherous. Gunshots suddenly rang out from somewhere and Merlin ducked and braced himself against the wall beneath the window. A bullet whizzed past his ear and thudded into the window casement. He waited a moment then edged carefully along the brickwork. The moon came out from behind some clouds and he saw his men lying flat twenty yards ahead. There was another shot and, to his surprise, he saw one of his men rise and return fire. Someone screamed and a heavy clattering sound followed. Merlin's heart was pounding as he skidded from his cover to a chimney pot ten yards further along. He shone his torch again and saw a man racing away in the distance with his officers in pursuit. A loud animal cry from below made Merlin jump; he went to the roof edge and pointed his torch down. A motionless body was spreadeagled in an alleyway and something was crawling over it. He had little religious belief these days but by reflex he made a sign of the cross. Then Johnson was shouting for him, and he turned and hurried on.

His men were on the roof of the furthest house, looking down. 'It's no good, sir' said Johnson. 'He's hopped it down the drainpipe. Cole here wanted to follow him down but I said it was too dangerous.'

'I'm sure I can manage it, sir. He looked like he was limping before he went down. If I go now, he won't have got far.'

Merlin edged forward and saw the drainpipe. 'Sorry, Constable. The Inspector is right. It's not a risk worth taking. We've bagged two of them, at least. The other fellow you were chasing has had it. From your bullet or the fall I'm not sure. Where did you get the gun?'

'One of those two inside was carrying it and I pocketed it,' answered Johnson.

'Good thing you did, or one or both of you might have copped it. There'll be some tedious questions to answer but you were clearly within your rights to fire.'

Back in the house, they found their two captives complaining loudly. Both men were heavily built. The older and taller of the two had a tuft of grey hair above each ear but was otherwise bald. He looked menacingly at Merlin. 'I should have known it would be you, you dago bastard.'

'Nice to see you too, Mr Young. Who's your handsome friend?'

The second man was younger with pock-marked olive skin, heavily oiled black hair, a snub nose and a thick moustache. Merlin was reminded of a picture of a young Joe Stalin he'd seen once.

'Ah, Yes. Let me guess. You'd be Boris Orlov. Our Bulgarian import. Pleased to meet you. Frank Merlin.'

The man launched a gobbet of spit at him, but Merlin had kept his distance and it fell short.

'Careful, please. I only just cleaned my shoes.' Merlin turned to the constable. 'Any idea how the others have got on downstairs?'

'One of the officers came up a moment ago, sir. There was only one other person in the house, as far as he could tell, but he got out through the back door and they lost him in the dark. They did, however, find something in the basement. Something he thought would please you.'

'That sounds intriguing. Have they called for an ambulance and transport?'

'Yes, sir. On the way.'

Merlin turned back to their captives. 'Anything to say before we get you off to the Yard? No? The constable here will continue to keep you company until the Black Maria arrives. Meanwhile, I suppose I'd better go and see what's in the basement.'

On the ground floor, one of the constables was busy tending to the injured man. He pointed to a door under the stairs. 'Down there, sir.'

Merlin led the way into a dark and narrow stairwell. The other constable was waiting for them at the bottom. A single bulb hung from the basement ceiling and revealed a room crammed with wooden crates. Some were covered with dirty white cloth, and others with green blankets. Johnson pulled off a cover. Candlesticks, candelabra and similar objects filled the crate to the top. Another uncovered crate held a treasure trove of silver and gold plate. A third was full of expensive-looking rugs. Merlin estimated there were around thirty crates in the room.

'It seems we have discovered Ali Baba's treasure with you cast in the role of Aladdin, Constable.'

The young officer blushed but the light was too dim for anyone to notice. 'There's a ceiling hatch over in the corner, sir. The goods must have been brought in through there. I looked outside. The hatch opens into a back alley, part of which is gated off.'

'I see. Well, we'll need some help sorting this stuff.' Footsteps sounded outside. 'Ah. With luck that's it arriving now.'

Three uniformed officers came in. Merlin knew one of them. 'Bloody hell, Vernon, is that you? How the hell are you? Must be four or five years at least.'

'Six, sir. Blackmail case in Hoxton. You weren't quite so grand then.'

Merlin looked at Johnson and Cole as he slapped the man on the back. 'Sergeant Hooper and I go way back. We were in the Met football team together fifteen or so years ago. Finest wing half I've ever seen.'

'You weren't such a bad player yourself, Chief Inspector.'

Merlin sighed. 'Happy days, Vernon. We'll have to make time to catch up at some point. For the moment, though, unfortunately, there's a ton of work to do. I'd appreciate it if you could take charge of the scene. Once forensics have done a once over I'll need you to take a full inventory. Once we've got the villains upstairs on their way to the Yard, and our wounded man off to hospital, the constable here and his two fellow officers can stay and help you. That alright?'

It was teatime on a bleak autumn day. The cold, the solitude, and the relentless soughing of the wind in the trees were wearing the young woman's nerves down. And she was afraid. Her eyes darted nervously back and forth between the front door and the solitary window on the other side of the room. The lamplight ebbed and flowed. She was in a part of the deep countryside where electrical power was unpredictable. The Jane Austen she'd been reading had been set aside. She was just sitting. Sitting and waiting. A flash of lightning illuminated the room and put her heart in her mouth. She hurried over to the door to check yet again that it was securely locked.

The wood fire had almost gone out. There were more logs in a shed behind the cottage but she couldn't contemplate going outside. Thunder rolled and there was another flash of lightning. She thought she saw a figure outlined in the yard. A third flash confirmed someone was there. A man was approaching the door. She waited with bated breath for a knock, but none came. Then a fist exploded through the glass of the window. The fist held a knife. She screamed.

'And cut it! Wonderful Jean, darling. And you Michael. And very well done effects. We'll take a little break there. Back in fifteen everybody.'

An elegant middle-aged man appeared from behind the cottage wall and crossed the film set to his co-star. 'Very good scream, darling. Am I really so frightening?'

Jean Parker, a striking blonde with large oval green eyes and a small but full-lipped mouth laughed. Her laughter had a certain musicality to it. It was one of the many things Michael Adair found attractive in her.

'You are a terrifying ogre, Mr Adair. Or so I understand from the script.'

Adair leaned towards her and kissed her on both cheeks.

'None of that, please. You're going to cause extra work for make-up.' Emil Kaplan, the director, waved an admonishing finger then sat down in the canvas chair bearing his name and wiped his perspiring forehead with a handkerchief. He reached into his jacket pocket and took out a hip flask. 'Drink you two?'

'Too early for me, Emil' said the actress.

'I'll take one, old chap.' Adair took a swig and then another. 'Very nice too. Talisker if I'm not mistaken?'

'Special Reserve 1931. I'm down to my last case.'

'You poor darling.' Jean Parker sat on the left of the director and Adair on the right. She yawned. It was only nine thirty but they'd already been on set for three hours. 'Will it be another early start on Monday?'

'Afraid so, my dear. You know Victor's desperate to get the film in ze can as soon as possible.' Kaplan had almost eliminated all signs of his Hungarian accent during the thirteen years he had worked in England. He looked, dressed and sounded as if he had been to Eton and Cambridge. There was, still, the very occasional slip.

Adair crossed his legs. 'I don't believe I'm in the first scene you have scheduled for Monday morning, old chap.'

'Quite right, Michael. You can come in at nine.'

'So kind.' Adair produced a cigarette case and lit up. As he did so he glanced at his reflection in the polished silver cover. He had been a preposterously good-looking young man, with high cheek-bones, soft large brown eyes and a strong cleft chin. He was now 42 and ageing well, with only the odd wrinkle here or there bearing witness to a hedonistic and pampered film star's life. As his eyes moved on to the exquisite face of his co-star and lover there was a loud bang from the rear of the studio. He turned to see a flurry of technicians congregating around a lighting gantry which had collapsed to the ground. An angry male voice roared out from the gloom.

'Watch out, for goddam sake. That's expensive equipment. Not to mention you might have killed someone.'

The culprit, a young stagehand, slunk away and the owner of the voice bustled out of the shadows and towards the set. Clouds of cigar smoke accompanied him.

'So there you all are. How goes it?'

Unlike Kaplan, Victor Goldsmith could never be mistaken for an Englishman. His accented voice however had an assuredness and charm which was very British, the fruit of many years spent in the company of the English-monied and aristocratic classes.

'Are we still on schedule, Emil?'

Kaplan rose to shake his boss's hand. 'Almost, Victor. We have a couple of days to make up but "Murder at Midnight" should be wrapped before Christmas as you wish.'

Adair rose languidly from his chair. 'Are we still going with that title, Victor. It has always seemed a little banal to me.'

'Banal?' Goldsmith pronounced it to rhyme with 'ale'. 'You always are one for the fancy words, aren't you Michael? Well, yes, I like the title "banal" or not. Titles with "murder" or "death" in them usually do well in my experience, eh Emil? Besides, that was the title of the book on which the film is based, and the "banal" title didn't stop it being a runaway bestseller, now did it?'

Adair held his hands up defensively. 'Sorry, Victor. Forget I said anything. You're the boss after all.'

7

Goldsmith turned back to Kaplan. 'I understand we are running over budget?'

'Only by about five per cent, Victor.'

'"Only five per cent" is a lot of money, Emil.'

'Not in the same league as Swanton, though.'

Goldsmith threw his hands in the air. 'My God, Swanton. Don't remind me of him, Emil! That film went over by thirty per cent.'

'That was . . . unfortunate.'

Goldsmith glared. 'Unfortunate! It was a bloody disaster.' He looked at Jean Parker and his features softened. 'You are looking particularly wonderful today, my dear. Glowing indeed.'

'Why, thank you, good sir.'

Goldsmith grasped the actress's right hand and kissed it. Goldsmith was a portly man of medium height, dressed today, as always, in a charcoal grey three piece suit, a fob watch hanging at his round belly. His thick hair was black with flecks of grey and he had strikingly bushy eyebrows. His face had the broad and blunt rough features of the Lithuanian peasant smallholder he might have been. It was 'a face of character', as his dear wife put it. And Viktor Shimon Goldschmidt had indeed required a good deal of character, not to mention balls of steel, to make his long and successful journey away from the impoverished shtetl of his birth. A journey which had brought him in due course to this advanced studio complex by the banks of the Thames, a few miles to the west of Windsor, and to the exalted position of Chairman, Managing Director and principal shareholder of Silver Screen Studios, one of Britain's leading film companies.

A blanket of smoke briefly obscured Goldsmith's face. When it appeared again, he was looking at Adair. 'Yes, Michael. Thirty per cent over budget on a simple little Archie Tate film. How could anyone do that?'

'Hard to imagine his type of humour requiring lavish expenditure.'

'Quite so, Michael. A simple little film set in the country. A

8

little location work in Somerset, the rest in the studio. A supporting cast of his usual old music hall buddies, a handsome supporting leading man and a few pretty girls. No expensive actors apart from Tate himself. Hard to imagine going a penny over budget on such a picture. But Swanton managed it comfortably. If I did a really thorough audit, I'd no doubt find a good portion of the overspend went down his throat. However, he knows I won't bother because he's Archie's favourite crony and the film will make a bomb anyway.'

A studio hand brought a fourth canvas chair into which Goldsmith carefully eased his large backside. 'So all is going well? This little film noir should grab the audience's attention, I think, eh Emil?'

'I hope so, Victor.'

Goldsmith's overgrown brows rose. '"Hope" Emil? I do not deal in "hope"! I deal in certainty. Certainty of success. Oh, yes, I'll concede there has been the odd failure along the way but overall, I think, my record speaks for itself. I have had to make compromises, naturally. By putting out Tate's vulgar humour I make the profits to invest in films of higher quality like this one, or that new Dickens film I have you pencilled in for shortly, Emil.'

Michael Adair looked ingratiatingly at Goldsmith. 'I'm in that one, too, aren't I?'

'Yes, Michael, as you know very well. I've already advanced you half the fee, haven't I?'

Adair turned away awkwardly.

'And you too, Jean darling. I haven't quite worked out the rest of the casting for *Bleak House* yet. I'm hoping to get Priestley to do some work on the screenplay.' Goldsmith clapped his hands excitedly. 'That will be one in the eye for the Kordas! I love them all dearly but I detest their presumption that they are the only British producers capable of creating great artistic films. I'm going to out-Korda the Kordas! I'll raise Silver Screen Studios above them, above that baker Rank, above Balcon, above them all. You'll see.'

9

Goldsmith took a final puff on his cigar then snapped a finger. A lackey hurried over to remove the stub. The portly producer got to his feet. 'Well, I'll let you all get back to work. I'm sure you'll get a lot done today. I believe that ....' A young messenger hurried up and interrupted him with a telegram. Goldsmith found his spectacles and read it. Then he frowned, stuffed the cable in his pocket and disappeared without another word.

Merlin's old Swiss office clock had just cuckooed ten o'clock when Merlin came through the door. He threw his hat and coat onto the coat stand then fell into his chair. His eyes closed and he considered the morning so far. The raid had been a success, but when he thought about the guns he realised how lucky they'd been. Things could have gone disastrously wrong. Fortunately, it looked like the injured constable was not badly hurt, and they had a roomful of stolen goods and two relatively big fish gangsters in custody.

He opened his eyes and saw the framed photograph now taking pride of place on his desk. His wedding day on a sultry August morning just over three months before. Somehow or other, the dark outfit Sonia had worn had successfully disguised her pregnancy, although all in attendance had been perfectly aware of her circumstances. He picked up the frame. The black and white photograph could not really do justice to Sonia, with her glorious auburn hair and charming freckled cheeks. She still looked gorgeous and he didn't look too bad either, he thought, with all due modesty. Merlin's barbershop visit on the wedding day morning had eradicated most of the grey specks from his hair. His face had angular features, a noble straight nose, and a generous mouth. He looked good as his lively eyes looked down from his six feet plus on his beautiful new bride. They looked what they were – a very happy couple. Others in the photo outside Chelsea Register Office included Sergeant Sam Bridges, his best man, and his wife, Iris. Assistant Commissioner Gatehouse was there in morning suit and wing-collar, displaying one of his gummy smiles to the camera and accompanied by Mrs Gatehouse. Merlin's brother Charlie was on the right in his wheelchair with wife and young son behind, and next to them were Sonia's parents and brother Jan, smart in his RAF pilot's uniform. Peter Johnson was there on the left, without Mrs Johnson who was out of London. WPC Clare Robinson and her new barrister beau were to Johnson's right, while the heads of DC Tommy Cole and a few other friends could just be seen in the back row.

Merlin suddenly realised he hadn't spoken to Sonia since Tuesday. He'd had a ton of work but that was no excuse. She'd given birth, a little prematurely, three weeks ago to a fine baby boy. All had gone smoothly, but Sonia was naturally anxious as a first time mother. Because Merlin was very busy, they had decided it might be best for Sonia to spend the first few weeks of the baby's life with her parents. Accordingly they arranged for Sonia and the boy to travel to the North of England where her parents had now settled. Sonia and her family were refugees from Poland who had managed to get away just before the Nazi invasion. Her Jewish father, Peter Sieczko, had been a highly-regarded metallurgist in Warsaw, but had struggled to get a job in England. Eventually, in the summer of 1941, he'd obtained a good position at an aircraft component factory just outside Manchester. He and his wife had rented a comfortable little cottage in open countryside not far from the factory, and the new grandparents were delighted to take Sonia and the baby in for a few weeks.

As Merlin was considering what would be the best time to call her, the telephone rang and the stern voice of the AC's secretary, Miss Stimson, came on the line. 'Chief Inspector Merlin? Mr Gatehouse would appreciate a word.'

'I've only just got in. Can you give me half an hour?'

'I rather think he would like to see you immediately.'

Merlin put the phone down with a grunt of irritation then set off on the short journey upstairs to the AC's office. Ignoring the secretary's cold stare, he walked through her outside office, knocked perfunctorily on the AC's door, and entered without waiting for a reply.

Assistant Commissioner Gatehouse was a gaunt, lanky man in late middle age, attired in his usual uniform of black jacket, striped trousers, wing collar and dull dark tie. He was at his desk, peering at a document held about an inch away from him. He glanced up. 'Ah, there you are, Chief Inspector. Come and sit down.' He put the document down with a sigh of annoyance. 'I think I need new spectacles. Either that or whoever typed this has a typewriter with smaller characters than my secretary's machine.'

'Something interesting?'

'Not particularly. It's a paper from the Home Office. They are increasing their budget for internment of enemy aliens.'

'They're expecting to round up more?'

'It appears so.' He looked intently at Merlin. 'Anyway . . . to business. I gather your raid this morning went well?'

The AC had an extraordinarily efficient bush telegraph, the speed of which never ceased to amaze Merlin. 'I think you could say so, sir. The only qualification on its success might be that we arrested only two of the five criminals in the house.'

'One man died, I believe?'

'Yes, sir.'

'How?'

'The two men trying to escape on the roof had revolvers and were shooting at us. Johnson had removed a gun from one of the men already apprehended and used it to return fire. He downed one of the men who then fell from the roof. The second fellow escaped down a drainpipe, and another escaped through the back of the house. The good thing is that the men we caught are quite high up in the gang. And, as you've no doubt heard, we found a large stash of stolen goods.'

The AC looked pleased. His lips parted, revealing mottled gums and an array of yellow teeth. 'Glad to hear it, Frank. A most disgusting racket if ever there was one. Preying on unfortunates in such a foul way. Utterly deplorable. Deplorable!'

'Yes, sir.'

The racket in question was an increasingly pervasive wartime swindle. The country was overflowing with refugees from Europe. Many Jews and others unpopular with Hitler or Stalin had escaped to Britain, just like Merlin's own dear Sonia. The majority had arrived destitute or close to destitute, but some had managed to get their money and possessions to Britain. Most of the refugees had suffered at the hands of organisations like the SS, the Gestapo or the KGB. In consequence the sight of uniformed figures of authority, even the bottle blue of the British constabulary, was a matter for dread. The gangsters' evil scheme exploited this fear. They targeted refugee families known to possess something worth having. Uniformed thugs, representing themselves as police officers, would visit their houses, query the authenticity of the family's papers and insist they come away for questioning. The petrified refugees would be driven away to some distant place while other gang members would move in to their empty homes and ransack them. Young and Orlov managed one such racket and Merlin had been on their trail for several weeks.

After a period of little progress, they'd got lucky. Johnson had received a tip off from one of his snitches. A disgruntled employee of an antiques dealer had got drunk in a West End pub. His boss had been fencing goods stolen in this way, and the drunken man hadn't thought it was right. He'd been pulled in and quickly spilled all he knew. Names had been disclosed and in due course Merlin had got a handle on the location of their base in the East End. The raid had followed.

'Has work begun on matching these goods to their owners, Frank?'

'As you can imagine, that is a going to be a laborious process but it's under way.'

The AC impatiently picked up a pencil and tapped it on his teeth, a habit which Merlin found extremely irritating. 'Do you think this fellow, Young, will spill the beans?'

'He's a hardened crook, sir. Been around Billy Hill and Joe Abela for a while. We might have more luck with Orlov. He's a little newer on the block.'

13

The AC tapped his teeth again. 'Billy Hill. Think this is one of his?' Hill was thought by the police to be the criminal kingpin of London, with fingers in many pies.

'I'm pretty sure Young reports directly to Joseph Abela, who has his own outfit. They are all, however, beholden to Hill in one way or another. It would be wonderful to get evidence against the top people but you know how they run things.'

'At several arms' length?'

'Yes.'

To Merlin's relief, the AC put the pencil down. 'It's funny, isn't it, Frank? When the war began, we all thought there'd be a falling off of gang activity as everyone put their backs to the war effort. Whereas . . .'

'The opposite has happened.'

'Yes. Gang crime is booming. Crime in general is booming. Billy Hill is raking it in from the black market and other rackets. The Maltese gangs are making a bomb from prostitution and vice. Then there are the Italian gangs around Hatton Garden and all the rest.'

'It's disappointing, sir.'

The AC banged his fist on the desk. 'Disappointing? It's bloody heartbreaking.' He got up and strolled over to the window. A brisk wind was propelling dark clouds south westward over the river and the London County Council offices opposite. On his right, the AC could see crowds of well-wrapped up men and women hurrying back and forth over Westminster Bridge. Further to his right he could just see Big Ben, one proud survivor of the Blitz, towering over the bomb-damaged Houses of Parliament. He returned to his desk with a shake of the head. 'Got a name for the young boy yet?'

'We are inclining to Harry.'

'After your father?'

'Yes. I told Sonia I would be perfectly happy with Peter, which is her father's name, or indeed several others, but she said she liked Harry best.'

14

'That wasn't your father's original name, of course.'

'No, sir.'

Merlin's father had been a Spanish sailor who settled down with an English girl in London's East End before the Great War. He had been born Javier Merino but eventually, fed up with the endless mangling of his name by the locals, had Anglicised it to Harry Merlin and his children, Francisco, Carlos and Maria had become Frank, Charlie and Mary.

The AC gave Merlin an awkward look. Thinking of Merlin's slightly exotic origins always made him uncomfortable. He changed the subject. 'Well, at least things at the Yard are a little easier for you now you've got everyone back.'

'I don't think I'd say *easier* exactly, sir, but it is good to have my full team around me.'

For several weeks earlier in the year, Merlin had been deprived of two of his men. Inspector Johnson had been seconded to MI5's investigation of Rudolf Hess, Hitler's deputy, who had mysteriously flown solo to Scotland in May for reasons still as yet unclear. Cole had gone away under an unfortunate cloud. The AC had disapproved of a blossoming relationship between Cole and the only woman member of Merlin's team, WPC Clare Robinson, who also happened to be the AC's niece. Cole was a working class Londoner. The AC did not consider the liaison an appropriate match and had posted Cole out of the way to Portsmouth CID for a few months. The move had been a success from the AC's viewpoint, as the pair had split up. Merlin had, however, found the AC's behaviour distasteful and unnecessarily disruptive.

'Cole behaving himself, is he?'

'How do you mean, sir?'

'In regards to my niece.'

'Oh. Yes, as far as I can tell the two officers are maintaining a cordial professional relationship. Perhaps there has been a small element of strain on Cole's side, but it has not affected his work.'

'Good. Yes . . . ah . . . well, Clare seems perfectly happy now with her barrister friend Rutherford.'

'Does she now?'

The AC looked a little discomfited, as if he now regretted raising the subject. 'Does, er, does Cole have a new lady friend?'

'Not that I am aware. He spends much of his spare time attending evening classes. He's become very keen on self-improvement. He's a good boy.'

'Ah. Yes. Good for him.' The AC picked up the file he'd been reading earlier. 'One of the reasons for raising the internment budget is that the Government expect we'll have many more enemy aliens in the near future.'

'And who would they be, sir?'

The AC tut-tutted. 'Come on now, Frank. I know you've had a lot on your mind recently but the developing situation in the Far East cannot have escaped you.'

'Well, of course I've read the newspapers but are things really getting that bad?'

'They are. My friends in the Foreign Office say things could blow up any day. The Japanese have taken things too far with their intensive militarisation and aggression against neighbours. The Americans have tried to rein them in peaceably with oil sanctions and the like but there's a limit to what can be achieved that way.'

'I read somewhere the other day that American–Japanese negotiations were going well.'

The AC snorted. 'Whoever wrote that doesn't know what he's talking about. There's an outside chance war can be avoided but the Foreign Office view is that the Japs are stringing the Americans along while they continue to strengthen their position. If things do blow up, our people in Singapore, Malaysia, Hong Kong, and so on will be in a badly exposed position. Australia too.'

Merlin stifled a yawn.

The AC's cheeks flushed. 'Not boring you, am I Chief Inspector?'

Merlin's face also flushed. 'Not at all, sir, but may I remind you, I have been up since four this morning. And I was here until eleven last night.' He stood up. 'Now, if you'll forgive me, I have a lot of work to be getting on with.'

The AC waved a placatory hand. 'Sorry, Frank.' The gravy-coloured teeth appeared again. 'I'm afraid my temper is a bit short these days with all the pressures on us. I was out of order. Of course you must get off to your office. I was just going to say, Frank, on a slightly brighter note, that one good thing might come out of it.'

'Out of what, sir?'

'Out of a Japanese declaration of war on the Americans. If that happens, it's hard to think the Germans won't ally themselves with the Japanese. In such circumstances, Mr Churchill will be bound to get what he's been striving for all along.'

'What's that, sir?'

'Why, America's entry into our war of course!'

Chargé d'Affaires Ikuru winced with pain as he acknowledged the arrival of his Second Secretary with a curt bow. He had awoken early with a toothache and the pain had increased steadily throughout the morning. It hadn't helped that he'd consumed all of a disgusting full English breakfast at Claridge's, but manners would not allow him to refuse. His host, Alexander Cadogan, the head of the Foreign Office, was difficult enough as it was without unnecessary rudeness on his part. It was hard to think of a time when Anglo-Japanese relations had been more strained. The British Government was fully behind the punitive sanctions imposed on Japan by Franklin Roosevelt. There was little of substance Ikuru could say in reply to Cadogan's probing questions about Japanese intentions. He had confined himself as far as possible to non-committal diplomatic platitudes. Naturally he was a master of such wordplay, otherwise he would never have advanced so far in the service of His Imperial Majesty. He was also only a deputy, acting on behalf of an absent Ambassador who'd been recalled to Japan in the summer. As such it was easier for him to prevaricate when opinions were sought.

As the Second Secretary bowed deeply to him for a second time,

Ikuru reached down to retrieve a small bottle from a drawer in his desk. He always kept a bottle of laudanum close to hand as he was a man prone to minor afflictions. If it wasn't toothache, it was a migraine or sinus trouble or a back strain or something else. He poured a measure of the medicine into a small glass and drank as his young underling seated himself nervously on the opposite side of the desk.

'Are you alright, sir?'

'Just a rotten tooth. Nothing too serious.'

'I am very sorry. My wife swears by nutmeg and turmeric for such an ailment.'

'Does she now? Thank you but I'll stick to the fruit of the poppy.' Ikuru adjusted his wing collar, then pulled his chair closer to the desk. 'What have you for me?'

'The overnight messages from Tokyo have been decoded, sir.'

'And?'

The Second Secretary placed a file on the desk and removed a sheet of paper. 'There is an extremely important message.'

'Given the current state of affairs, I'd be surprised if there were not. Well?'

The gilt Louis XV clock by the window began to chime the hour. The young diplomat waited until the final eleventh strike then began to read. 'Honoured and esteemed . . .'

'You can skip all the flummery. Just get to the meat.'

'In summary, the message informs Your Excellency that negotiations with the Americans do not proceed well.'

'That's hardly news is it?' Ikuru scoffed.

The Second Secretary continued. 'There is no question of His Imperial Majesty making any further concessions.'

'The endgame is in sight.'

'There follows a reference to further new emergency codes which are detailed in accompanying overnight communications.'

Ikuru unthinkingly touched his inflamed tooth and stifled a cry as he caught the nerve. He drank the rest of his laudanum glass. 'Why new codes?'

18

'In case we are required to destroy our cipher machines and codebooks.'

'I thought we already had such codes.'

'They were deemed inadequate.'

Ikuru sighed. 'Do I personally need to know the details?'

'Not really, sir. But if you are interested, the coded words are to be broadcast in Japanese short wave news bulletins. They relate to winds.'

'Winds? How so?'

'If diplomatic relations are about to be broken off completely with regard, for example, to the United States, the bulletin will contain a reference to "east wind rain".'

'Breaking off relations equates to a declaration of war, I presume.'

'You presume correctly, sir.'

'Here, pass it to me.' Ikuru put on his reading glasses and looked carefully through the message. 'So, the most important phrase for us is "west wind clear". When we hear that we'll know that we are about to be at war with our British hosts.'

'Yes, sir.'

There was an awkward silence before the Second Secretary spoke again. 'If we have to vacate the Embassy at short notice there is a special coded file in the Chancery covering such an eventuality. Shall I have it decoded and brought to you, sir?'

'I suppose so.'

'Do you think there would be any difficulties about our . . . our making a safe departure?'

Ikuru looked amused. 'Do you mean are we likely to be strung up and lynched? I think not. The British are a civilised race.' He looked down at his hands for a moment. 'Then again if our security forces somehow manage to do something like blow up the King, who knows? They love their royals as much as we do ours, if not more.' The tooth made him wince again. 'However, I think the chances of that happening must be pretty slim.'

'Where would we go, sir?'

'Well no doubt this special file will tell us. Portugal I'd guess. They still have scheduled commercial flights there after all.'

'That's what I thought.'

'Is there anything else, Second Secretary? You don't quite seem yourself today. Of course we are living through very worrying times, but you must take heart. We are a great nation. If the Emperor determines on war we shall no doubt acquit ourselves with courage and honour and prevail. I like England and the English, but there it is. If they choose to side with the Americans and deny us our rightful place in the world, they must bear the consequences.'

The Second Secretary rose slowly to his feet, picked up his papers, and bowed. 'Of course you are right, sir. Long live the Emperor! Long live Japan!'

Filming had stopped for lunch and Michael Adair had quickly made his way to the bar in the studio canteen. He had a stiff pink gin in hand and was looking forward to a leisurely afternoon as he had no more scenes to film that day. His first drink disappeared swiftly as did his second. The alcohol was having its usual calming effect and pushing his many worries to the back of his mind. He looked at his watch. Jean Parker had said she'd join him, but was uncharacteristically late.

The barman caught his attention. 'Mr Adair, sir. The telephone for you.'

'Who is it?'

'Miss Laura Curzon.'

Adair was surprised. His hand jerked and a few drops of his third gin sprinkled the counter.

'Would you like to take it in the back office?'

'Thanks, Johnny.'

Adair left his drink and followed the barman into a small room off the kitchen. There was a telephone on a small table. Strangely he felt he had to steel himself to pick up the receiver. 'Laura, darling. How are you?'

'Fine, thank you Michael.'

'More to the point, where are you? You sound awfully close.'

'I'm home in the flat.'

'When did you get back from California?'

'I landed on Wednesday night. The journey was awful. I flew in a freezing and very basic cargo plane. It was either that or a tedious long haul via South America, West Africa and Lisbon. However, I really think I might travel that way next time. If there is a next time, that is.'

'What do you mean?'

'You haven't heard? Ah, but then you never do read the trade papers, do you? The film collapsed. That's why I'm back.'

Laura Curzon was Adair's estranged wife. She was a rising screen star of great poise and beauty and had been in California since the summer preparing to star opposite James Stewart in her first major Hollywood film.

Adair had in fact heard the odd whisper about Laura having difficulties in California, but had been too bound up with his own problems and his thrilling liaison with Jean Parker to pay much attention. 'I'm so sorry, Laura. What happened?'

'The story put out is that Stewart's participation was blocked.'

'What do you mean?'

'Well, as I think you know, Jimmy enlisted in the US Army Air Corps a few months ago. Max Flack, the producer, said he'd only been permitted by the authorities to appear because of the film's military content but at the very last minute someone high-up had withdrawn that permission. "No Stewart, no film" Flack then said.'

'You poor darling. How disappointing.'

'There was a little more to it, actually, but I won't bore you with that. It was a wonderful opportunity to lose but it's no good crying over spilt milk. I have to get back into the swing of things back here. So it's bye bye palm trees, swimming pools and sun; and hello rain, fog and snow.'

'Didn't you try and see if Korda could get you something else, seeing he's out there?'

21

'I did, but he thought I'd be better off returning to home ground. It was he who organised my place on the flight home.'

'Good old Alex. Sunning himself in California while we battle on here.' Adair wished he'd brought his drink with him. He wasn't very good at words of commiseration. After a pause he asked 'So what are your plans now?'

'I think I'll go to Gus Cowan's party tomorrow night. Show my face and let everyone know I'm back. No doubt there'll be some tart comments but I shall brazen them out. Are you going?'

'I . . . I don't think so, Laura. Gus and I weren't on the best of terms after the last film I did with him, as you know. It would be nice to see you, though. Perhaps we could meet for lunch on Sunday?'

'Alright. Call me tomorrow and we'll arrange where. I'd better get on. Toodle-oo!'

Back in the canteen Adair saw Jean Parker looking for him. He hurried over and they found a nice table overlooking the studio lawn and the river beyond.

'What have you got on after lunch, darling?'

'The scene in the station where the guard warns me about you.'

'Oh, yes, and naturally you do not heed the warning.'

Jean leaned forward and placed her hand in his. 'Yes, idiot that I am.'

He bent to kiss her fingers then picked up the menu. 'So what shall we eat? I don't think I'm up for another toad in the hole. The one yesterday tasted like cardboard.'

Jean Parker was quick to decide. 'I'm going to have the omelette. It was just about edible the last time I had it. And I . . .' She was distracted as an elderly actress, well-known for her rudeness, barged past, nearly taking their table-cloth with her. There was no hint of apology. Adair made a face.

'There goes Hermione, the old battle axe. Victor was telling me how Larry and Noel hate her. They were all together in a stage production on Shaftesbury Avenue a while back and she managed to upstage them frequently.'

22

'Quite an achievement to upstage those two at all, let alone frequently' said Jean.

Adair smiled then looked at the menu again. He chose the vegetable pie. 'Better not to ask what the vegetables are, I think.' He beckoned a waitress and they placed their orders. As the girl headed off to the kitchen, Adair saw her pass a plump man in a loud brown-checked suit. He was heading in their direction. 'Oh, God. Look who's coming.'

Jean turned to see the famous comedian Archie Tate approaching, beaming at them with his trademark stupid grin. Following behind was a tall, big-framed woman in a dark green coat and matching flowery hat.

'Michael, me old pal.' He made a small bow. 'And who do we have here? None other than the beauteous Jean Parker. Two of your favourite stars, Mother. Say hello, then.'

'Pleased to meet you both, I'm sure.' Tate's mother, like son, had a Lancastrian accent, although hers was broader. 'Oh, they make a fine couple, don't they chuck? My chucky here always speaks well of you, Miss Parker. I liked you very much in that film you did with him when you were just starting out. What was it called? Oh, yes. *The Cat's Cradle* wasn't it Archie?'

'*The Cat's Cream*, Mother. 1938. We had a grand time, didn't we love?'

Jean Parker didn't respond. It was an experience she didn't care to recall. Archie Tate was notorious for his wandering hands.

'Course, I've never had the pleasure of working with Mr Adair here. Perhaps I shall, though. You never know. Maybe you'll consider appearing in a proper popular film? You've had a couple of flops in the arty end of the market, haven't you, Michael? Be a good move for you to appear in a film which makes a lot of money for once, eh? All my films make a lot of money, you know. That's why good old Victor gives me a lot of leeway here and does his best to keep me sweet. He knows any of the other British studios would take me on at the snap of a finger.' Tate snapped his own fingers to illustrate his point. His stupid grin had now disappeared

23

and his prominent front teeth had become less evident. His pudgy face was dominated by a wide crooked mouth and large, saucer eyes. His nose was small and upturned. He had overly long brown curly hair and some saw in him a resemblance to Harpo Marx, although Tate would bridle at the suggestion. 'Anyway, I just wanted to introduce my mother. I've taken her to see Victor and now I'm taking her back to town to do a bit of Christmas shopping. Remember what I said, Michael. I get Victor to pay the right people well, you know. Think about it. Cheerie-bye!'

Adair and Jean Parker watched as the odd couple processed out through the crowded tables to accompanying cheers and a spontaneous round of applause.

'Horrible man,' said Jean.

'Indeed he is.' Adair sighed as, despite himself, he wondered just how much a Tate film might pay. 'Here's the food.'

'We'd better tuck in. I'm due back on set in twenty-five minutes.'

After they'd eaten, Adair suggested a plan for later. 'Shall I pick you up from your place at nine tonight? I could book us a table at Quaglino's.'

'I'm sorry, Michael. My father left a message earlier while we were on set. My mother is feeling a little poorly. Nothing too serious, apparently, but he's keen that I go down to Sussex and visit over the weekend.'

'Oh. I see. Sorry to hear that.'

'My driver's going to take me there when I'm finished for the afternoon.'

'Oh, well. You have to go of course.'

'Will you go to Cowan's party?'

'No.'

'Even if you're at a loose end?'

'There's a new James M Cain book out. *Mildred Pierce*. I'll go and buy a copy tomorrow and curl up with it over the weekend. When will you be back in town?'

'Late Sunday afternoon, I should think.'

'Will you call me then?'

'Of course.'

Adair leaned forward and cupped her chin in his hand. He pulled her towards him and kissed her firmly on the lips. 'Love you darling.'

'Love you too.'

The blue Bentley turned into Farringdon Road, then pulled up smoothly to the kerb a hundred yards on. Victor Goldsmith stepped out onto the pavement and looked up at the imposing red brick building which housed the headquarters of the London Providential Insurance Company. His nose twitched as the pungent smells of the nearby Smithfield Meat Market wafted in his direction. He turned to his driver. 'I'm not sure how long I'll be, Ted. Might be half an hour. Might be two.'

Ted Morris, a beefy former Regimental Sergeant Major of the Coldstream Guards, had been at his boss's side for nearly ten years as driver, handyman, and general factotum. Goldsmith trusted him implicitly. 'Not to worry, sir. I'll be here come what may.'

Goldsmith hurried up the steps to the main door. Crossing the marble floor of the building's cavernous lobby, he was recognised by a liveried porter and escorted deferentially to the senior management's elevator. There he was greeted in turn by the elderly lift operator. 'Good to see you again, Mr Goldsmith.' The inner lift door clanged shut and they set off for the twentieth floor. 'Got any nice pictures for us to look forward to?'

'I have a few films in production. The most promising I think is a thriller called *Murder at Midnight* starring Michael Adair and Jean Parker.'

'My wife likes them both and she loves a good murder story, so that'll be right up her street. I'm a comedy man myself. I read in the paper there's a new Archie Tate. He's one of yours, ain't he?'

'That's right.'

The old man chuckled. 'I love him. He really gets to me, he does. You can forget your Trinders, your Formbys, your Hays and your Marx Brothers. Archie's the one for me.'

25

The lift drew to a halt. 'Well, I hope you enjoy his film.' The operator touched the peak of his cap and opened the wire caging. Goldsmith stepped out onto the thick pile carpeting of the insurance company's executive floor. A young blonde secretary was waiting for him.

'Mr Goldsmith?'

'Good afternoon, young lady. You're new here, aren't you?'

'Yes, sir. I'm Miss Ramsden's replacement. She retired last month. I'm Miss Taylor. The Chairman is awaiting you in the Board Room.'

Miss Taylor led Goldsmith down a long corridor. She had a good figure and Goldsmith enjoyed the view. In years gone by, he would have given his business card as a matter of course to a pretty girl like this. Offers of a screen test and dinner would have followed as preliminaries to the inevitable attempt at seduction. Now, however, he was a happily married man and no longer played the field.

'Here we are, sir.' She pushed through a double door and escorted Goldsmith into a richly furnished rectangular room. Two men were seated at the far end of a long mahogany table. The window behind them had a fine view of St Paul's Cathedral.

'Victor. Welcome.' The neat little man who spoke was the Chairman of the Board, Herbert Wilkinson. Two licks of Brylcreemed black hair were combed over a very pink cranium. A small beard covered his prominent chin. To his left sat Eric Carlton, the Managing Director, a man whose frame was as considerable as his Chairman's was slight. His large eyes bulged from behind a pair of pince-nez spectacles perched precariously on his round red nose. Wilkinson indicated a chair opposite him. 'Please.'

The London Providential Insurance Company had been Goldsmith's principal financial backers since the middle of the previous decade. After the trailblazing success of Alexander Korda in attracting a major City institution, the Prudential, to back his film company, Goldsmith had been quick to follow suit. The British Government had been trying to persuade major UK finance houses to support the burgeoning national film industry for some time. As tales of the excellent returns being made by American backers of the Hollywood studios continued to cross the Atlantic, this pressure eventually told. Goldsmith found he was pushing at an open door when he approached the London Providential. Nearly a million pounds' worth of loan finance had been forthcoming and, through various equity and preferential participations, the insurance company had received a healthy yield on its investment every year.

The Providential's funding had enabled Goldsmith to develop and expand his business to the point where, if not quite a match for Korda and his state-of-the-art studio at Denham, Silver Screen Studios could certainly be regarded as the equal of the thriving studios at Ealing and Shepperton. He'd been lucky enough to strike gold fairly early on when he'd managed to pinch Archie Tate from a competitor and then had gone from strength to strength. In the past four years he'd been able to broaden the studio's range and improve the quality of its productions. He had now reached a stage where he was able to attract the best British stars as well as the occasional glamorous Hollywood performer.

Given this successful record, Goldsmith's relations with Wilkinson and his colleagues had always been extremely amicable. Today, however, he detected a palpable tension in the air. He attempted to diffuse it. 'You fellows look pretty sombre today. Perhaps one of these would cheer you up?' He reached inside his jacket and flourished three gigantic Havana cigars. 'I got these from the Prime Minister the other day. I gave him a private screening of last year's King John movie, which he loved. They come from the supplies Roosevelt gave him when they met up in Newfoundland in the summer.'

Wilkinson declined with a pained smile and Carlton did likewise.

Goldsmith shrugged. 'Alright, suit yourselves.' He pocketed two cigars and prepared to light one for himself. 'You don't mind, do you?' Wilkinson looked as if he did but Goldsmith went ahead anyway.

'Well, Herbert, to what do I owe this unexpected pleasure? Our regular quarterly meeting isn't due until the end of January.'

'You are right, of course, but this meeting is . . . is not . . . is not a regular meeting as such. It has a . . . a special agenda.'

'Special agenda, eh? That sounds a little ominous. Very well. Sounds like you need to get something off your chest.' He drew on his cigar then expelled a swirling trail of smoke behind him. 'Fire away, then.'

Wilkinson referred to a small notepad on the table in front of him. 'There are . . . um . . . two items on the agenda. The first relates to another relationship of ours. In the film industry, that is.' Wilkinson turned to his colleague. 'Eric, why don't you brief Victor on that?'

Carlton nodded. 'As you know, Victor, in addition to our relationship with Silver Screen Studios, we have had involvements with other film companies in recent years.'

'Yes, of course I know all about those. Your natural attempts to replicate the success you have had with me.'

Carlton's nose twitched and his spectacles wobbled. 'We have two such relationships of significance. The first is with Jacob Meyer. That business was performing well but, as you know, his studio was commandeered in May by the Government for war work. We are rather stuck there until . . .'

'Until Hitler's had it.'

'Quite. Until . . . um . . . that person has received his comeuppance.'

Goldsmith pointed a finger at Carlton. ' "Come-uppance". I like that. I might use it in a film. Perhaps you should become a scriptwriter, Eric? I pay writers better than most, you know.'

'I think not, Victor. So that relationship is not working out well for us at the moment.'

'I'm sure his namesake, Louis B, to whom Jacob likes to pretend he is related, would never have ended up in such a position. He'd have paid a backhander to someone in the Civil Service to ensure the Government looked elsewhere for its film facilities.

I might remind you that I did warn you about backing that schmuck.'

'So you did, Victor, but it's not often you have a kind word for any of your competitors, is it?'

'That's not true, Eric. I respect the Kordas and maintain cordial relations with them. And there are others.'

'What about Gus Cowan. How are your relations with him?'

'We have our disagreements but I count him a friend. We work together occasionally.'

'His is the second of our significant film involvements, as you know.'

'Yes.' Goldsmith looked sharply at Carlton. 'Ah. I think I get the picture. All this is leading up to you telling me you are having difficulties with Gus, isn't it? Well, I'd be happy to have a word with him, if you like. However, I don't really see what your problems with Mayer and Cowan have to do with me.'

Carlton adjusted his spectacles. 'Bear with me please. Let me explain. We put a lot of money behind Cowan. Not as much as we gave you but more than we provided to Mayer. When we backed Cowan he was on a good run with several hits here and one in America. We stepped into the breach when for some reason he fell out with his Canadian financier.' Carlton glanced at Wilkinson. 'We never did really find out what happened there. "Operational disagreements" we were told.'

Goldsmith smirked. 'Could mean anything with someone like Gus.'

'Just so. In any event, emboldened by our success with you we took the plunge and got behind him. Unfortunately . . .'

'Look I know he's had one or two stinkers recently. It happens to us all from time to time. But he's had some great successes too. There was that spy film with Robert Donat which went like a bomb and then . . .'

'Yes, alright Victor. Cowan has had some hits and some misses. The problem is that there were some . . . some weaknesses in our contractual arrangements. It has come to light that Cowan

29

exploited these weaknesses and, with the aid of creative accounting, ensured that we only had a small piece of the hit films and a large piece of the misses.'

'Goodness me.'

Wilkinson responded irritably. 'Dammit, Victor. Please don't play the innocent with us. You know very well that all sorts of tricks can be played with figures in the film industry. Clearly the company managers who negotiated with Cowan were no match for him and his accountants. Suffice to say, they have all been sacked. The situation they have left behind is dire. Our finance department has calculated that we are owed almost a quarter of a million pounds.'

Goldsmith whistled. 'A lot of money, then. Well, as I said, if you want me to have a word with . . .'

'That will not be necessary, Victor. The matter is now with our lawyers.'

'But perhaps with a bit of effort and goodwill, Cowan might be persuaded . . .'

'It is a legal matter now, Victor. There is no goodwill existing between us and Cowan and the law must take its course.'

'Still, I . . .'

Wilkinson held up a hand. 'Now, if you don't mind, we'll move on to item two on the agenda. Naturally, when we reported the Cowan situation to our directors they were shocked. A protracted debate has taken place within the board over recent weeks. In addition to our own difficult experience, we learned on the City grapevine that all was not smooth sailing in the Prudential's relationship with Korda. Over-spending, reduced profitability – we don't know exactly but there is unhappiness. Eventually, in light of all the circumstances, the board decided that the London Prudential should withdraw completely from engagement with the film industry.'

Goldsmith looked quizzically at Wilkinson as he puffed his cigar. '"Withdraw from engagement"? You must remember I'm just a Lithuanian peasant. What exactly does that mean for Silver Screen Studios?'

Carlton replied, 'It means, Victor, I'm sorry to say, that our business relationship is at an end. Furthermore, as the board has instructed us to act with all haste, we shall be strictly applying the termination provisions of our agreements with you. Accordingly we shall be looking for prompt repayment of our loans. It would be best for both of us, obviously, if you could find an alternative source of finance to make us whole, assuming you can't resolve the matter personally. If that can't be done, we shall have to arrange an orderly liquidation of assets.'

It took a lot to silence Victor Goldsmith, but Carlton's words had succeeded. When he was finally able to find words, he said 'Surely, as gentlemen of honour, we can discuss a practical and sensible procedure of disengagement. I have three films in production, with more to start in the new year. The new Archie Tate is coming out imminently and requires promotional investment. I can't simply pull-up sticks and bring everything to a shuddering halt. I'll need a good six months to sort out new arrangements and give you what you require.'

Wilkinson pursed his lips. 'Of course, Victor, we are all gentlemen. However six months is completely out of the question. The board made it abundantly clear to Eric and me that our own jobs were on the line here if we did not implement their decision promptly and clear up the mess.'

'But, Herbert, that mess is not my mess, is it? It's Cowan's and yours. Your involvement with me has been a great success. This is insanity!'

Wilkinson leaned back and gazed at the chandelier above as he considered his words. He sighed. 'Look, Victor, I don't want to get all legalistic with you but if you examine our contracts you'll find we have a pretty watertight position. Unfortunately the same does not apply with Cowan. We have security on your studio and all physical assets and we have liens on all the completed films. We have learned from your advanced and innovative thinking that even if a film loses money when released it can turn out to be a profitable asset in the long run, with additional releases and the

31

possible advent of things like television after we have won this damned war. Thus we feel comfortable that we shall recover our money if we have to distrain on you. Having said that, you are a man of huge ability not to mention substantial personal wealth. You have a host of powerful and rich friends who might help. We are not going to walk in on you with the bailiffs tomorrow.' Wilkinson and Carlton exchanged an inscrutable look. 'I think we can give you a couple of weeks to come up with a plan.'

'What exactly does "come up with a plan" mean?'

'What it says. Tell us how you're going to repay us.'

'I'll need two months.'

'Three weeks maximum. Repayment within six.'

'And what about the financing of the films currently in production?'

'All new credit ceases from today.' Wilkinson looked down and scribbled an addendum to his notes. 'I'm sure you'll have no difficulty bringing those productions in with your own resources. Now I think that's all.'

The producer rose slowly to his feet. He felt as if the earth had opened up beneath him. 'Very well. If that's how it must be, I wish you good day.' He ignored the extended hands of the two executives and made for the door. Making his way out, Victor Goldsmith had no thought for the beauty of the secretary, nor time for the small talk of the lift man. He was a chastened and worried man.

It was freezing in Court 14 of the Old Bailey. The heating had gone on the blink after lunch. Mr Justice Chivers made a mental note to bring a hot water bottle on Monday, in case repairs hadn't been effected. He shivered and glanced hopefully at the clock at the back of the court to find that it was only ten to four. He looked down testily at the defence barrister in the well of the court.

'Is that your last question, Mr Brooke?'

'Yes, m'lud.'

'Anything in re-examination, Mr Fuller.'

'No, m'lud.'

'Well, I know we are meant to go until four, but I think we might call an end to proceedings now in the circumstances. Thank you, Sergeant Bridges. You may step down from the box. Members of the jury, you are reminded that you are not to discuss the details of this case with anyone over the weekend.' He got to his feet, the barristers and court officials bowed their heads, and the men in the dock rose. As he made his exit, he reflected that the jury warning on this occasion was superfluous. The case was cast iron and the defendants were clearly going down.

Bridges was thinking exactly the same as he passed through the lobby on his way to the street. He crossed the road and turned to look up at the north-western corner of the Bailey which was still heavily clad in scaffolding. Work continued to repair the heavy damage inflicted on the building by the German bombers back in May. Two court employees had been killed and a courtroom and many surrounding areas obliterated, but the dispensation of justice continued at the heart of the British criminal judicial system. Bridges's eyes moved up beyond the scaffolding and saw the famous statue of Justice with her sword and scales still presiding over the building from the cupola.

He felt a tug on his jacket and turned to find the prosecuting barrister, Geoffrey Fuller QC. The men working on the building were making a considerable racket but Fuller's booming bass easily eclipsed the clamour of drills and tools. 'Well done, Sergeant. We should have this all neatly wrapped up by Tuesday at the latest.'

Fuller was prosecuting a case of ration book forgery on a large scale. Bridges had been a principal witness against the gang responsible. The principal 'inkman' was a wily customer called Simmons, whom Merlin and Bridges had been trying to nail for some time. Before the war he'd been known as the best forger of counterfeit notes in the game. He'd always somehow managed to avoid conviction and it would be very satisfying to put him behind bars at last.

'It'll be good to have Simmons out of the way for a long time.'

'So it will, Sergeant. But he's still small fry compared with the people in the background, isn't he? You and I know that Billy Hill and his friends were behind Simmons. To have those crooks in the dock one day, now that would be the thing!'

'So it would, sir, but you know we'll get nothing from Simmons and the others. They want to live.'

'As we've discussed many times before, Sergeant. We must be happy with what we get. You're going back to the Yard, I presume?'

'Yes, sir. I need to catch up with Mr Merlin. My day in court here meant I missed out on an important raid this morning.'

The barrister removed his wig and scratched his curly thatch of straw-coloured hair, which was exactly the same shade and texture as the policeman's. With their hair, similar rugby player builds and rosy complexions, the two men could easily be taken for brothers were it not for the sharp contrast of their speaking voices: Fuller's plummy Etonian tones against Bridges's moderated Cockney.

'Sorry to hear that, Sergeant. However, given how much crime there is in London these day, I'm sure you won't have to wait long for another raid.' Fuller buttoned his coat and hailed a passing taxi. 'I must be off. I have to make a five thirty train to Bicester. Family weekend in rural Oxfordshire to look forward to.' He patted Bridges on the back and disappeared into the cab, leaving the sergeant to hop on a bus to Westminster.

Merlin was just putting the telephone down when Bridges got back to the office. He had finally spoken to Sonia. She and the baby boy were well, and had managed a couple of uninterrupted nights' sleep since Merlin had last called. Sonia's parents were coping and the only fly in the ointment was that her mother was over-protective of the baby. This was beginning to get on Sonia's nerves. There had been a letter from her brother Jan, a pilot in one of the RAF's Polish Squadrons. There was little detail, as was to be expected, but he was happily fit and well. Sonia had thought she detected a hint of boredom behind the lines of his letter. The Luftwaffe had largely withdrawn from British skies after May, and the wintry weather limited the scope of longer range RAF operations. She guessed he didn't have much to do. At the end of the call, Sonia had asked hopefully whether Merlin could travel up to see them on Saturday, but Merlin had had to say no. The conversation had thus, unfortunately, ended on a downbeat.

'How'd it go, Sam?'

Bridges took a seat. 'Verdict in Monday or Tuesday, most likely.'

'And that will be . . . ?'

'The defence have been trying their best to cloud the issue with technical points. Judge doesn't seem to think much of them. Mr Fuller thinks it's open and shut. Guilty on all counts.'

'How is Simmons looking?'

'Miserable.'

'Good.' Merlin drummed his fingers on the desk and looked off to the window.

'I was in and out of the office this morning before you got back. How did the raid go?' Bridges could see that his boss's mind was elsewhere.

It took a while for Merlin to respond. 'Sorry, Sergeant. I was just chatting to Sonia. Thinking about her made me forget you were out of the loop. Actually, it went pretty well.' Merlin gave Bridges a quick run-down of the morning's events.

'All good then, sir.'

'Up to a point. We've made a start on the interrogations of Young and Orlov. As you'd expect, they're not being very cooperative.'

'What about the men who got away?'

'No news.'

The main radiator in the room made a loud growling noise. '*Madre de Dios*! I hope the heating isn't about to conk out like it did last winter.'

'The Old Bailey was pretty parky.'

'I bet it was with all that building work going on.' He leaned back in his chair and regarded his sergeant. 'All well on the home front?'

'Not so bad. We still have the occasional bad night with the baby. You're lucky to be missing out on all that at the moment.'

'Not for long. How old is yours now?'

'He just turned one.'

'I didn't realise the sleepless nights could go on so long.'

'Depends on the baby, of course. You can be lucky.'

Merlin raised two crossed fingers. 'And Iris? How is she?'

'She's fit and well but has the usual bee in her bonnet.'

'And what particular bee is in her bonnet at the moment?'

'Her nephew, Dan.'

'The one who joined the navy a few months back?'

'That's the one. He's been posted on his first ship. *The Prince of Wales.*'

'That's a spanking new vessel, isn't it? I was reading about it somewhere the other day.'

'Yes. It's just been sent to the Far East. At least, that's what Dan thought was going to happen when we saw him last. He was full of excitement, of course. Iris wasn't. Every day she scours the papers for news. The situation out there is not doing wonders for her mood. I've told her that, worrying as it is, we are in the same boat as thousands of British families. She's as good as anyone at the old British stiff upper lip but I know it's eating at her. Thing is she has a very close relationship with Dan. More like a mother than an aunt, after Iris's sister died and his father did a runner.'

'I know how she feels, Sam. It was terrible when my brother Charlie was over in France. I thank God every day he got back safely from Dunkirk, albeit at the cost of his leg.'

Bridges was contemplative for a while before saying 'Doesn't feel right having to worry about a young lad like Dan. It should be me out there fighting.'

Merlin dipped his head in sympathy. He knew how disappointed the sergeant had been when the military medics had vetoed his enlistment in the forces for the bizarre reason of his having a sixth toe on one of his feet. Merlin too, although in his forties, had been keen to enlist, and had been unhappy to have been prevented from doing so by the AC.

'Never mind, Sam. As the man upstairs says, we are soldiers in another way. You remember what he told me?' Merlin imitated the AC's languid drawl. '"Without an effective police force, Chief Inspector, chaos will ensue – and domestic chaos is worth a hundred divisions to Herr Hitler."'

The office door suddenly opened. There was the AC, looking a little confused. 'I could have sworn I heard another voice in here. A strangely familiar one.'

'No, sir. Just us two.'

The AC gave Merlin an odd look. 'Hmm. Well, good day to you both. I'm off for a weekend of beagling in the country, but as always feel free to telephone if you need me.'

Merlin and Bridges held their breath as they listened to the footsteps travelling down the corridor and then on down the stairs. Then they burst out laughing.

'That was a little too close for comfort, Sam.'

Chapter Two

The Royal Australian Air Force Hudson bomber had taken off from Kota Baru early in the morning. It was on its routine daily reconnaissance mission of the South China Sea. The pilot, Flight Lieutenant Ramsey, a bluff Queenslander known to one and all as 'Bull' was in a good mood, as he usually was when up in the air. He loved flying. He loved seeing the blue of the sea and the blue of the sky all laid out before him. His mood was bolstered this morning by the solid night's sleep he had enjoyed and the hearty cooked breakfast in his belly. Not a man of few words, he had enthused at length since take-off about the beauty of the day and the world to his navigator before launching into a detailed reminiscence of the occasion in Sydney league cricket when he had caught and bowled the young Don Bradman. It was not the first time the navigator, an amiable young man called Frederickson, had heard the story and almost certainly not the last. Further back in the plane were Gunners Weir and Wilson.

It was mid-morning by the time Bull Ramsey had finally exhausted all the possibilities of his cricketing adventures and had fallen silent. He suddenly heard a shout from the back of the plane but the words were drowned by the noise of the engines. Gunner Weir came up to the cockpit to repeat his message. 'Japs, sir. At least I think they're Japs. Three ships on our right at North, North East.' Weir, a scrawny intense young man had made it his task to memorise the RAAF manuals depicting all known vessels of all major powers, and Ramsey had found his knowledge pretty reliable. 'They are well off but they are either destroyers or cruisers.'

Williamson, the older of the two gunners, came up to voice his agreement. 'Definitely Japs. Heading on a westerly course.'

Ramsey turned the aircraft a few degrees so they could get a better view. He picked up his binoculars. 'I see them. A small detachment of vessels. Might be significant, might not. Best call it in, Freddie.'

Frederickson did as ordered and the flight continued on its original easterly course. Twenty minutes later the navigator whistled and pointed to his left. 'Will you look at that?'

Ramsey turned, only to be blinded momentarily as the sun reappeared from behind a cloud. Seconds later the sun was obscured once more and the pilot saw what Miller was looking at. 'Struth, Freddy! Quite a convoy. How many do you think?'

'Twenty-five. Maybe more.'

Ramsey turned his head and shouted to the gunners. 'Do you see them, you two? Japs again?'

Weir returned to the cockpit. 'Yes, sir. Japanese destroyers, cruisers and support vessels heading west.'

Frederickson consulted the map on his knees and performed some calculations. 'Approximately 380 miles east of the mainland. They could be off Malaysia or Thailand by tomorrow.'

Ramsey scratched his chin and stared back out at the distant vessels. 'Call it in Freddy. Call it in pronto!'

It was past eight, late for him, when Merlin crawled wearily out of bed and ran himself a bath. As he lay back in the soapy warmth he reflected on his long Friday. The aftermath of the raid had gone reasonably well. Sergeant Hooper had been extremely efficient and to Merlin's amazement a full inventory of the stolen goods had arrived on his desk by seven in the evening. It was clear that Young and Orlov were nailed and would be going down for a long time. His long interrogations of the men had, however, led

39

nowhere in terms of catching bigger fish. As usual, it was proving impossible to get the soldiers to squeal on their generals. As he towelled himself dry, he decided not to continue questioning them over the weekend. He'd just lay the charges, get them packed off on remand to Wormwood Scrubs, and let them sweat. Perhaps a few days contemplating the prospect of years in prison might undermine one or both of them.

He put on one of the new navy suits he'd recently acquired from Moss Brothers under Sonia's supervision. From the same West End shopping trip, he picked out a crisp white Asser and Turnbull shirt and a muted red tie. He looked at himself in the mirror. 'Tall, dark and oh so very handsome' was Sonia's routine compliment to him. He wondered what Alice, his first wife, would think of his new domestic arrangements. Poor Alice. She would have loved to have Merlin's children. He thought of her only occasionally now, but hoped that was only natural. There used to be a picture of her in his bedroom but he had relegated it to a drawer when Sonia came on the scene. Not that he thought Sonia would've complained if he'd kept it out. She wasn't the type to be jealous of a dead woman.

In the kitchen he made himself a piece of toast. He only had smidgeons of butter and jam to spread on it. His supplies of food and drink were running low in Sonia's absence. He had no time to shop and to wait in long queues for rationed provisions. Up until recently he could have counted on getting a proper breakfast at Tony's café, just round the corner from the Yard. However, Tony, a Londoner of Italian origins, had closed down Merlin's favourite greasy spoon in September. Because of his background, Tony had faced internment as an Italian alien earlier in the year. Merlin had pulled a few strings to save him from that fate but after the experience, Tony had become depressed and lost his zest for life. He'd eventually shut up shop and taken his family off to live somewhere up North. Merlin missed him. There was talk of someone reopening the café but nothing had happened yet.

Merlin had lived in his Chelsea apartment block close to the river since early 1940, when his friend Jack Stewart had persuaded him to quit the single room off the King's Road which he'd occupied since Alice's death. Merlin had been left a modestly wealthy widower and could afford something better, as Jack had pointed out many times. Eventually, Merlin had taken the plunge and paid a tidy sum for the lease on this mansion flat. It was a more than comfortable place for one, and perfectly acceptable for two. What it was going to be like for three, he had yet to find out. Merlin had found it difficult being back on his own again, even if only for a few weeks. 'Must be love, I suppose,' he muttered to himself as he went through the door and started down the stairs.

Out on the street he took a left turn and headed towards Sloane Square Tube Station. A thin mist was rolling in off the river and it was another bitter day. He skipped around some icy puddles in front of the shell of a neighbouring house bombed back in the spring. If Merlin didn't have a police car with him, he usually took the bus to work or walked. For the past week, however, water-main repairs on the King's Road had been playing havoc with the bus service so today he'd reverted to the Tube. He bought his ticket and hurried down the escalator. Odd signs of the station's recent spell as an air-raid shelter still remained, but the six-month lull in bombing meant things were now looking close to normal.

Hitler's airborne blitzkrieg on London had lasted from September 1939 to May 1940. It had ended just before the Nazis invaded Russia. The general view was that after the population's plucky endurance of the bombing and the magnificent performance of the RAF, Hitler had concluded that an invasion wasn't going to be as easy as he thought and, in any event, he had other fish to fry. He needed the planes that had been battering Britain to support the massive attack on Russia he launched in June of 1941. The country had thus received some very welcome breathing space. Sporadic German raids on towns and ports outside London did continue and the air raid sirens wailed every so often to keep people on their toes, but no significant bomb damage had been seen in the capital for six months.

It was the weekend and the train was not crowded. Merlin got a seat and began to read the newspaper he'd picked up at the station kiosk. One of the headlines told him that Britain had formally declared war on Finland, Hungary and Romania. He wasn't sure he cared about Hungary and Romania, but he had some sympathy with the Finns. Merlin knew they'd been subjected to years of aggression from the Russians who had battled over the centuries to incorporate Finland into the Russian Empire. Stalin's policy had been no different to that of his imperial predecessors in this, and the Finns had found themselves between the Devil and the Deep Blue Sea, or rather between two Devils. They had plumped for the German Devil.

A second headline story was about a secret contingent war plan conceived, allegedly, by Roosevelt which had been leaked to the press. American isolationists like Ford and Lindbergh were having a field day, claiming this showed the President had wanted all along to drag the US into the war against the Germans, contrary to many promises otherwise. There was also more speculation on the progress of America's ongoing talks with Japan. Cordell Hull, the US Secretary of State, had given a pessimistic speech on the subject.

Merlin flicked through a couple more flimsy pages. Newsprint was in short supply, as were many other things. He saw a short piece about the forthcoming new Archie Tate film and thought of Sonia. He didn't care for Tate himself, but he was one of several music hall-style comedians whom Sonia found hilarious. Max Miller, Tommy Handley, Tommy Trinder, The Crazy Gang. She loved them all. Merlin found it difficult to fathom how a young Polish refugee could follow and enjoy the innuendo-laden humour of very English comics like these. He gave up a prayer that the Tate film would somehow escape Sonia's notice.

When he resurfaced in Parliament Square, it had started to rain. He looked over at the bomb-damaged Houses of Parliament. He still hadn't quite got used to the sight. It was in May that the Luftwaffe's incendiary bombs had destroyed the Commons

Chamber and set Westminster Hall ablaze. The Commons, after a brief sojourn in Church House by the Abbey, now sat in the Lords Chamber, which had survived the attack relatively undamaged. The Lords themselves now had to hold sittings in their own Robing Room. Bridges had been obliged to do some security work in Parliament at the end of the summer and had painted the picture colourfully for Merlin.

'All these toffs, sir, your Dukes and Earls and Barons, not forgetting the Archbishops and Bishops, all crowded together in a small space with no room to swing a cat. I found it very funny, I'm sorry to say. Mr Churchill and the MPs nice and cosy in the Lords Chamber and the peers kicked out into the changing room. Mind you, that's how it should be, to my way of thinking.'

Merlin walked towards the Embankment, passing the sad, boarded-up façade of Tony's Café, and turned left to cover the short distance to the Yard. As he went through the gates, he saw DI Johnson ahead of him and picked up pace to catch up.

Victor Goldsmith woke just as Merlin was getting to work. His sleep had been fitful and his head was pounding. Much like the policeman, he was normally an early riser. He had, however, hosted a dinner party the night before at his Mayfair residence and, unusually for him, had overdone things a little. He blamed his overindulgence on the insurance people. Those idiots at the London Providential had ruined his day and his night. He would have to pull his finger out to make sure they didn't ruin his life.

He pressed a bell by his side and, within seconds, the butler appeared. 'I'll skip the eggs today, Davide. Just a lemon tea and some toast for me.' Davide disappeared and Goldsmith tried not to think of Herbert Wilkinson and his fat sidekick Carlton. He failed.

After breakfast, he instructed his butler to pull back the curtains. 'Let's see what kind of a day it is. Cold and wet, I'll bet.' The curtains were parted and his forecast proved correct. He sighed. 'Any idea what Valerie has planned for the day?'

Davide was a neat little Frenchman. He consulted a small

43

notebook. 'According to her maid, Madame has luncheon arranged at the Ritz for one.'

'With?'

'The Duchess of Castlemore and the Marquise de Baillon. Valentine is coming to the house at eleven to prepare Madame's hair. After lunch her maid anticipates taking a rest prior to accompanying you to Mr Cowan's party tonight.'

Goldsmith opened a drawer in his bedside cabinet and took out a box of pills. Davide opened a nearby bottle of Evian and poured a glass. Goldsmith downed four pills. 'I really don't know why Valerie spends so much time with those two scroungers. Grand enough titles but without two pennies to rub together.'

'Madame's maid says Madame believes they all have things in common.'

Goldsmith pursed his lips. 'She's right there. They have a common interest in money and the spending of it. I can forgive it in my wife but not the others. And drink! They all like to drink. Speaking of which, I'd better warn Valerie to take it easy at lunch if she wants to enjoy Gus's bash tonight.'

'A much sought after invitation I understand, sir.'

'I'm sure it will be pretty high falutin'.'

The butler looked confused.

'That's how Will Rogers used to describe Hollywood parties he didn't want to attend. "Too high falutin' for little old me, Victor. I'll just stay at home and griddle a few steaks on the barbecue." He was a character. Can't believe he's been dead these six years now. Anyway, for your benefit perhaps the word to use is "chic". Then again, that's probably not the word for something associated with Gus Cowan.'

Mention of Cowan got his blood pressure rising again. He would do better this morning to forget the man whose financial finagling had put him in such a mess. He closed his eyes.

'Will you be rising now, sir?'

'Give me another half an hour. I have some thinking to do. You can lay out the usual clothes.'

Davide inclined his head and slipped away. As the door shut, Goldsmith began to consider his position in detail. The world knew him as a successful entrepreneur in a fast-growing and glamorous business. He lived a life of extreme luxury and was to all appearances a very wealthy man. However, smoke and mirrors had played as much of a part in his life as in his films. Ever since he'd become an entrepreneur he'd lived well, even when, like Valerie's titled friends, he'd not had two pennies to rub together himself. He had learned from others in show business to avoid the display of failings, either of confidence or means. He learned to stay at the best hotels, to eat at the best restaurants, to wear the best clothes, and to make sure he always had a beautiful girl in tow. Credit could always be acquired by the exercise of a pugnacious charm, Peters could be robbed to pay Pauls and, in extremis, dud cheques could be employed. This stratagem had worked for Korda, for Spiegel, for Cowan and many others. So far, it had worked for Goldsmith too.

He had spent his childhood years in poverty. Survival had been a struggle. Born in 1888 in a Jewish hovel at the very bottom of society's ladder, he had the advantages of a sharp brain and great capacity for hard work. His road from Lithuanian poverty to his present position at the pinnacle of the British film industry had been a long and hard one. His progression, however, had been steady and frequently blessed by luck. He left school to work as a local shop assistant. Then he became accounts clerk for the shop. Then accounts clerk for a bigger shop, a department store in the capital. The store owner there soon promoted him to buyer. Goldsmith acquired a good working knowledge of the French language in evening classes and this prompted the store owner to send him to Paris as ladies' fashion buyer. Over time in this position he became friendly with several French fashion models. He took a chance, quit his job and started a model agency. Finance was begged and borrowed from various sources and he got the business off the ground. With a little judicious bribery he'd managed to avoid an army call up for the Great War and continued to build the agency steadily. In 1919 a couple of his models were cast in a film and he gained his entrée into the world of film. His agency began to handle film stars as well as models and soon he diversified further into film production, then direction. He was successful, and in due course his growing reputation in France gave him a chance at Hollywood. A number of happy and profitable years had followed there before he'd suffered some serious setbacks. This turn of events had prompted his move to England in the hope of better luck, which he most certainly got.

While Goldsmith had achieved great success and prominence in Britain as a film man, other business ventures on the side proved less rewarding. A string of poor investments depleted his personal finances. He had an expensive wife and two useless spendthrift sons. His company's cash flow funded a lavish lifestyle but the fact was that his personal wealth outside of films was much smaller than people thought. His credit, too, had become stretched. His substantial personal bank lines were now all at their limits and those limits were unlikely to be increased as and when the London Providential's decision became known. Thus, the bailing out of Silver Screen Productions from his own resources was out of the question.

Goldsmith's head was still aching as he swallowed another pill. He decided the coming day could be postponed no longer and eased himself out of bed. After turning things over in his mind, he had realised there was a quick fix available to him. It wasn't a particularly palatable fix, but given the short time frame he'd been given, it might be his best and only option. He would have to consider making the call.

It was one o'clock and Young and Orlov had just been transported to Wormwood Scrubs. Contrary to Merlin's earlier intent, he had launched, at Johnson's instigation, one further round of interrogation. It had proved another waste of time and after the Black Maria had driven away, Merlin had given Johnson and Cole the rest of the day off.

Merlin shared a sandwich lunch with Bridges. Afterwards he sat wondering whether, now that the weekend was his own, a quick trip to see Sonia might after all be possible. He took a copy of the timetables down from the shelf under the cuckoo clock. Long railway journeys were notoriously slow and uncomfortable these days, crammed as the trains were with soldiers shuttling around the country, and weekend travel was the worst. Bridges said he had a friend at Euston who could tell him what state the lines were in. After making the call he made a thumbs down sign.

'There are repair works on the Manchester line today. My mate says you'll be lucky to get there in ten hours. Same tomorrow coming back.'

'That settles that then.' He put the timetables away. 'You're fine to go home if you want, Sam.'

'I thought I might stay and do some catching up. Paperwork has been piling up while I've been stuck at the Old Bailey, and besides Iris has gone off with the baby to visit a cousin in Tooting.'

Merlin hated paperwork but offered to help. 'I've got nothing else on.' It took them a while to deal with everything to the sergeant's satisfaction. When they'd finished, Merlin got to his feet. 'Sitting down this long isn't good for me.' He winced as he stretched out his arms.

'The old bullet wound playing up again, sir?'

'Not today. Just a stiff back and old age.' He raised a hand and mimicked taking a drink. 'Fancy a beer in the Red Lion? I could murder a pint.' Bridges agreed enthusiastically and they were just about to leave when the telephone rang. Merlin sighed. 'I suppose we'd better take it.'

Bridges picked up the receiver and exchanged a few words before saying to Merlin. 'Desk downstairs, sir. Some bloke calling from Westminster Coroner's Office. Wants an urgent word with a detective. I can deal with it if you like and you can get off home.'

'No, it's alright. I'll speak to the fellow and see what he has to say. Do we have a name?'

'Wright, sir.'

A flicker of recognition passed over Merlin's face. 'Name rings a bell. I've had dealings with a pathologist of that name before.' He took the telephone from the sergeant. The line clicked a couple of times and then Merlin heard a well-spoken voice. 'Detective Chief Inspector Merlin? This is Anthony Wright. Do you remember me?'

'I do indeed, sir. Messy shooting in 1938, wasn't it?'

'So it was. How are you keeping?'

'Not so bad. I'm told you have something urgent to discuss?'

'I do. A police matter, I believe. Let me explain. I was called out during the night to help out at the morgue. There was a sudden influx of bodies. Happened all the time during the Blitz of course, but it's been relatively quiet lately. The thing is . . .' Wright broke off. Merlin could hear some sort of commotion in the background. Wright came back on the line a short while later. 'Sorry about that. People anxious to look at the bodies for identification purposes. They've been escorted into another room.'

'You were saying.'

'Yes. So I've been here all night and all day with colleagues examining corpses and verifying causes of death. We've had a total of twenty-five bodies to look at. All found under a collapsed building in Victoria.'

'The building collapsed last night?'

'Yes. Well, actually, it's a little more complicated than that. Two adjacent office buildings were hit by bombs in May. One collapsed straight away but the other, the Costello Building, stayed upright, although severely damaged. It was possible back then to remove the casualties from the adjacent building but the Costello was deemed too dangerous to enter. The authorities have been dilly-dallying since May about whether to pull it down or not but the collapse has taken the decision from them.'

'So the clearance of the Costello Building has now been possible and that's where your bodies have come from?'

'Yes. They're still at it but I understand they're nearly finished. We haven't had a new body for two hours so I'm thinking the twenty-five figure is close to final.'

'And what prompted you to call us?'

Wright took a deep breath. 'One of the bodies uncovered is that of a young girl. A teenager. I'm afraid I don't think she was killed in the bombing. I suspect foul play.'

'Right, sir. We're on our way.' Merlin put the phone down. 'We'll have to wait for our quick pint, Sam. Come on.'

Cole wasn't quite sure what to do with the free Saturday Merlin had given him. In the end he decided on a walk up West and the pictures. After a brisk walk around Hyde Park and a Lyons Corner House pie and mash, he headed for Leicester Square to see what film took his fancy. One of the cinemas on the north side of the square was showing Hitchcock's latest, *Suspicion*, with Cary Grant and Joan Fontaine. He felt a twinge of nostalgic regret. It had not been so long ago that he'd taken Clare Robinson to a Hitchcock film, *Rebecca*, at this very cinema. They'd become an item shortly after. Cole felt his temper rising again at the thought of the treatment he'd received from Clare's uncle, the AC. Cole was not good enough for his beautiful privately-educated niece, and the AC had ruthlessly taken steps to part them.

The main practical consequence of the AC's rough treatment was that Cole had embarked on a major programme of self-improvement. He might be working class and lack the benefits of an Eton education, but he would show Gatehouse what was what and become the smartest and most knowledgeable constable in the Yard. He had taken up night-classes and become particularly interested in British history. He was doing a class at the moment about the English Civil War and found that he was fascinated by Cromwell. A few nights ago, he'd struck up conversation with a pretty Irish girl in the class and they'd engaged in a heated but civilised argument about the Protector's vices and virtues. For the first time since parting with Clare, he had felt attracted to someone. He'd have to build up his courage and ask her out.

He turned away from the Hitchcock hoarding and checked out the next cinema on the square. This one was showing a film starring and made by a fellow called Welles. Cole had read about Welles and the pandemonium he'd caused in America with a scary radio version of The *War of the Worlds*. He decided if Welles could have listeners running for the hills with a little radio programme, he must have something. The film was called *Citizen Kane* and he bought a ticket.

Merlin's nostrils flared as he encountered the depressingly familiar mortuary smells. It had been a few months since he'd last had the experience. In front of the policemen were a number of sheet-covered trolleys carrying, Merlin presumed, the latest arrivals to the morgue. A man appeared at the far end of the room pushing another covered trolley and headed towards them.

'Chief Inspector. Good to see you again. And your colleague is?'

'Detective Sergeant Bridges, sir. Pleased to meet you, Mr Wright.'

Wright was a dapper-looking man who exuded a bouncy energy. He removed his white medical coat to reveal a loud emerald green twill suit. Merlin was a little taken aback. Wright looked down. 'Yes, a bit much, isn't it? However, I just had my birthday and this was my wife's present so wearing it is obligatory I'm afraid. I'm about to join her for a country weekend, bodies allowing of course. Lost half of the weekend already but one lives in hope.' He parked his trolley up against the wall, then removed the sheet. The bare remains of a young girl were revealed. After a moment's hesitation, the policemen moved closer and had a careful look.

'Her face doesn't look as I'd expect.' said Merlin.

'Yes, Chief Inspector. Remarkable, isn't it? The head and neck are in amazingly good condition considering the corpse is presumably around six months old.'

'How come?' asked Merlin.

'Hydrated lime, or you might know it better as slaked lime. She has significant traces on her. The lime has the effect of preservation in the way that you see. It's an effect not too dissimilar from mummification. A strange effect I know, but I think you can make out enough to tell that she must have been a pretty little thing.'

'Hmm. If you say so, Mr Wright. You think she was a teenager?'

'I do. There are a number of physical factors which tell me this is the body of a girl aged somewhere between fourteen and sixteen. I could go through them if you wish.'

'I'll take your word for it. No doubt they'll be listed in your report?'

'They will. If I were pressed to an exact age, I'd say fifteen. In any event, the most important thing from your perspective is that this odd state of preservation prompted me to do a more thorough post mortem than I otherwise might. This led me to identify something crucial.'

'That being?'

'That being, Chief Inspector, that the girl was strangled. There is a fractured hyoid bone.' Wright pointed to the girl's neck. 'It is highly unusual for that bone to be fractured for any other cause than strangulation. We are too late, of course, for other traditional indicators of strangulation, such as bruising or petechiae.'

'Petechiae, sir?' Bridges asked.

'Small red or purple spots on the skin, Sergeant. Caused by broken capillary blood vessels. A side effect of strangulation. The bone fracture, however, is convincing for me.'

Merlin bent down to the body. 'Well, that's good work, Mr Wright, but why the lime? Quick lime I could understand but . . .'

'Quite so, Chief Inspector. A murderer might want to cover the face of his victim in quicklime to accelerate decomposition and forestall identification. My guess is that the murderer is a rather ignorant man and doesn't know the difference between quicklime and hydrated lime, which has the opposite effect to what he was seeking.'

Merlin took a pace back from the trolley. 'He wouldn't be the first killer in this war to think a bomb ruin might be a good place to hide a body. I'm sure a number of murders have been covered up in that way, with victims being wrongly categorised as bomb casualties. However, the murderer here can't have trusted to that chance completely, hence the lime. I admire your diligence, Mr Wright.'

Wright tilted his head in acknowledgement of the compliment and re-covered the body. 'So that's why I called you, gentlemen. I'll be happy to testify but I'm thinking you'll have a very difficult job getting someone to court for this.' He pointed behind him. 'I've got the girl's clothing in the office back there. Everything's filthy and ragged of course.' He disappeared briefly and returned with a straw shopping bag. 'This is all I could find to put them in. They'll be covered with my fingerprints now, but I'm sure it's too late for anyone else's to be found and identified.' He reached into the bag. 'The only things on her were a few coins and this scrap of paper.' Wright handed the paper to Merlin. 'I believe it's part of some kind of food wrapping. You can make out a couple of letters. An "E" and a "Y" I think.'

Merlin looked at the wrapper briefly before passing it to Bridges. 'Well, thank you very much, sir. And well done again.'

'Let me see you out.'

Out on the street, Wright shook hands then hailed a passing taxi. The policemen got into their car and Bridges turned on the ignition. 'Funny chap, sir. Bit like a nervous ferret.'

'A clever ferret, though.' Merlin suddenly felt ashamed. The war was desensitising him. Here he was exchanging minor pleasantries with Bridges when only a few minutes before he'd been looking at the cadaver of a poor murdered girl. He sighed. The war was making death very commonplace.

Bridges pulled out into the road.

'We'd better get Robinson onto the missing person files. She's a whiz at that.'

'Have you forgotten, sir? She's off on that forensic course in Edinburgh. The AC told me you'd cleared it so I couldn't raise any objection.'

'Blast it, Sergeant!' he said irritably. 'I wish you'd double-checked with me. The AC mentioned something in passing a week or so ago and I didn't register it was going to happen so quickly. Has she already gone?'

'Took the sleeper last night, sir. She put in a long day's work on those West End smash and grabs we've been working on, then went straight to the station.'

'Alright, we'll have to get Cole onto it. Come on. Let's be off. Let's have that drink when we get back. I need one.'

Chapter Three

Sunday December 7ᵗʰ 1941

From the terrace of his permanent suite at the Dorchester Hotel, Gus Cowan watched as the early morning light brought the park trees slowly into relief. Clad still in the white-jacketed evening suit in which he'd hosted his party, he relaxed back into a lounger, smoking one of his favourite Turkish cigarettes and cradling a large Napoleon brandy. He'd mislaid his watch but guessed it was somewhere between seven and eight. There was a hoar frost and he had a thick blanket to hand, but ignored it. The winters of his Moravian youth, almost Arctic in their intensity, had made him largely impervious to extremes of cold. He turned his head for an instant. The bedroom window further along the terrace was slightly ajar and he could hear the gentle snoring of one or other of his young night time companions. For some reason he hadn't yet availed himself of their charms. He was usually ready for action at any time, regardless of alcoholic intake. Something, however, had put him off his stroke.

What had it been? Was it the unattractive sight of so many drunken women? The newly returned Laura Curzon and Victor Goldsmith's wife, Valerie, had certainly made spectacles of themselves. Nothing turned him off more than the sight of an intoxicated woman. It wasn't that, though, he was sure. Was it the writ served on him just before the party began? No. Writs were as confetti to him. He'd dealt with hundreds of them over the years.

Meaningless pieces of paper. No, he suddenly realised what it was. It was the completely unexpected violence of Goldsmith's tirade when they'd found themselves alone together in the gents. It was that which had disturbed his equilibrium.

He had first known Goldsmith in Hollywood when they had competed in pitching low budget movies to the smaller studios like Columbia and Universal. European emigrés, particularly the Eastern European ones, tended to congregate together socially and more often than not at a card table. It was in a game of gin-rummy at Anatole Litvak's place that they'd first come across each other. Despite the fact that they were deadly competitors, a grudging sort of friendship had developed. It was not the sort of friendship which precluded the one from shafting the other in business but it did have its positive side. When they met, Goldsmith was ahead in the Hollywood game. He had arrived in California earlier and, Cowan had to concede, possessed the wider range of talents. He could both direct and produce, had a better eye for talent, and possessed considerably more charm. Cowan was little more than a hustler. A very good hustler, but a hustler all the same. His greatest attribute as a film producer then and now was relentlessness. He had that in spades.

Goldsmith had decided to transfer to England in the early 30s. He'd had a bad run and become disillusioned with Hollywood. Cowan followed a few years later, leaving a large cast of angry creditors in his wake. In England the two men had seen quite a bit of each other from the outset and maintained cordial relations. They agreed not to tread on each other's toes, gave each other the odd tip, and tried to avoid bad-mouthing each other. While not quite in Goldsmith's league, Cowan had raced well up the producing ranks by the time the war began. He was now a top ten producer. His ambition was to get into the top three.

In the summer, the two men had agreed to collaborate on a film for the first time. A bright young defector from Michael Balcon's Ealing Studios had brought Cowan an excellent script about the young Shakespeare. Cowan had liked it because it had the potential to be something of a bawdy romp, while Goldsmith, who was keen to buy the script from him, appreciated its high artistic potential. In the end they had compromised by agreeing a co-production, which was scheduled for shooting at Silver Screen Studios in the second half of the coming year.

So, given their good relationship, why had Goldsmith been so angry with him? Why had he overreacted about a few accounting irregularities, and what was it to him anyway? Financial creativity was all part of the game in their industry, and Victor knew that as well as anyone. He might like to pretend he was whiter than white, but Cowan knew different. His present chief accountant, Isaac Steiner, had previously been Victor's accountant.

Cowan was supremely relaxed about the writs the London Providential were showering on him. Steiner had assured him that his position was watertight and he'd already secured a new backer, a star-struck Scottish industrialist, to replace the oafs at the insurance company. He was sorry if his financial manipulations had somehow caused Goldsmith discomfort, although Goldsmith had given no indication of what that discomfort might be. But then Victor was a big boy. He would be able to weather any storm which came along. There would be another financial stooge waiting around the corner soon, if required. Meanwhile, Goldsmith could do a bit of ducking and diving if needs be, just as the two of them had been doing on and off all their working lives.

Suddenly he realised that the gentle snoring had stopped. His ears pricked up at the sound of pattering footsteps somewhere inside. Standing up, he finished his brandy and stubbed out his cigarette on the bronze statue of a nymph behind him. He opened the French doors and undid his tie. 'Are you up, my darlings? Ready for a little fun with Uncle Gus?'

Merlin had been intent on going into the Yard first thing to make a start on identifying the Victoria girl, but after thinking about it, he realised he'd be able to achieve very little on a Sunday. It was

56

also the case that the girl's body had been lying in the rubble for six months already, and another day's delay in investigating her murder would be neither here nor there. He could do with a break, and when Bridges called to find out his plans he told him to inform everyone they had the day off. Then he relaxed back into his chair to decide what to do with his unforeseen day of leisure. It had been a while since he'd visited the local pub on a Sunday and it took no time for him to think of the person he'd most like to see for a lunchtime drink.

Proud Scot and Merlin's closest friend, Jack Stewart spent a heroic spell of service as a senior London Auxiliary Fire Service officer during the Blitz. He'd since been posted to the North of England to help improve the AFS operations in Liverpool and Manchester. After several months away, Merlin knew he'd just returned to London but they hadn't reconnected yet. He gave him a call.

Stewart was at home and free and more than willing, so they arranged to meet at The Surprise at one. Once there, they secured a quiet table at the back of the pub and settled down cheerfully with their pints of London Pride.

'Been a while, Jack.'

'That it has, Frank. It's great to see you again. You look well. Fatherhood and marriage must be suiting you.'

Merlin wiped some froth from his lips. 'I haven't really had much fathering to do so far. Immediately after the boy's birth we decided it best for Sonia to go to her parents for the baby's first few weeks. She's there now.'

'Sounds sensible.'

'I feel pretty useless in the circumstances.'

'As would I.' Stewart looked thoughtfully at his pint. 'Sorry I couldn't make the wedding. I had quite a bit on my plate.'

'No need for apologies. There's a war on, isn't there?' The two men grimaced at the well-worn cliché.

Stewart was a handsome man of similar height and build to Merlin, although he carried a few extra pounds of muscle. He had a well-chiselled face and wavy red-brown hair. He was a keen ladies man when he had the opportunity.

'I'm sure Sam did a much better job than I would have as best man.'

'He was a safe pair of hands. No crude jokes or embarrassing stories.'

'You think I'd have done that to you?' Stewart pursed his lips.

'We'll never know now, will we?' Merlin winked. 'Anyway, how was it? Your northern posting?'

'To tell the truth, Frank, it was bloody boring. We had the odd little bit of activity but it was like a tea party compared with the Blitz. I was very busy but mostly with administrative matters. Lots of politics to deal with, of course. Politics, as you know, is not my metier.'

'You'd probably have found London a little boring if you'd stayed. Not a serious raid since May.'

'I know. Boredom apart, it was obviously a bloody good thing Hitler fancied himself the superior of Napoleon and attacked Russia.'

'And what is it the AFS have you doing now you're back in The Smoke?' Merlin drank some beer.

'I'm running a station again, which is much more up my street. I hoped to get my old Chelsea station back but it's in good hands apparently. They've given me Victoria, instead.'

'That's funny. I was in Victoria last night. Looks like we have a murder there.'

'Oh, yes?'

'Girl found dead in a collapsed building. Been there for a while but the pathologist thinks she was strangled.'

'Where was she found exactly?'

'Place called the Costello Building.'

'Hmm. I know about that place. I'm not starting until tomorrow but I've been keeping tabs on things. Several of my new men were involved in clearing the place.'

'That's very interesting, Jack. I'd like to have a word with whoever found the body.'

'Why don't you come over tomorrow?' Stewart took out a pencil and scribbled something on the cigarette packet he'd just emptied of its last Navy Cut. 'Here's the number. Call me first thing.' He picked up their now empty glasses and headed off to the counter. Merlin reflected on the many pleasant hours the two men had passed in The Surprise. They had first met on the football field in the 20s and had become fast friends. They had remained close over the years and had become even closer when Merlin's first wife succumbed to leukaemia. Stewart had been a brick and Merlin would never forget.

Stewart returned with two replenished glasses and a couple of meat pies. 'Thought you might be feeling peckish, Frank. I know I am.'

Merlin examined his pie carefully. 'Think it's safe?'

'Reckon there might be a bit of dog inside?' He dug his fork into the centre of his pie and tried it. 'Tastes fine. But what if there is a little canine content? A seafaring friend of mine told me way back that dogs are some sort of delicacy out in Korea. Come on. Tuck in!' Little reassured by Stewart's comments, Merlin took a small bite. It tasted good and he took another.

The pies were dispatched in short order. Stewart grunted with pleasure. 'That certainly did the trick. You know, I was in a pub in Liverpool a couple of months ago and a pissed countryman of mine was going on about how he'd never tried a haggis and would love to do so. I hate haggis and told him so. Almost ended up in fisticuffs we did. Anyway if you want a food product with dodgy ingredients, look no further. God knows what rubbish people put in their haggises. I thought of giving him a quick burst of Robbie Burns' famous poem on the subject but it would have been wasted on him.' The two men enjoyed a deep love of poetry and liked to engage in friendly competitions to test their mutual knowledge.

'It won't be wasted on me. Let's hear it, then' Merlin asked.

Stewart mopped up a stray morsel of pie he'd missed on his plate. 'Och, I don't know. It will probably sound like gibberish to you.'

Merlin smirked. 'Most things you say sound like gibberish to me, Jack.'

'Very funny, Frank Merlin. Alright, you asked for it. I'll just rinse my larynx.' Stewart took a couple of gulps of beer then, as was his wont when reciting, placed his hand on his heart.

> Fair fa' your honest, sonsie face,
> Great chieftain o' the puddin'-race!
> Aboon them a' ye tak your place,
> Painch, tripe or thairm
> Weel are ye worthy o'a grace
> As lang's my arm.

Stewart beamed at Merlin. 'So what do you think?'

'As far as I can tell, Burns seems to be rather positive about the haggis. Maybe I'll try it with you, one day. When the war's over.'

Winston Churchill had passed as pleasant a weekend as possible given the dire circumstances of the country he led. He had been at Chequers, the Prime Minister's official country residence. For a while, after the German bombing had started, both Chequers and his own rural retreat in Kent had been declared off-limits for security reasons. Both properties, set in open countryside, had been deemed too vulnerable to air attack. Now that the German bombing threat had diminished, greater latitude was being offered and he was grateful to be able to use Chequers again.

It was Sunday evening and he was dining with two of his favourite Americans. Gil Winant had succeeded Joe Kennedy as American Ambassador in March and was infinitely more supportive of the British war effort than his defeatist predecessor. Avercll Harriman was a wealthy financier and businessman whom Roosevelt had appointed as his special envoy to Europe. Also dining tonight were Harriman's daughter, Katherine, the PM's naval assistant, Tommy Thompson, and Thompson's private secretary,

John Martin. Despite the congenial company, Churchill was not his normal ebullient self. His guests could only presume the pressures and anxieties of his office were weighing particularly heavily tonight. It was not often that Churchill let the mask slip, but there were a host of things to worry about. Most pressing was the situation in the Far East. There had been reports of Japanese flotillas steaming towards the Malayan peninsula. The PM was awaiting further confirmations about what was happening. Winant had been able to divine further specific matters of concern over the pre-dinner cocktails. Churchill had enquired whether the USA would declare war on the Japanese if they attacked British possessions but made no move against America. The Ambassador had only been able to give a formulaic response that such a decision would be up to Congress. Churchill's reaction of brooding silence had opened Winant's eyes. The man was clearly, and naturally, worried that Britain might shortly be fighting a war on two fronts while the Americans continued to stand aside.

The good food and wine at dinner had not had its usual revivifying effect on the PM and he was sitting silently, head in hands, when his valet, Sawyers, as was the normal routine, brought in a radio so that his master and the guests could listen to the BBC nine o' clock news. Sawyers plugged in the wireless and turned the on dial. When the machine had eventually warmed up, the characterful refined voice of Alvar Lidell filled the room. He read out some discouraging news about British progress in North Africa, then more positive news about Russian resistance to the Nazis on the Eastern Front. As Lidell moved on to provide more details about these opening headlines and other items, conversation around the table began to pick up and the radio became secondary. Suddenly, however, the private secretary Martin stood up. 'Did you hear that? Something about an attack on American ships?' There was a shaking of heads and everyone looked at each other enquiringly.

In the silence, Sawyers emerged from the shadows at the back of the room. As usual, there was little deference in his words.

61

'Didn't you 'ear? Japs have attacked some American base in Hawaii. Gold Harbour or something it was called.'

'Good God! Pearl Harbour!' exclaimed Harriman.

'Aye, that's the one. Pearl Harbour.'

Churchill reached out to the radio and turned the volume up. He was suddenly alert with a gleam in his eye. Lidell was repeating the headlines and the newsflash of the attack had been moved to the top of the order.

'Japanese aircraft are reported to have attacked Pearl Harbour, the American naval base, in Hawaii. Naval and military targets elsewhere in Hawaii have also been raided. The White House said details are still coming in.'

The company sat in stunned silence for a moment before an ebullient Churchill leaned forward to pound the table with his fist. 'We shall declare war on Japan immediately, Ambassador.'

Winant held up a hand of caution. 'Prime Minister, I think we should await further confirmation before any action is taken.'

The PM leaned back in his chair and folded his hands over his rotund stomach. 'It is my understanding that the information broadcast over the radio emanates from the US Government. What further confirmation is required?'

'Don't you think we should get a more direct source than the BBC?'

Churchill pondered for a moment before replying. 'Indeed I do, Mr Ambassador. Martin? Please make arrangements to get Mr Roosevelt on the telephone at once.'

Fifteen minutes later, a telephone was brought, plugged in, and placed on the dining table. Churchill looked at Gil Winant who was seated on his right. 'You speak first, Mr Ambassador.'

Winant picked up the receiver. 'Mr President.' He listened as Roosevelt gave him a summary of what he knew. Then the telephone was passed to the Prime Minister.

'Franklin, my dear fellow.'

'Winston? It's true I'm afraid. The Japanese Air Force have attacked our most important naval base. I don't want to go into too much detail in case this is an insecure line, but the fact is that we are all in the same boat now. I shall go to Congress tomorrow and request a declaration of war against Japan.'

Churchill's jaw jutted out in its familiar way. 'And we shall follow suit within the hour. And we must meet Mr President. Very soon. I shall come to you.'

When the call had ended, Churchill's cheerful exhilaration was clear for all to see. The Japanese action would bring the United States into Britain's war at last. He could see light at the end of the tunnel for the first time. It would take time, guts, blood, sacrifice and superhuman effort, but with Britain and America in harness, Hitler's days were numbered. Of this he had no doubt.

Chapter Four

It was still dark when Merlin left the flat on Monday morning. The overnight rain had stopped and the forecast had promised a crisp sunny day, so he decided to walk to work. The exercise, he thought, should help clear the mild hangover he'd acquired from his outing with Jack Stewart.

He was crossing Buckingham Gate when the sun rose. Entering St James's Park, he glanced back at the Palace and wondered what their majesties might be up to today. He chuckled to himself as he remembered the bizarre situation Johnson and Cole had got themselves into during the Blitz. For reasons Merlin couldn't quite remember, the two policemen had found themselves in the Palace forecourt with a group of firefighters. All of a sudden the King himself had appeared and chatted freely with them for a while until the Queen had come along and hurried him off to a place of greater safety.

The brightening sky put a spring in Merlin's step. When he reached Parliament Square he got a newspaper. The shocking headline pulled him up sharp. He read the story twice before turning onto the Embankment and entering the Yard. He was still in something of a daze when he got to his office and almost didn't notice the AC who was hovering down the corridor.

'What news, eh Frank?' The AC had a broad grin on his face.

'Pearl Harbour, you mean? I've only just heard about it.'

'Have you been hibernating? It's been all over the radio since last night.'

Merlin shrugged and pushed at the door. He acknowledged Bridges who was already at the little desk by the window which was his to use when he chose.

Seeing the AC follow his boss in, the sergeant asked, 'Shall I make myself scarce, sir?'

The AC waved a hand at Bridges. 'That won't be necessary, Sergeant. Just a passing visit of no great import.'

Merlin sat at his desk. 'You seem very cheerful today, sir.'

The AC sat down. 'And why not, Frank? The Emperor Hirohito has done us a great favour.'

'I doubt all those dead and wounded servicemen in Hawaii would see it that way.'

The AC shifted a little uncomfortably in his chair. 'No, of course they wouldn't. Of course. But one has to look at the big picture. With America on our side in the war, our situation has improved enormously.'

'And what about all of our own people now at risk in the Far East. People in places like Malaysia, Burma, Hong Kong?'

'Yes, yes. There are negatives of course, and lives have been lost and will continue to be lost. But can't you see it, Frank? This could be a critical turning point in the war.' Merlin said nothing and the two men stared awkwardly at each other for an uncomfortable few seconds until the AC got abruptly to his feet. He sniffed irritably. 'I can see you're not in the mood to discuss the news sensibly.' He went to the door where he paused to say, 'I understand you have a new murder on your hands. Be sure to keep me posted.'

When he was gone Bridges asked, 'Were you intending to get up his nose sir, or did it just happen by accident?'

'Hmm.' Merlin rested his hands on the desk, 'I didn't really mean to antagonise him. It's just I haven't really had enough time to digest this news. Maybe he's right and the attack is a good thing in the long run, but I can't help thinking of the great loss of life and the danger our people in the East are facing.'

Bridges came over to the desk and sat down, a folder in his hand. 'Iris is in a state, as you might imagine.'

'Of course, Sam. Sorry I hadn't thought about your nephew.'

'I was very glad to get out of the house this morning, to tell the truth. It's hard to know what to say. Poor Dan is on a Fleet flagship in what's about to become a war zone. He's right in the firing line, isn't he?'

'I suppose he is. I'm not sure I'd know what to say to Iris either.' Merlin saw Johnson and Cole at the door. 'Join us please, gentlemen. We were just discussing the attack on Pearl Harbour.' For the first time Merlin noticed the file in the sergeant's hand. 'You have something for us, Sam?'

'Mr Wright's report. It was delivered just before you got in, sir.'

'That was very quick. Perhaps he didn't make his weekend in the country after all.' Merlin took the file from Bridges and leafed through it. There was nothing new in the post-mortem summary, but there was much more detail to support Wright's findings, and several photographs. When Merlin had had a good look, he passed the file across the desk to Inspector Johnson and Constable Cole. 'The sergeant has briefed you on our new case I presume?'

Johnson nodded. 'He rang me yesterday and I told the constable.'

Cole was looking uncomfortable as he flipped through the photographs.

'Not very nice, I know, Constable, but there's more to see of the girl than we would normally expect after six months or so,' said Merlin.

'The sergeant told us about the lime, sir,' said Johnson.

'Yes. A strange mistake on the part of the murderer it seems. Generally, however, we've very little to work with. We do have the girl's clothes. Where are they, Sergeant?'

Bridges retrieved the straw bag from under his table. 'I've not touched anything. Presumed you'd want it sent off to forensics.'

'We should, I suppose, though it's probably too late for them to find anything. What about that wrapping paper in her pocket?'

Bridges reached into the bag. 'Here, Sergeant. Take them out with these tweezers, just in case.'

Bridges extracted the scrap of paper and placed it on the desk. There was one straight side and three jagged ones. Faint though they were, three whitish capital letters showed clearly set against a brown background. There was an 'E' and a 'Y'. The 'Y' was followed by what looked like an apostrophe and then came an 'S'. After all three officers had looked for a while at the paper from various angles, Cole tentatively raised his hand.

'Yes, Cole?'

'I think I know what it is, sir.'

'Please enlighten us.'

'It's a chocolate bar wrapper, sir. The letters are the last three letters of the brand.'

'Not Cadbury's or Fry's, then. What is it?'

'It's a Hershey's Bar, sir. An American brand of chocolate.'

'Don't think I've heard of that. You two?'

Johnson and Bridges shook their heads.

'Are you sure, Cole?'

'Yes, sir. I know about it because my sister had a fling with a Yank before the war. A sailor off a boat being repaired in the Pool of London. There was a Saturday afternoon when they were alone in the house with me. My mum was out working. For obvious reasons they wanted me to make myself scarce and I was being awkward, so the sailor gave me a bribe. A bar of chocolate. A Hershey's Bar.'

'And you recognise this as the remnant of a Hershey's Bar wrapper?'

'I do, sir. Chocolate was a real luxury. The Hershey's Bar naturally sticks out in my mind.'

'Are these available in our shops?'

'I don't think so. Maybe some fancy ones. This sailor bloke made a big fuss, bragging about how much better American chocolate was than ours and what a lucky boy I was.'

The office window was open a crack and Merlin could hear

some loud shouting. Probably something military, he thought. Detachments of soldiers were frequent sights near Parliament these days. 'So our girl had an American chocolate wrapper on her. What does that signify? Cole?'

'That she had an American friend?'

'Or was American herself?' suggested Johnson.

'I wonder.' Merlin picked up the pathologist's report. 'Generally speaking, Americans have much better dentistry than us. In here Wright says her teeth were "in good condition".' Merlin paused to think. 'As we have so very little to go on, perhaps it might be worth a visit to the American Embassy. Find out if they've got any missing American girls of the right age.'

'Wouldn't they have already passed such missing person cases to us?' As he spoke Johnson stroked his upper lip. In the early days of the war, he had sported a neat little moustache. The AC had got him to shave it as it made him think of the Führer. Merlin knew Johnson still felt a little naked without it.

'It's possible some may have slipped between the cracks. It can't do any harm to ask, anyway.'

Merlin returned to Wright's report. 'Estimated age 14 to 15. Height five feet two. Weight when alive estimated at six to seven stone. Distinguishing marks, none. Hair fairish brown. Eyes . . . well the eyes are gone. Wright thinks the clothes she was wearing were of reasonable quality. White blouse, tweed skirt. Remnants of nylons on her legs. As we know, nylons are at a premium these days. Underwear . . .' Merlin noticed Cole blushing. 'Come, now, Constable, you're not too delicate for this job are you? Normal underwear again of decent quality.' He closed the file and sat back. 'Really we haven't got much, have we? We had more to work on with that Irish girl last summer.'

'Bridget Healy.'

'Yes, Sergeant. The botched abortion case which happened while the Inspector and Cole were away. At least poor Miss Healey had a bit of a toe missing to distinguish her.' He looked at Cole. 'Constable, with WPC Robinson away, the leg work on this is yours. You know the routine. Ring around all the central London nicks starting with Victoria. See who's on the missing rosters. If you have no luck, extend your enquiries to the suburbs. Inspector, you deal with the American Embassy. As for you, Sergeant, by the strangest of coincidences, Jack Stewart is taking charge at Victoria Fire Station today. You come there with me. We should be able to speak to some of the men involved in the search and clearance of the Costello Building.'

David Seltzer, a white-haired man who looked much older than his fifty years, was, as usual, wearing two pairs of spectacles – one lodged on his forehead and the other on his nose. He twitched nervously as he reorganised the large pile of papers he'd just set down on his boss's desk.

'Well. How's it looking? Have you come up with a plan?' Goldsmith could not conceal the impatience in his voice. Seltzer was a good accountant but there was something about him which got under Goldsmith's skin. Seltzer's predecessor, Isaac Steiner, had been younger and more personable, for an accountant at least. It was a pity he and Isaac had fallen out about money. He had always had a habit of underpaying his closest henchmen. Valerie chided him about it, and she was right to do so. Not only had he lost an excellent figures man in Steiner, but Cowan had immediately snapped him up for his company. Isaac would have been worth his weight in gold at a time like this. Seltzer was solid but not as creative as Steiner.

'I'm just going over a few final things. If you could just bear with me.' The accountant frantically searched for something in the pages of one of the files.

Goldsmith swung his swivel chair around 180 degrees to face the main window. He had a good view of the picturesque studio lawn which led down to the river. The head of Silver Screen Studios had two offices in his film complex. There was this one, located high above the main film set, and another, a grander affair, in the Administrative Block which he used for entertaining financial and movie bigwigs. He liked the one above the set best. He liked to be in the middle of things, with only a quick walk down the stairs to the action. The two other Silver Screen sets were close as well, located in the adjacent building. If he opened the internal window to the left of his desk, he could hear all the studio buzz below. Today the clinking of glasses, the hubbub of party extras, and the music of a small orchestra, interspersed with the shouted instructions of Emil Kaplan and his assistants, filtered up to him. He recalled they were shooting an early scene of *Murder at Midnight* set in a London nightclub.

The task given Seltzer, when Goldsmith had called the accountant at his Northwood home on Sunday morning, was to produce a major cost-cutting plan for Silver Screen over the next six months. That was the time he thought he needed to refinance his business.

The sound of Seltzer clearing his throat made Goldsmith swing his chair round. 'You're ready?'

The accountant swapped his spectacles around. 'I have formulated a number of proposals and suggestions, sir. I'm not sure if you'll like them all.'

'Before we start, I hope you're not going to propose anything which will impinge on my routine level of expenses?'

Seltzer extracted a couple of sheets from his pile of papers, screwed them up and threw both with surprising accuracy into the wicker basket by the office door.

'Bravo, David! You have hidden talents.'

Seltzer's mouth contorted itself strangely. An odd wheezing noise emanated from his mouth. He was registering amusement.

'So what do you propose we cut, Mr Chief Accountant?'

'I take it you do not wish to cancel any of the current or forthcoming productions?'

'You take it correctly. As you well know, a cancellation of any film would undermine confidence and bring further financial pressure on us. Confidence is essential if we are to get through the next few months. I'm sure the London Providential's action will become known at some point, but as long as we continue to churn out films, the damage can be limited. People will think I'm rolling in it and can support the studio myself. They'll think if I need one, a new backer will be easily found. And, of course, that is my fervent hope. The maintenance of a full roster is thus essential but no doubt a little judicious adjustment of timings and timetables can produce reasonable savings.'

'I have taken the liberty of factoring in a few "judicious adjustments" as you call them.'

'Good. Good. So what else have you got?'

Seltzer consulted the sheet of paper sitting on top of his pile. 'First of all there is the talent. On the current productions, all the actors excepting the extras, who are paid daily, have received only part of their agreed fee.'

'With the exception of Adair whose total fee I, like an idiot, paid up front.'

'Indeed, sir, with that exception. I propose to defer paying the balances to everyone else. *Murder at Midnight* has only two weeks shooting to go. People will not start asking for their balances until after the film is in the can. We could easily string them out for a while. It's being Christmas will help.'

'And we can do the same with the other productions. I made most of the actors anyway. They'll just have to lump it. What about those behind the screen?'

'You probably want to keep the editors happy until the films are completed. Otherwise I propose . . .'

'Stringing them out, too? I'm sure we'll manage. As for the directors, Emil is a man of means and he's in my pocket anyway. The other fellows are young, up and coming. They'll wait for their money if I say so. As for the 1942 films we'll have to back-end as many of our contracts as possible. Most likely have to sweeten the deals a little too to get everyone to agree.'

'Yes, sir. You know very well how to go about such things, but I have made some estimates of what savings we might be able to achieve during the crucial period.'

'Good. What else?'

Seltzer proceeded to go through a long list of detailed cost-cutting or cost-saving measures which Goldsmith, after some careful cross-examination, decided to approve in their entirety. He lit the cigar he had been promising himself as a treat all morning, and sent a long trail of blue smoke off to the ceiling. The room was unventilated, save for the small part-open internal window, and Seltzer began to cough.

'Alright, alright, David. I know you've got asthma. Off you go. Thank you and I'd appreciate, as Mr Churchill inscribes all his memos, "Action this day"!'

Seltzer was almost out of the door when Goldsmith remembered something. 'David. You made no mention of insurance.'

'I gave it some thought but decided you'd only wish to discontinue the premiums as an act of last resort.'

Goldsmith heard his stomach rumbling. He had been too wound up to eat any breakfast and the morning was well-advanced. 'You were right. We must keep up the premiums. Who knows? Some helpful chap might burn down the studio or bump off one of the stars. That would provide a nice windfall.'

Seltzer looked nervously at his boss, unsure if he was joking or not.

Goldsmith maintained a poker face. 'Off you go then. Tell Gloria to come in, will you?'

Gloria appeared instantly, notebook and pencil in hand. Gloria Broome was a buxom peroxide blonde of thirty-five years who had been at Goldsmith's side for most of the decade he'd been in England. She had auditioned for the part of a secretary in one of his early British productions. Her acting had been atrocious but she'd displayed excellent secretarial skills and he'd taken her on. She had soon become an essential cog in the management of his business and personal life. Although privy to most of his secrets, she had not yet been informed about his latest difficulties. She had quickly surmised, however, that something was wrong. Gloria was a perkily attractive woman, and Goldsmith had often been tempted to cross the line with her. He knew, however, that an affair would put their working relationship at risk and congratulated himself that, so far at least, he had not succumbed to temptation.

'Can you get me a plate of sandwiches and a glass of lemonade from the canteen. And before you go, please dial this number and put it through.' He handed her a scribbled telephone number.

Gloria looked at the number and pursed her lips. 'Things that bad are they? What's the problem?'

Goldsmith picked up one of the awards with which his office was cluttered. It was a bronze statuette of a rearing horse which had been awarded him in Spain for a 1933 quota quickie called *Sangria*. It honoured the positive image the film had given of Spain, albeit the film production team had never left the confines of Twickenham Studios. It was ironic that the country portrayed so well was shortly after plunged into a bloody and horrific civil war. He stroked the bronze figure for a moment then looked back at Gloria. The fact was, good as all Seltzer's proposals were, they were not enough to give him peace of mind. To achieve peace of mind, the unpalatable measure he'd been pondering must be taken forward.

'I'll tell you all about it when you've got the sandwiches. For now, just get the number.'

His secretary retreated and a light on his phone soon started flashing. He picked up the receiver. A heavily accented voice came on the line. 'Victor. Long time. Good to hear from you. How may I assist?'

Merlin's planned morning visit to the fire station was delayed by a call from the AC. 'I bit on one of Miss Stimson's homemade ginger biscuits, Frank, and jarred a nerve. I'm in agony. My dentist says he can fit me in now but at no other time today. I'm due at an important Home Office meeting. You'll have to go in my place. It's about third columnists.' Merlin argued but the AC wouldn't budge.

73

The meeting lasted over three hours. There were two other senior policemen present along with a gaggle of civil servants. In the chair was the relatively new Home Secretary, Herbert Morrison. Merlin thought Morrison, a pugnacious and effective Labour machine politician, an improvement on his predecessor, a dour establishment automaton called Anderson. The principal purpose of the meeting was to discuss the legal nuts and bolts of dealing with suspected spies and fellow-travellers like the Mosleyites. It was all pretty boring and Merlin found he had little to contribute. The one part of the discussion which piqued his interest was Japan's new hostile status. The civil service had made a preliminary list of Japanese residents in Britain, but there weren't enough staff available to properly assess the risks posed by each individual. Morrison advised the safest option, in the circumstances, was to arrest them all.

Merlin and Bridges finally got to Victoria at two. They were just in time to hear Jack Stewart make his first address to his men. Merlin noticed he made a great effort to tone down his Scottish accent. The speech was met with a solid round of applause and the men dispersed. Stewart saw the policemen on the side of the room.

'Got your message, Frank. It's probably for the best you're late. I've had a very busy morning.' Stewart put a hand on Bridges's shoulder. 'Good to see you, Sergeant. I understand you did a great job at the wedding. You'll have to give me a rerun of your best man's speech some time. I'd like to know how easy a time you gave Frankie boy here!'

'Good to see you too, Jack' said Bridges a little stiffly.

'Why don't the two of you come and see my grand new office?'

They followed Stewart behind some fire engines and down a corridor. His office was cramped, with a small desk, and three rickety chairs.

'Apparently I'll get a filing cabinet if I'm a good boy! No, it's not really that bad. There's a bigger office for me up front but it's being painted. Take a pew. I have to say it's wonderful to be back in harness at a station again. There may be no bombers at the moment but there seems to be plenty to be getting on with. The bomb damage to utilities continues to be a big headache. A week ago, a gas main exploded around the corner and set a street of houses on fire. Five people killed. There's going to be much more of that sort of thing, I think. And, of course, we still have damaged buildings collapsing all over the place, as you know.'

'Speaking of which, Jack, do you know the fire officers involved with the Costello Building?'

'Better than that. I found the two officers who dug your girl out.' Stewart turned to the door. 'Sharp, Miller. In here if you please.'

Two firemen squeezed into the room. They both looked to be in their fifties. Miller had a face carpeted with moles and was the taller and tougher-looking of the two. Sharp, balding, weak-chinned and bespectacled, looked like a bank clerk.

Stewart introduced the policemen and explained why they were there. 'Any help you can give the officers will be gratefully appreciated. Frank?'

'I appreciate your time, gentlemen. We are investigating the death of one of the people found in the Costello. A teenage girl. Mr Stewart says it was you who found her?'

'We discovered three girls that night.' Miller's voice was as ragged as his face. 'They were the only girls found so I guess one must be yours.'

'Show them Wright's photograph, Sergeant.'

Bridges took it from his pocket and the firemen leaned forward to look.

'That's the last body we dug up. It was I who saw her first.' said Sharp, who was much better spoken than his partner. 'She was trapped under some collapsed wooden joists. It was rather strange, actually. Above the wood was a section of wall which had fallen there from a higher storey. It had a red arrow on it which was pointing at the body. A rather creepy coincidence.'

'Were you both working here in May when the building was bombed?' asked Merlin.

75

Miller replied. 'I was, but Sharpie here wasn't a fireman then. I got called out on the job. As you know, the Costello and the place next door, the Blythe building, were 'it. The Blythe was flattened while the Costello was badly damaged but remained standin'. It took some time to put the fires out but when that 'ad been done we went in with the ARP and other emergency workers to search for survivors and bodies in both buildings. After a few hours of lookin', a bunch of jobsworths turned up and told us to stop working in the Costello. They said they was worried it would fall down on us. We did as we were told and the site's been fenced off ever since. Well, until Friday that is. I think . . .'

Sharp interrupted. 'As I understand it, Mr Merlin, the building would normally have been pulled down in a controlled fashion straight after the bombing, but that didn't happen. Mr Stewart's predecessor said there was some politics involved. Some bureaucratic wrangle. Something about the building having special significance, historical maybe, but no one has been able to explain what that was. Regardless, it was bound to come down one day soon.'

'I see. Thank you. So coming back to Friday night, what happened after you first discovered the body?'

'I called to Max here come and help me get her out.'

Bridges looked at Miller and couldn't help smiling. 'You are really called Max Miller?'

Miller chuckled. 'Nah. Max is a nickname, innit? I'm really John, but that's too boring for my mates.'

Sharp continued. 'So Max came over to help and we got the poor thing out. It wasn't too difficult as we were mainly dealing with wood and light rubble. There wasn't any heavy masonry to shift.'

'Did you find anything unusual, out of the ordinary, near the body?' asked Bridges.

'Nah,' said Miller. 'Only the normal sort of clutter you find in these bombed-out buildings. Broken glass, piping, tangled wiring, cigarette packets . . .'

76

Sharp interrupted his partner. 'I suppose you might say the cig-arette packets were a little out of the ordinary. Some of them, anyway.'

'How so, Mr Sharp?' asked Merlin.

'Well in amongst the Player's and Rothmans and so on, there was a foreign brand. I'm not a smoker myself. What was it, Max?'

'Yank ciggies. Couple o' packets of Camel. Four cigarettes left in total.'

'What did you do with them?'

'Picked 'em up and smoked 'em when I got a chance. Can't say they were that great but a smoke's a smoke isn't it?'

'Anything else you observed?'

Sharp looked thoughtful. 'Well, it did occur to both of us that the corpse was . . . er . . . in rather good condition . . . considering how long it must have been lying there.'

'You're right, Mr Sharp. There was a reason which I'll let Mr Stewart tell you later.' The policemen asked a few more questions but the firemen had nothing interesting to tell them and they were allowed to return to their duties.

'Sorry, Frank. Don't think you got much there.' said Stewart.

'No need to apologise, Jack. They saw what they saw. It's possible the American cigarettes might be of interest. We found an American chocolate wrapper on her. I suppose it's an odd coincidence. It might be worth checking if there were any American businesses located in the Costello Building. If so, per-haps the girl had some involvement there.' Merlin got to his feet. 'Anyway, thanks, Jack. We'll leave you to your new job. Good luck!'

They sat together in a secluded corner at the back of the steam room. The Monday afternoon regulars at the Porchester Baths knew well enough to give them a wide berth. Joseph Abela, the shorter, plumper, and darker of the two, had been operating on the wrong side of the law in London for over thirty years, ever since his arrival from Malta. The other, Billy Hill, was younger, thinner, taller, and a Londoner born and bred. Despite his relative youth, he was the senior of the two. A crook since childhood, he had been a very successful pre-war gangster in London. The onset of war had taken his power to another level, and he relished the opportunity to become king of the black market.

Joe Abela, whose harsh accent had been moderated only slightly by thirty years in London, ran his own powerful gang but deferred to, and paid tribute to, Billy Hill. Much as he detested being in this position, he knew he was not strong enough to cross the criminal king. Yet.

'How's business, Joe?'

'Can't complain, Billy. And you?'

'Fair to middling. Anything to report?'

Abela took as deep a breath as the swirling hot wet air would allow him. 'You heard about the little setback in Shoreditch last week?' Abela knew there was no point trying to hide unfortunate developments from Hill.

'Of course. Merlin again?'

Abela felt his towel unravelling and pulled it tighter around his waist. 'Yes.'

'He's proving a tiresome bastard these days. Buggered up one of my better forging operations the other day. My guys are about to get long sentences.'

'Ever tried giving him a bung?'

'I got someone to try a couple of times before the war. Nothing doing. He's as straight as Nelson's column.'

'Hmm.' Abela lifted his hefty buttocks and moved a few inches along the tiles. 'I suppose other means are out of the question?'

'It's never in our interest to use violence against the coppers, as you know.' A note of irritation showed in Hill's voice. 'And it's a good job your shooters didn't hit the target the other night. That would have been a disaster. Tell your boys the guns are only for show when it comes to the police.'

'You heard who he pulled in?'

'Young and Orlov, wasn't it?'

'Yeah. It was Spencer who bought it and Mellor and Finlay who got away.'

'Not a good day then. Where are those two now?'

'Salted away out of town until things die down.'

'That'll be a while I should think. Young and Orlov are sound?'

'Of course. They'll keep their mouths shut.'

'I presume you've got things covered if there's a chance they don't?'

'Yeah. I've got eyes on them at the Scrubs from both angles. Jailbirds and screws. Merlin won't get a dicky bird out of them, don't you worry.'

Abela picked up the pail of cold water behind him and tipped it over his head. 'Oof! Mother of God, that's cold.'

Hill edged away with a sniff of distaste to avoid the water sluicing off his colleague. 'I suppose we should thank our lucky stars not all the coppers are like Merlin.'

'You're right there, Billy. My whoring business certainly benefits from that.'

'Speaking of whoring, how's your supply chain going? Still finding plenty of new product for the punters? Demand is growing all the time, eh?'

'No sign of goods running out yet. Still plenty of fresh girls keen to join the Piccadilly Commandos.'

'And if they're not keen you get them in anyway with your scouts on the street. If they're pretty enough, of course.'

'Yeah. But we only go for the waifs and strays. Can't be doing with girls who have families.'

Hill grunted his approval. 'Things still kosher with the Messinas?'

The Messinas were Abela's main competitors in the vice market. Hill chose not to involve himself directly in prostitution, although he benefitted indirectly through Abela and others. The Messinas were the biggest in a market dominated by Maltese gangsters.

Abela sighed. 'My cousins seem content with the current state of play. We still have the occasional disagreement but nothing too serious. They generally cooperate. Even give me business occasionally.'

'Really? I didn't know that.'

Abela immediately regretted telling Hill something he didn't know, even though the revelation was unlikely to harm him.

'Tell me more.'

'Every so often they pass on customers they think I can handle better.'

'Like who?'

A jet of hot steam from somewhere below blasted Abela's privates and rendered him temporarily speechless. When recovered he replied, 'For example, I got a rich customer from them last year whose taste runs to young girls.'

'What counts as young these days?'

'Better not fix a number, Billy, but, as it happens, I've developed something of a speciality in this area. Quite a lot of men have tastes of this kind. Well-known ones too, but I won't mention names. Anyway, this rich customer has unusual interests.'

'You mean in addition to liking young girls?'

'Fact is he fancies himself as a bit of a Devil-worshipper. Wants the girls to take part in his black magic ceremonies. You can probably imagine what goes on.'

'My imagination is already running riot. Is it safe for the girls?'

'I had the odd one disappear on me without proper explanation.'

'But he paid you well enough, you didn't ask questions?'

'Yeah.'

'And why didn't the Messinas want his business? Sounds very lucrative.'

'It's hilarious. They said they didn't want to deal with him because of their religious beliefs. Said, as devout Catholics, it wasn't the business for them.'

'Ha, ha! Religious beliefs, my arse. With the things they get up to! So they think they've got things squared with God, but bring the Devil into it . . . what a shower!'

80

'So there it is. This chap is very good business. Holds a Black Sabbath, or whatever you call it, every few weeks. There's one coming up this weekend in fact.'

'Never been the superstitious sort have you, Joe?'

'Not me! No. Vampires, ghosts and devils don't lose me any sleep. I suppose being in our line of business gives us er . . . what's the word . . . oh, yeah . . . perspective. Mind, I do enjoy a good horror once in a while. Saw a good one the other day. Boris Karloff. *The Devil Commands* I think it was called.'

Hill grunted. 'I had a cousin of his in one of my crews before the war. Name of Pratt. That was the family name. Boris Karloff was really William Pratt. Changed it when he went to Hollywood.'

'A good move, obviously.' Abela paused to burp. 'Excuse me, Billy. Too much for lunch again.'

'You really should take care of what you eat before coming to a place like this, Joe. Man of your build might have a heart attack.'

'Point taken.'

'Still running your loan book?'

'I am. Not a problem for you, is it, Billy?'

'No. So long as I get my cut. I do a little in that area too, as you know, but there's plenty of business out there for everyone. Where do you find your . . . your customers?'

'All over.'

'Large amounts?'

'Sometimes. I know a few big-shots who need the occasional helping hand. Funnily enough I heard from one of them today.'

'Hmm.' Hill eased himself to his feet. 'Well this has all been rather jolly, Joe, but I think I'd better be getting back.' Unlike Abela, who had been perspiring copiously throughout, Hill had barely broken sweat.

'I might stay for another twenty minutes.' Abela replied, grasping his belly. 'I could do with shifting some of this.'

'You do that, Joseph. It's been good chatting.' Hill patted Abela's shoulder. 'Something you said made me think. I may have a

81

few new customers for you. Influential types who might like the occasional runout with the best of your young girls.'

'Of course, Billy. My pleasure.'

'And knowing our customers' vices might occasionally be turned to mutual benefit, if you get my drift?'

'Sure, Billy. You scratch my back, I scratch yours.'

Hill tightened the towel wrapped around his waist. 'That's the way the world goes round, ain't it, my friend?'

Chapter Five

The morning newspaper headlines were again full of the Far East. It was now known that at the same time as the attack on Pearl Harbour, the Japanese had also launched massive offensives against Malaysia and Hong Kong. Climbing the stairs to his office, Merlin was thinking of what the AC had said and reflecting that the price to pay for having America in the war was going to be a heavy one.

The sight of Bridges bent over his desk prompted uncomfortable thoughts closer to home. 'Morning, Sergeant.'

'Sir.' Bridges was typing something and spoke without looking up.

'More awful news from the Far East.'

'Yes, sir. Terrible.'

'How is Iris taking it?'

'Badly. I . . .'

Before Bridges could say any more the telephone rang. Merlin looked apologetically at the sergeant and answered. It was the AC.

Gatehouse was at his desk, fiddling irritably with his collar and tie. Merlin never understood why the AC persisted in wearing a detachable wing collar. Merlin associated it in his mind with the late unlamented Prime Minister, Neville Chamberlain. Over a few drinks one night, he had suggested the AC

83

become a little more up to date but the suggestion had been given short shrift.

'There you are Frank.' The AC gave up on his collar. 'Sorry to bother you so early but something of the utmost importance has come up.' He waved Merlin into a seat.

'I had the Commissioner on the line earlier. There has been an unfortunate . . . ah . . . incident.'

'What kind of incident?'

'Have you, by any chance, heard of someone called Laura Curzon?'

Merlin thought for a moment. 'The name does ring a bell. She's a film actress, isn't she?'

'Yes, but "was" is unfortunately now the appropriate word. She was found dead on the pavement outside her apartment building this morning, having apparently fallen from a great height. She had a flat on the seventh floor.'

'How did it happen?'

'Well that is the question. Her penthouse apartment has a terrace. It is to be presumed that she fell from that. She was in quite a mess as you can imagine.'

'Accident? Suicide?'

'We don't know.'

'No witnesses, then?'

'No.'

'And you're telling me about this because . . . ?'

'Well, obviously there has to be a police investigation and the Commissioner was extremely keen I put my best man on the case.'

'Why is the Commissioner getting directly involved?'

'He's friendly with some powerful people in the film industry. One of them contacted him and requested he take a personal interest in the case. As I say, he told me to put our best man on the job. He specifically asked for you.'

Merlin's face darkened. 'You're not being serious are you, sir? I'm very sorry for the poor lady but you know I have the fullest of plates at present. There are other good officers available. That new chap, Sandford, was only complaining to me the other day that he hadn't been assigned anything he could really get his teeth into. Why don't . . .'

The AC interrupted sharply. 'It is my prerogative, Chief Inspector, to allocate our assignments. I promised the Commissioner you would handle the case and handle the case you will.'

An uneasy silence followed. When the AC spoke again, his tone had softened. 'Look Frank, I'm not so keen on the Commissioner getting involved in cases in this way either, but you have to understand. I can't just ignore him.'

'And he's got involved because he's mates with some movie mogul and because the victim is a fancy film star?'

'Well, yes. You know how the Commissioner likes to mix with the great and the good. He's been going to some of the Prime Minister's picture nights and that's how he's made these new friends. Have you heard of the Korda brothers?'

'I've heard of Alexander Korda. Produced those Charles Laughton films about Henry the Eighth and Rembrandt. And that big science fiction one.'

'*Things to Come*. A strange film, but then HG Wells is a strange man. Miss Curzon was quite close to him and his brother, Vincent. Alexander Korda is away in America at the moment. It was Vincent who called the Commissioner this morning.'

'Is there any hidden agenda?'

'What do you mean, Frank?'

'Some nasty circumstances around the death which require hushing up?'

The AC pursed his lips. 'That's a little cynical.'

'Sorry, but I imagine these film bigwigs like to avoid lurid headlines. Very bad for business. Perhaps it's not the best policeman wanted, but the most compliant.'

The AC was amused. 'If the Commissioner wanted someone compliant, you'd be the last name on his list.'

Merlin gave a resigned shrug. 'Very well, sir. If you insist, I shall . . . comply. But what about my other cases? We've got the gangsters in the Scrubs, the various criminal enterprises we're tracking, and now this girl in Victoria . . .'

'I know, I know. Important cases all. I'm not asking you to set any of them aside but I think it would be wisest for now to give this Curzon case top priority. You'll probably find it's all very straightforward and only take you a day or two to sort.'

'Very well, sir. Of course if I find it's more complex and something fishy has gone on, I shall pursue the facts with full vigour, regardless of any embarrassment to the powers that be.'

'Of course you will, Frank.' The AC handed Merlin a piece of paper. 'Here's the address.'

'Alright. Stop it there. Michael, are you alright?'

Michael Adair pulled out of his clinch with Jean Parker and fell back heavily into one of the armchairs on the set. Their scene was meant to be taking place in a flat in the Albany, Piccadilly, one of London's smartest addresses. Art was imitating life insofar as Adair had once himself been a resident of the Albany, before his marriage to Laura Curzon. He'd kept the place on when he'd moved into her Mayfair flat, but unfortunately the Albany had been bombed in the Blitz and his flat was no more. When he'd split up with Laura he'd found a nice house nearby but he looked back on his time at the Albany as a golden period in his life, and this scene was making him feel maudlin. He had other problems too.

'Just a little headache, Emil. I'll take a couple of pills and be fine in a minute. These lights don't help.'

Kaplan moved closer to the actor. 'Did you have a heavy night, Michael? You look a bit pasty. Good job we're not shooting this in colour. Even so, I think you could do with a bit of sprucing up.' He turned and called out 'Make-up!'

A young brunette hurried over and went to work on a grumbling Adair. When she'd finished Kaplan viewed the actor through his viewfinder. 'That's better. Now, let's do that scene again.'

Everyone got back into position but just as the cameras were about to start rolling, Goldsmith's secretary appeared and interrupted the director. 'I'm very sorry, Mr Kaplan, but there's an urgent call upstairs.'

'Oh, really Gloria. Surely it can wait until I have this scene in the bag? Did Victor send you?'

'He's not in, Mr Kaplan, but I think he'd have wanted me to tell you. It's an urgent message for Mr Adair.'

'For me? Who is it?' asked the actor.

'Mr Vincent Korda.'

Kaplan shook his head. 'Shit, Gloria. He's probably just trying to discuss some other film with Michael.'

'I'm sorry, I don't think that's right. Mr Korda was quite clear that it was not a business call.'

Adair looked puzzled. 'Well, I'd better speak to him, Emil. I'll try and be as quick as I can.'

Kaplan threw his script to the floor in frustration then flounced off set.

In Goldsmith's office, Adair sat at the desk and took the telephone receiver from Gloria, who disappeared to her own office. 'Vincent. What a pleasant surprise.'

'I'm afraid, Michael, that what I have to tell you is far from pleasant.' Korda's accent was as thickly Hungarian as it had ever been. 'I take it, then, you've not heard the news?'

'What news?'

'You must brace yourself, my friend. It's Laura. Poor Laura is dead.'

'Laura? Dead? B . . . but that can't be. I've just seen her. She's . . . she's as fit a . . . a fiddle.'

'Believe me, Michael, she's dead. She fell from her flat. A terrible accident. I . . .' Korda paused as Adair began to sob. 'Courage, Michael. I know you recently had your differences but I can understand what a dreadful shock it is. Such a beautiful woman, cut down in her prime.'

Korda waited for Adair to regain control of himself. The sobbing eventually stopped. 'Michael . . .'

Adair said quietly 'I must go to the flat.'

'That's a bad idea, Michael. The place will soon be crawling with police and . . .'

'Police. Why police?'

'Come now, Michael. The authorities are bound to investigate an incident like this. They'll need to determine whether what happened was an accident or suicide or . . . foul play.'

'Suicide? Foul play? What are you talking about? It's that damned fence, that's what it is. I must have told her a million times to raise and strengthen it!'

'Please keep calm, Michael. I'm sure you're right and it was some kind of terrible accident. However, to ensure everything is investigated properly and discreetly, I've taken the precaution of speaking to my friend, the Metropolitan Police Commissioner, and asked that they put their best man on the job. A fellow called Merlin. Brilliant officer, apparently.'

'I . . . I understand. But can't I see her?'

'Well . . . Michael, not to put too fine a point on it, if someone falls to the pavement from such a height they are . . . they are not going to look . . . to look their best.' Silence followed. 'Michael? Michael? Are you still there?'

There was a deep sigh at the other end of the line. 'My God, yes. Seven stories she'd have fallen. My God. The poor thing. You're right, Vincent. I'll stay here. I don't think I can go back to work, though.'

'Of course you can't. You must go home and rest.'

'I'll do that . . . and . . . thank you, Vincent. It was good of you to take it upon yourself to tell me.'

'Well, Laura was very dear to me and Alex, as you know. We shall all miss her very much.'

South China Sea

'Able Seaman Ross?'

'Yes, sir.'

'I'd be obliged if you could clean these glasses for me. Something seems to be obscuring the right lens.'

'Right you are, sir.' The glasses in question were an impressive pair of state-of-the-art binoculars, the Barr and Stroud CF41 model, to be precise. Ross took them from their owner, Sir Thomas Phillips, recently appointed Admiral of the Fleet, and, handling the equipment as if it were a sacred relic, polished both lenses carefully. The two men were part of a group of naval officers and ratings gathered on the bridge of the Royal Navy's latest pride and joy, the battleship HMS *Prince of Wales*, commissioned only eleven months before. Danny Ross found himself in this exalted company because one of the Admiral's senior adjutants, Captain Mitchell, had taken a shine to him. Apparently Mitchell's brother had served in the police with Ross's uncle, Sam Bridges, a few years back. The brother's respect and affection for Bridges had been communicated and thus Ross, a lowly rating, had been afforded this fascinating first-hand view of the command deck of a major ship of the line.

The vessel had moored in Singapore on Friday, four days earlier. On Monday she and all the other ships in harbour had come under enemy bomb attack from the Japanese. The ship's anti-aircraft guns had been called into action for the first time since the spring. No damage had been sustained, but Phillips had decided it would be wisest to seek the protection of the open sea. Thus, the *Prince of Wales*, accompanied by a few smaller Navy vessels, had steamed out of harbour and was now heading on a north-easterly course through the South China Sea.

The binoculars duly cleaned, Ross returned them to the Admiral. For a military supremo, Phillips was a surprisingly diminutive man. His nickname below decks was 'Tom Thumb'. He seemed a decent enough fellow to Ross, to whom he spoke in a polite but distant fashion.

The sun would be setting shortly, Ross thought. The sky was an exotic mix of purple, yellow and blue, and was unlike anything he'd ever seen in an English sky. As he enjoyed the spectacle, he became aware of black specks emerging from a bank of dark clouds to the right. He was not alone in seeing them. Captain Mitchell nudged the Admiral's arm.

'Forty degrees to starboard, sir. Looks like reconnaissance.'

The Admiral swung his binoculars around. 'Seaplanes. I can see three I think. Or is it that a fourth?'

'There are four, sir.' Mitchell disappeared and returned with a Navy catalogue of Japanese military equipment in hand. He flicked through it quickly. 'Asoki E13A most likely.'

'Whatever they are, Captain, they'll be around for a while I'm sure. We might have to do a little manoeuvring to confuse them about our heading. The storm that's getting up might help us.' Phillips turned to Ross. 'Able Seaman, it looks like it's going to be a long night. This might be a good moment for you to grab a quick bite to eat.'

Ross saluted then headed downstairs. The smell of overcooked vegetables wafted up to him as he descended to the mess.

Laura Curzon's apartment block was called Seymour Mansions and was located in a street just off Park Lane. It was a modern building and like most in the area oozed opulence.

'One of those art deco places you like, sir' said Bridges as they got out of the car.

Merlin looked up. 'Not the best example of the style perhaps, but attractive enough.'

The pavement in front of the building was clear. 'Looks like they've already moved the body, sir.'

'Yes. A pity.'

An ambulance was parked outside.

'Look, sir.' Bridges pointed to a body-sized bloodstain a few yards to the right of the entrance and close to the kerb.

They both had a good look before entering the building. In the grand thickly-carpeted lobby they found two ambulance men and a police constable standing over a stretcher. There was a blanket on the stretcher and they could tell a body lay underneath from the arm poking out on the side.

'Gentlemen. DCI Merlin and DS Bridges. Might I ask who had the clever idea of moving the body?'

The constable inclined his head towards the reception desk beyond him where two men in matching striped trousers and black-tailed jackets were being harangued by a woman in a mink coat.

The constable spoke. 'Purvis, sir. Mayfair station. The porters brought the body in. It was on the carpet covered by a tarpaulin when I got here. You can see the mess it caused over there. These two lads arrived with the ambulance a few minutes later. They put her on the stretcher and covered her properly. The head porter said he didn't think it was right to leave her out on the street.'

'I suppose that's understandable, but I'd have liked to see the body where it fell.' He turned to the ambulance men. 'Any particular observations regarding the body?'

'Apart from her being as dead as a dodo, sir, no' said the man nearest him.

'Thank you for that. Any sign of the police doctor yet? Constable?'

'On his way, sir.'

'I see. I suppose it's not . . .' Merlin was finding it increasingly difficult to think as the voice of the woman at the porter's desk continued to boom out.

'It's a disgrace, Jackson. A dead body in the lobby. An utter disgrace! I shall be complaining most vociferously to the management. Of course this is what happens when you allow theatrical riffraff into the place. Disreputable characters with uncontrollable passions. This silly unhappy girl decides to jump from the roof and splatter herself over the pavement. Then you decide to bring her in and ruin the carpet. Deplorable! Quite deplorable!'

Merlin had had quite enough and walked over to the porter's desk. The woman looked to be in her seventies. The eyes of several small stuffed birds stared balefully out at him from the ridiculous feathery hat she was wearing. The Chief Inspector tried to be as polite as he could. 'Madam, I'd be grateful if you would calm down. I've just arrived from Scotland Yard to deal with this sad incident. Unless you're in a position to provide me with material evidence about Miss Curzon's death, I'd be obliged if you withdraw so I may interview the porters.'

The woman was silenced and after a long withering glare of contempt, turned and made for the exit.

The older porter looked very grateful. 'Thank you, sir. Jackson's the name. Arnold Jackson. Head Porter.' Jackson was a solid-looking fellow, with the bearing of an ex-military man. He sported a bushy brown moustache and reminded Merlin of Lord Kitchener in his famous recruitment poster of the Great War. 'That was Mrs Cavendish. Stockbroker's widow. Never tires of making a fuss.'

'Right old bag,' said the other porter, a sullen youth who looked as if he wasn't long out of school.

'Now then, Baxter. There's no need for that.' Jackson turned to Merlin and to Bridges, who had now joined his boss. 'Forgive him, gentlemen. He's new to the job. Manners need a little work. You'll be wanting to question us now?'

'We shall. Was it you who found the body, Mr Jackson?'

'No, it was young Baxter here. He got to work first and I was a few minutes after him.'

'What time would that have been?'

'I got in just after six. The lad said he got here about ten minutes earlier.'

'Yeah,' grunted the young man.

'You don't have a night porterage service here, Mr Jackson?' Bridges asked.

'No, we don't cover nights at the moment. I lost my former colleague to the services five weeks ago. He was responsible for the nights. Baxter here has only been with us for a short while, as I said. He's learning the ropes and the management agreed that we just provide a day service until he's trained. I can't do nights myself, unfortunately, as I have an invalid wife at home.'

Jackson turned to Baxter. He was an unprepossessing young

man with a pimply face and a head of untidy greasy brown hair. 'Why don't you go to the kitchen, lad, and make a pot of tea.' Baxter sloped off and Jackson drew closer to Merlin. 'With the war on, it's very difficult to attract the right calibre of person. He's a bright enough fellow but it's going to take a while to get him in shape.'

'Was it Baxter who moved the body?'

'No, Chief Inspector. I decided to do that. I'm sorry if that was wrong but I couldn't just leave her out there for all and sundry to gawp at. We carried the body in as soon as I'd called the police and threw a tarpaulin over her. Then, I'm afraid the lad was sick and we had some tidying up to do. The young constable over there got here about twenty minutes after I made the call. He asked the questions you just asked then got in touch with his station. He'd been expecting reinforcements from there but was told some detectives were on their way from Scotland Yard. And here you are.'

'What time did you knock off last night?'

'Six. I was a little earlier than usual as I was meeting some friends.'

'And your colleague?'

Baxter reappeared with the news that there was no tea.

'You pillock! I told you to get some yesterday afternoon. Sorry gentlemen.'

Merlin shrugged. He didn't want tea anyway.

'The officer wants to know what time you left last night. Weren't you waiting for some friends or something?'

Baxter examined a fingernail carefully before answering. 'Yeah. I was later than usual because of that.'

'When did your friends turn up?'

Baxter's eyes avoided Merlin's. 'Around eight o'clock, give or take.'

'And you were both on duty all day and in a position to see all the comings and goings in the building?'

'Apart from our separate one hour lunch breaks, yes,' said Jackson.

'Did Miss Curzon receive any visitors while you were here?'

'I didn't see anyone myself.' Jackson looked enquiringly at Baxter.

'Nor me.'

'She lives . . . sorry . . . lived alone?'

'Yes, sir,' replied Jackson 'but her husband lived here until they split up.'

'Who is her husband?'

'Michael Adair. The actor. They parted before she went to America.'

'I see. Well we can go into that in more detail later.'

'Is the front door locked when the porters are off duty, Mr Jackson?' asked Bridges.

'Yes, sir. Of course, the residents all have their own front door keys.'

'What about visitors?'

'In the absence of a porter to allow entry there are speaking tubes for communication with residents.'

'And is there some way the door-catch can be released without the resident having to come down to open the door?'

'No, Sergeant. They have to come down to allow visitors entrance.'

Merlin looked towards the rear of the lobby where there was a door bearing a 'No Entry' sign. 'Where does that go?'

'That leads to the storage area and the rear delivery door.'

'Is that the only other means of entry to the building?'

'Yes, sir. The tradesman's entrance opens onto the mews behind. There's no other way in.'

'And the back door is always locked, except when in use?'

'Of course, sir. I always make sure it's locked after any delivery and I always double check it's locked when I leave in the evening.' Jackson looked puzzled. 'Excuse me, Chief Inspector, but I'm not sure I understand how that's relevant. The poor thing fell from her terrace. Either it was an accident or she killed herself. What does it matter about access to the building?'

94

'It's our job to gather as much information as we can, Mr Jackson. Sometimes what seems irrelevant at the outset can prove very important. We'll need to go over all this more thoroughly with you both later. However . . .' he turned to Bridges 'I suppose we can't put off viewing the body any more. Let's get it over with, then.'

They walked over to the stretcher and, at a nod from Merlin, the ambulance men removed the blanket. Merlin had seen plenty of the horrifying things violence could do to a body, first in the trenches of the Great War, and then in some twenty years of police service. Laura Curzon's wrecked body would rank with the worst. The delicately chiselled features of one of Britain's most beautiful film stars had been smashed almost to pulp. Her broken limbs were twisted at unnatural angles. Her right arm was in pieces and Merlin had a vision of the petrified woman holding it out ahead of her as she plummeted to the pavement.

Jackson came over to join them.

'No scream reported by a resident, Mr Jackson?'

'Not so far, sir, but I've only seen a few people this morning, and none of them were keen to loiter in the lobby. Apart from Mrs Cavendish, that is, and she didn't mention a scream.'

'We'll be canvassing all the residents in due course.'

'You will?'

'We have to.'

'Don't think the building managers will be happy about residents being disturbed.'

'Well, they'll just have to lump it won't they?' Merlin glanced at Bridges who looked a little shaken. 'I suppose the only comforting thing I can think to say, Sergeant, is that it would have been over very quickly.'

'That it would, sir.'

Merlin took a deep breath and bent down to examine the dead woman's clothing. She had died wearing pale blue silk pyjamas and matching dressing gown. 'Nice stuff. Probably cost as much as a top-notch suit from Gieves and Hawkes. The material must be quite resilient. The only parts that have ripped are around the legs.'

'There's a little rip just at the top of the jacket, sir.'

Merlin bent closer. 'So there is, Sergeant. Doesn't look like something caused by the fall. More like someone's pulled at it. Hmm. Well, no doubt we'll get a full report on this from forensics. Did you find any footwear, Mr Jackson.'

'No, sir.'

'You, Constable Purvis?'

'I had a good look around on the pavement and on the road, sir. I didn't find anything else of Miss Curzon's.'

Merlin took a last look at the body then asked the ambulance men to cover it. 'As soon as the police doctor's done his bit, get the body off to the Central Morgue.' He straightened up and turned. 'And now for the apartment.'

Tommy Cole had the room to himself. 'Room' was really too grand a word for this small cubby hole down the corridor from Merlin's office. It contained a small table on which he and Robinson, and Bridges when he felt like a break from his boss, could work. The kettle and tea were also there.

Johnson had his own office nearby, a decent sized room he'd been given on his return from the MI5 secondment in the summer.

Merlin had briefed everyone about the new case before heading off to Mayfair with the sergeant. The constable had seen and admired Laura Curzon in several films and was very sorry to hear of her death. He was not, however, sorry to miss out on the visit to her flat, keen as he was to crack on with his investigations in the Victoria case. Since Monday morning he'd been busy going through his list of London police stations to see if there was a match for the Victoria girl in the missing person files. He'd now been in touch with more than half of the list but had yet to generate a single possibility. It didn't help that the girl didn't have any distinguishing features and that the photos of her mummified face were not that great. Bridges had told him that a specialist artist had been asked to work on a drawing of what the girl might have looked like alive. Cole knew the man being used was very good at what he did. For now, however, all he had to give the other station officers apart from a dodgy photo was the girl's estimated age, her build, and a description of her ragged clothes. And, for what it was worth, the American chocolate wrapper. That tenuous link had sent Johnson off to the American Embassy where, to Cole's mild irritation, he had made some progress. The Embassy had details of a missing American family who had a daughter of the right age. Johnson was now following up the lead.

From along the corridor, Cole could hear Merlin's weird old cuckoo clock chirping midday. His mum had been poorly and hadn't been up to making his usual cooked breakfast that morning. He was famished but wanted to keep going a little longer. There were a couple of inner London stations which hadn't yet responded to his messages. He'd call them again before starting on the stations in the suburbs. After lunch he'd change focus for a while and, as the sergeant had requested, look into which companies were operating in the Costello Building before the bombing. Satisfied with his new plan of campaign, he picked up the phone and dialled the number for Wandsworth police station.

Laura Curzon's flat was just as Merlin would have expected a film star's flat to be. Her grand and spacious drawing room was packed with lavish furnishings and the walls were plastered with fascinating movie memorabilia and expensive artwork. On one wall there were numerous photographs picturing Laura with the giants of the British screen – Olivier, Leigh, Oberon, Laughton, Donat, and Harrison among them. Another wall had Laura in company with great Hollywood figures like Grant, Gable, Tracy, Stewart, Cagney, and Astaire. The most striking image for Merlin, however, was the large oil portrait of the late actress above the fireplace. Merlin put on his reading glasses and read the artist's signature at the bottom. 'Impressive, Sergeant. A Sickert.'

'A what, sir?'

'This painting. It's by Walter Sickert. A very fine artist.'

'Art isn't my strong point, I have to say. I do like a good drawing, though. Iris and I went to an exhibition before the war. There was a clever drawing of a rhinoceros. German fellow did it. Can't remember his name but it had the most fantastic detail.'

'Dürer. A great artist. You surprise me, Sergeant.'

Bridges raised an eyebrow. 'Because I've got good taste?'

'No. You said art was not a strong point. In that context, your remembering and liking such a fine work surprised me. There's no need to take offence. I've always credited you with good taste. As regards your wife for example.'

'So you have, sir. But hadn't we best forget art and taste for now and get on, sir?' He took a couple of pairs of gloves out of his pocket and handed one to his boss.

'Got a pair for the constable?' Constable Purvis had accompanied them to the flat.

'You know me, sir. I always carry spares.' Bridges handed another set to Purvis.

The three policemen set to. As well as the drawing room and a very modern kitchen, the flat had two large bedrooms – one decorated in pale blue, the other pale green. The blue bedroom had clearly been in use while the green one looked unoccupied. Merlin saw nothing immediately untoward in the bedrooms but there were signs of some disturbance in the drawing room. He found a broken crystal tumbler under a coffee table, and in an alcove at the back, where there was a small dining table, a couple of chairs had been overturned. Two other unbroken crystal tumblers, smelling of whisky, sat on the coffee table as did an ashtray holding a couple of lipstick-stained cigarette butts. There were also a couple of used champagne flutes on a side table in the alcove beside an empty bottle of Krug. A large drinks cabinet, full of all kinds of liquor and doors open, stood nearby. Next to the drinks cabinet was a small antique desk.

Bridges and Purvis started going through the bedroom drawers and cupboards while Merlin decided to go out on the terrace. A chill wind was blowing outside and he pulled up his coat collar. The terrace was a good size, almost as large as the drawing room. In the centre was a green metal garden table and matching chairs. One of the six chairs was on its side. Merlin noticed a slipper beneath the table. It was the same pale blue colour as Miss Curzon's nightwear. He picked it up and put it on the table. The terrace balcony was an odd affair, partly brick, partly iron. The metal part was in the form of an ornate balustrade about six feet long which broke the brick wall in the middle. The brick part of the balcony came up to Merlin's waist but the balustrade was about a foot shorter. Merlin thought he'd certainly want it raised if he lived there. It wobbled a little too when he took hold of it.

Bridges joined him, an apprehensive look on his face. Merlin knew Bridges wasn't particularly keen on heights. 'Not a bad view, Sam.' Over a jumble of rooftops, they could see the tops of trees in Hyde Park.

'Be better in a few months when the leaves are out.'

Merlin put a hand on the balustrade again and jiggled it for the sergeant's benefit. 'What do you reckon to this?'

Bridges took a nervous step back. 'Watch out, sir. Not the safest of fences, is it?' The balustrade had quite an intricate swirling pattern and the sergeant noticed something caught up in a curling piece of metal near the top. 'There's something there, sir.'

Merlin saw what Bridges was looking at and removed it. 'Piece of thread. From a suit at a guess.'

'Man's suit or woman's?'

'Impossible to say. There's not much of it but it seems quite a robust thread. Could be from a coat, I suppose. We'll see what forensics make of it.' Just to the right of the balustrade there was a large empty flowerpot. Merlin thought he could see something white wedged behind it and bent down. 'A handkerchief, Sergeant. Good quality. Ah. See. There's a monogram.' At one corner there was a capital 'C' sewn in red.

' "C" for Curzon, sir?'

'I suppose.' Merlin had another look behind the pot and this time saw the matching slipper, which must have been underneath the handkerchief. He showed it to Bridges. 'I found its partner over there under the table. Odd isn't it, that she somehow lost her footwear before the fall?'

The two men went over to the metal table and Merlin put the slipper together with its partner. Bridges took possession of the slippers and the thread and put them in the small bag he was carrying.

'Find anything in the flat?'

'There's quite a bit of personal correspondence in her desk. I'll get forensics to bag it. I . . .'

Purvis burst through the French doors and interrupted them. 'I just found this in a bedroom cupboard.' He was carrying a brown paper bag which was leaking some sort of white powder. He looked at Merlin. 'Any idea what it is, sir?'

Merlin took the bag, opened it and sniffed. 'Hmm. It's definitely not talcum powder. Something a little more powerful, I think. In which bedroom did you find it?'

'The blue one, sir. In a hat box.'

Merlin looked at the balustrade and the overturned garden chair and put his nose to the bag again. He was beginning to get the feeling this case wasn't going to be as straightforward as the AC had suggested.

Marcus Waring loved browsing in old bookshops. The previous year he had found a particularly interesting shop off Charing Cross Road. It had a wonderfully eclectic stock of books and, in particular, boasted a fine collection of volumes relating to the occult, a subject with which Waring was obsessed. Since the discovery, Waring had become by far the odd little Hungarian shop owner's biggest and most important customer. He was normally given carte blanche to idle away the hours digging through the stock, after shop hours if he wanted. Today, however, was an exception.

'I'm very sorry, sir, but I have to shut up shop dead on five today. I'm meeting some compatriots of mine for an early drink, then dinner.'

Waring leaned back in one of the shop's two comfortable armchairs. 'That's fine, Mr Faludy. Not to worry. May I ask where you are dining? No.' He raised a hand. 'Let me guess. The Gay Hussar?'

Mr Faludy looked surprised. 'How did you know, sir?'

'It's the only good Hungarian restaurant in London, to my knowledge at least. I had some very fine dumplings and duck when I last went a couple of years back. A word of advice; be very careful what you say. A friend of mine tells me it's a favourite haunt of spies and revolutionaries.'

Faludy stroked his grey side-whiskers thoughtfully. 'I shall be very careful indeed, Mr Waring.'

Waring held up a dusty volume he'd been perusing. '*The Key of Solomon the King.*'

'Ah, yes, the Mathers translation of 1889.'

'Very interesting. I'll take it.' He indicated the pile of books on the table next to him. 'These too.' He got to his feet. 'I'll send someone round to pick them up but I'll settle now.'

The Hungarian made a quick review of the books then gave Waring a price.

'That includes my usual discount?'

'Of course, Mr Waring. A twenty per cent reduction for you.'

Waring took out his wallet and handed over some notes. 'I'll bid you good day then, Mr Faludy. Enjoy your meal!'

'I will, sir. And thank you.'

Waring turned out of the shop, and walked via Charing Cross Road towards Trafalgar Square. Opposite the National Portrait Gallery he hailed a taxi and gave the driver his Kensington address.

Marcus Waring was in his early forties but could pass as younger. He was careful of his appearance and clothes. His usual style was colourful, slightly old-fashioned formality. Today he was wearing a striped three piece suit, pink shirt, mauve tie, and spats. A large fob watch hung from his waistcoat, and his sleek dark brown hair was parted in the centre. He had a small angular face, with neat features all in proportion. The thinnest of pencil moustaches decorated his upper lip.

He was a very wealthy man, more through chance than skill or ability. Several years before, after two male first cousins had suffered fatal climbing accidents, he had become the sole heir to an uncle's substantial fortune. The heartbroken old man had survived his sons for only a short time and thus, in 1937, Waring had come into his inheritance, an estate valued at just over one and a quarter million pounds. At the time, Waring had been working in the City of London as a not particularly successful stockbroker and promoter of speculative business ventures. After his good fortune, Waring continued to keep his hand in as a promoter and enjoyed the occasional modest success. The blue chip stock and property portfolios bequeathed by his uncle, however, still formed the bulk of his wealth.

Between 1937 and the outbreak of war, Waring had engaged in a number of rich man's hobbies, like hunting boar in France and sailing large boats in the Mediterranean. Now that most such pursuits were closed off for the duration, he had had to find other interests. The study of the occult had become by far the most important of these, and it was this subject which was in the forefront of his mind as the taxi pulled up to his house. The next major event on his occult calendar was the ceremony on Sunday. He had hosted many ceremonies over the past eighteen months. They had been stimulating and satisfying, but he had increasingly felt something was lacking. That 'something' was authenticity. Book knowledge was one thing but he felt he needed the advice of a master of the black arts to set up a truly fulfilling Mass. Now he knew he had found the right man to advise him. A friend had put him in touch with Aleister Crowley, the notorious Satanist. With Crowley's involvement, the quality of the ceremonies was bound to rise to another level.

As soon as Waring was inside the house, he went straight to the hallway telephone. It was important he speak to Crowley and confirm he would be at the following day's lunch. And there was

102

something else he needed to confirm. The supplier of his young ladies was always very reliable but Waring was a worrier. He wanted to check one more time that all was well in hand. The ceremony needed the girls. He decided to make that call first.

'Make yourself comfortable, Mr Jackson.' Merlin pointed to one of Laura Curzon's comfortable pale blue sofas.

'Rather stand, sir, if you don't mind. I'd never presume to sit there when she was alive and it certainly doesn't seem right now she's dead.'

'An admirable sentiment, Mr Jackson, but you'd actually be doing me a favour. Police work is hard on the feet and I'd like to sit down. And it will be easier to talk if we're on the same level.'

The porter grudgingly conceded the point and sat down next to Merlin and Bridges. Purvis remained standing by the door.

'I'd be grateful to know a little more about Miss Curzon's domestic circumstances.' Merlin had been a little surprised by the earlier mention of a husband. That development in Miss Curzon's life had somehow passed him by. He knew of Michael Adair and had seen him in a couple of films. He'd played pretty much the same character in both – a drily witty upper class toff with a cruel streak. Something in the Rex Harrison mould, he remembered thinking. Was the man in person like the character he portrayed? It seemed more than likely he was going to find out.

'And you say Miss Curzon had been away in America for a while until last week?'

'Yes, sir.'

'Has Mr Adair been resident here while she's been away?'

'No sir. As I said, they are separated.'

'So they were only together for a relatively short time?'

'Shortish, yes. I think they got hitched in 1940. They met on a film together, I read in the *Daily Mail*. Something about Cavaliers and Roundheads.' Jackson's forehead creased with concentration. '*The Royal Oak* it was called. That's the tree Charles the Second hid in. Before he got his throne back. Adair was the King.'

'Has Mr Adair visited the flat at all in Miss Curzon's absence?'

'He's still got a key. I've seen him a few times.'

'Where does he live now?'

'I've got a forwarding address from him downstairs. Some-where in St James's.'

'Perhaps you could provide that to the sergeant later?'

'Of course, sir.'

'Any idea if their separation was amicable or not?'

'I can't rightly say. Their next door neighbour, Mrs Cavendish whom you met downstairs, she complained a few times earlier in the year of being disturbed by rows. But what newly married couple doesn't have the odd row? And, as you've seen for yourselves, Mrs Cavendish is the complaining type so . . .'

'It's not clear what weight, if any, to attach to her comments?'

'Exactly, sir.'

'Was Adair alone when he visited?'

'Mostly, when I saw him. There was one time . . .'

'Yes?'

'One time last month I saw him with another pretty actress. Jean Parker. They were in the flat a couple of hours. They didn't . . . er . . .' Jackson shifted uncomfortably in his seat 'they didn't stay the night.'

'I see. When exactly did Miss Curzon go to America?'

'That would have been in July. Second half. I can check the exact date for you in my notebook downstairs.'

'Thank you.'

'She was all excitement as she was going to make a film in Hollywood she told me. She'd been over and had some parts there before, and she knew all the big stars, as you can see from the photographs here, but she said this was a big step up. A large part in a major film. She expected to be in Hollywood for a very long time.'

'So her return was premature?'

'Yes. I was very surprised to see her. I asked out of politeness but she just shrugged and said "Change of plans."'

'No further explanation?'

'No.'

'Had she fallen ill, perhaps?' asked Bridges.

'Seemed right as rain to me.'

Merlin stroked his chin. 'When was the separation exactly?'

'Just before Miss Curzon went away. Leastways that's when Mr Adair gave me his new address.'

'And these rows Miss Cavendish says she heard. Assuming for the moment she wasn't making them up. Was there any suggestion of violence?'

'No, sir. She just complained about the racket.'

'Well, we'll see what she has to tell us.' Merlin paused to allow Bridges to catch up with the notes he was taking. 'So, what about Miss Curzon as a person? I always imagine actors and actresses as outgoing people, though I suppose they can't all be like that.'

'Oh, she was outgoing alright. Life and soul of the party type for sure.'

'She liked a drink?'

'Oh yes. Him too. Saw them both one over the eight several times. Do you think drink might have had something to do with her fall?'

'Well, it's clear that drink had been drunk, not to mention other substances.' Merlin did not elaborate for Jackson's benefit and decided to bring a halt to the questioning for the moment. 'No doubt we'll be talking again, Mr Jackson, and following up with Baxter of course. Thank you.'

As Jackson left, Merlin turned to Bridges. 'If you could handle the door to door with Purvis, Sergeant? I'd like to . . .'

The Chief Inspector was interrupted by the arrival of Inspector Armstrong and his forensic team. Armstrong was the senior and best forensics officer at the Yard.

'Here you are Denis. I didn't expect you'd be coming yourself.'

'Morning. Got a message from on high insisting I be present. Nasty business. I saw the body downstairs. The police doctor arrived with us and is having a look. What are you thinking?'

'All possibilities are on the table for now, Denis. Accident, suicide, manslaughter, murder. I'm keeping an open mind.'

'No doubt you'll get to the bottom of it, Frank. You always do. Found anything of interest in your initial search?'

'We found a bag of what I'm pretty sure is cocaine in a cupboard. The sergeant has a few items for you. You'll see some overturned chairs and a smashed glass. I'm not clear yet what that signifies. Drunken clumsiness . . . or worse.'

Armstrong got his notebook out and set his team to work. Merlin left Bridges in charge of the scene and headed back to the Yard.

Victor Goldsmith was brooding. He was sitting in a booth of the Dorchester bar where he had just had his first investor meeting. It had been unsatisfactory. Norman Addleshaw was a Yorkshire engineering magnate. He was worth many millions and would soon be worth many more from his new armaments partnership with the Government. Archie Tate, a close friend of the industrialist, had told Goldsmith many times of Addleshaw's interest in putting money into films. Although he hadn't needed Addleshaw's money at the time, the producer had taken the trouble to check him out. What he'd learned did not surprise him.

The man had a reputation as a tyrannical boss who was shifty and difficult to deal with. This was only to be expected from a man who had risen from nothing, but didn't recommend him as a desirable business partner. Now, however, Goldsmith couldn't afford to be too choosy and had arranged a meeting. Addleshaw turned out to be truly awful. Blunt, vulgar and fractious, Goldsmith knew he would be the type to hang around the studio questioning decisions, interfering with scripts and, like Tate, pestering female talent. However, he expressed interest in investing and, awful as he was, Goldsmith realised he couldn't reject him immediately. He'd have to keep him in play until better alternatives came along.

What alternatives? There was potential in the City, but news of the London Providential betrayal, if it came out, would limit the possibilities. There were people in Hollywood, Canada and Wall Street whom he could tap, but then he would have to travel. Phone calls would not be enough, and that was a problem. Always brave and fearless in business matters, he was a physical coward. The sights he had seen in the ghettoes of his homeland long ago had affected him profoundly. Of the numerous poor souls he'd seen murdered, many had exhibited courage, but what good had it done them? They had still died horribly. The lesson he learned was to avoid all physical danger. And there was definitely physical danger in flying the Atlantic in 1941. The journey had to be made on rattling and freezing military aircraft which were easy prey to the Luftwaffe. Such a journey was not for him, nor were the longer more roundabout routes via Africa and Brazil.

Goldsmith drank the remains of his whisky and contemplated ordering another. As he considered, his eyes glanced up to see a familiar face at the entrance to the bar. Archie Tate saw him immediately and waved before setting out in his direction.

'Victor, my lad. What are you doing here all on your own?'

'Having a nightcap at the end of a long day. You?'

'I've been giving me old mum a little treat. As you know I've got my own place nearby but occasionally she likes a slap up meal and the luxury of a suite in a top notch hotel so that's what I've given her tonight. She's just gone up and I thought I'd come and see what's what in here.' Tate sat down. 'I see your glass is empty. What's your poison?'

'Scotch and soda, please. Black and White.'

'Coming up. I'll have the same.' Tate waved at a waiter and placed the order. He turned and grinned. 'So what's up today, Victor?'

'You heard about Laura Curzon?'

Tate's face became serious. 'I did. Terrible. She was looking in the pink at Cowan's party. It's a rum old world when pretty young things can be snatched away like that. How's Adair taking it?'

'Upset, of course. I've had to give him a few days off filming.'

'I saw him the other day in the studio canteen. With Jean Parker. They looked pretty cosy.'

Goldsmith shrugged. 'You know Michael. Never one to let the grass grow under his feet.'

'It were never going to last were it? Him and Laura I mean. He always had a roving eye and she weren't averse to a bit of fun herself.'

Goldsmith stroked his chin. 'They were certainly very hot for each other for a while. Perhaps they'd have managed to get back together if she hadn't gone off to Hollywood.'

Tate rested his hands on his bulging stomach. 'Hollywood didn't work out for the lass, did it? I heard Jimmy Stewart dropped her in the soup by pulling out at the last minute. Tough luck.'

'Vincent Korda told me there might have been something more to it. She could be difficult.'

'Aye, she had a good temper on her, especially when she'd been on the pop. Or . . .' Tate put a finger to his nose 'the dope. Still, she were a good little actress.'

The drinks arrived and they clinked glasses. 'So how did the meeting go?'

'What meeting?'

Tate chuckled. 'No need to be cagey with me, Victor. Do you think my old mate Norman Addleshaw would meet you without telling me?'

Goldsmith pulled a cigarette case from his jacket pocket and tapped it irritably.

'By heck, Victor, that's a cracker of a case. Where'd you get it?'

The case was twenty-four carat gold and embedded with diamonds. 'It was a birthday present from Valerie.'

'Nice. If I ever get 'itched I hope I 'ave a wife who buys me stuff like that.'

'The experience is not necessarily so thrilling when the present is paid for out of one's own money.' Goldsmith held out the case.

'Better not. Mother can't abide cigarettes. She'll smell 'em on me and give me merry hell.'

'You don't have to smoke it now, Archie. Take a few for later. It's a German brand so, for obvious reasons, impossible to get hold of currently. A delightful Oriental blend.'

Tate weakened. 'Alright, Victor. If you twist my arm. Ta very much.' He grabbed a handful.

'How long is your mother staying?'

'She's back off to Blackpool in the morning. I'll be a free man then. For a few days at least.' Tate leaned back in his chair and loosened one of his braces. 'So what happened, then? With Addle-shaw. I was surprised you wanted to see him. You never wanted to give him the time of day before.'

'No, you have that wrong, my friend. I definitely took on board what you said. I always planned to get together with him but . . . you know . . . pressure of work.'

'Oh aye.' Tate gave Goldsmith a sharp look. 'I always assumed you thought Norman too much of a bloody awkward Northerner like me to have as an investor.'

Goldsmith lit himself a cigarette. 'I know from our many con-tract negotiations, Archie, that you can be a difficult and tight-fisted bugger, but then I'm probably not so different. I guess we've known each other for too long for it to matter. If you must know, I found Norman quite . . . er . . . sympathetic. It's possible we could do business together.'

'Ha! Norman Addleshaw "sympathetic". That's a joke.' Tate looked down at his drink and shifted awkwardly in his seat. 'However . . . you're seeing him did set me to thinking.'

'Oh?'

'Yes. I thought to myself that if Victor Goldsmith was prepared to contemplate an investment by the likes of Addleshaw, he must be in need of new money. That's what I thought.'

Goldsmith examined his fingernails carefully and said nothing.

'Then I thought to myself that perhaps Victor's current backers, those lardy-da insurance people, might be playing games. Perhaps they're not happy with returns, budget overruns, whatever. Of course I know my little comic gems make you and your company a lot of money, but sometimes that money gets wasted on other artsy fartsy stuff put out by the studio.'

Goldsmith frowned. 'There's no need to be rude, Archie.'

'Come now, Victor.' Tate winked. 'You'll take a little teasing from your number one box office star, won't you? Of course you will! Anyway, I'll get to the point. My thinking led me to a decision.'

'And what decision is that, Archie?'

'To tell you that if you're in some sort of financial bind, or if all is well but you just want to take in new money, forget Norman Addleshaw. Look no further. I'm your man.'

Goldsmith's eyes widened in surprise.

'I know. I know. You weren't expecting that, were you?'

'But, Archie . . .'

'I've got the money, you know. I'm pretty good at investing, as it happens. I've turned the income from my films to good account. I won't bore you with the details but I've grown my earnings by a factor of ten at least. I was doing well before 1939 but I've done even better since the war began. Norman's a handy friend to have. I've made a killing in the stocks of various companies which have secured Government contracts. The fact is, Victor, Archie Tate has got the kind of lolly you need for the film game.'

'But . . .'

'I know what you're going to say. Another awkward bugger like Addleshaw. But remember what we were just talking about. We've been business partners of a different sort for years and done very well for each other. I think . . .'

Goldsmith raised a hand. 'Alright, Archie. As you often say to me, hold your horses. What you've proposed does come as a surprise, but you shouldn't assume it's an unwelcome one. Let me first emphasise most forcefully that there are no financial difficulties. The business is in excellent shape. It's just that I can see opportunities and would like to expand. Expansion requires money. The insurance people have been good to me but I've never liked putting all my eggs in one basket. Hence the interest in new investors.

110

Now, if you really want to be considered, I shall treat your interest with all seriousness. Some might say it's a conflict of interest for talent to partner in a studio, but Chaplin, Fairbanks, and Pickford didn't do so badly when they set up United Artists together, did they?'

'Well, by 'eck, Victor, I'm so glad you say that.' Tate reached across the table and patted Goldsmith's arm enthusiastically. 'I think we should drink to that!' A waiter swiftly brought them refills and they clinked glasses again. 'This scotch tastes all the better for what you just said, Victor. So!' He swirled the drink around in its glass. 'How much are you looking for?'

Goldsmith paused to make some calculations. He didn't want to frighten Tate with too large a figure but didn't want to quote a figure too low given the scale of his problems. He took a couple of puffs of his cigarette then said: 'Between a hundred and a hundred and fifty thousand pounds. Per investor that is. I might consider allowing two or three new people in at that mark.'

Tate's mouth turned down. Goldsmith thought for a moment he'd gone too high but the comic's face quickly brightened. 'Aye, that's the sort of money I thought you'd be talking. How much of the company would a hundred thousand pounds buy?'

Victor Goldsmith relaxed. 'Well, now, Archie. Let's see . . .'

Chapter Six

It was overcast and miserable outside. Merlin had all the office lights on. He had bought a packet of Everton Mints on his way into work and popped one in his mouth. For years he'd been hooked on Fisherman's Friends, powerful lozenges which reeked of eucalyptus. Sonia detested the smell so he'd been obliged to give them up. The mints were his milder replacements.

Ten minutes later, his team had all gathered around his desk. 'Why don't you kick off with the Curzon case, Sergeant? Tell everyone what we have.'

'Righto, sir. I think everyone knows the bare facts of Miss Curzon's death. The DCI and I went to her Mayfair flat yesterday. This is what we have learned so far.' He consulted his notes. 'One. Miss Curzon had been away in Los Angeles since July. She had only returned to the country last Wednesday.

'Two. She was married to, though estranged from, the film actor Michael Adair. Our initial understanding is that their parting was amicable. A neighbour, however, reported occasional rows before the split. According to the porter this neighbour, Mrs Cavendish, is a busybody and prone to exaggeration. When I questioned her, though, she was adamant about what she heard. More pertinently, perhaps, she told me she'd heard raised voices coming from Miss Curzon's flat on the night of her death. The voices of a man and a woman between eight and nine o'clock. She couldn't hear any of the words, though.

'Three. We found a bag of what forensics has confirmed to be cocaine in one of Miss Curzon's bedroom cupboards and traces of the drug elsewhere in the flat. There were empty drinks glasses and bottles in the drawing room. Signs too of some disturbance – overturned chairs, a smashed glass, et cetera. There are two bedrooms but only one appeared to be in use. There were some items of interest on the terrace which forensics now have. A snagged thread. A handkerchief. We haven't heard back from forensics yet so I don't know if they found any other interesting evidence.

'Four. We interviewed the senior porter, Mr Jackson, but have yet to speak in detail to his assistant, Baxter. He's on my list for today. We did a thorough door to door of the building tenants. We didn't find everyone at home, but we saw something like three quarters of them. Nothing. No one heard a scream or saw any-thing suspicious. If Miss Curzon had visitors, none of the tenants saw them.

'Five. At night time when the porters aren't around, visitors can only get through the front door when tenants come down to physically let them in. There is a tradesmen's entrance at the back of the building which is the only other access point. The porters have the key and check to make sure it is closed in the evening. I haven't examined the entrance myself yet. That's on my list of things to do.

'Six. Around the roof terrace there is a wall, mostly of brick but with a central part that is in metal only. This metal fencing is lower than the brick part and doesn't seem very secure, although it doesn't appear to be damaged. It would not be diffi-cult to fall over.'

'So a simple accident is quite credible?' asked Inspector Johnson.

'Yes. And if Miss Curzon was drunk or doped or both . . .'

'If she was really gone that could explain the signs of disturb-ance,' said Merlin.

'How many drinks glasses were there, Sergeant?' It was Johnson again.

'In addition to the broken glass, sir, two whisky tumblers and two champagne flutes.'

'So she must have had at least one visitor. Maybe more.'

'Looks like it, Inspector. That's it, Sergeant?'

'For now, sir.'

'Thank you. So all possibilities open. The flimsy fence, Miss Curzon drunk. A regrettable accident? Suicide? Signs of visitors. Signs of commotion. Foul play. We must keep our minds open.' Merlin's eyes moved from Bridges to Johnson to Cole and back again. 'You got Adair's new address from the porter, Sergeant?'

'Sir.'

'We'd better see him next and find out what he has to say.'

South China Sea

Danny Ross hung tightly to the spar of timber which was serving as his life raft. The cries of the injured and dying kept him company as night descended. His head throbbed, his legs ached, and he'd swallowed a gallon or two of sea water, but for now he was one of the lucky ones. He was alive. He guessed that the nearest men in the water were some forty yards off and he caught an occasional glimpse of lights in the distance as he bobbed up and down in the swell. The water was feeling colder and he kept kicking his legs to keep his circulation going. He was losing track of time but thought it was at least three hours since the Prince of Wales had completed its final death throes and sunk to the ocean floor.

Exhaustion was beginning to overcome him when he was roused by the sound of cheering. Then he thought he could hear an engine. Eventually the lights of a low-flying aircraft appeared on his left. The sudden release of a flare revealed its RAF insignia. His hopes rose. It had to be a reconnaissance plane sent out from Singapore or some other Malaysian base to assess the situation. His throat was too dry to manage a cheer but he waved. The pilot circled the wreckage for a while then disappeared back into the darkness.

They'd sighted the first bomber mid-morning. Ross had quickly realised things were serious from the reaction of the officers on the bridge. Not that there was any show of fear. Just gritted teeth and faces of steely resolve. Briefly he had thought of his Aunt Iris, who had fought so hard to stop him signing up. 'Sam will be able to get you into the police. You'll be alright there. No need to be a hero. Be sensible!' He'd thought of her safely tucked up in that nice little Battersea semi, with Sam and the baby, just as the bombs had begun to fall. He had a grandstand view of the initial action from his position on the bridge. The first wave of bombers had concentrated their attack on HMS *Repulse* but with little effect. The second wave, mostly torpedo bombers, targeted both *Repulse* and the *Prince of Wales*. It took them a while to get their range but eventually a bomb had hit home, destroying the *Prince of Wales's* propeller shaft. Other Japanese hits had followed in quick succession. Within the hour the flagship had begun to list and the guns been disabled. *Repulse*'s situation had deteriorated similarly and it was not long before the two vessels had been swallowed by the waves.

The ocean swell rolled and Ross's head went under the water yet again. He hauled himself back up, heaving and coughing. Things were looking bleak. He knew from the officers' talk on the bridge that there were other British vessels in the vicinity of their flotilla. Perhaps they'd all been sunk as well? If rescuers were on their way, would he be able to survive long enough? As he'd waited to jump from the ship there'd been talk of sharks. There had been a number of worrying ripples in the water. He noticed another and froze. Something was certainly heading in his direction. When it was about five yards away, to his immense relief, a head popped above the water, then a hand which reached out to grasp the spar.

'Room for two on this vessel?'

The man's face was obscured by oil but Ross recognised the voice. 'Alright, Wilf?'

'Wotcha Danny boy. Bit of a lark this, ain't it? If I'd known we were going for a swim I'd have packed my trunks.'

Wilfred Watson was an irrepressibly chirpy gunner from Hackney who'd bunked close to Ross. 'Got to keep smiling, as me old Pa used to say, however shitty the mess you're in.'

'I'm not sure he had a mess as shitty as this in mind.'

'Don't get yourself down, Danny boy.' Watson pointed to his left. 'See those lights out there? I'll bet they're destroyers of ours on the way to pick us up.'

Ross could see nothing.

'Didn't you see that ship earlier? The *Express*?'

'No. I missed it. Must have been too busy stopping myself from drowning.'

'She managed to take a few men on board before she had to pull away. One of those lights is 'er, I think.'

'What about sharks, Wilf?'

Watson's voice lost some of its confidence. 'Sharks. Yeah.'

'You've seen one?'

'No, but when I was over there . . .' he jerked his head to the right 'I heard someone screaming "Shark".'

'And?'

'Dunno. The screaming stopped.'

The two men fell silent. Ross could see Wilf's lights now. They seemed to be getting closer but maybe that was an illusion. His thoughts returned once more to Iris and Sam in their cosy little London house.

'So, Cole, moving on from the Curzon case, why don't you tell us where you are in your efforts to identify our Victoria girl?'

'I'm afraid, sir, that I haven't much progress to report. I've drawn an almost complete blank with the police missing person files. I used the window of the twelve months up until May of this year. I did eventually get a couple of matches only to find the girls were subsequently accounted for. The only real lead I have, and it's not a strong one, came from Wandsworth. An orphanage was bombed around this time last year. Most of the kids resident there had been evacuated previously to the country but twenty-two were still in place at the time of the bombing. Six of this group are known to have survived the attack, and ten to have died. That left six unaccounted for, of whom three were teenage girls.'

'Any chance they could have been killed by the bombs but were just unidentifiable?'

'The local sergeant thinks not, sir. He seems pretty certain all the bodies were retrieved and that these six children escaped and are out there somewhere.'

'Do we have the names of the children?'

'Yes and no, sir.'

Merlin looked confused. 'Beg pardon, Constable?'

'Sergeant Owens, the Wandsworth officer I'm dealing with. He . . .'

'He has the names?'

'Half the names, to be accurate.'

'Please explain.'

'After the bombing, those orphanage files left intact were moved to a temporary storage facility, a hut by the river, which was itself then hit in another raid. The file containing details of the twenty-two children who survived the original bombing was damaged in that raid. Basically the list was torn in half by the bomb blast. The half that remains has the children's Christian names only. The authorities were able to match surnames to the sixteen children identified as dead or surviving. However, as regards the other six, no one knows the surnames.'

'Weren't there any surviving Barnardo's employees who could help?'

'All the staff died in the bombing.'

'No parents or relatives came looking for their children?'

'No, sir. We are talking about orphans mostly, although I understand some of the children had family from whom they had been somehow parted. But no, no one came looking.'

'I suppose that's a dead end, then.' Merlin had a quick glance at

Bridges. The sergeant had been a Barnardo's orphan himself, though he didn't care to be reminded of it.

'Not necessarily, sir. Sergeant Owens thinks it's worth having another look around the hut. He said, as they were in the middle of the Blitz and swamped at the time, they didn't manage a very thorough search. He thinks it's possible the surname half of the list survived the blast and is somewhere in the hut. He'd be happy to have another look if we wanted.'

'I have to say this seems quite a long shot, Constable, but I suppose it's worth a few hours of your time to follow it up. Get yourself over to Wandsworth and tell Owens that I'd appreciate him pulling out all the stops.'

'Yes, sir.'

'Anything further?'

'At Sergeant Bridges's request, I checked out the businesses operating in the Costello Building before it was bombed.'

'And?'

'There were two American corporate tenants. One was the Alpha Elevator Company Incorporated of Madison, Wisconsin.'

'Madison, Wisconsin, eh? Home of the great Frank Lloyd Wright.'

'Who, sir?'

'A brilliant American architect of Welsh extraction, Constable.' His team stared back at him blankly. 'Philistines, all of you. Never mind. He's probably not our murderer. Carry on, Cole.'

'The second American tenant was a company called Cowan Productions. A film company. Alpha Elevator doesn't appear to have relocated in London since the bombing but the Cowan company has a new office in Shepherd Market.'

'Well, I don't think we're quite up to sending an officer to Wisconsin, but Shepherd Market is within our reach. Inspector, you alright for that?'

'Of course, sir.'

'Anything further on your missing American family?'

'I have a little more detail, sir. The daughter in the family is thought to be around sixteen. The father, Gerald Washburn, is

118

some sort of itinerant evangelist who got into trouble in America before the war and escaped to Europe, ending up in London in 1939. The man is a fraudster according to the American Embassy. He had some scheme going in London duping people into giving money to his bogus religious charity. When he got found out he did a runner. That was in February. It's believed he took his wife, two sons and daughter with him. There are civil and criminal proceedings pending against him in Southwark and the police have him on a wanted list.'

'Do Southwark have any leads yet, Inspector?'

'Not yet, sir. Should I involve myself directly with their investigations?'

Merlin thought for a moment. 'On balance, I'd say no. Let's tell Southwark and the Embassy that we have a keen interest in hearing of any further developments and leave it at that for now.' He popped another mint in his mouth. 'Alright, there's plenty to do. Let's get going.'

The policemen parked the car on Pall Mall and turned down a narrow alleyway close to the junction with St James's Street. Halfway along the alley, they turned right. At the end of a dead end street sat a charming little Georgian house; Michael Adair's new home.

The actor's hair was not quite as immaculate as it was on screen, nor was the skin on his face as smooth and unwrinkled, but it was most certainly Michael Adair who opened the door to Merlin and Bridges. Though clearly not at his best, he remained a very good-looking man, with the powerful presence one would expect of a major film star. Dressed in a navy silk robe and smelling strongly of whisky, he looked down at his feet as Merlin made his introductions. Then he led the policemen up a flight of stairs and into a snug wood-panelled drawing room. A fire was burning merrily and the actor invited them to join him in the antique brown leather armchairs around the fireplace. A low oak table separated the policemen from Adair. It was covered with old magazines, most featuring the beautiful face of Laura Curzon.

'Forgive me, gentlemen. I was indulging in a little nostalgia. Laura was, as you can see, a very beautiful woman.'

Merlin stretched out a hand. 'May I, sir?'

'Of course.'

Merlin picked up a three-year-old copy of *Picture Post* whose cover featured Miss Curzon in what looked like eighteenth-century period costume.

'That's the Dick Turpin film she did with George Sanders. I was offered Sanders's part but had to decline. I was engaged elsewhere. Pity. I'd have met Laura much earlier then and . . .' There was a catch in his throat. 'Maybe things would have turned out differently between us.'

Laura Curzon had been a fine-boned beauty of the classic English type. High cheekbones, a firm chin and narrow nose, with bright and intelligent blue eyes and a sultry full-lipped pout. The *Picture Post* photograph was in black and white but he knew from her colour films, not to mention his brief recent acquaintance with her in the flesh, that Laura Curzon's hair was of a rich auburn colour quite like Sonia's. He looked hard at the face before passing the magazine on to Bridges. 'A very beautiful and talented woman, Mr Adair. Our deepest condolences.'

Adair waved a hand in acknowledgement and turned morosely to the fire.

'As you know we are investigating Miss Curzon's death. I'm afraid we need to ask you a few questions.'

Adair turned back to Merlin. 'If you must.'

'Do you have any thoughts on what happened?'

Adair sighed. 'I think it was an accident. No doubt you've seen how unacceptable the metal fencing on the terrace is. I suggested many times that we raise and strengthen it but for some inexplicable reason she always said she liked it as it was.'

'Yes we noticed the fence. Clearly an accidental fall is a possibility. However, there are other things I am bound to consider. Do you think she might have killed herself?'

'Not Laura. Not her,' said Adair vehemently.

'You seem very certain. May I ask why?'

Adair paused as he lit himself a cigarette and placed it in a distinctive zebra-striped holder. 'I was married to the woman, Chief Inspector. I knew her! She wasn't the type to do herself in. She was always so very positive.'

'Forgive me, Mr Adair, but it's my understanding that you and Miss Curzon separated in the summer, just before she went to America for several months. How can you know about her recent mental and emotional state? Perhaps your split made her very unhappy? Perhaps other things happened to make her unhappy?'

Adair's nostrils expelled two jets of blue smoke and he looked again into the fire. 'We parted very much as friends and that remained the case. I can assure you that nothing in our relationship or its ending would have made her suicidal. She had got over me. As to other causes of unhappiness, there was the disappointment of what happened in America of course but . . .'

'Can you tell us about that?'

'She was cast in a major new Hollywood film. The producers pulled the plug. Her co-star, James Stewart, had to withdraw and they decided, in the circumstances, to cancel the production.'

'And how do you know this, sir?'

'Laura told me.'

'On the telephone?'

'On the telephone and in person. I spoke to her by phone on Friday and once over the weekend. Then I saw her on Monday.'

'Did you now?'

'Yes. I went round to her flat for an evening drink. We had planned to have lunch on Sunday but she cried off. She was very tired after her journey and also said she had a sore throat. I agreed instead to pop round the following day. She seemed right as rain apart from her throat. She was disappointed about the film, and there's no doubt it was a blow to her career, but she was resilient. She suggested there had been other problems in America but nothing to worry about. She already had irons in the fire and was certainly not suicidal, to my mind anyway.'

121

Merlin leaned forward. 'When exactly did you arrive at her flat?'

'I'd say about sevenish. Maybe seven fifteen.'

'And you left when?'

'I was only there forty-five minutes or so. Perhaps a little longer.'

'I see. And Miss Curzon seemed fine?'

'Yes, as I said. We had a sociable drink together and then I left.'

'You had another engagement?'

'No. I could see she was still tired from her transatlantic journey and I knew she'd also had a late night at a party on Saturday. And she had a sore throat, as I mentioned. So I left her to have an early night.'

Merlin regarded Adair carefully. 'I'm sorry to ask this question again, sir, but you insist that there was no . . . no strain in your relations of any sort?'

Adair's cheeks flushed. 'Damn it no, as I've already said!' He jumped to his feet and strode over to a well-supplied drinks cabinet near the window. He made himself a large pink gin before returning to his chair. 'Look, Merlin, if you're trying to suggest our relations were bad enough for Laura to kill herself . . . or worse, for me to push her to her death . . . you are most definitely barking up the wrong tree.'

'My questions tend only to getting to the truth of things, sir,' replied Merlin. 'The flat at Seymour Mansions. Miss Curzon owned it?'

'She held a long lease. It was her place before the marriage.' Adair sipped his gin. Merlin noticed his hand was shaking. 'I had a set in the Albany which I retained when I moved in with her. Unfortunately the Jerries blew it to pieces. Otherwise I'd be there now. I rented this place in the summer after we split up.'

'May I ask the reason for the split?'

Adair sighed. 'Really? Do you *really* need to know about these personal matters? I can tell you we were very deeply in love for a while but the acting profession is not conducive to marital bliss. After the wedding, we were often apart for long periods working on different films. An occupational hazard. In such circumstances, there can be . . . distractions.'

'I see. And you succumbed to these . . . distractions?'

'I did and so, in due course, did she.'

'So it was infidelity which drove you apart?'

'If you want one single thing, then yes, I suppose it was.'

'And you planned to divorce?'

'Yes, but there was no rush.'

'You both agreed amicably about that?'

'We did. Her California opportunity came up and we agreed to wait and sort it out on her return. I spoke to her a few times in America on the telephone and there was no mention of her changing her mind.'

'Did you discuss it on Monday night?'

'We didn't.'

'I'm sorry to persist, but I want to have this crystal clear. There was no question of the two of you being at odds on this matter? Of you wanting to get a divorce quickly so you could marry someone else? You have a new relationship with another actress, I believe?'

Adair stroked the hem of his dressing gown distractedly then looked up. 'I see you've been quick off the mark digging into my affairs, Chief Inspector.'

Merlin shrugged. 'The head porter told us in passing, sir.'

'Good old Jackson.' Adair frowned at Merlin. 'I see the picture you're trying to paint, Chief Inspector. Lovelorn wife wishes for reconciliation with estranged husband. Thwarts husband who wants to move on and marry anew. To get his way, dastardly husband pushes wife to her death from great height. I think I played a character like that in repertory years ago. It's poppycock.'

Merlin sighed. 'I hope it is but . . .' He waited while Adair went to get a second drink. When the actor was back in his seat, he asked, 'Could you please tell me a little more about Miss Curzon's behaviour in the marriage. You said she was unfaithful too.'

Adair looked for a moment as if he was going to lose his temper but he managed to rein himself in. 'The profession is notoriously promiscuous,' he said sharply. 'Beautiful women and handsome men abound. Temptation was . . . *is* . . . great. She succumbed.'

'As did you. Was that early on in your marriage?'

'Pretty early. She only succumbed in the latter stages of our relationship, I believe. Initially I had thought we were modern enough to weather the occasional infidelity. Contrary to my expectation, Laura turned out to be the jealous type. I tried to restrain myself but when I failed she eventually took up with other men to get back at me.'

'Do you know who her lovers were?'

'No. I didn't ask questions and she kept the details to herself. One hears the odd rumour of course, but I made a point of ignoring such things.'

'Was she seeing someone when she left for America?'

'I don't believe so, as she told me she hoped to meet someone new over there.'

'And meanwhile you have found yourself another beautiful actress girlfriend. Another marriage in the offing? After all, there's nothing to hold you back now, is there?'

Adair gave Merlin a look of disgust but made no reply.

Merlin felt a twinge from an old bullet wound but the pain quickly subsided. 'Let's move on. I'd like to have as full a picture as possible of Miss Curzon's activities after her return from America last Wednesday. I know now you spoke to her a couple of times by phone and saw her on Monday. Do you know what else she got up to in the few days she was back?'

'Well there was Gus Cowan's big party on Saturday night. She went to that.'

'Cowan?' Merlin exchanged a look of recognition with Bridges. 'That would be the film producer of Cowan Productions.'

'Yes. That's the chap. He had a big bash at The Dorchester. He's always holding grand parties.'

'Did she tell you about it on Monday night?'

'She mentioned it briefly. She saw some mutual acquaintances of ours.'

'She enjoyed herself?'

'She always loved a good party.'

'She didn't mention anything which upset her there?'

'No.'

'Did she tell you about anything else she'd done after her return?'

'She implied she'd had some business meetings without being specific about who or when.'

'I see. Anything else you discussed at the flat?'

'We talked about the war. And what happened to her in America, as I said. She joked that the American Air Force must have known Pearl Harbour was coming and that's why Stewart got pulled off the picture.'

'Any discussion of the divorce?'

'I already told you. No.'

'You say Miss Curzon always liked a good party. Was she a heavy drinker?' asked Bridges.

Adair's cigarette had gone out and he relit it, this time not bothering with the holder. He took a long draw on it before answering. 'That depends on what you call heavy, Sergeant. She liked a drink and could hold her liquor. Is that a good enough answer for you?'

'What about other stimulants?' Bridges continued.

Adair's eyes narrowed. 'What do you mean?'

'Drugs, dope, cocaine?'

'I don't know what she got up to in America, but in my company she only took alcohol.'

'You don't take drugs yourself then?'

'Certainly not, Sergeant.'

'One other question from me, sir.' Bridges flipped through his notebook until he found the relevant page. 'The lady next door, Mrs Cavendish, says she heard raised voices in the flat somewhere between eight and nine. Did you have an argument during your visit to the flat?'

'That old bat. I shouldn't listen to anything she says. She's always imagining noises and disturbances to complain about. No, we didn't argue, and in any event I was gone by eight or there-abouts. Laura had a bad throat as well so wasn't even capable of raising her voice.'

'Was Miss Curzon drunk when you got there?' Merlin asked.

'She may have had a glass of something before I arrived but no, I wouldn't say "drunk". However she was good at holding her drink, as I said.'

'Was a glass dropped or chairs overturned while you were there?'

'Goodness, no.'

'Did you go out on the terrace at all while you were there?'

'No. It was a freezing night. Why would I?'

Merlin looked at Bridges.

'Anything else, Sergeant?'

'I don't think so, sir. For the moment at least.'

Merlin got to his feet and thanked the actor for his time. Adair was both relieved and aggrieved as he accompanied the officers down the stairs. He couldn't resist a parting shot as the policemen went out onto the street. 'I think you'll realise in due course, Merlin, that this distasteful grilling was completely unnecessary. Laura's death was neither suicide nor foul play. It was an accident and I'll look forward to your apology when the investigation duly reaches that conclusion.'

Johnson chose to make his way to Shepherd Market on foot. The skies above had brightened a little and he thought rain unlikely. His route took him along Whitehall to Trafalgar Square and then on to Piccadilly. When he got to Green Park Tube Station, he paused to look across the road at the In and Out Club. The impressive neoclassical building had been the home at one time of Lord Palmerston, one of the country's most colourful Victorian Prime Ministers.

The DI spent much of the little spare time he had reading. For most of the year he had been living a bachelor's life in the family flat in Pimlico. Over a year before, he and his wife Dora had reluctantly decided she should escape the dangers of the Blitz and go to stay with her parents on Tyneside. She had returned in June, when the German bombing campaign appeared to have stalled, but her stay had proved short-lived. Dora's father had suffered a serious fall in August at the shipyard and she'd returned home to help her mother. A few weeks later, her mother had suffered a bad stroke. With both parents in a pretty bad way, Johnson wasn't sure when he'd get her back.

During this long period of domestic solitude, books had been Johnson's salvation. Latterly, partly prompted by discussions with Cole about his evening class studies, Johnson had become interested in history, in particular the Victorian period. Hence the draw of Palmerston's old home. He idled for longer than he should, thinking about the biography of the man he'd just read. Then he picked up his feet again only to find his path now blocked. The pedestrians ahead were held up by a military party turning from the road into Green Park. It was a company of soldiers with a couple of field guns, marshalled by a squad of mounted policemen. The sight of military men going about their business in London, common as it now was, never failed to unsettle him. Important as Johnson knew his police work to be in the war effort, he could never quite rid himself of the guilt that he wasn't doing his bit in the forces, a feeling shared by many of his colleagues at the Yard.

Shepherd Market was not a particularly salubrious place, even though it was situated in one of London's smartest districts. To many Londoners it's most notable feature was prostitution. Some girls congregated near the Grapes pub on the east side, others around Hertford Street on the west. Johnson was fully familiar with all of this as he had been a young beat constable in the area nine years before. He remembered how, when he started out, the girls would all scatter instantly on his approach. Over time, they'd become less fearful of him and would stand their ground, teasing him. Since the police policy at the time was pretty velvet-gloved, this was not so surprising. The standing instruction of the sergeant at the Mayfair station had been 'Just move 'em on. We know they'll be back but it's right to remind them, and the residents, that we have our eyes open. This game has been going on in Shepherd Market since it was built two hundred or so years ago and no doubt it will be going on two hundred years from now.' He blushed as he remembered the ribaldry his name had provoked amongst the girls. 'Anyone need a Johnnie? If you do there's one coming down the road.' His eventual transfer to a more refined part of London had been a relief.

The film company office was in Market Mews. A gold-lettered sign on the front door of the terraced house read 'Cowan Productions Ltd' and a number of other affiliated companies were listed in smaller letters beneath. The brass knocker on the door was in the shape of a film camera. He banged it a couple of times and a young blonde appeared. He showed his warrant and the girl led him upstairs to a large reception area, the walls were plastered with movie posters.

'And who is it you want to see, sir?'

'Whoever's in charge.'

'That would be Mr Cowan, but unfortunately he's out. Mr Steiner, the chief accountant, is here if you'd like to see him.' The girl's accent was a strange mix of Cockney and something else. Johnson guessed she was an East Ender who'd had a few not particularly effective elocution lessons. Looking at her tight blouse and skirt, her buxom figure and pretty face, he doubted she'd been recruited purely for her secretarial skills. A call was made and she led him to a simply furnished meeting room whose window overlooked an Italian restaurant Johnson remembered patronising years ago. After a brief wait, a skinny, swarthy man with thick glasses joined him.

'Isaac Steiner.' He thrust a surprisingly large hand across the table. 'Pleased to meet you, Inspector.' He sat down. 'How may I assist.'

'I am making some routine enquiries in connection with your old offices.'

Steiner scratched his head and dislodged a few flakes of dandruff from his bushy hair. 'You mean the old offices in Victoria?'

'Yes, sir. In the Costello Building.'

'All rubble now, I believe. I heard it finally collapsed the other day.'

'It did. We are taking an interest because a body was found in the ruins.'

'Was that surprising? I would have thought many bodies were found in the ruins.'

'They were but in this instance we are looking for a murderer.'

'I see. And the murderer isn't to be found wearing a moustache and living several hundred miles to our east?'

'No. This girl's killer is in London.'

Steiner shrugged. 'Very well but what does that have to do with us, Inspector?'

'I'll come on to that but I have a few general questions first. How many employees do you have here, Mr Steiner?'

'Seven. We run a tight ship. Apart from Mr Cowan and myself, there is young Mandy at reception, Mr Cowan's secretary, my secretary, my assistant, and a driver.'

'And did you all work previously at the place in Victoria?'

'No. I am a recent recruit as are most of the others. The only survivors here of the old office are Mr Cowan and his secretary, Miss Ryman. The others went their separate ways.'

'I presume you have a record of those people?'

'Of course.'

'Could you . . .'

'Provide a list? Certainly, but why?'

'We are interested because . . .'

Steiner had turned to the door. They could hear heavy footsteps approaching. Then the door burst open. A heavily built man in a brown check suit stood grinning in the doorway.

'Inspector Johnson, I presume?' The man made a face. 'My God, I sound like Spencer Tracy in that terrible movie about Livingston and Stanley. You know the one Steiner, don't you? "Doctor Livingstone, I presume?"'

Steiner stared back blankly at his boss. 'No, sir.'

129

'No? Well, what the hell. You're only an accountant after all. I'm sure the Inspector gets the reference?'

'I do, sir. A very good film.'

'You know, Zanuck promised me a chunk of that movie, the bastard, then reneged. What do you think of that?'

Johnson felt no reply was required.

The man in the doorway looked towards Steiner and asked, 'So what's this all about?'

'The Inspector is making enquiries about the old office in Victoria. Apparently a murdered body has been found in the ruins.'

'Has it indeed? Well, you'd better come along to my office now, Inspector. I'll answer your questions and Mr Steiner here can get back to his abacus beads and slide rules. Follow me.'

Cole preferred getting around London on his bike, if he could. Wandsworth was a fair distance and it took him an hour. As he was leaning his bicycle up against the wood fencing in the yard of the local police station, he saw a burly uniformed officer approaching.

'DC Cole, is it?'

'Sergeant Owens?'

'Aye.' They shook hands. 'You seem a little puffed.'

'Wandsworth is further than you think.'

'It's a good old trip from Westminster that's true, and more difficult these days with all the bomb damage cluttering up the roads. I've cycled the journey a few times when I've had business with your fellows, or to see my daughter.' The sergeant's accent had been moderated by many years in London but his Welsh origins were still apparent.

'You have a daughter living in Westminster?'

'Working, not living. She's a constable at the Yard like you.'

Cole had a flash of recognition. 'Glenys Owens?'

'The very same. Lovely girl . . . but then I would say that, wouldn't I? You know her?'

Cole smiled awkwardly. Glenys Owens was a pleasant but

130

rather homely girl who worked on the switchboard. He had been told she had a bit of a crush on him. 'Can't say I know her really, but I've spoken to her.'

'So you must have. I'm hoping they move her from the switchboard soon so she can get some proper experience. Anyway, you're not here to talk about my daughter.' He started walking back towards the station building.

'It's good of you to help us out,' Cole said, following Owens's quick steps.

'You're welcome. Truth is, the thought that those kids might be out there on the streets, destitute and starving, has been playing on my mind for months. I'm glad to have another go at helping find them. I've got one of my constables to help. Derek Hands. An apter surname would be "Shovels" as that's what his hands are like. We'll go and get him then head off for the storage hut. It's a fifteen-minute walk.'

Three hours later the three policemen were choking with dust, filthy, perspiring and frustrated. Their prize was eluding them. The hut was close to the Thames on a site which had been home to a number of industrial units, nearly all now flattened by the Luftwaffe. From one cracked window they could see Hurlingham Park over the river, from another, Putney Bridge. The small structure was battered but standing. There were big gaps in the brickwork, a wide gash in the metal roof, and numerous signs of fire and water damage. The remains of several rusting metal filing cabinets were scattered in among general debris on the floor. They had painstakingly searched through everything without success, and were beginning to lose heart.

The sergeant wiped the sweat from his forehead and leaned on his shovel. 'It looks like we're going to be unlucky.'

'Let's give it a little longer, Sarge,' suggested Constable Hands. 'You never know.'

They all agreed to stick at it for another half-hour and set to again.

The half-hour was nearly up when Cole straightened up with a grunt of pain.

'Alright, son?'

'It's just a rick in the neck, Sergeant. A hangover from my days as an athlete. I'll be alright in a sec.' He turned his neck to and fro to ease the pain and as he did so stared up at the gap in the roof. His eyes shifted to the skylight window next to the hole. The glass had long gone from the frame but some wire meshing remained. He thought he could see something caught up in it. Material of some sort. He looked hard, then pointed up. 'What do you think that is?'

The other two officers followed his finger. 'A rag?' Hands volunteered.

Sergeant Owens squinted. 'Hard to tell. Why don't we move that thing under the skylight.' Owens indicated the only undamaged filing cabinet in the hut.

'If you want me to stand on it, Sarge, I don't think it will take my weight,' said Hands.

'No, but it might take Cole's.' The three men dragged the cabinet over and Cole clambered up. The metal creaked but the cabinet held. Cole steadied himself then reached out. He stretched as far as he could but was still an inch or so short.

'Here. Try this. It should give you a bit more height.' Earlier in the search Hands had dug a big old leather bible out of the rubble. It seemed pretty solid and Cole set it down on the top of the cabinet. He stepped up, the book held, and he reached up again. Now he could just get his fingers to the material. He went on tiptoe and pulled carefully. Slowly the tangled material came away but as he grasped it, the cabinet wobbled and he lost his balance. He fell, fortunately, into Hands's outstretched arms. When Cole got to his feet, he passed what he had in his hand to the sergeant who said: 'It's too dark in here. Let's step outside.'

An upturned wooden crate stood a few yards from the hut. There was just enough room for the three of them to sit. Their discovery turned out to be a grubby piece of paper which must have been blown upwards into the skylight by the bomb blast.

Its entanglement in the meshing seemed to have preserved it quite well. The sergeant held it up to the light. One edge was jagged. It looked like it was part of a larger sheet of paper which had been ripped. To one side of the jagged edge, there was a vertical line of typed words. It looked like a list. The type had faded but the words could just about be read. The one at the top read Evans. Owens pulled the list of the children's Christian names out of his pocket and held out the two pieces of paper side by side. They matched.

When Goldsmith awoke that morning he had a sore throat, runny nose and a bad headache. He should have done as his wife advised and spent a day in bed. Instead he got dressed, skipped breakfast and went to his study to read over a couple of the scripts he planned to film in the first six months of 1942. One, a Robert Donat vehicle, aimed to exploit the actor's success in Hitchcock's *Thirty-Nine Steps*. The story revolved around a Nazi spy working undercover in the London headquarters of an unspecified European Government in Exile. Donat was to play an Oxford professor caught up unwittingly in the German spy ring. Ideally, Goldsmith would have got Hitchcock to direct but the man had decamped to Hollywood and probably wasn't coming back. It might be an idea to bring in some new blood to direct the film. There were a couple of up-and-coming men, Reed and Lean, on whom he'd had his eye for a while. He would see them both and form a view.

The second script was a dramatisation of *Bleak House*, the Dickens film he'd been discussing at the studio with Kaplan and the others. Unlike the Donat script, which was ready to go, this was not in good shape, and Goldsmith had arranged to have lunch with JB Priestley just after Christmas to see if he'd agree to rewrite it. The author would be expensive, but quality always was.

Just after one, Ted Morris appeared carrying a steaming mug of something.

'Your missus told me you were under the weather, boss. Thought you might appreciate one of my specials.'

'Usual ingredients?'

'Yep! Large dollop of single malt, small dollop of honey, couple of cloves, egg yolk, slice of lemon and piping hot water.' Morris placed the drink on Goldsmith's desk.

The producer took a sip. 'Perfect. Which malt?'

'Lagavulin.'

'Good choice.' His throat immediately felt a little better. 'Why don't you tell me what you've been up to this morning.'

Morris took a seat and crossed his long legs. 'Thanks boss. I was told you wouldn't need me today, so I took the Bentley to the garage to sort out a couple of problems.'

'I thought there wasn't a mechanical problem under the sun you couldn't fix yourself?'

Morris had a rumbling laugh which sounded rather like water going down a plug hole. 'I needed some parts. Without the parts, not even I can perform.'

'As the eunuch said to the actress.'

'Bah-boom!' More water disappeared down the plug hole. 'Anyway, boss, I've something for you.' Morris slid an envelope across the desk. 'Just after I parked the car outside, a fellow came over and gave me this. Said you'd be expecting it.'

Goldsmith weighed the envelope in his hand, and immediately realised what was inside. When he opened it a key fell out. If the routine hadn't changed, it would open locker thirty-nine in the left luggage room at Victoria station. In the locker would be the first instalment of Goldsmith's cash loan from Joe Abela. Further instalments would be deposited there at weekly intervals and in a month he would have the full amount.

Now he was faced with a quandary. He had serious investment interest from two parties. Neither Tate nor Addleshaw were ideal partners, but their money would be a hell of a lot cheaper than Abela's. Should he trust to one or both of them coming through and reject Abela's money? Or should he take it by way of insurance?'

Morris remembered the last time a key had been delivered like this. 'Want me to go to the locker, boss?'

Goldsmith drank some more of Morris's hot drink and looked thoughtfully towards the window. 'Pull the curtains, Ted. Let's see what type of day it is.'

Morris did as asked and sunlight streamed into the room.

Goldsmith got to his feet with a grunt of satisfaction. 'The sun is shining and your drink has revived me. Perhaps, once again, all is well with the world.'

'And the locker?'

'Leave it for now, Ted. I need to think.'

'Hungry, boss?'

'You know, for the first time today, I am. A smoked salmon sandwich would go down well.'

Back in Wandsworth the officers were in Sergeant Owens's room at the police station. The two parts of the children's list had been put together and they now had the full names. Twenty-two in total, with six not accounted for. Six children. Three boys. Three girls. Grace Roper, Ida Walker and Vera Rogers.

'Pity we haven't got the ages,' said Cole.

'We ought to be able to find that information somewhere now we have the names,' said Owens.

'Happy to go through the local council files, sir,' volunteered Hands. 'Those that survived the bombing, that is.'

'Thank you, Constable. And there's always Somerset House.'

'I'll handle that, Sergeant,' said Cole. 'I'll head back, now. Probably be too late for Somerset House when I get back this afternoon, but I'll be round there first thing tomorrow. Thank you both very much for your help.'

'Pleasure, lad. Let's hope it's not all a wild goose chase. Oh, and if you see my Glenys, tell her hello from me.'

There was an envelope on Merlin's chair when he and Bridges returned from Adair's house. Merlin opened it and found a memo from the Governor of Wormwood Scrubs:

To: DCI Frank Merlin
From: Governor WS
Re: Prisoner on Remand Boris Orlov

I had an approach last night from the above prisoner. Orlov wanted to arrange an urgent meeting with you. I would have telephoned you regarding this first thing this morning but by chance AC Gatehouse called me at 8.30 on another matter, and when I mentioned the prisoner's request, he told me you would be far too busy for a meeting today and that I should send you a memorandum.

I called Orlov to my office this morning to question him. He was extremely agitated and seemed wary of opening up to me. However, he eventually told me he'd decided to provide you with some of the information you wanted. He appreciated this would place him in danger.

Unlike some of my prison service colleagues, I do not keep my head in the ground. I know very well that violent criminals on the outside have their stooges behind prison walls. After seeing him, therefore, I put him in solitary as a protective measure.

When do you think you will have time to see him? Would you prefer that I send him to the Yard or are you happy to see him here? Either way I suggest speed is of the essence. No doubt gossip will spread about him being in solitary and some people may draw the wrong conclusions. For the moment I have put it about that he is being punished for attacking a guard.

With warm regards
Gordon Cleverly, Governor

Purple blotches appeared on Merlin's cheeks and he slammed the memorandum down on the desk. 'Unbelievable! *Madre de Dios*! How dare he interfere? Here. Look at this, Sergeant.'

By the time Bridges had read the memo, Merlin was at the threshold of the AC's office. He ignored the stern secretary and barged straight in. Gatehouse was standing near the window, a golf putter in hand, lining up a ball. His target was a metal ash tray near the desk. The AC ignored the interruption and struck the ball firmly into the hole.

'By Jove, Frank. Good shot, eh?' The AC looked up at Merlin and waited for the compliment. None was forthcoming, and it didn't take long for him to gauge Merlin's mood. 'I think we'd better sit down.'

'I just received a memorandum from the Governor of Wormwood Scrubs.'

'Ah yes. Cleverly. Good man.'

'It concerned a prisoner called Orlov who communicated an urgent desire to see me.'

'Yes. So the Governor told me.'

'And you took it upon yourself, sir, to tell him I'd be too busy to see the man today.'

'Well obviously you have the Curzon case to deal with as a matter of priority.'

Merlin struggled but failed to find the right words in response.

'Was that not correct, Frank?'

Merlin found his voice. 'Do you not think, sir, that I should be allowed to calculate my priorities for myself?'

'Of course, Frank, but I was just trying to relieve some of the pressure on you.'

'This man Orlov might be about to spill the beans on his gang masters.'

'Let us hope so but the story he wants to tell today will more than likely be the same he tells tomorrow.'

'That's not the point, sir. News might get out. The man is in prison and if he's decided to squeal he's in great danger. You should not have advised the Governor as you did.'

The AC's tone hardened. 'I did what was right, Chief Inspector. Pursuant to the Commissioner's instruction, the speedy resolution of the Curzon investigation is our top priority. I did not want to impede your work in that regard.'

'A visit to the Scrubs will be no such impediment.'

An awkward silence followed. Merlin counted to ten and calmed himself. 'My officers have the Curzon case well in hand. The case will not suffer if I take time out to go to the prison.'

'Is there news regarding Miss Curzon?'

'Progress is being made. I'm not sure, though, that her death is quite as straightforward as you and the Commissioner would like.'

'Are you basing that view on evidence or intuition?'

'Both. We interviewed the husband this morning.'

'And?'

'Can't say I took to him. Said some odd things. Seemed under pressure.'

'The man's just lost his wife, for goodness sake, Frank. Not bound to be at his best, is he?'

'She was about to become his ex-wife.'

'Was she indeed?'

'Adair was very thin-skinned. He reacted very aggressively to some of my questions. His demeanour was . . . suspect.'

'But, goodness, Frank, you can't think he had anything to do with her death?'

'Probably not, but . . . we'll see.'

'What did he think happened to the woman?'

'He said it must have been an accident. Said she wasn't the suicidal type. We did notice that part of the fencing on the roof terrace was quite low.'

'Well there you are. Poor fencing, unfortunate fall. Sad but simple. I'm sure the Commissioner and his friends would be happy to see it all wrapped up quickly on that basis.'

'I'm sure they would, sir, but there was definitely something fishy about Adair.'

The AC looked sharply at Merlin. 'I know, as always, you'll investigate everything thoroughly and properly, but I hope you won't go out of your way to over complicate matters or dig around unnecessarily out of . . . out of spite against the Commissioner.'

'Do you really think I'd do that?'

The AC thought for a moment, then shook his head.

'Thank you, sir. Now, if you don't mind . . .' Merlin got to his feet.

'Look, Frank, I know you are not very keen on the Commissioner but there are valid reasons for him to stick his oar in here. He told me last night it was important to protect what is a valuable part of the country's social and economic fabric. The success of the British film industry is important to morale and the Exchequer. Thus, it would be better if the facts of this case don't in any way cause embarrassment to that industry.' The AC stuck out his chin. 'However, Frank, should those facts prove otherwise, I shall not gainsay or undermine you. Indeed, when have I ever done anything like that?'

Merlin could think of several occasions but now was not the time to mention them. 'Very good, sir, but I really must get going now.'

The prison was a bleak Victorian edifice a mile to the north of Shepherd's Bush. Merlin remembered playing football years ago on the open ground beyond the building.

They were greeted by a senior prison officer and hurriedly conducted through a maze of clanging doors and corridors to the Governor's surprisingly warm and comfortable office.

'It's been a long time, Frank.'

'You're looking well, Gordon. Last time we met was that regimental reunion in the City, I think.'

'Yes. 1937 that would have been.' Gordon Cleverly and Merlin were the same age. The Governor's fair hair had receded an inch or two since Merlin had last seen him, and his face looked more creased, but he was still a fine figure of a man, looking in much the same physical shape as when he'd played international rugby twenty years before. As well as being a first rate sportsman he had been first rate academically too, and Merlin had never really understood why he'd devoted himself to the distinctly unglamorous life of the prison service. All he could think was that Cleverly's devout Christianity must have had something to do with it.

Merlin introduced Bridges and they sat down in three battered armchairs close to the fire. Cleverly leaned forward and looked gravely at Merlin. 'I was very sorry to hear about Alice.'

Merlin shrugged. 'It's a while ago now, Gordon but thank you.'

Cleverly's face brightened. 'However, I understand your life has now taken a better turn and that congratulations are in order?'

Merlin shifted uncomfortably in his chair. 'Yes. Thank you again.'

'I'd love to be able to catch up in more detail some time, Frank, but I know you are pressed. I haven't seen Orlov again so I've nothing more to add to what I said in my memo. Shall I get him in here?'

'I think this might be a little too cosy, Gordon. A basic interview room will suffice, if you've got one free.'

'Of course. Please bear with me.' Cleverly disappeared for a while then returned looking apologetic. 'One of my officers has pointed out that if you use one of our normal interview rooms, you'll be obliged to walk through the centre of the prison to the other side of the building and will no doubt be seen by some prisoners. Gossip is already rife on Orlov's solitary confinement. I think it would be wisest to give you one of the rooms along the corridor here. It's a file storage room but has a table and chairs and is suitably bleak.'

'That will be fine, Gordon. Will Orlov be seen by many when he's brought here?'

'He won't be seen by any prisoners. The solitary cells are on this side of the building below where we are.'

'Would you like to sit in?'

'No. It's kind but I'll let you professionals get on with it. Just bear with me again while I make sure the room is in order.' He disappeared again.

'So you served with him, sir?' asked Bridges.

'We were in the same regiment. In Ypres and a few other hell-holes. A very brave man. Got the Military Cross for rescuing some of his company from no man's land. Many thought he should have received the big one.'

'The VC you mean?'

'Yes. Story was he was denied the Victoria Cross because he was too outspoken to his superiors. He's never been one to suffer fools gladly.'

Bridges said nothing. He had heard similar things about Merlin's military service.

The Governor returned. 'They're bringing him up now.'

'Thanks. The other man arrested along with Orlov. Walter Young. Had any peeps out of him?'

'If you mean about helping you out; no. If you mean in connection with Orlov; one of my officers heard him discussing Orlov's move to solitary with another inmate. They seem to have accepted that he struck an officer. For now, at least.'

'Good.' Merlin looked at his watch.

'Sorry, Frank. My secretary will come in a second and tell us when he's in place.' Cleverly crossed his long legs and sighed. 'Worrying events out East, eh?'

'Very.'

'I have some friends in the War Office. They're not very optimistic. The distance the Japs covered to attack Pearl Harbour was immense. Opens up a whole new range of possibilities in warfare.'

'Yes, Gordon. I don't . . .'

Merlin was interrupted by the arrival of Cleverly's secretary. Orlov was in the interview room.

Johnson and Cole were comparing notes in Merlin's office. Cole went first and told the Inspector everything that had happened in Wandsworth.

'Well done, Constable. A good bit of investigative work you've done there. Let's hope it wasn't a waste of time? It's still quite a long shot.'

Cole shrugged. 'As Mr Merlin says, you can only work with what you've got. And you, sir? How'd you get on with the film company?'

Johnson thoughtfully tugged at an earlobe. 'There are seven employees of Cowan Productions at the Shepherd Market office. Of them, only Cowan himself and his secretary worked at the previous office in the Costello Building. I'm waiting on a list of the other employees in Victoria.'

'Do we know if anyone looking like our girl worked there?'

'Obviously, only Cowan and his secretary would be able to tell us. I didn't get to see the secretary, as she was out on an errand. Cowan says he doesn't know.'

'What's Cowan like, sir?'

'Mr Cowan is an imposing, verbose and domineering sort of man. It was a struggle to get a word in edgeways. The moment I sat down in the his office I was subjected to a torrent of verbiage about his brilliance as a film producer, his genius as a scriptwriter and editor, his ability to spot talent, his friendships with the great and good, his love of Britain and his great admiration for the London constabulary. I did manage to get some questions in but didn't get far. It wasn't so much that he refused to answer my questions as that he wouldn't give them proper consideration.' Johnson attempted an American accent, ' "I have employees all over the place – here and abroad – some are young, some are old. You can't expect me to recall them all, particularly people like office girls. Do you know, since the Victoria office was bombed I have made three films. Spring 1940 is a lifetime ago for me." '

'Good accent, sir. Perhaps you should have a go at the films.'

Johnson made a small bow.

'Anything about the chocolate wrapper, sir?'

'More in the same vein.' Johnson returned to character. ' "Chocolate? You're asking me about chocolate? What the hell do I know about chocolate? Sure I like a little from time to time. Do I look like a man who is concerned about his waistline? Hershey's? Sure I know Hershey's. It's nice enough. So is your Cadbury's. Then there's that bar with the kids' heads. Five Boys, that's it. I'm quite partial to that one. Do I hand out chocolate bars to children?

142

No I don't. They don't sell Hershey's here anyway." That's as far as I got on that.'

'Are you going to try and speak to the secretary?'

'I guess so.' Johnson sighed. 'I know Cowan is a long shot too, Constable, but he struck me as pretty shifty. As we've got little else to go on, I'm going to dig a little further.'

Orlov's few nights under lock and key had had their effect. Bloodshot eyes, papery pale skin, cold sores on his lips. There were dark shadows under his eyes and Merlin doubted he'd had much sleep.

'Please for cigarette, Merlin? I am gasping, as you say.' Orlov waved a couple of nicotine stained fingers in front of him.

'That's Chief Inspector Merlin to you, matey,' snapped Bridges.

Orlov glowered at the sergeant and muttered something under his breath.

'It's alright, Sergeant. We can run to a cigarette for our friend, I think.' Bridges went out to cadge a packet of cigarettes from someone. He returned with three loose cigarettes and gave one and a box of matches to the Bulgarian. Orlov lit up, hands trembling. 'Bad case of the shakes you've got there, Boris.'

Orlov made a sour face. 'Try a few days in here yourself, Chief Inspector. See how you get on.'

'First time behind bars, is it?'

'Yes.'

'You've had a good run, then. Your luck was bound to turn. There's a long stretch in prospect for you now.'

Orlov looked grim and took a pull on his cigarette. He watched as the smoke spiralled slowly up towards a small grille in the ceiling. 'Maybe. I suppose depends, eh?' he finally answered.

'Depends on what?'

'On whether I help you out.'

'And how will you do that?'

The Bulgarian ran a hand through his unkempt hair.

'I rat on Walter and the others. What if I do that?'

143

'That might help you. The inside story on Young would be very interesting. As to "others", whom exactly do you have in mind?'

'Young is my main boss. You know that. His boss is Joe Abela. His boss Billy Hill. Hill I never met. I can tell nothing against him. Young, Abela, others in the Abela gang . . . Have spent much time with them. Heard many things. Done many things. Can tell you.'

Merlin gave Orlov a long, hard look. 'Why the change of mind?'

Orlov sent more smoke spirals to the ceiling. 'Have simple choice. Inform or die.'

'Why are you so certain you'll die?'

'I am a foreigner. Sure I am hard man and can handle myself but have been thinking. I am no use to Abela, Hill in here. They have no loyalty to me. I have a temper. If I fall out with someone, no one will protect me. Young, he never really like me. Sees me as threat. No. I will not last in prison long.'

'I see.'

'If I tell you what I know I want deal. I walk free. Have protection. New life.'

Merlin moved his chair a little closer to the table. 'We'll see. I'll need clearance from my superiors for any deal. I'll support such a thing if it's reasonable and I'm assured of the quality of your information.'

'If you want as they say, a taste, concerning what I know, I can give you, but I need to know for certain from above you can deal.' Orlov stubbed out his cigarette and looked greedily at the other cigarettes on the table in front of Bridges.

Merlin slid one over to Orlov, then got up. He walked the few paces to the room's only window. Looking out through the bars, he saw an empty courtyard below and the other prison wings opposite. A sparrow landed on the window ledge and took an inquisitive look at him before fluttering away. Merlin thought for a while before returning to the table. 'Let's negotiate a deal then, but before we do I'll seek a general clearance from my boss to make sure we're not wasting our time.'

'I was law student long time ago, Chief Inspector. In Sofia. One must always negotiate, yes?'

'You surprise me, Boris. We'll be off now. I'll be back as soon as I've got the nod.'

Orlov reached out for Merlin's hand and squeezed it. 'Soon as you can. Am not safe here.'

'You ought to be safe enough in solitary.'

'Here, I am safe nowhere. Please hurry.'

Joe Abela removed the knuckle-duster, took out his handkerchief and wiped the blood away. He reached into the glove compartment where he kept emergency medical supplies and found the iodine. Wincing, he applied it to the cuts on his fist.

When his ministrations were completed to his satisfaction, he leaned forward and tapped his driver's back. 'Alright, Harry. Let's go 'ome.'

'Which home, boss? The missus or Glenda's?'

Mrs Lia Abela lived with the two young Abela children in a substantial detached house on Wimbledon Common. Glenda Travis, Joe Abela's mistress, had a smart two-bedroom mansion flat in South Kensington.

'Glenda's. I can't be fagged with the journey south of the river. You can call Lia later from a box and tell her I've had a busy day and am spending the night in the office.' Abela ran his crime kingdom from a flat above a barber's shop in Clerkenwell. The rooms included a comfortable master bedroom.

'Hand alright, boss?'

'Stings a bit. I'm annoyed with myself, getting personally involved in the rough stuff like that. Should be above that sort of thing now. Felt I owed that cheating bastard a bit of personal attention, though. For old times' sake.'

The 'cheating bastard' in question was an unfortunate called Enoch James. Once an important member of Abela's gang, greed or jealousy or both had driven him to do the unthinkable and switch to a competitor. He'd compounded his treachery by enabling his new bosses to get the jump on a big bank robbery Abela had been planning. It had taken a while to track James down, but today they'd finally got hold of him and punishment had been exacted. Now, his battered face the texture of mashed potato, he lay breathing his last in a metal coffin bound shortly for the bottom of the Thames. Abela had had some fun with Enoch over the years. They'd seen things the same way and Abela had enjoyed Enoch's wicked sense of humour. Betrayal was, however, a serious business and the penalty had to be severe.

Abela reached into the door side-pocket and took out a half-bottle of Johnnie Walker and a small bag of cocaine. After a snort and a liberal pull of whisky he began to feel much better. As the car pulled away, he lay back on the plush red leather and, to get Enoch James out of his head, began to think about practical matters. Practical business matters.

Joseph Abela liked to think of himself as a modern business-man. He kept up with the latest business books. He knew all about optimum organisational structures, the advantages of successful delegation, management motivation and the rest. In his mind he saw his business as a corporate entity. There was the holding company at the top, which he managed, and beneath lay the operating divisions with their own managing directors. There were the two divisions in which he took the closest interest, Vice and Finance, and in which he doubled as his own MD. Then there was the Protection Division, run by the clever bruiser, Oswald Chappell. The Robbery Division, which handled straightforward robberies and the business's various fraudulent wartime schemes, had two bosses, Paddy Lynch and Walter Young. Then, finally, there was the Pharmaceutical Division, run by the man in front of him, Harry Gough.

After another slug of whisky he considered the most pressing of the operational decisions on his agenda. Walter Young was behind bars. He'd already had his best brief looking at the case and it looked pretty certain the man was going down for a long time. There was always the option of springing him, as they'd organised for Ozzie Chappell a year before, but Abela thought it would generate too much heat if they made a habit of it. So, he'd either have to put Paddy Lynch in sole charge of Robbery or find him a partner. It was a tough decision. Orlov would have been the obvious candidate for promotion but Abela had lost him too.

Abela was now completely relaxed. A soothing warm glow had come over him and he'd have nodded off if Gough hadn't suddenly shouted at him.

'Boss. I forgot. While you were having your fun with Enoch, I called the office from the warehouse. Betty said Billy'd been on the blower. He seemed pretty keen to talk to you about something.'

Abela swore under his breath. Despite the outwardly good relations he was keen to maintain, he really didn't like Billy Hill. He yearned to break free of the Hill yoke. 'I'll call him tomorrow.' It was pitch dark outside and all he could see was his faint reflection in the car window. 'On second thoughts, Harry, let's give Glenda a miss. I fancy a trip to Maisie's place. She told me the other day she was expecting a bunch of new girls. Let's go and see if they've arrived. Perhaps we can run one or two of them in?'

Chapter Seven

Thursday December 11th 1941

The old man contemplated the time-worn reflection staring back at him from the dressing-table mirror. Beneath the large hairless dome of his head, the hooded eyes still had much of their magnetic power and menace, and the face was still striking despite the ravages of age. He turned away suddenly as a car horn sounded outside. Then he smiled to himself. For 'the wickedest man in the world', as he was still known to some, to take fright at such a petty thing was rather ridiculous. He stood up, removed his bathrobe and walked naked into the tiny bathroom of his new home – a modest Hanover Square serviced apartment. The bathroom had a mirror, a full-length one. He sighed at the sight of his sagging pot belly and flaccid manhood. There was no point in denying it. He was well past his prime. He scratched his testicles. Sex had been hugely important in his life. Sex with women. Sex with men. Sex with – well there had been that close shave with a goat in one of his occult ceremonies but thankfully he had thought better of it. Drugs had been a great source of pleasure too. Sex. Drugs. And, of course, religion. Dark religion. His own religion. And writing about all these things. All sources of pleasure but if he had to choose one above others, it was sex. His powers in that area were, however, undoubtedly waning. He was sixty-six. Too young to be on the scrap heap yet, surely? For Aleister Crowley. 'The Beast', as the Northcliffe press had dubbed him. He, above all others, shouldn't be subject to the pattern of decline which applied to ordinary men. Beatrice, the latest in a long, long line of lovers, was doing her best to keep the machinery functioning, but it wasn't easy. He sighed as he reached out to turn on the shower. Stoicism was the only answer, of course. And acceptance. But he had never had much time for such virtues, if virtues they were.

After the shower, Crowley dressed himself and went through to the small living room. On the old scratched desk, a pile of correspondence awaited his attention. He had only been in Hanover Square for four weeks and not many of his acquaintance were aware of his new address. Most of the letters were thus ones forwarded from his previous residence in Torquay, the majority being bills which he peremptorily tossed into the waste basket. Much of the rest ended up in the same place. Eventually there remained only one letter. The envelope had been addressed only with his name and been left for him on the lobby table the evening before. He opened it, took out the welcome sum of money enclosed, and read.

Dear Aleister,

Thank you very much for agreeing at short notice to meet me for lunch yesterday. I very much enjoyed our discussion. The exposure to your evidently vast knowledge of the occult and related matters was fascinating and illuminating. On the subject of your new religion 'Thelema', I'm afraid much of what you said went over my head but I wish you luck with it.

I very much appreciate your numerous suggested improvements and amendments to my little 'order of service', so to speak, for the ceremony planned for Sunday night. I'm sorry that you feel unable to take up the leading role I had envisaged but am delighted that you have agreed to be a participant. As mentioned, I would very much like you to be a regular counsellor to me on these matters, on a remunerated basis of course. In the hope that you will accede to my request, I enclose an advance of £10.

I very much look forward to seeing you on Sunday night. I shall be serving drinks from 7.30 ahead of the evening's proceedings.

With warmest regards
Marcus Waring

PS I'm also having some friends for dinner at my house on Friday night. Would be delighted if you could join us then.

Waring had been courting him for a long time, deluging him with correspondence in Torquay and then London. Initially cool to his approaches, Crowley had finally given in, despite his view that Waring was not a truly serious Devil-worshipper. While Waring had clearly read widely on the occult, and had conducted many black rites, he lacked a proper intellectual appreciation of the underlying spirituality of his acts of worship. It seemed to Crowley that Waring was interested more in the orgiastic and climactic elements of Devil worship than anything else. The man had spoken with lascivious relish of those parts of the ceremonies involving young flesh.

In recent years, Crowley had actually become a little bored with Satanism. His current religious interests were complex and embraced many strands of pagan belief, but did not encompass the deification of Beelzebub. He was prepared to give Waring ceremonial advice, but wouldn't be telling him that in all his years of practising the dark arts he hadn't managed to raise as much as a minor demon, let alone the Devil himself. He had decided to help for the money, pure and simple, although he would enjoy the show of naked beauties as much as the next man. Crowley had never been lucky financially. Apart from a few all too brief interludes, he had spent his life scrabbling for cash. If Waring insisted on being his financial benefactor at this late stage of his life, Crowley would not object.

He put the letter and the money away in a drawer and went to make himself a hot herbal concoction in the kitchenette. Back in the drawing room, he sank into his one shabby armchair and sipped his drink. It occurred to him that other advantages might accrue from his relationship with Waring. The man was wealthy and well-connected. Perhaps Crowley, through Waring, would meet other influential men who could be persuaded to support his latest, more advanced work. The thought that news might get out of his involvement again in the rites of the occult did not worry him. A few months earlier, the traitor and Nazi propagandist William Joyce, known to all as Lord Haw Haw, had referred to Crowley in one of his notorious broadcasts from Germany. Joyce had joked that as a recent National Prayer Day in Britain had clearly failed to remove the Nazi threat, perhaps a Black Mass celebrated by Crowley in Westminster Abbey would do the trick. His popular reputation was at rock bottom. It could fall no further.

He finished his drink and went over to the window. As he watched, an attractive young woman crossed the road below. He thought of Beatrice, closed his eyes and remembered their last union. Something stirred below and life suddenly began to seem better.

It was Winston Churchill's custom, when possible, to remain in bed until mid-morning. Sawyers would bring him a cooked breakfast on a tray. The meal would be accompanied by a weak whisky and water to get his system going. The latest ministerial red boxes would be brought for his attention, and he would work through them. On this morning, he had just begun to read a Home Office paper on criminal exploitation of the black market when his bedside telephone rang.

'Pound here, Prime Minister.' Admiral Sir Dudley Pound was the First Sea Lord. Minor pleasantries were exchanged. Churchill thought the man sounded a little subdued.

'Speak up, Dudley. We have a bad line.'

Pound raised his voice and repeated himself.

'That's better,' said Churchill. 'Tell me quickly what you're calling about in case the line fades again.'

'I'm afraid I have very bad news to report, sir. Her Majesty's Ships, the *Prince of Wales* and *Repulse*, have both been sunk by the Japanese. By aircraft attack. Tom Phillips is missing, presumed dead.'

The eggs Churchill had just consumed almost made a reappearance. 'Are you sure of your information, First Sea Lord?'

'Sadly, I am. There is no doubt at all.'

Churchill could find no words and set down the receiver in a daze. His spirits, raised high in recent days by the American entry into the war, plunged. Only a few weeks before, the *Prince of Wales* had carried him across the ocean to Newfoundland for his first wartime meeting with Roosevelt. He knew Phillips and many of his officers. He had a terribly vivid image in his mind of the diminutive Admiral going down valiantly with his ship. The dreadful thought occurred that there was hardly a battle-worthy British or American ship present in the great vastness of the Pacific Ocean.

His eyes rose to see Sawyers loitering by the bedroom door. He pulled himself together. 'Run my bath, if you please. I'm getting up. I'll be going to the House very shortly.'

'Something upset you, has it?'

'The worst of news. The very worst! And once you've got the bath running, refill my drink will you? And make it a strong one.'

'You're sure this Orlov fellow is going to play straight and give us the goods, Frank?'

Merlin had a fuzzy head and was slow to respond. He'd returned from the Scrubs with Bridges the night before to find Johnson and Cole waiting in the office, and on a whim they'd all repaired to The Red Lion. After a quick run through of developments, Merlin had insisted they enjoy their drinks without discussing work. Instead they'd talked of football, of Cole's night classes, of Johnson's books and of Iris's originality as a cook at this time of rationing and shortages. They'd all ended up merry and Merlin was paying the price this morning.

152

'Feeling under the weather, Frank?'

'No, sir. I'm fine. Busy, that's all.'

The AC remarked sagely. 'A policeman's lot in wartime London is not an easy one. Any idea when Sonia will be returning to London to support you?'

'Soon, I hope. We're certainly aiming to spend Christmas together.'

'Yes, that's not far away now is it? Is Sonia getting used to motherhood?'

'She is. How easily will I get used to fatherhood? That's the question.'

The AC leaned across to pat his Chief Inspector's forearm benignly. 'You'll do fine, Frank, I'm sure.' He chuckled and Merlin got a strong whiff of the AC's habitually overpowering bad breath. 'Going back to Orlov, if the fellow is going to get a free pass out of jail, he'd better be giving us first grade stuff about Abela and his cronies.'

'He knows that's what we expect.'

'If it works out and we end up nailing Abela, d'you think in turn, through him, we'll get a real shot at Hill?'

'That would be great but let's not count our chickens. Remember how much influence Hill wields.' Both men knew Hill had several bent coppers in his pocket. The AC had tried a couple of runs at force corruption but had not received the necessary backing from above. 'Do I take it that I have your approval to proceed with Orlov, sir?'

'Yes, alright Frank but I'll need to put the Commissioner in the picture. Can you hold off until I've done that? I don't expect him to object but I need to do it for form's sake.'

Merlin sighed. 'Speed really is of the essence here, sir but very well. You'll let me know as soon as . . .'

'Of course. Any more on the Curzon case?'

Merlin sighed. 'The day is young, sir. However it did occur to me that Orlov might be able to help us out there.'

'On the Curzon case? How?'

'The Abela gang deal in drugs. Big time. Perhaps he knows who Miss Curzon's suppliers were?'

'If it was Abela's people you mean?'

'If not, he might know what other gang was involved. There would presumably be a lot of competition to service high profile people like her.'

'Maybe. Are you thinking now that the drugs might have had something to do with her death?'

'Drugs and violence often go together, sir.'

Valerie Goldsmith liked to laugh. She was laughing now as her companion, the Duchess of Castlemore, completed her hilarious story about outrageous adventures at a recent party in Ireland.

The women were enjoying a morning coffee at the Ritz, after which they would embark on one of their regular Bond Street shopping expeditions. Despite the Duchess's grand title, she came from an ordinary background. The Duchess had been born Peggy Mullins, the eldest child of an impoverished Church of Ireland vicar in Cork. She was very attractive in a Celtic way – wavy red hair, sparkling green eyes, and a scattering of freckles on nose and cheeks. It was the freckles which had first drawn the attention of Johnny Fitzalan, at the time Marquess of Greenstone and heir to the dukedom of Castlemore, when Peggy was nanny to his sister's children in the old family castle in south west Ireland. They were married in short order. The Castlemore estate was not a rich one and every passing year presented newer and tougher financial challenges. Her husband, now the Duke, was able to support Peggy in solid comfort in Ireland but he baulked at financing expensive shopping binges and socialising in London. Luckily for the Duchess, Valerie Goldsmith was happy to make free with her husband's money and step into the breach.

'Goodness me, Peggy? Was she aware half the house party had seen her bare backside wobbling into the trees as she chased after the gardener?'

The Duchess giggled. 'She must have been but I have to say she

154

carried it off very well at breakfast the following morning. Not a hint of embarrassment. Just bit the butler's head off about the temperature of the kedgeree and greeted everyone amiably at the table as if everything was absolutely tickety-boo.'

Valerie Goldsmith laughed heartily again. She too had risen from lowly beginnings. The youngest daughter of a Hampshire butcher, she was blessed with a voluptuous figure, flowing golden locks, and the face of a cheeky angel. At nineteen, she'd been plucked from a West End chorus line by one of Victor Goldsmith's talent recruiters and put into the movies. She had swiftly graduated from small roles to big ones, and from carefree dalliances with young actors to a more serious dalliance with Goldsmith himself. During a cruise on Goldsmith's boat in the Mediterranean, a few months before the Abdication, she had accepted his proposal and soon thereafter become the second Mrs Goldsmith. She had no interest in providing Goldsmith with more children nor, she soon realised, in continuing a film career. The life she now enjoyed was a carefree one of extravagant spending, grand parties and social climbing. She was a sensible woman and knew it was important to stay on her husband's right side. She didn't find this difficult. Her cheerful disposition and wide range of bedroom skills seemed to be enough to keep him happy. She remained completely faithful, and knew he did his best to do likewise, although she was aware of the occasional lapse. Valerie finally regained her composure and turned to look out into the lobby. 'Where on earth is Louise?'

Louise, Marquise de Baillon, was the third of their little gang. An older woman by several years, she was the wife of a French exile recently attached to the Free French Command in London. Unlike her two friends, she was no beauty. Her greatest attribute was an uncanny knack for rooting out the juiciest scandals in London society and sharing them with her friends.

The Duchess surreptitiously topped up the coffees with a tot from the half-bottle of Drambuie she always kept in her bag. 'Louise's husband is having De Gaulle and some other French bigwigs to dinner at their place. She said she'd try and get here but I'd wager that the preparation of the dinner arrangements has got on top of her.'

'Oh God, I didn't realise.' Valerie giggled. 'The thought of Louise entertaining on a grand scale in that little flat of theirs is hilarious. And she doesn't know how to boil an egg! Has she got caterers in?'

'I don't know. And if she has, where will she put them?' The Duchess helped herself to the last of the delightful Ritz macaroons and became serious. 'Anything more on poor Laura?'

'Victor tells me Scotland Yard are on the case. Vincent Korda pulled some strings to ensure her death was investigated by some-one good.'

'Why did Korda get involved?'

Valerie waved imperiously at a waiter and ordered more coffee. 'She did a few films for the brothers. Both Alex and Vincent have always had soft spots for her. Platonic only. Or so she claimed.'

'My hairdresser said the story was she'd committed suicide.'

Valerie shook her head. 'I'll never believe that. I saw her at Cowan's party on Saturday. She was on good form.'

The Duchess crinkled her nose. 'I know you, Valerie, my darling. No doubt you were having a whale of a time at that party. When you are stuck into the Pol Roger and fully in the swing of things, you think the whole world is on good form!'

'That was quite uncalled for, my dear.' Valerie pursed her lips. 'I was perfectly sober on the three or four occasions I spoke to her. She was very jolly and smiling sweetly at everyone. Later on I saw her dancing gaily with the host and others.'

'Dancing with Gus Cowan? Ugh! Rather her than me.'

'Oh, come on, Peggy. He's not so bad. And he throws a good party.'

'You know exactly what he's like.' The Duchess gave Valerie a knowing look.

Valerie shrugged. 'So what if he's a lecherous ogre? Plenty of those around, especially in the film industry. If Gus tried it on

156

with Laura, I'm sure she was perfectly capable of giving him the elbow.' Her eyebrows rose. 'Come to think of it, I did see him glaring at her rather fiercely at one point later on. Maybe she'd given him the elbow just then?'

The Duchess patted her lips with a napkin. 'I suppose we should count our blessings regarding our other halves. They might not be the greatest lookers in the world but they have class and are perfect gentlemen.'

'Most of the time anyway.' Valerie put her handbag on the table. 'Now, it's clear Louise isn't coming. Let's get away and do some shopping.'

'Cole is at Somerset House, Peter?' asked Merlin. He was in his office with Johnson and Bridges.

'Since first thing.'

'Alright.' Merlin's eyes fell, as they often did, on his larger paperweight, a replica of the Eiffel Tower bought on a pre-war trip with his first wife. He briefly thought of their excitement as they reached the viewing platform and gazed out entranced at the city of Paris that lay before them. Happy memories. He returned to the present and picked up paper and pen. 'Time for a quick stock-take, I think. I'll just jot a few things down. Bear with me.'

Bridges and Johnson waited patiently as Merlin covered a sheet of paper then checked what he'd written. Eventually he looked up at them. 'So this is what I've got:

'One. The Victoria Case.

We have the names of three missing girls from the Wandsworth Barnardo's. Cole is seeking further information.

'Minor progress re the Cowan Victoria office. Question is whether anyone resembling our girl worked for Cowan or had any dealings with him or the office? Inspector Johnson not taken with Cowan and would like to pursue further. Next steps me to interview Cowan and Johnson to see secretary.

'Other possible lines of enquiry. Who else had offices in the Costello Building . . .' Merlin looked up. 'You know, tracking down and interviewing people from the other offices is going to require a lot of legwork and resource. I don't think we have the capacity at the moment. I'm going to park it for now. We'll revisit if our other enquiries come to nothing.' He returned to his notes. 'The missing American family. Will wait on Southwark police and Embassy who know of our interest.

'Two. The Curzon Case.

'Cause of fall? Accident, suicide or foul play? What have we got?

'Adair in flat on evening of death. Says he left early. Twitchy in interview. Directly raised idea of him pushing Miss Curzon off roof to deny it. Adair a suspect?

'Evidence of neighbour that raised voices or argument in middle of evening between 8 and 9.

'Accident theory supported by dodgy fencing.

'Cocaine in flat presumably for Miss Curzon's use. Anecdotal evidence she was a drinker. Possibility substances contributed to accidental fall? Who supplied drugs? Could Orlov help on that?

'Relevance of other items of evidence. Thread in fence. Monogrammed handkerchief. Smashed glasses, slippers, overturned chairs.

'Next steps –

'Find out more about Miss Curzon's state of mind.

'Dig into Adair.

'Find drug supplier.'

Merlin looked up again. 'I've no doubt missed something so suggestions or corrections gratefully received. I haven't covered the Orlov Case as you both know the state of play there and there's nothing to be done at the moment while we await the Commissioner's clearance. So . . . ?'

It was Bridges who responded first. 'On the Curzon Case, there's more to be done at Seymour Mansions which you haven't mentioned. There's the young porter still to see. I meant to do that yesterday but what with Adair, then Orlov, I didn't manage it.

There are also a few residents who were out when we did the rounds. I'd also like to look into the building access points in more detail.'

'All important, Sergeant. You'd better get round there this morning.'

Johnson said, 'I understand why you want to leave off investigating other Costello offices for the moment but what about finding a building manager or porter who worked there? They might remember seeing a teenage girl around the place.'

'Good idea, Inspector. Ask Cole to add that to his list if and when he has the time.'

'Regarding Miss Curzon's state of mind, sir,' Johnson continued. 'It would be useful to get more information about her behaviour at the big party on Saturday night.'

'Contact Adair, Inspector. I think he's back at work today so you'll need to get the studio number. He should be able to give you a name or two of friends of Miss Curzon who were at the party.'

'It would also be helpful to know more about what happened in America.'

Merlin thought for a moment. 'She must have had an agent. He must know something. I'll track him down.'

'Maybe Cowan knows something too?'

'He might, Inspector. I'll ask when I see him. Anything else? Sergeant?'

'We still haven't a full report from forensics. Apart from the items you listed we need to know whether they found anything of interest on the nightwear she was wearing when she fell. And there were the personal papers they took from her desk . . .'

'Alright. You liaise with forensics later today and find where we are on everything.' Merlin put the note away. 'So off you go to Seymour Mansions, Sergeant. Inspector, you ring Adair and get a name. I'll try and identify Miss Curzon's agent and then track down Cowan.'

'It also occurs to me that it would be useful to know what Adair gets up to over the next few days,' said Bridges.

'So it would, Sergeant, but we haven't got the manpower to put a tail on him.'

'What about when Robinson gets back? She could pick up on Cole's work and he could . . .'

'Nice idea, Sergeant, but . . . well, we'll see. When is Robinson coming back?'

'Course finishes tomorrow, I think, sir, so presumably Saturday.'

'Good. We need her. I . . .'

There was a knock at the door and, before Merlin could answer, a duty desk officer poked his head around the frame. 'Envelope for the sergeant, sir. Marked urgent.'

Bridges opened the envelope and read the message. 'It's from the Bailey.' He made a thumbs up sign. 'The jury has returned a guilty verdict in the forgery case. All defendants guilty on all counts.'

Merlin got up to pat Bridges on the back. 'That's excellent news, Sam. No doubt it was your great performance in the witness box which clinched it.'

Bridges blushed. 'I don't know about that, sir.'

'Never refuse praise, Sam. It's a rare thing in this place.'

Goldsmith was still dithering about Abela's locker key. He didn't really want to make the decision to refuse Abela's money until speaking again to Tate and Addleshaw. He'd telephoned them but neither had been available. Tate was in rehearsals for a BBC variety show while Addleshaw was on a train to Leeds.

He needed to get the dilemma out of his mind for now so he picked up the *Bleak House* script he'd been looking at the previous day. He'd promised Adair a starring part but he wasn't sure there was a good match for him amongst the characters. He knew he'd think he was too young to play Jarndyce and he was definitely too old for Richard Carstone. Sir Leicester Dedlock, perhaps . . . ? Jean Parker could play Esther or maybe Ada. Basil Rathbone would probably make a very good Jarndyce. And

Tulkinghorn the lawyer? Charles Laughton perhaps, if he could get him out from Korda's clutches. As he was running over the various candidates in his mind he heard the bang of the front door and the clatter of high-heels.

'Darling. Is that you?' he called out. The study door flew open and his beautiful wife entered.

'Victor, my love. You look a lot better.' She shimmied over to her husband's desk then leaned across to give him a peck on the cheek.

'I had another of Ted's concoctions. It seems to have done the trick.' He relaxed back into his chair. 'You look very cheerful. Where have you been?'

His wife settled into an armchair by the window. 'Oh, the usual. Coffee and shopping with Peggy.'

'Oh, yes?' Goldsmith's face clouded. 'You know, darling, I'm . . . um . . . in the process of switching banks at the moment. That means the chequebook you have will not work after today. I'll have a new one for you in a few days. You'll have to delay your next expedition until . . .'

'You silly boy . . .' His wife crossed her legs and afforded Goldsmith a brief but enticing glimpse of thigh. 'You have accounts at all my favourite shops. I don't need a chequebook to shop.'

'Oh yes. Silly me.' With luck his finances should be back to normal soon, and there was no point upsetting Valerie over the expense of a few baubles. 'What was I thinking?'

As Valerie smoothly got up from the armchair, Goldsmith remembered the message. 'I forgot, my dear. You had a call earlier. The police want to talk to you about Laura. It was someone from Scotland Yard. I guessed you'd be back by now so I told them to come at half past three.'

'Oh poor Laura. It's so sad. But I have to admit to a feeling of excitement. I don't think I've ever spoken to anyone from Scotland Yard before.'

'Didn't you speak to Inspector Lestrange of the Yard in that Sherlock Holmes film we did a few years ago?'

161

'Very funny, Victor. I wonder who else they're speaking to. And why me?'

'At a guess, I'd say they want to know about her recent state of mind from a friend. You spent time with her on Saturday. They'll want to know if she was down. Depressed. Suicidal.'

'She seemed absolutely normal to me.'

'Then that's what you tell them.'

Valerie's brow wrinkled. 'She could be moody, of course.'

'Being prey to moods doesn't necessarily signify depression, my darling. If it did most people in our industry would qualify as depressives.'

Valerie suddenly looked at her watch, gasped, and jumped to her feet. 'I'd better get on and change. Got to look my best for Scotland Yard, eh my love?'

When he was on his own, Merlin put in a call to Eddie Butterworth, a freelance reporter he knew who dealt mainly in show business tittle tattle. Merlin generally gave members of the press a wide berth, but Eddie was a regular at his Chelsea local, and they had become friends.

'Frankie, old boy! How are you and where've you been? I haven't seen you in months. Changed pubs, have you?'

'No, Eddie. Just busy. I have managed the occasional weekend visit, though. I was there on Sunday as a matter of fact.'

'I'm not around much weekends these days. Got a new *friend* with a country cottage near Henley.'

Butterworth liked the ladies and had a high turnover of girlfriends. 'This one serious, Eddie?'

'Who knows? She's lasted since September so far.'

Merlin whistled. 'Long-term relationship, then.'

'Ha! We'll see. Speaking of long-term relationships I gather you got spliced in the summer. I was very hurt not to get an invite.'

'I apologise. Family and work colleagues only.'

'Chah! Only teasing. I wish you every happiness. Now am I right in thinking this isn't a simple social call. If you need something best tell me sharpish as I've got a press call to get to. Some new show Binkie Beaumont's putting on in Shaftesbury Avenue.'

'Laura Curzon. What can you tell me about her?'

'Oh, you're investigating that are you? Sad business. Can't say I ever got particularly close to her. Not much of a one for hobnobbing with newspapermen, although I understand she could be the life and soul of the party in the right company. Pretty girl, of course. I really don't know much more than your average newspaper reader. Got married a year or two ago to that arrogant prick Michael Adair. Rumoured to have had a rather open marriage, on his part at least. Split up in the summer before she left to star in a film in Hollywood. Mysteriously returned last week when the film was cancelled. I'm sure you know all that.'

'What's the gossip about her death?'

'Most seem to think it was an accident but I have heard the word suicide mentioned. If you know what happened already, I'd be most grateful for enlightenment.'

'You know I can't do that, Eddie.'

'Of course you can't, but if you get to the point when you can, an early tip to your old friend would be much appreciated.'

'I hear you. There's one simple question you might be able to answer for me. Who was her agent?'

'Hmm, let me think. I'll go and get my little red book. Hang on a mo'.' When Butterworth got back on the line he had what Merlin wanted. 'The Hilton Agency. They're in Soho somewhere. David Hilton. I know him only by reputation. Quite a big hitter. Said to be larger than life. He's a cousin of Tennent, the theatrical impresario who just died. Story goes he gave Hilton a leg up when he was starting out. The man is bound to know what's what about Laura.'

'Thanks, Eddie.'

'I'd better scoot, Frank. Hope to see you in The Surprise some time.'

Merlin went over to the shelf beneath the cuckoo clock and

pulled out the E to H edition of the London telephone directory. He quickly found Hilton's number and office address in Wardour Street and made a note. He'd contact the office shortly, but first he had another important call to make. He dialled the number Johnson had given him.

'Cowan Productions.' It was a man's voice.

'Mr Cowan, please. This is DCI Merlin.'

'He's out.'

'To whom am I speaking?'

'Steiner. Chief Accountant.'

'I see. Well, Mr Steiner, I'd very much like to see Mr Cowan.'

'What for? Another copper's already seen him.'

'I'm in charge of the investigation and need to see Mr Cowan myself.'

'I see. The boss is at lunch.'

'When will he be back?'

'Who knows? Lunch is a big deal for him. Quite often he never returns.'

'Do you know where he's eating?'

'He didn't tell me.'

'Does he have a regular place?'

After a long silence, there was a reluctant sigh. 'Wilton's on Jermyn Street is his favourite but I'd prefer it if you didn't say I told you.'

'Alright, Alright. That's enough for now.' Emil Kaplan spat out the unlit cigar stub he'd been grinding on frustratedly for the past couple of hours. 'For Christ's sake, Michael, what's up with you? You've been like a wet blanket all morning. We're all very sorry about Laura, but for Christ's sake, you're meant to be a professional. You've had a couple of days off to grieve. Now's the time to get back on the bike.' The set was a crowded first class railway compartment on a train waiting to leave Paddington Station. It was an expensive scene with eight actors in total and a complicated set. Kaplan looked pleadingly to his lead actress. 'Jean, darling, can't you do something to crank Michael up?'

The actress pulled Adair to the side and started whispering to him. Kaplan turned away to see Goldsmith's secretary approaching.

'Hello, Gloria. I hope you're not going to drag Adair away again. I'm having enough difficulties as it is.'

'No, it's you I want this time, Mr Kaplan. Mr Goldsmith would like a word. You can take his call on the telephone by the door.'

'Victor?'

'How goes it, Emil?'

'Terribly. Michael isn't up to it at all.'

'We aren't going to get this in the can before Christmas, are we?'

'I'm trying my best. He's completely lethargic. It's like directing a lump of wood.'

'Get him on the line. Let me see what I can do.'

A grumbling Adair was brought to the telephone.

'What's the problem, my friend?'

Adair groaned. 'You know.'

'Laura?'

'I just can't seem to get her out of my head.'

Goldsmith counted to ten. 'Look, Michael. Let's speak plainly. What happened was terrible but you must have a sense of perspective. Your marriage was over. When it was in progress you were shtupping girls all over the place. It is not as if you and Laura were the lovers of the century, is it?'

'What would you know, Victor?'

'Have you been drinking, Michael?'

'What if I have?'

'Dope?'

Adair made no reply. 'Look Michael. I am a very understanding man. I know people don't realise how pressurised the life of a leading man can be. Stardom can be a two-edged sword. The higher you rise and all that. But . . .' Goldsmith's voice took on an abrasive edge. 'I was very instrumental in your rise and I can be just as instrumental in your fall. I have been a very good friend to you. Money scrapes, business scrapes, women scrapes. I've helped you deal with them all. Now pull yourself together. I cannot afford to have any more delays in the completion of this film. My patience is at its limit and if you fuck this film up, I shall make it my business to fuck you up!'

'Don't threaten me you little Jewish . . .'

Goldsmith cut Adair short. 'Think very carefully before you say another word, Michael. Take a deep breath. Why don't you call that lovely girl Jean over? Gloria and I can go and get some lunch in the canteen and you can have my office to yourselves for an hour or so. Lock the door and relax. Have some fun. She's a beautiful girl and you are a lucky man. Do whatever it takes to restore your equilibrium.' He paused. 'Then return to the set and do your bloody job!'

Adair made no reply.

'I'll take that as a "yes thank you very much, Victor". Now, off you go.'

The plush drawing room into which Johnson was ushered was all whites and yellows and it looked like Valerie Goldsmith had dressed to match the décor with yellow necklace, white shoes and a creamy clinging woollen dress which displayed her figure to full advantage. She focussed her beautiful large grey eyes on Johnson and he felt a little overwhelmed.

'Is it just you then?' Mrs Goldsmith looked enquiringly over Johnson's shoulder.

'I'm . . . I'm afraid so, ma'am. You were expecting more?'

'I was, rather. I always understood detectives ran in pairs. You know. Holmes and Watson, Poirot and Hastings. Nick and Nora Charles.'

'Sorry to disappoint.'

'Oh not at all, Inspector. I'm sure just the one of you will suffice.' She guided him to a seating area by the window.

'We do often run in pairs but are a little stretched at the moment.'

She gave him a sympathetic look. 'No doubt you've lost some officers to the forces?'

'We have, ma'am.'

'That must be hard with all that's going on. Now I'd offer you refreshment but I have a feeling you'd prefer to get down to business straightaway.'

'Yes, please.'

'So how can I help you?'

'You and Laura Curzon were good friends?'

Valerie looked down and her face became suitably grave. 'We were. Such a terrible tragedy.' She plucked a small handkerchief from the cuff of her dress and dabbed an eye. 'I still can't quite believe it.'

'You knew her well?'

'We started out in films at the same time.'

'What was her background?'

'You know, Inspector, that was always a bit of a mystery. She would never really talk about it. Curzon was a stage name, of course, but she was more than happy for people to think it was her real name and she had some connection with the aristocratic Curzons. You know. The Viceroy of India and all that.'

'Did you ever know her real name?'

'No. Never.'

'Or anything at all about her family?'

'No. All she admitted to me was that, like me, she'd come from very ordinary stock. She'd been lucky and a kind sponsor had seen her talent and backed it somehow.'

'Were you of the same age?'

'I was a couple of years older. We were both pretty early starters. I did my first film at twenty, she at nineteen. We met on a movie set. We had middling parts in a stupid little comedy.' Her eyes crinkled with amusement. 'I probably shouldn't say that as it was a film of my dear husband's. Then we were in another film together, an eighteenth-century period piece. All crinolines and lace. She had a bigger part than me then. Her career took off more meteorically than mine, but that didn't stop us being friends. She had no side to her, as they say.'

'How would you describe her character?'

'Unpretentious. Good fun. Happy-go-lucky. Very sociable. She could have the occasional tantrum but don't we all?'

'And men?'

'Men? What do you think, Inspector? She was a gorgeous looking woman. Men were buzzing around her all the time. I don't believe however that there was anything particularly serious until she was around twenty-two or twenty-three. She got keen on a young art director. Name of . . . ah, yes . . . name of Beatty. Stephen Beatty. Unlucky fellow. Got killed in a car crash. There were a few other relationships, but nothing serious again until Michael Adair came on the scene a couple of years ago.'

'You know Mr Adair?'

'Of course. I've never made a film with him but he's starred in a few for my husband. He's doing one right now.' She turned her head to the door, as if checking for eavesdroppers, and lowered her voice. 'I'm afraid I think he's a bit of a shit, if you pardon my French. My husband's known him for a long time. They've had some successes together and he has a bit of a soft spot for him. I have no time for the man, though.'

'Can you elaborate?'

'I don't think my husband would appreciate my dishing too much dirt on one of his major stars. Let's just say the male acting profession is full of womanisers. However, there are womanisers and then there are *womanisers*, if you get my meaning?'

'I'm not sure I do.'

Mrs Goldsmith looked at the door again. 'There are womanisers like my husband, Inspector. He is the better sort of womaniser. He could not live without women but he's a romantic and, if in a relationship, a loyal and supportive partner. Adair is the worst type of womaniser. He likes women but for the wrong reasons. He doesn't particularly care for their company. He lusts after them and his pursuit of them is a game. Each woman is a challenge, but once he has succeeded in his aim he loses interest. He doesn't stay with any woman long.'

'He was with Miss Curzon for a long time, wasn't he?'

'If you call eighteen months or so a long time. There was another factor at play there, though.'

'What was that?'

'Self-interest. When they first got together, his previous two films had been duds. One for Victor, who predictably forgave him, and one for Gus Cowan, who didn't. Her recent films, by contrast, had all been hits. The news of their romance took people's minds off his failures and as a couple they attracted a lot of positive publicity. Then she persuaded the Kordas to give him top male billing in her next film which turned out to be another success.'

'She saved his career?'

Valerie paused to brush a piece of fluff from the arm of her dress. 'I'm not sure I'd go as far as that, but she certainly gave it a boost. Chances are he'd have bounced back without her help. He's a talented actor – comedy, tragedy, romance – he can do them all. But she was definitely good for him. The funny thing is that after that hit film together, she went on to make a couple of duds of her own. That's why the American opportunity was so timely.'

'And the marriage itself. What do you know of that?'

'It followed a predictable pattern. After a short honeymoon period he started chasing other women, usually the co-stars of whichever film he was making. Jean Parker is the latest. A smart girl. I like her, actually, and thought she'd see through him pretty quickly. Apparently not. But then, he is a very attractive and entertaining man.'

'How did Miss Curzon cope?'

'Initially she was furious but he had his hooks into her and she didn't want to give up so easily. After a while, gossip had it, she started playing the field herself but still they remained together. However, the arrival of the American offer brought things to a head, I think, and they decided to call it a day.'

Johnson paused to consult his notes, then continued. 'Miss Curzon's death may well have been an accident but we have to consider the possibility of suicide. The breakdown of her marriage was, presumably, very upsetting for her. Do you think that might have had any bearing on what happened?'

'I doubt it. They were both in agreement about splitting and everything seemed reasonably friendly. You must remember, she had risen to the top of her profession from nothing. She was a tough cookie as the Yanks say.' Mrs Goldsmith looked down thoughtfully at her heavily beringed hands. 'That said, and Victor would probably kill me for telling you this, if Laura did kill herself because of Michael, it wouldn't have been the first suicide in his life.'

Johnson sat up. 'What do you mean?'

'Michael had a spell in Hollywood when he was younger. In the late twenties, early thirties. He had a girlfriend, a young starlet, who overdosed on sleeping pills. It was the subject of considerable gossip in Los Angeles at the time, although the studio managed to keep it out of the press. Victor was out there then and helped Michael out. The girl was called Daisy Thompson. She fell for Michael hook, line and sinker. He treated her badly and broke things off rather cruelly. She decided she couldn't live without him and killed herself. Victor doesn't like to talk about it. I asked Michael about it once. He just went white and changed the subject.'

'Were there any criminal or civil proceedings?'

'I don't believe so. Just a hurried and unpublicised inquest.'

'Hmm.' Johnson scribbled some notes. 'I take it you saw Miss Curzon at the big party in the Dorchester on Saturday night?'

'At Gus Cowan's party? Yes I did. She seemed very jolly.'

'Was she accompanied?'

'No.'

'Mr Adair wasn't there, he says.'

'I didn't see him. He and Cowan aren't the best of friends these days.'

'Do you know if Miss Curzon had a boyfriend in America?'

'She didn't mention anyone on Saturday and I've heard nothing to that effect. Obviously the flow of gossip from the States is more limited than it used to be, what with the war and everything.'

'I see. Well this is all very useful. I have one final question for you. Did you know that Miss Curzon had a drug habit?'

Valerie glanced awkwardly away. 'I'm . . . I'm sorry, Inspector, but it seems somehow . . . somehow a little disloyal to a departed friend to discuss things which might have been . . . um . . . illegal.'

'The fact is, Mrs Goldsmith, we found drugs in her flat. Whether she broke the law is neither here nor there now. I only ask in case it had any bearing on her death.'

'I see.' She sighed. 'Well, yes, Laura did have a habit. Cocaine I believe. I am not an expert on types and varieties. More of a martini and champagne girl myself.'

'Did Mr Adair share her habit?'

'I don't know for certain but I wouldn't be surprised. I find it hard to think that there's any kind of hedonistic activity Michael hasn't tried. Victor implied there'd been occasional problems on set.'

'I suppose you wouldn't have any idea about how she got the drugs?'

'No idea at all, I'm afraid, Inspector. You'd be better off asking Michael that, don't you think?'

Cole hurried into Merlin's office and was disappointed to find the room empty. He had made progress at Somerset House and was keen to tell his bosses about it. He waited ten minutes, but no one appeared. Feeling it wasn't quite right to loiter on his own in the boss's office, he wandered down the corridor to the cubby-hole. He was hungry. It was well into the afternoon and he'd eaten nothing all day. He wasn't quite hungry enough, though, to eat the mouldy piece of Swiss Roll someone had left on a plate by the kettle. He made himself a cup of tea and read over his notes.

Ida Walker, Vera Rogers and Grace Roper. He'd found birth certificates for them all in the Somerset House records. And one death certificate. Grace Enid Roper, born in a house in Tower

Hamlets in January 1926 had died of tuberculosis in Tooting Hospital on September 26th 1941. Vera Irene Rogers had been born on Boxing Day 1926 to Nancy and Arthur Rogers of Cropley Street, Hoxton at the St Leonard's Hospital. Ida Walker had been born on June 15th 1926 in St Thomas's Hospital to Mary and Sidney Walker of Spicer Lane, Vauxhall. After finishing his tea, Cole would have to get on his bike again. Although the girls had been living in an orphanage, it didn't necessarily follow that there weren't parents or family still around. And if the old addresses yielded nothing there still might be neighbours who could help. He decided to cycle first to Hoxton, the more distant of the two locations.

Merlin had been to Wilton's years before with Alice. December 1936. It was quite easy to remember the month as it wasn't long after the King's abdication. Unfortunately, Alice hadn't liked it. Too stuffy and upper class, she'd said, which was a little strange coming from the daughter of a judge and granddaughter of a baronet. He had begged to differ. He liked the atmosphere, the food, the wine, everything. He could still remember what he'd had – Colchester Oysters, Dover Sole, and Apple Crumble, all washed down with a fine Meursault.

As he turned the corner into Jermyn Street, he wondered whether the place would have changed much over the past five years. Timelessness was a major attraction of some of these long-lived establishments and as he came through the door and cast his eye around, he was pleased to see all was as before.

Merlin had confirmation from the restaurant that Cowan was lunching there. Now on arrival, he was told the meal was nearing completion. He took a stool at the bar and ordered a lemonade. His decision to collar Cowan at the restaurant had not been taken without some misgivings. Merlin would have much preferred an interview at the Shepherd Market office or the Yard, but that might take another day or two to arrange, if Cowan chose to be uncooperative. Better, Merlin decided to crack on and take the bull by the horns. Rather than interrupt Cowan at his meal, though, he thought it wiser to catch the man on his way out. No one could exit the restaurant without passing the bar. If Cowan played ball, the *maitre d'* had given Merlin use one of the private dining rooms for his interview.

The liqueur and coffee stage of Cowan's meal took longer than Merlin would have hoped. The producer finally appeared three quarters of an hour later. Merlin recognised him from a newspaper cutting Johnson had shown him earlier. He was accompanied by a very pretty young brunette. Merlin tapped his shoulder as he was waiting for their coats. 'Mr Cowan?'

'Maybe. Who wants him?'

Merlin introduced himself.

'Another goddam copper! Look, I already told the other guy I know nothing about the people working in our old office and I don't hold an English concession for Hershey Bars. Didn't he report back?'

'He did, thank you sir. However, I have some different questions for you.'

Cowan looked disgruntled. 'See here, Chief Inspector, I don't take kindly to being doorstepped in public like this. What was to stop you ringing my office for an appointment?'

'I did, sir, but they weren't sure if you'd be going back there today. I was forced to take the initiative. I'm sorry but we need to get on with our enquiries.'

'Well, I think it's a hell of an imposition.' Cowan's look of disgruntlement turned into one of curiosity. 'So what are these different questions you have?'

'They concern Laura Curzon.'

Cowan's eyes narrowed. 'Do they now?' He mulled Merlin's words over in his mind for a moment then told the cloakroom attendant to keep his coat. He turned to the girl and gave her some cash and her coat. 'Here you go, sweetie. Get yourself a taxi and I'll see you at the hotel later. I gotta see this guy, I suppose.'

★

173

The sergeant stood uncomfortably close to the railing of Laura Curzon's terrace and listened to the distant rumbling of the traffic at Marble Arch. Sam Bridges hated heights. At the age of seven he'd gone on an orphanage outing to the funfair and got stuck on a broken big wheel. He'd had to wait an hour in a high wind on a rickety chair at the top as workmen had worked at fixing the problem. A whiny boy called Clive, who'd cried buckets throughout, had shared the ordeal with him. Bridges had since avoided heights whenever possible. In this instance, however, it was impossible. A thorough further examination of the terrace was required, and he did not shirk his duty. As it happened, when he'd gone over everything again, he'd found nothing new and with a huge sigh went back inside.

'So, Mr Jackson, you say your assistant has resigned?'

The head porter took a step forward. 'Yes, sir. He turned up the day after Miss Curzon's death, picked up whatever belongings he kept here and told me I could stuff my job. Said it was too boring and he'd received better offers. "Boring?" I replies. "A famous film star falls to her death from her apartment. We have police and everyone crawling all over the place. You call that boring?" He just shrugged and cleared off.'

'Had he given any indication before that he might quit?'

'No. He did plenty of complaining, mind. And he fancied himself. Said more than once he was cut out for better things. He was quite a pain and in normal times I might have got shot of him myself. But these aren't normal times and it's hard to get good people for this sort of job. It's not such a bad way to make a living, you know. It's nice and secure and you meet a good class of person . . . and some not so good.' He looked towards Mrs Cavendish's flat.

'Hmmm.' Bridges rolled his eyes. He'd just spent half an hour with the tiresome woman going over her statement one more time. Her story remained the same. She'd heard voices in the Curzon flat between eight and nine but heard or seen nothing else out of the ordinary. She'd retired to bed at nine fifteen and taken a sleeping pill. No, she hadn't heard screaming later on. She had a list of minor grievances against her next door neighbours and indeed against most of her neighbours but nothing which had any relevance to the police investigation.

Prior to seeing Mrs Cavendish, Bridges had caught up with the tenants he and Purvis had missed on Tuesday. More blanks. He looked up again at the actress's portrait. She'd been a stunner for sure. 'Mr Merlin said this was by a very famous artist. Did you know that, Mr Jackson?'

'No, but that doesn't surprise me.'

Bridges took a seat. 'Baxter's abrupt departure seems fishy to me. So soon after Miss Curzon's death and before I'd had a chance to question him properly. Did he have something to hide, do you think?'

'No. He's just a stupid young boy. I can't believe he had anything to do with Miss Curzon's death if that's what you're thinking. But you can ask him yourself, you know. He may have quit his job but I've still got his home address. The details are downstairs.'

'Oh! That's very good. Maybe I'm being over-suspicious but that's part of my job. I'll get them from you later. Now, you said you'd show me the tradesman's entrance?'

'Of course. We'll use the stairs if you don't mind.'

Bridges followed Jackson out of the flat and along the corridor to a 'Staff Only' door. They walked down the seven flights and came out into a spacious high-ceilinged room. Boxes and crates were piled up against the walls.

'This is, as you can see, our loading bay and storage area. All deliveries come here and we store things like furniture and fittings and the like around the sides.' He pointed to the green garage door opposite them. 'Lorries drive into the mews behind and, if they're the right size, pull in. If they can't they park out there and wheel things in on our trolleys.'

'Is there a bell or buzzer outside?'

'Yes, it connects to the porter's desk.'

'And the garage door is electrified?'

'It is. The latest system. Controlled by that.' He pointed to a blue button on the wall to their right. To the left of the garage door there was a smaller red door.

'The red one's for people, obviously.'

'And what are the security arrangements?'

'There's a locking mechanism next to the blue button. It requires two keys which I hold. I always ensure everything is locked when the door is not in use and I double check it's secure when I leave in the evening.'

'And the red door?'

'That has a straightforward double lock. The key is in my possession and I, again, check it before I go home.'

'So no one can enter this way without your knowledge, and at night time both doors are securely locked?'

'Yes.'

'Have you checked they haven't been tampered with in any way?'

'I didn't specifically check after Miss Curzon's death but they've been used several times since and I'd have noticed if they had been.'

Bridges went to examine the doors closer up and Jackson followed him. 'And Baxter. How does, or rather did, he feature in the security arrangements?'

'He knew how it all worked, naturally, and if I wasn't around for some reason, he was responsible.'

'Did he have his own copies of the keys?'

'No, but I kept the keys in a locked drawer at the front desk and he had a spare key to that drawer.'

Bridges stepped back a couple of paces. 'Can I see the main door operate please?'

Jackson went over to press the blue button. The door slowly ratcheted up and folded into supports above. A gust of cold wind blew into the men's faces as they stepped onto the cobbles of the mews outside. There were a number of shops and workshops either side of the garage door and opposite. Bridges saw a car

176

mechanic's, a carpentry, a masonry, and an industrial plumber. Fifty yards or so to their left the mews hit a dead-end.

Back inside, Bridges said 'One thing is clear. If anyone did enter the building this way, it would be quite easy for that person to nip up the stairs and get to Miss Curzon's flat without being seen.'

The porter shrugged. 'Sure, but how would they get in without my say so.'

'Yes, I wonder.' Bridges looked thoughtfully at the garage door. 'I think I'll go back out into the mews and visit the people working there. Perhaps one or other of them noticed something unusual.'

'Will you want to come back in this way?'

'No. You lock up. When I've finished I'll come back round the front and get Baxter's address from you before I go.'

'So. Laura Curzon. Mr Cowan. What can you tell me?'

Cowan had ordered another glass of the dessert wine he'd had at lunch. He swirled the golden liquid around in its glass then raised it to his nose. 'Lovely aroma, Chief Inspector. Beaumes de Venise. From the southern part of the Rhône Valley. It's delicious. You should try some.' Merlin declined. 'Laura Curzon.' Cowan's sighed. 'A beautiful woman. Reasonably good actress. I first met her around '36 or '37 when she was cast to feature in one of my films. Lively sort of girl. I can't say we were particular friends. There are plenty of people who were closer to her than me.'

'A colleague of mine is meeting Mrs Valerie Goldsmith today to get a female perspective on Miss Curzon.'

'And you are seeing me for the male perspective?' Cowan chuckled. 'I would love to be able to give you a comprehensive view of Laura from the male perspective, if you get my drift, but that sadly never happened. Not for want of trying on my part, I have to say, but there was nothing doing. With most actresses, keeping a man like me sweet is a wise thing to do. Laura didn't think so but she was probably too much of a star at that time to feel she had to. Anyway, I withdrew gracefully when rebuffed and we remained on speaking terms.'

'You didn't contemplate some sort of revenge?'

'Goodness me no. Plenty more fish in the sea and I had other entanglements to keep me . . . satisfied. Perhaps if she'd been more accommodating I could have done a little more to further her Hollywood ambitions, but she got there anyway, didn't she?'

'Her Hollywood adventure didn't turn out so well, though, did it?'

'No. It seems not.' Cowan drank a little wine then looked into the glass thoughtfully.

'Do you know what really happened?'

'I've heard the story about Jimmy Stewart having to pull out and the movie being cancelled in consequence but I don't buy it. I know the producer, Max Flack. He's one of Zanuck's pals. A tough, creative and clever guy. If he had a script, a budget, and had already put big bucks into pre-production, as he must have, I don't believe he'd pull a film just because he lost one major star. With the studio system there are plenty of big contracted stars to hand. If you haven't got the right actor for the part you can always borrow one from another studio. He could easily have got another star name to step into Stewart's shoes.'

'So there must have been other reasons for the picture being cancelled?'

'Who knows? I had reason to speak to Max last week and asked him about it. He clammed up completely. "These things happen" was all he'd say.'

'Perhaps the production was closed because of something to do with Miss Curzon?'

The film producer shrugged. 'Look, I can't help you on this.'

'How was she at your party?'

'Pretty chipper. Seemed to be enjoying herself. She liked to enjoy herself.'

'We know she was partial to alcohol, if that's what you are implying. Other things too.'

'You know about the drugs already? Good detecting Merlin. Yes, she was a bit of a dope fiend but I don't think it ever got too out of hand.'

'Did it affect her work?'

'Not when she worked for me. I did hear the odd complaint about time-keeping but a lot of the talent are lousy at that. Generally speaking, in a bitchy business, people mostly spoke well of her.'

'Do you think she killed herself?'

'The vagaries of human nature never fail to surprise me, but she didn't seem that type to me. I suppose to flop as she did in Hollywood must have been very depressing. There was her failed marriage with that prick Adair. Perhaps she drank a skinful that night, smoked a little too much happy stuff? Who knows. It's possible.'

Merlin asked a few more questions but learned nothing new. Finally, as he prepared to get to his feet, he asked, 'Is there, perhaps, anything you'd care to add to what you said in answer to my Inspector's questions yesterday.'

Cowan finished his dessert wine and gave the Chief Inspector a weary, but mischievous look. 'Nope.'

'Thanks for your time, sir. I have an odd feeling we'll be meeting again.'

Archie Tate kept waving until the train disappeared from sight, although he knew his mother would have long since withdrawn her head from the window and taken out her knitting paraphernalia in readiness for the long journey north. He felt the usual mixed emotions as he headed back down the platform. He loved his mother dearly but her visits significantly limited his freedom of action. In the past year, a pattern had developed in which her living arrangements alternated so that she spent a week or so in London with her son, then a week or so at her seaside home in Blackpool. Tate would quite like to restrict the frequency of these visits to London but he'd never been able to get up the courage to tell her. At least now he had another week to himself and could have some fun.

Once he was back on the station concourse, he found the nearest telephone box. He rummaged through his pockets for his little address book. His most secret telephone numbers were on a page at the back. He found the number he wanted, paid in the coins and dialled. It was an odd personal tic of his that he always spoke out loud the phone number he was dialling. 'C . . . L . . . E . . . 4 . . . 1 . . . 8 . . . 7.' A gruff voice grunted in response and he pressed the 'A' button.

'Who's this?' asked the gruff voice.

'Um. It's . . . um . . . oh damn.' For his own security reasons he'd got the people to agree a communications code with him. The trouble was it changed every couple of months and he frequently forgot what was the correct one to use.

'Damn it all, hang on a sec.' He flipped through his diary again and with a sigh of relief found the list of alternate codes. 'It's Vinegar, here. I'd like two packages. Fresh product. Usual requirements and address. Nine o'clock tonight.'

'Standard terms?'

'Yes.'

'It shall be done. Good day to you.'

And there it was. His evening's entertainment arranged as quick as a flash. It would be just the thing to bring him relief and serenity in what was proving to be a very stressful week. He looked up at the big station clock as he stepped out of the box. It was nearly five and he had a meeting with his agent in half an hour. There was just enough time for a quick tot of rum at the station buffet. As he took a stool at the bar he wondered whether he should tell Hilton about his business discussions with Goldsmith. Could he trust Hilton to be discreet? Yes he probably could, but it was maybe still a little premature. He'd wait until pen was set to paper. Then the bragging could begin.

Merlin had his head in a file when Bridges entered the office, and responded belatedly to his sergeant's arrival. 'Sorry, Sam, I was miles away. Sit down. How'd you get on?'

'Baxter has suddenly quit his job and wasn't at the building. I thought it seemed a little fishy but now it seems even fishier. Jackson gave me his home address in Bethnal Green. I just went round there to find he'd cleared out of there too.'

'Reckon he knows something and doesn't want to talk?'

'Something seems wrong, doesn't it? Anyway, I'm going to do my best to track him down.'

'Pick up any new information otherwise?'

'Not really. I saw some of the apartment tenants we'd missed. Nothing to report. I also took the time to check out the rear entrance for myself. All seems pretty secure. Strong locks, double keys.'

'What was Baxter's involvement in security?'

'He was in charge if Jackson wasn't around.'

'So if he wasn't trustworthy . . . ?'

'Well, yes, that's why I'd better find him.'

'Speak to anyone else?'

'There are some workshops in the mews at the back of the building. I questioned people there. Again, nothing doing.'

Merlin stretched out his arms behind his neck and looked up at the ceiling. 'It's funny, isn't it, that no one heard a scream?'

'Do people scream when they jump to their deaths intentionally?'

'Suicide might provide the answer, but I'm reminded now of something Adair said. About Miss Curzon having a bad sore throat. Maybe she couldn't scream?'

Bridges shrugged and looked at the file on Merlin's desk. 'Anything new, sir?'

'Mr Wright had another look at the body and has sent us a longer, modified version of his pathological report. Most of it is the same but one new paragraph set me to thinking.' He opened the file and soon found what he was looking for. 'He observes that although the face and neck are well-preserved, for reasons we know, the rest of the body has decomposed naturally. He then comments: "Thus, I have not been able, for example, to discern whether the girl was a virgin, should that have any relevance to your investigation." '

'I suppose that's not surprising. Medically, I mean.'

'But the thing is, Sam, we have only focussed, so far, on the identification of the girl. We have given no thought at all yet to motive. This comment is a useful prompt to us. We may not know who she is but that doesn't mean we can't speculate on motive. Why was she killed? Was sex involved? How many murders of young women have we dealt with where the motive has been sexual?'

'Plenty.'

'So we need to broaden our thinking. If Cole draws a blank identifying the Victoria girl, perhaps we can get to her another way by concentrating on likely motives. If, for example, the motive was sexual, we have to think of the possible circumstances.' Merlin closed the file. 'Speaking of Cole, I wonder where the hell he is now. Any ideas, Sergeant?'

Hoxton had proved a disappointment. The road where the Rogers family had lived when their daughter Vera was born had been wiped out in the Blitz and Cole hadn't been able to find anyone living nearby who knew of them. Visits to the local police station and the hospital where Vera had been born had likewise proved fruitless.

Cole had more luck in Vauxhall. The Walker family were no longer living in Spicer Lane but a woman at the local corner shop was able to provide some information. She knew nothing of the general family circumstances but had dealings with Mary Walker, who was known locally as a competent seamstress. Mrs Walker had left the area a while ago but had visited the shop within the past year to place a card advert in the window. The advert was to inform her old Vauxhall customers that she was back in business and contactable at a new address in Holborn. To Cole's delight, that card was still in the window and he set off immediately for the new address.

Half an hour later the constable found himself in a long grubby street off Theobalds Road. This was an area of London where residences of the rich and famous jostled with those of the poor. Cole remembered an outing years before when his mother had pointed out the smart terraced house of Charles Dickens not very far from where he stood. That property was far from Dickensian, but the rickety old tenement he was looking at now could certainly qualify as such. In the pitch dark of the London blackout, Cole had his torch out. A stained wooden board by the doorway informed him that Number thirty-three was on the third floor. He could only hope Mrs Walker was still at this address.

He knocked on the door several times but there was no response. He was thinking of pushing a scribbled note through the letter box when a small, bald, bespectacled man opened the door of Number thirty-four.

He looked Cole up and down. 'Ye can bang all night if ye like, but ye'll get no answer.'

The constable showed the man his warrant card. 'I'm looking for a Mrs Mary Walker. Do I have the right place?'

'Aye, it's the right place, but she's away.'

'Do you know when she'll be back?'

'No, she did'nae tell me. She's probably gone to visit her sister. Somewhere out in Essex. She goes there from time to time.'

Cole's shoulders slumped a little. 'Do her visits last a long time?'

'Normally just two or three days.'

'I need to ask her a few family questions.'

'Och aye. Such as?'

'Whether she has a daughter.'

'Hmm.' A small dog of indeterminate breed appeared from behind the man's feet and started yapping. 'Whisht, Angus. It's only a policeman asking questions. Don't make such a fuss.' He picked the animal up. 'It's parky out here. Ye might as well come in for a sec.'

Cole was ushered into a gloomy sitting room. The man improved the lighting marginally by turning on a weak lamp. Papers, books and manuscripts were everywhere. The dog was dropped to the floor and the man cleared away enough of the debris to reveal two small armchairs.

'Sit yerself down. The name's McAllister. I did'nae catch the name on your card.'

'Cole. Detective Constable Cole.'

'I hope ye'll forgive the mess. I am a writer with slovenly habits. A Scottish writer that is, as ye may have been able to deduce.' The dog started barking again. 'Angus doesn't really like policemen. Me neither to tell the truth. I had a son. He's dead now. He had some bad experiences with the police. But ye look a nice enough fellow. I'll forget for the moment who ye represent.'

'That's very good of you. What do you write?'

'Westerns, mysteries, adventure stories. Whatever can earn me some money. Penny Dreadfuls they used to call them. As ye can probably tell from my surroundings, I don't get much more than pennies for them. Anyway, enough of that. Why are ye looking for Mary?'

'We discovered the body of a dead girl. A teenager. There's a chance, a slim chance, that she might be related to Mrs Rogers.'

'That's nae so good a reason.'

'Do you mind telling me what you know about her?

'Mary moved in next door about a year ago. That's how long I've known her. She's a reserved type but we are friends of a sort. We rely on each other for certain practical matters, as neighbours often do.'

'Family?'

'There's a husband from whom she's separated. A violent man. He visits her occasionally. I understand there were two bairns of the marriage. Girls. Several years apart. They both left home at some point. Ran away. Something to do with the father.'

'He was violent to them?'

'Something like that. Mary is sparing with the details.'

'Did you ever see any photographs of the girls?'

'No. If Mary has any they're not on display in her living room.'

'I understand she makes a living as a seamstress?'

'Aye, and she's a very good one by all accounts.' McAllister paused to give the dog a biscuit from his pocket. 'What exactly happened to this poor girl ye found, if I may ask?'

Cole explained the circumstances surrounding the discovery of the body and how the name of Ida Rogers had emerged.

'The poor wee lassie. What a terrible thing. However, if you don't mind me saying so, your evidence for thinking that Ida Rogers might be the dead girl seems a little . . . a little of a stretch.'

'I know, but we don't have much to go on.'

'Indeed. I've written enough detective stories to know that ye've got to follow up whatever lines of enquiry ye've got as best ye can.'

'Has Mrs Walker ever told you the names of her daughters?'

'She never did.'

'I see. You don't by any chance have a telephone number for her sister?'

'No, I'm sorry. I do have a key to Mary's flat, as she does mine, but I doubt it would be right allowing ye entry without her say so. It's not like she's suspected of a crime now, is it?'

'No, of course not. Can you tell me a little about the husband?'

'He comes around every so often. I usually know because there's often a noisy row and these walls are paper thin. Once or twice I've gone in to intervene but Mary's sent me packing. That's all I can say.'

Cole rose to his feet and the dog started barking again. 'I'm very grateful, Mr McAllister.' He wrote down his number at the Yard and gave it to the Scotsman. 'I'd be grateful if you could let me know when she returns.'

'Shouldn't I just tell her to contact ye?'

'She'll want you to tell her why. It would be better, I think, if I talk to her first.'

McAllister shut the dog up with another biscuit. 'Fair enough. There's a public phone box on the corner I use. I'll let ye know.'

The Goldsmiths had returned late from a film premiere in Leicester Square and Valerie had gone straight up to bed. Victor was about to join her when he heard the telephone ringing in his study. Tired as he was, the sound was not wholly unwelcome. It might be Addleshaw or Tate finally returning his calls. He picked up the receiver.

'Victor, my friend. Not too late for you, I hope?'

'Ah, Joe. No, of course not . . . what can I do for you?'

'A little birdie tells me that you have not yet drawn down on our recently agreed facility. You received the account access information, did you not?'

Goldsmith was slow to respond as he carefully considered his words.

'Are you still there, Victor?'

'I'm still here, Joe. Look, I've had a long day. Can we discuss this tomorrow?'

'There's nothing like the present, I find, in business. Did you get what I sent you?'

Goldsmith took a deep breath. 'Yes I did but look, Joe, it's just that . . . that some potential new investors have emerged. I might not need your money.'

This time it was Abela's turn to pause and consider his words. When, in due course, he spoke, his voice was freighted with menace. 'Look, Victor. I'm a simple businessman providing a range of services. In this instance, the service is commercial lending. Now it may be that my lending services are more expensive than your run of the mill bank, but my risks are commensurate. My competitors in the City document their loans. I don't, but the terms are clearly understood, and once a deal is struck, it is struck. The fact is we orally agreed a loan over the phone. We agreed an amount, a term and a rate of interest. We committed. I became bound to advance you the money and you became bound by my loan terms. If, for some reason, you now choose not to avail yourself of my funds, that's all fine and dandy but my normal terms still apply. According to those terms, if a customer of mine chooses not to drawdown on an agreed facility, the full interest is none the less payable for the full amount over the full term.'

Goldsmith suddenly felt in need of his medication. 'Look, Joe. Let's be reasonable about this. It was very good of you to agree to help but circumstances have . . .'

'You can stop right there, Victor. Don't talk about reasonableness to me. Do you think I've succeeded in what I do by being reasonable? You asked for dosh. Said you were in a bind. I agreed to accommodate you. We agreed the vig. Deal done. No turning back.'

'But Joe, we are talking about fifteen thousand pounds' worth of interest here. That's a ridiculous amount to pay for no money. Look. If the people come through with the money what about I pay you . . . let's say two thousand . . . we can call it an arrangement fee. How about that?'

'Let's call it nothing, Victor. I want the full interest.' The two men said nothing for a while until Abela broke the silence and moderated his tone. 'Look, Victor, be sensible. Why don't you just tell these investors of yours to bugger off for now? Take my money and pay the interest for real value received. Then you'll be in a much stronger position to negotiate new investment with cash in hand and your current problems behind you.'

'Maybe you're right, but you know what they say about the bird in the hand. The people I have may only be prepared to bite now. If they do . . .'

'Take everyone's money then. But whatever you choose I want the vigorish.'

'Look, Joe . . .'

'Nice chatting, my friend. Let me know by tomorrow whether you're using my money or not.' The line went dead.

Chapter Eight

Merlin had had a vivid dream. He'd been wandering alone through London on a night in the Blitz. Bombs had been raining down all around. A young girl had waved at him from behind a postbox, then run off. He'd chased her into the ruins of a huge house but all he'd found was an evil swirling black mist. He was shouting to warn the girl about it when he awoke.

His clock told him it was only four forty in the morning but he didn't feel like going back to sleep. He got up and went to make himself a coffee. All he had in the kitchen was Camp Coffee which was disgusting stuff but did have some reviving powers. Merlin took the drink to the living room and sat down in his favourite armchair. He leaned back and thought again of the Victoria girl. When he was in the middle of a puzzling case, he often came to this chair in the peaceful early hours to think. All he could hear was the whistling of the wind along the river and the occasional bark of a dog. It seemed ages now since the rumble of the Luft-waffe bombers had filled the night air, although it had only been a few months.

If the girl wasn't one of Cole's wandering orphanage girls there was a good chance she was someone similar. A young girl out on the streets. How would a teenage girl in that position survive? They were still waiting for the sketch artist's attempt at the girl's face. Merlin found it difficult to imagine what she had looked like alive from the viewing in the mortuary and the photos they had. Wright had thought she'd been pretty. Had she been capable of using feminine wiles to get by? Had she gone on the game?

For some reason Merlin had never quite understood, the prostitution and vice rackets of London were largely under the control of criminals from the British Mediterranean colony of Malta. He'd never been directly involved as a detective in combatting prostitution, but several of his investigations had crossed over into that world. As he sipped his coffee an idea came to him. He'd already thought that Orlov might be able to provide useful information about the drugs supplied to Laura Curzon. But the Abelas were big in vice too. Perhaps Orlov might have some insight into how a young kid could be sucked into that world. Another line of enquiry for him to pursue when they met later.

It was always an option, of course, to talk to colleagues in the Vice Squad. However, parts of that department were riddled with corruption and Merlin generally chose to give it a wide berth. There had been one vice officer whom Merlin had trusted, a friend of the sergeant's, Jim Toshack. Sadly, the man's incorruptibility had recently lost him his job in the department, and he was now languishing in a petty administrative role somewhere. It would be worth Bridges picking his brains over a pint, though.

When Merlin finished his drink and set the mug down by his feet, he noticed a book poking out from under his chair. It was the collection of Auden poems Stewart had lent him a while back. He opened it at random to a poem called 'The Night Mail.' It had accompanied a wonderful documentary he'd seen a year or two before. He read the first few lines aloud to himself.

> This is the night mail crossing the border,
> Bringing the cheque and the postal order,
> Letters for the rich, letters for the poor,
> The shop at the corner, the girl next door

He closed his eyes for a moment. The Victoria girl was someone's girl next door once. What really had happened to bring her short life to its tragic end?

Goldsmith was at the studio early. Whatever the extraneous financial problems, the business had to be monitored and managed. Two of his three current productions were going smoothly, but the third and most important one, *Murder at Midnight* continued to be problematic. Adair was back at work today, but Goldsmith knew things weren't going well. From the studio floor below he had heard many loud shouts and complaints. He asked Gloria to check when the next break was due and tell Kaplan to come up then. Fifteen minutes later Kaplan appeared.

'There you are, Emil. I know you're busy and I won't detain you long. I think there's time though for a quick cup of tea and one of those excellent bagels from the canteen. Gloria is already on the case.'

'I haven't eaten, so a bagel will be more than welcome, thank you. You are looking well this morning.'

Goldsmith felt far from well but wasn't going to admit it. 'Valerie keeps me young. You don't look so bad yourself.'

Kaplan was always well turned-out. He wore a bright crimson cravat above his white silk shirt. A matching handkerchief was planted in the top pocket of his elegantly tailored blue blazer. The blazer boasted an ornate badge which Goldsmith knew to be that of an exclusive social cricket club for which Kaplan often played. The director often boasted that he must be the only Hungarian Jew to have scored a fifty at Lords. Goldsmith frowned as he recalled the wretched attempts of his own boys to master the rudiments of that stupid game at boarding school. They had been as useless at cricket as they'd turned out to be at everything else, save for the spending or losing of money.

'How is Adair this morning?'

'On the plus side he was in on time and his attitude is a little better but his acting is still lifeless. And he's still whining about Laura.'

Goldsmith threw his hands in the air. 'Laura! Laura! You'd think he'd be happy not having to worry about expensive divorce lawyers and financial settlements.' Goldsmith looked thoughtfully at Kaplan. 'You don't think he did it, Emil . . . and all this is for show?'

'Did it?'

'Pushed Laura off the balcony. In a fit of temper. You know as well as I that he's got a terrible temper. Perhaps this behaviour is all some sort of act to deflect . . .' Goldsmith was interrupted by Gloria's arrival with the refreshments.

'Help yourself, Emil. Don't stint. I need you to be strong.' Goldsmith thrummed his fingers on the desk as Kaplan hungrily bit into a bagel. 'Michael has always treated his women badly, you know. Remember that cute little thing in Hollywood he drove to suicide. Maybe he took things into his own hands this time?'

'But why?' asked Kaplan, through a mouthful of crumbs. 'They'd already split up. Amicably I thought. What did they have to fight about? Do you really think he'd kill her to avoid having to pay a divorce settlement?'

Goldsmith sighed. 'In reality there wouldn't have been much of a settlement for Laura, given the messy state of Michael's finances. Maybe it's the other way round. Laura was pretty wealthy in her own right, and had good advisors. Perhaps he thought there was a pile of money to come into from her and that's why he bumped her off?'

'Victor, come on, you've been making movies for too long. The story you're suggesting would make a wonderful movie. A great film noir! However, I bet you, when the dust settles, this will just turn out to have been an unfortunate accident.'

Goldsmith stroked his chin. 'Of course you're right, Emil. I'm sure it was all a simple accident. The trouble is, it isn't that hard to think the worst of Michael. He and I have been close for many years. A number of my earliest British hits were with him as you know. Because of our history together, there's no doubt I indulge him but I have to admit his behaviour is getting progressively worse. Valerie thinks he's an ass. I have to say I'm beginning to agree with her.'

Kaplan wiped his mouth and got to his feet. 'I'm sorry, Victor but I must get on. Thanks for the bagel. What do you suggest I do about him?'

'Is there much scope still to shoot around him for the next few days?'

'A little. There were a few of his scenes I was leaving to the end and a few reshoots of scenes he's not in which I'd like to do.'

'Bring forward the reshoots and give him the rest of today off.'

'I'll lose some time making fresh setups.'

'So be it. I know you'll do your best. At a stretch, how long before you absolutely need him back?'

Kaplan did some quick calculations. 'We could just about manage without him until Wednesday. Thursday at the latest. We might have to work over the weekend, though.'

'Try not to. The overtime costs will be crippling.'

'I'll try, Victor. I'll try.'

Bridges got into the office a little later than usual. Merlin thought he didn't look himself. 'Anything up, Sam?'

'You've not seen the papers, sir, or caught the radio?'

'Afraid not. Only spare time I had, my head was in a book. What's the news?'

'The Japs have sunk the *Prince of Wales* and *Repulse*. Somewhere off Malaya.'

'I'm so sorry.' The two men struggled for words. Merlin came round the desk and gave Bridges an awkward pat on the back. 'Anything said about survivors?'

'Nothing yet. The radio said there were other British ships in the area who would report further. Iris has been completely floored by the news, as you can imagine. It wasn't very easy getting out of the house this morning, hence my lateness. Sorry.'

'Goodness, don't worry about that. In fact, I think you should turn round right now and get back to her.'

'That's kind of you, sir, but no. There's far too much to deal with here. Anyway, the neighbours were rallying round when I left. To be honest, I think I've run out of things I can say to her. She'll be well looked after. My place is here.'

'Well . . . if you're sure.' Merlin returned to his chair. 'Any sign of the others?'

'I saw Cole down the corridor when I came in. He said DI Johnson had gone off to the dentist with a bad toothache. According to Cole, the Inspector was intending to soldier on but the AC saw that he was in pain and insisted he go. Arranged for him to see his own dentist in fact. The AC's dentist I mean.'

'Really? That was good of him. Let's hope the dentist doesn't take too much time.'

Cole appeared at the door.

'Constable. Just the man. Sit down. The sergeant and I are eager to know how you got on yesterday.'

Cole proceeded to report on all that had happened the day before.

When he'd finished, Merlin gave him an appreciative look. 'Good work. Sounds like you've hit a dead end in Hoxton, though?'

'I've asked the local police to keep an eye out, but I'm not hopeful.'

'So it's looking like Ida Walker or nothing. Let's hope Mrs Walker returns to London shortly.'

'Don't forget the American family, sir,' said Bridges.

'There is that too, I suppose.' Merlin glanced towards the window. It was beginning to rain. 'I had a thought this morning. Let's assume for the moment our girl was Ida Walker or someone like her. A displaced orphan teenage girl. Homeless and penniless roaming the streets of London with no recourse to family or friends. Wouldn't that sort of girl be a great target for pimps?

'If she was pretty, I suppose, sir,' said Cole.

'Doesn't have to be that pretty, considering some of the

working girls I've seen hanging round Piccadilly at night,' added Bridges.

'Well, pretty or not, I think we should put some effort into investigating that possibility. I have a few ideas. Seen anything of Jim Toshack recently, Sergeant?'

'Saw him a couple of weeks ago. He's working in records out in Hounslow, poor chap.'

'A waste of a good officer. Give him a call. Tell him you'd like a chat. Preferably today.'

'Sir.'

'Oh, and I've had some relatively good news on Orlov. The Commissioner has cleared us to make a deal with him, but his clearance is conditional on my having a lawyer with me when I do so. To ensure everything agreed goes by the book.'

'That's alright, isn't it, sir?'

'Yes Sergeant but it means we can't get down to the nitty gritty with Orlov until tomorrow. That's when the designated Home Office lawyer is first available. That said I still aim to see Orlov today. I'll stay off the weightier matters but I want to ask him about the Abela drugs business. And the Abelas are big in prostitution. Perhaps Orlov can give us insights into how they recruit girls in that business.' Merlin scratched his forehead. 'There was one other thing on my mind . . . what was it . . . oh, yes. Where the heck is the artist's drawing, Sergeant? He's taking far too long.'

'Top of my list for today, sir.'

Johnson finally got out of the dentist's at one o'clock. He'd had a back tooth removed and two fillings. His mouth was numb but he felt much better. For the first time since he'd transferred to the Yard, he felt in the AC's debt. He wouldn't have done anything about his toothache if he hadn't bumped into Gatehouse. Now he was very pleased he had. And to have the treatment on the AC's slate, that was quite something.

The rain had stopped and he decided to walk back to the Yard. He turned down Mount Street, right onto South Audley Street, then left on Curzon Street. He wasn't far from Shepherd Market when he saw her entering a café a few yards ahead of him. He'd only seen Cowan's secretary very briefly but was sure it was her. Miss Ryman. He held back for a second then followed her in. He sat a table four away from hers, ordered a glass of Tizer, pulled his hat down and watched and waited.

Miss Ryman looked to be in her mid-thirties, and her plump lunch companion looked to be of similar age. Old school friends perhaps? They ordered sandwiches and tea, then started to natter. Despite it being lunchtime, the café was quite empty and he found he could hear most of their conversation. Miss Ryman was doing most of the talking. She was angry about her job and had a long list of complaints against her boss. There were his tantrums, his temper, his ingratitude and his wandering hands. Eventually she told her friend she'd had it with Cowan. Just half an hour before, she'd given in her notice.

When Miss Ryman's diatribe had finished, and her companion had managed to get in a few words of commiseration, they paid the bill and parted with a hug. The friend headed east towards Piccadilly while Miss Ryman headed in the opposite direction. Johnson followed. The woman crossed Park Lane, and entered the park. She walked briskly down a path leading to the Serpentine and, halfway along the lake, sat down on a bench. She'd kept some crusts from her lunch and started distributing them to the ducks and geese. Then she lit a cigarette. Johnson decided it was time to make his move.

'Miss Ryman? How are you? Do you remember me?'

She looked him up and down. 'I'm not sure that I do.'

He took out his warrant card. 'DI Johnson. I was in your office on Wednesday to see Mr Cowan.'

Her eyes narrowed. 'Oh, yes. I think I remember now.'

'May I sit down?'

'Please yourself. It's a free country. For now at least . . .' She was a rather severe-looking woman but Johnson could just about see why she might have been under threat from Cowan's wandering hands. Her nose was perhaps a little overlong and her brown hair perhaps a little too short, but she had big warm brown eyes and an attractive bow-lipped mouth.

As Johnson sat down, the secretary became fidgety, crossing and uncrossing her legs two or three times and transferring her cigarette nervously from one hand to the other. Finally she spoke. 'Now the rain's stopped it's really quite nice, isn't it? I can't quite believe it's only two weeks until Christmas.'

'Yes, very mild. Very different from the last few Christmases.' There was an awkward pause. 'I wonder if I might ask you a few questions. They are straightforward enough and won't take long. I had originally hoped to speak to you after my interview with Mr Cowan, but was told you'd gone out for the day.'

She drew on her cigarette. 'Oh, yes. Mr Cowan sent me off in a car to drop a script off to someone in Windsor. I don't know why an ordinary messenger couldn't have taken it but he said it was for some important man and it would look better if I took it. What is it you want to know?'

'Just some information regarding your old office in Victoria. Where you worked before the place was bombed. I understand you and Mr Cowan are the only current members of staff who used to work there?'

She smiled. Her face was prettier when she smiled. 'That's correct, although I hate to think what Mr Cowan would say if he heard himself described as a member of staff. They were good offices. Nicer than what we have now. And better situated. A short walk from the Army and Navy Stores which was very handy. A nicer class of person altogether round there. There are some quite odd people round Shepherd Market, not to mention . . .' she blushed 'the ladies of the night.'

'As I know only too well. I used to be a beat copper round there. Who else worked with you at the old office?'

She counted silently on her fingers. 'There were four others. Reg, the office boy, Edie, the receptionist, Hecht, Steiner's predecessor as accountant, and Hecht's ancient secretary, Gladys.'

'No young office girls?'

'I suppose you could class Edie as an office girl.'

'How old was Edie?'

'Twenty-one or thereabouts.'

'No other younger girls? No part-timers?'

'Is that what you're interested in? Any young girls who may have passed through the office?'

'Yes.'

'For whatever purpose?'

'Yes.'

She stubbed out her cigarette on the bench and became thoughtful. Eventually she turned to face Johnson. 'Look, Inspector, you ought to know that I just resigned my position as Mr Cowan's secretary. I have my reasons. Good reasons. He is not an easy man to work for and I'm afraid I reached the end of my tether. You might therefore think that what I'm about to say is motivated by malice towards the man. I can assure you it is not.'

'I believe you.'

'The fact is my boss's behaviour often goes beyond the pale.' She sighed. 'Fat and ugly as he is, Mr Cowan is something of a ladies man. It's the money, power and glamour of the film industry which attracts them, of course. And the chance of getting into the movies. He takes maximum advantage of his position. When we were in the old office, he often brought girls there. There was a steady stream. Some young actresses or models on the make, other professionals . . . if you know what I mean.'

'Like the girls in Shepherd Market?'

'Quite so. He was quite shameless about it. Didn't mind who knew. Sometimes it was impossible to tell which girl was professional or not. I could tell most of the time, though.'

'Does he still do this? Bring girls to the new office?'

'Once in a while, but since we moved to Shepherd Market, he seems to have become . . . oh what's the word . . . circumspect. More circumspect. I'm not sure why.'

'I see. Can you tell me more?'

'At the Victoria office, if he brought girls it tended to happen in the afternoon. After a good lunch or before a good dinner. Sometimes there might just be one, but usually there were more. Three or four sometimes. If he got busy, of course, they'd have nothing to do but loll around bored where I was and get under my feet. Occasionally I'd try and get them to help out in some minor way, tidy up files or the like. Once in a blue moon, one of them would.'

'And you mention this because . . . ?'

'I remember one girl who did help me like that. A sweet little thing she was. Professional though, I'm pretty sure. The thing is, all these girls were made up to the nines but . . .'

'Yes?'

'This girl was pretty young, I'm sure.'

'Below the age of consent?'

The secretary glanced nervously down at her hands. 'I don't want to get Cowan into trouble. I may have quit but . . .' She looked off towards the nearby Serpentine bathing area. A couple of all-season lady swimmers were resolutely ploughing through the freezing water. 'I think I made a mistake telling you all this. I may dislike the man but I don't want to get him sent to jail. How do I know what age the girls were? Look, I should have asked this earlier, I know, but what exactly are you investigating?'

Johnson held up his hands. 'You're right, Miss Ryman. I should have told you before. We are interested in the Costello offices because we just found a young girl, a teenager, dead – strangled – in the ruins of the building.'

'Goodness. How terrible!'

'There were a couple of American items on or near her body. This prompted us to find out if any offices in the building had American connections.'

Miss Ryman looked away. 'I see. Well we had American connections and I've just told you about Cowan's girls.'

'Yes.'

'But none of those girls really spent much time in the building. It's not as if they lived there.' She looked down at her hands again

'I can't really imagine Mr Cowan as a murderer. He's no angel, but . . .'

The clouds had disappeared completely now and the low sun was shining directly into their eyes. Johnson pulled his hat down. 'Look, I can agree the link is pretty tenuous but can I just ask you a couple more questions?'

She sighed. 'Alright.'

'Does Mr Cowan smoke?'

'Like the proverbial chimney. Mostly cigars, but also cigarettes.'

'American cigarettes?'

'His favourites are some evil-smelling Turkish brand but he smokes some American brands too.'

'Camel?'

'I've seen him with a pack of those, I think.'

'Does he have a sweet tooth?'

'Of course.'

'Chocolate?'

'Yes.'

'Any particular make he favours.'

'I think he likes them all. British, Swiss, American. I'm not sure where he gets them but he seems to have a ready supply. He's got a number of people at the Dorchester Hotel running errands for him. They probably get his chocolate in too.'

'Have you ever seen him eating something called a Hershey's Bar?'

'I'm not sure.' She thought for a moment. 'I am somehow aware of the brand. It's American, isn't it? No, I can't say. He likes expensive chocolate. Is that expensive?'

'I don't believe it is. In America at least.' Johnson looked out to the lake. On the far bank, a man and a little boy were attempting to fly a kite. Miss Ryman followed his gaze. 'Looks like they're having fun.'

'I was always hopeless with kites myself. Oh! See? There it goes. They've got it up.' The kite took flight but quickly fell to the ground. 'That's what used to happen to mine.' Johnson turned back to face Miss Ryman. 'It's been very good of you to speak to me. I'm sorry to impose but would it be possible for you to make a visit to Scotland Yard tomorrow?'

'Wh . . . what for?' she asked nervously.

'We are getting an artist's impression of the girl today, hopefully. I would count it a great favour if you could just have a look and see if it resembles any of the girls you saw with Cowan.'

'Don't you have a photograph of the body?'

'I think it's better you look at the drawing.'

'Oh.' She reflected for a moment. 'Alright, Inspector. It's in a good cause, I suppose. What time do you want me?'

'Eleven?' He gave her his card. 'I never did learn your Christian name, Miss Ryman.'

'It's Joan, Inspector. Joan Ryman.'

David Hilton's palatial office was on the middle floor of an eighteenth-century house just off Soho Square. Hilton reached across his oversized desk to shake hands. 'Good to meet you, Chief Inspector. I've heard a lot about you. I'm friends with your Mr Gatehouse. The AC and I share a passion for beagling. He speaks very highly of you.'

'That's good to know, sir.' Merlin had enjoyed the humorous hunting books of RS Surtees when young, and Hilton reminded him of Surtees' hero, Jorrocks. A burly man in a brown tweed three piece suit, he had thick mutton-chop whiskers sprouting from his ruddy cheeks and a genial manner. He was not at all what Merlin expected in a show business agent.

'I presume you want to talk about poor Laura?' His face became sombre. 'So sad. A beautiful star cut down in her prime. Whoever would have expected it? I am at your disposal, Chief Inspector. What do you want to know?'

'Well, sir, one possibility we have to consider is suicide. Could you ever imagine Miss Curzon ending her own life?'

'Frankly, no.' Hilton stroked his chin. 'I'm sure you already know a lot about Laura. A charming, happy go lucky girl.

Gorgeous. Good actress. Not perhaps in the first rank but good enough to be a leading lady on both sides of the Atlantic. Like most of us she had a few demons. Liked a drink. One or two other bad habits.'

'If you're thinking about the cocaine, sir, we know about that.'

'Yes. Well. I didn't approve but she always seemed to be reasonably in control of her vices. They didn't control her, as is often the case.'

'Any other demons? Demons from her past perhaps?'

'Not that I'm aware. She never told me about her past. She liked it to be a mystery.'

'Do you know how she became an actress?'

'There was some fellow who helped her but I never heard his name. She came onto my books when she was twenty-three and already reasonably well-established in the acting profession. Whoever taught her did a pretty good job. She was stylish, accomplished, and charismatic.'

'Curzon was a stage name. Do you know her real name?'

'No. She never volunteered it and I had no reason to press her. She was a decent and honest client. If she didn't want me to know it, that was fine by me.'

'We know she was unhappily married.'

'Yes. Michael Adair. That was completely predictable. I warned her but she wouldn't listen. It was bound to come to a bad end, but I doubt it had anything to do with her death. She seemed completely over it when she left for America in the summer.'

'America. Do you know what happened there?'

'Ah yes, America.' He tapped a folder on his desk. 'People often underestimate me, you know, Chief Inspector. When I'm not working I enjoy leading the life of an English country gentleman. Some people in the business make fun of my rural hobbies and think I'm old-fashioned and naïve. The fact is, I have plied this cut-throat trade successfully for many years in London, Los Angeles and New York. I have an excellent network of industry contacts whom I use to advance or protect my clients. If ill befalls one of

201

them and the reasons are covered up I usually have the resources to get to the bottom of things.'

'I understand, sir, but how does that bear on Miss Curzon?'

'I suppose you've been told the Jimmy Stewart story?'

'Yes.'

'There was more to it than that.' He pulled his chair closer to the desk and opened the folder. 'The reason put about was that Stewart's withdrawal for reasons of military service meant the film had to be mothballed. A reasonably plausible reason.'

'I've talked to Gus Cowan. He thought the reason rather weak. Said Stewart could have easily been replaced with a credible alternative.'

'The ghastly Mr Gus Cowan is correct. I first heard this story from Laura herself a few days before she flew back. It didn't sound right to me. So I looked into the matter and have found the real story. It's all in here.' He pointed to the folder. 'I spent a few years in Hollywood myself in the early 30s. I made many good friends, amongst whom was an excellent private detective. A real Sam Spade. I asked him to look into the matter. I received this report from him on the teleprinter last Friday. I was going to discuss it with Laura this week, but . . .' Hilton shrugged. 'I was going to tell her there were strong grounds for litigation.'

'What does the report say?'

'You are welcome to read the whole thing but, as you're obviously a busy man, let me summarise it. The lead producer of the film, Max Flack, like most of his ilk in Hollywood, expects sexual favours from his actresses as a matter of course. Most comply. Some don't and pay a penalty. On Laura's arrival in California, Flack made his expectations of her clear. She refused. He continued to pressure her for weeks and she continued to rebuff him. He became furious and his fury was compounded when he discovered she was having a fling with a jazz musician.'

'He doesn't like jazz musicians?'

'He doesn't, particularly if they are of what he regards as the wrong colour.'

'Ah.'

'He went berserk. At that point Stewart pulled out. Although he could have had the pick of five major stars to replace Stewart, he cancelled the film. My detective has no doubt that he did so as an act of revenge against Laura.'

'Wasn't that cutting off his nose to spite his face?'

'He will have lost some money, put some other noses out of joint, and received bad press. However, he still has the benefit of all the work done on the script and pre-production and can easily revive the film any time in the future with a new cast. Meanwhile he's a very big fish with a host of other productions to be getting on with.'

'The ways of the film world are strange indeed.'

'Strange and frequently unpleasant.' Hilton tidied the folder and put it away in a desk-drawer. 'So, that's what really happened and the whole experience must have been quite devastating for her. Flack was heard several times threatening to ruin her career. There was talk of leaking details of her relationship with the musician to the press. This would probably have led to her becoming box office poison in the southern states.'

'How much did Miss Curzon know about all this?'

'I don't know. I never had the chance to ask her.'

'This is a terrible story. Doesn't it make you want to reconsider what you said earlier about suicide?'

Hilton shrugged. 'Nasty and worrying as this is, she was a tough and resilient woman. Her nature would have been to fight back, not to kill herself.' Hilton brooded for a moment before speaking again. 'There is one other thing that's been worrying me, though. Something you should know.'

'Yes?'

Hilton retrieved another folder from his desk. This one was tied with a pink ribbon.

'A legal document, Mr Hilton?'

'An insurance policy.'

'May I?'

203

'Be my guest.'

Merlin took his time to read the document carefully. When he'd finished, he said 'I see. So what's the story?'

'About a year ago, when all seemed well in the marriage, Laura gave me a copy of this for safekeeping. She and Michael shared a solicitor who'd organised the policy and had his own copy, but she thought it sensible for a reliable third party like me to have a copy too. I was surprised and queried the wisdom of the policy. Her answer was that Michael had been keen on the idea and she hadn't liked to argue. As you've seen, it is a joint life insurance policy through which, on the death of one or other party, the survivor is to receive the substantial sum of sixty thousand pounds. I did remind Laura of the existence of this policy after the split and just before she went to America, but she said it could be dealt with on her return, along with all the other divorce matters.'

'Do you know if the premium payments are current?'

'I presume so. I understood they were Michael's responsibility.'

'Does it pay out on a suicide?'

'You are not the first to person to ask me that.'

'Oh?'

'Michael rang me yesterday. He couldn't get hold of the solicitor and knew I had a copy of the policy. I told him I wasn't a lawyer so my opinion would be worthless.'

'The policy doesn't mention suicide, does it?'

'No. It refers to the event of death without specifying cause.'

'Thank you for telling me, sir. That's certainly added another level of complexity to the case. May I take the respective documents with me?'

'Of course.'

A couple more nasty sores had erupted on Orlov's lips, and he was fingering these gingerly as he sat down at the table. Despite the sores he looked better than before as he'd had access to razor and comb.

'On your own today, Mr Merlin?'

'Sergeant Bridges is attending other business.'

'Have we a deal?'

'We do. However, the Commissioner wants a lawyer in with us at the first meeting to assess your level of cooperation and make sure all is agreed properly. If he's satisfied you are genuine, the Commissioner is prepared to allow a move from this prison to a better location. That man is only available tomorrow so we'll have to make a proper start then.'

Orlov banged the table and looked away angrily. 'Christ, Merlin. You'd better get on with it. You know I am not safe here. He must not trust you much, this Commissioner fellow.'

'It's no skin off my nose, Orlov, if he wants to send someone along. As long as I get my interviews, and you cooperate fully, I'm happy. However, as I'm here now, I might as well ask you a few preliminary questions.'

'About?'

'Prostitution and drugs.'

Orlov muttered something under his breath. Merlin doubted it was complimentary. 'I have nothing to do with such things. I am thief, not pimp or dealer.'

'I realise that. But the people you work for have significant business in those lines, don't they?'

The Bulgarian shrugged. 'Maybe. How come questions cannot wait until tomorrow when you have the other man?'

'I have some active cases where your help might be useful.'

Orlov glowered. 'You hurry for others but not to deal with me?'

Merlin didn't reply. The Bulgarian eventually shrugged. 'Alright. I show goodwill, as you say. What do you want to know?'

'How about a little history first? You arrived in England when?'

'December 1934. Worked my passage here on merchant ship out of Istanbul. Then skipped ship in docks. December twentieth. I remember date as was my birthday.'

'Where did you first live?'

'A cousin put me up. In Dalston.'

'What did you do for a living?'

Orlov sniggered. 'What you think I did? I became a crook and thief just like at home.'

'With Joe Abela's gang?'

'No. Not straightway.'

'Who did you work for before Abela?'

'Most chicken-shit outfits at the beginning. Then I hooked up with Messinas.' The Bulgarian's face suddenly clouded over. 'Look here, Merlin, you not trying to pin some old stuff on me now? You've already got me where you want me. What's the point accusing me of another crime?'

'Relax. I'm looking for information only. We have our deal. There'll be no more charges. All you need to do is cooperate. Now, the Messinas. They're the biggest players in prostitution. What did you do for them? You said earlier you were no pimp.'

'And I tell truth. I was just muscle. Worked mostly for Eugenio Messina. Kept an eye on the pimps. Dealt with out of order customers. That sort of thing.'

'What ages were the girls?'

'You think I was in habit of checking their birth certificates?'

'No.'

Orlov shrugged. 'All ages. From teenagers to forties. One or two maybe even older.'

'I'm more interested in the younger girls. Did the Messinas run under-age girls?'

'I suppose. It's hard to tell with young girls. Covered in make-up they can look older.' He paused to consider. 'Now I think about, I remember Eugenio having worries about this subject. I heard him once talking to his brothers about some customers wanting very young girls. He said that was not business he wanted to do. Others argued with him and he lost his temper. No child prostitutes, he said, and that was that. As boss, his word was final.'

'I see. And you joined the Abelas after the Messinas?'

'Yes.'

'And what do you know of their vice business?'

'Nothing. Except Joe is in direct charge himself.'

'And do you think he'd have scruples about running under-age prostitutes?'

'Sorry. What is "scruples"?'

'Would Joe Abela not want to do that sort of business?'

'Joe Abela would put his own mother to work as prostitute, if money good enough.'

'Where'd he get the girls?'

'All over place.'

'Alright, where'd he get the younger girls. Off the streets?'

'Again, all over place. I think he had some people working streets to find good girls. "Easy pickings" I remember some man say. Get stray girls, feed up and put to work. Lots of stray girls out there.'

'I see. Do you remember any names of these people working the streets?'

'No. Not my business to know.'

'Have a think before we meet tomorrow. It would be very helpful.'

Orlov shrugged again.

'And Abela's drugs? What about that business?'

'No. Never involved. Don't know who run it. Don't know no names.'

'Alright. Have a think about that too, will you?'

'Sure. I'll try. But what I really know is robbing and thieving. That what our deal is about.'

'I know, Boris, and I'm very much looking forward to what you have to say on those subjects.'

Marcus Waring was enjoying a sherry in his drawing room when he heard the tinkle of the front door bell. Seconds later his valet, Richards, entered.

'Mr Adair is asking if you are in, sir.'

There was a time when Waring would have been thrilled to welcome a film star into his house. That time had long passed when it came to Michael Adair. The man had become a pest. It wasn't Waring's fault that the tiresome actor had no head for business. He drained his drink and sighed. He knew he'd better see him. The guests wouldn't be arriving for a while yet, and if he didn't meet him now, he'd only return at some more inconvenient time. Besides, he thought grudgingly, the man had just lost his wife and some allowance was probably due.

'I'll see him. Take him into the study and give him a sherry. I'll be there shortly.'

An exquisite Louis XIV Boulle clock sat on the mantelpiece of the book-lined room. It was chiming even when Waring joined his unwanted guest. 'Good to see you, Michael. Come, let's sit over by the fire.'

Adair eyed Waring nervously as they took their seats. 'It's very good of you to see me at such short notice, Marcus.'

'And why wouldn't I make the effort for a good friend at this sad time. My deepest condolences. I presume you have been taking things easy?'

'Thanks. Yes, the studio has given me a few days. I went in today and tried to work, but it's so hard to concentrate.'

'Poor you. And poor Laura, of course.'

Adair stroked his glass. 'Everyone knows we had split up but we remained the best of friends. I was with her on Monday. She was her vibrant jolly self, then a few hours later . . .' His sherry went in a single gulp.

'Um . . . a refill, perhaps, Michael?'

'Please.' The valet was summoned to replenish Adair's glass.

'Your servants seemed very busy when I was waiting in the hall, Marcus. You're entertaining?'

'Just a few friends for dinner. You're aware of my interest in the occult?'

'I am.'

'I have the infamous Aleister Crowley coming. I'm hoping he might be persuaded to give a little talk on the subject of . . .'

'Hocus pocus?'

Waring stiffened. 'Be obliged if you wouldn't call it that, old chap.'

Adair reddened. 'Sorry. Marcus. I don't know where that came from. Wrong choice of words. I know you take all that stuff very seriously. Please forgive me. Didn't mean to offend. Not quite myself at the moment.'

'No offence taken, Michael. However, good as it is to see you, my guests will be arriving shortly. Is this a purely social call or is there something in particular you wish to discuss?'

Adair darted an anxious look at his host. 'As a matter of fact, there is. I know it's not long since we last discussed this and you told me I had to be patient until Easter, but I'm in a bit of a bind. I would really appreciate it if . . .'

'Michael, Michael . . .' Waring interrupted. 'Do I really have to run over all that stuff again? You know the situation. Nothing has changed. The company is strapped for cash at present. If you are to get any money back we have to wait for a new round of investment. We plan to organise that but can't do anything until April when the latest audited figures are released. There's a good chance I'll be able to arrange for you to be taken out then, though I doubt there'll be any profit in it for you.'

Waring's approach to business was much influenced by his late uncle's words of wisdom. 'Be sure to put as little of your own money into your ventures as you can, my boy. Get the maximum possible from other people, but award yourself a large carried interest as the promoter.' Waring could easily have given up his business activities but he still enjoyed the thrill of the chase. Some of his ventures came off, others didn't. It didn't really matter to him. He was insulated by his wealth and by the fact he put very little personal money at risk. Success or failure did, however, matter very much to the investors he cultivated. Many had large sums at stake and Adair was one such. He had excitedly invested more than he could afford in a specialist engineering company which Waring had promoted as the beneficiary of significant new technology under development. The technology, however, was proving difficult to apply practically and an investment return was looking further off than promised. Meanwhile Adair was in a desperate financial bind and Waring could see the panic in his eyes.

'Look here, Marcus. I understand the company might be constrained at the moment but, dammit all, you got me into the damn thing and made all sorts of promises. It was meant to be booming by now. If the company can't do anything for me, perhaps you can. You're rolling in it after all. You could buy my shares from me. What about that for an idea?'

Waring thought of his uncle. 'I think not, old chap. You just need to hang on for a few months. All will . . .'

'Alright then. How about a loan? You know I'm good for the money. I've got a string of films lined up. It's just that I've got a . . . I've got a temporary embarrassment '

'Look, I'm sorry. I won't deny I'm comfortable but I'm afraid most of my wealth is tied up in illiquid assets and trusts. I don't maintain large cash balances.' Waring noticed that Adair's hands were trembling. 'Surely your great supporter Victor Goldsmith could help you out with a salary advance from your next film?'

Adair stared back at him in silence. How was Waring to know that the actor had already pulled that trick several times over? He jerked awkwardly to his feet, dropping his sherry glass in the process, and lurched towards the door. Moments later Waring heard the front door slam shut.

Chapter Nine

'Any more news from the Far East, Sam? I've not seen a paper yet.'

'There are reports of survivors being picked up by our ships. No details beyond that.'

'Well, that's something.'

'Radio said significant casualties are expected.'

'Hmm. Not so good. Iris any calmer?'

'Not really. No reason for her to be. Kept me up half the night pacing around.'

As before, Merlin found himself at a loss. He settled at his desk and decided to change the subject. 'I missed you yesterday when I got back from the Scrubs.'

'Yes. The AC got me to run a few errands and then I had a drink with Jim Toshack.'

'Oh good. Tell me about it in a minute. First let me fill you in on Hilton and Orlov.'

When he'd heard everything, Bridges said: 'I don't know quite what to say about Hilton's information, sir. Despite everyone saying she wasn't the suicidal type, the detail of what she went through does make you think. As regards the policy, I suppose we'd better see the solicitor who arranged it.'

'Yes. Can you add that to your list? Now what did Toshack have to say?'

'He had something which might help us. Before he got kicked

out of Vice, he'd acquired a potentially useful source. A man who'd worked for the Abelas in their prostitution racket. Jim hadn't really got far with the man when he got fired from the department.'

'How do we get to speak to him?'

'Jim doesn't have an address or telephone number for him. The man was naturally very cautious. They only met once, at a church south of the river. Jim suggested we try there. He's given me the address.'

'The source's name?'

'Madeley. Vincent Madeley. If you're thinking of checking him out in the records, there's nothing on him, according to Jim. Somehow he has a clean slate.'

'And what exactly did he say to Toshack? What was his reason for wanting to flip?'

'Said he'd packed in the game out of disgust at the gang's increasing involvement in what he called "child prostitution". Said waifs and strays were being targeted and pulled off the streets to meet the growing customer demand.'

Merlin banged his hand excitedly on the table. 'This is right on the money! I hope Toshack didn't tell his superiors about the man.'

'He didn't. They are unaware as far as he knows.'

'Good. Let's fit in a visit to this church today, if we can.' Merlin opened a drawer and found himself an Everton Mint to suck. 'What about that artist's drawing?'

'We have it, sir. There was some cock-up at the morgue and the artist didn't get access to the body until Wednesday morning. Then he took his time as he's a bit of a perfectionist. He drew on Mr Wright's knowledge as well. Anyway, we have his work now. He's done several sketches with variations in hairstyle, different angles and so on.'

Johnson appeared.

'Teeth alright now, Peter? I have to admit, I was hoping I'd see you back here yesterday but . . .'

'Sorry, sir. I did return in the afternoon when you were out only to find an MI5 man waiting for me. I was wanted in St James's to help them with some of the work I did on the Hess case in the summer. You know what these people are like. He was pretty insistent and when I got there they kept me pretty late.'

'No need to apologise, Inspector. You had no choice. We seem to be making progress. Let me . . .'

'Before you do anything, sir, can I ask if we have that artist's drawing yet?'

'Yes, we were just talking about it.'

'Good. I have someone I'd like to show it to. I had an odd bit of luck yesterday after seeing the dentist. I was walking near Shepherd Market when I saw . . .'

Goldsmith was in his study at home. He was angry and frustrated. Norman Addleshaw had finally returned his call. The man had been all enthusiasm at their Dorchester meeting. Now it seemed he was either manoeuvring to get a bargain basement deal or was cooling on the idea of the investment. At their initial meeting, he'd said he was happy to take Silver Screen's accounts as they stood. Now he wanted a fresh audit of the last three years by his own accountants. And he'd introduced a number of other onerous requirements. Had he got wind of the London Providential's withdrawal and taken fright? The man was bound to have excellent contacts in the City of London. If the Providential's decision had already leaked, things were going to become even more difficult. It was true that Addleshaw was far from the ideal partner, but there was a comfort to knowing he was there in the last resort.

He took a few deep breaths and gradually regained his equilibrium. There was no need to panic. He still had Tate and, if needs be, Abela. The comic had also been difficult to pin down in the past few days, but they'd spoken earlier and had agreed to meet up. If Goldsmith could seal a firm deal by the end of the day, the legal could be completed at a push by Wednesday and money flow by the end of the week.

His wife suddenly appeared, looking very pleased with herself.

She was wearing a new blue dress and her best jewels. She performed a quick twirl. 'So what do you think, darling?'

'You look wonderful!'

'Thank you, my love! I'm lunching with the girls at the Criterion. I might be there a while. It's the Duchess's birthday and I'm in a martini mood. I hope you're not going to spend all day in this stuffy room checking your box office takings or whatever it is you do in here. You must take a nice walk in the park. You need to take more exercise, as I keep saying. I worry about your health, you know, darling Victor.'

Goldsmith thought this a little rich from someone who was about to consume a barrel load of lunchtime cocktails, but kept his thoughts to himself. 'Of course, my dear. I'll go for a walk, don't you worry. Now go and have a lovely time.'

After Valerie left, he decided to tend to his correspondence. The first letter he picked up had been hand-delivered that morning. He recognised the handwriting immediately. It was Adair's and Goldsmith guessed correctly that it was about money. His letters nearly always were. He read it with growing irritation. Adair proposed to sign up for a further two films beyond the two in the New Year already contracted. If he could be paid his money for these films up front, he was prepared to halve his normal fees. There was no reference to his recent poor behaviour or any suggestion of an apology.

Goldsmith leaned back in his chair and brooded. Something inside him had finally snapped in regard to the actor. Here he was coping with a life and death business crisis and Adair was still chivvying him for money while screwing him royally every day at the studio. 'Enough is enough', he muttered to himself. He tore the letter up and threw it into the waste paper basket. Adair had made his last film for Silver Screen Productions.

The Home Office lawyer was called Briers, and Merlin had arranged to meet him at the prison at half past eleven. Merlin hoped he might grab a little time with Orlov beforehand so he got there with Bridges an hour early. The moment he saw the Governor's face he knew something was wrong.

'You don't look so good, Gordon. What's up?'

'I'm sorry, Frank. Orlov is dead.'

The news completely knocked the wind out of Merlin. He was at a complete loss for words.

'You'd better sit down, Frank. Here.' Merlin and his equally stunned sergeant did as they were told and sat at the Governor's desk. 'You'll want to know how he died, but it's not absolutely clear yet. An officer went to check on him in his cell about an hour ago to get him ready for your visit. He was laid out on the floor in a pool of vomit. The prison doctor was called and his first thought was poison. We'll have to wait for the post-mortem for confirmation.'

Merlin finally found his voice. 'How could he be poisoned in a solitary cell?'

'The man had to eat. The food is sent from the kitchen. There are a large number of kitchen workers.'

'You've interviewed them?'

'In progress now. We are already aware, however, that a kitchen worker who was in earlier has left before the end of his shift.'

Merlin sighed. 'Now, there's a thing. And I'll bet he's a very recent recruit?'

'Yes.'

'Don't you vet these people?'

'We do our best. We take references but we haven't got the resources to delve very deeply into people's backgrounds. Obviously we don't take on people we know to have criminal records but, as you know, a lot of paperwork was destroyed in the Blitz. And there is a war on.'

Merlin groaned. 'Please Gordon, not that one. The war can't be responsible for every cock-up, can it?'

'Sorry, Frank '

'Well, that's it then. However it was done, I'm sure there'll be nothing to tie in the Billy Hills and Joe Abelas of this world with

Orlov's death. Perhaps you'll find your errant kitchen worker, but he'll not know enough to finger the big boys. We've lost a great chance to get at those people.' He banged a fist on the Governor's desk in his frustration. 'Sorry, Gordon. I blame myself. I should have followed my intuition, ignored my superiors and held him at the Yard from the outset.'

'Don't be silly, Frank. If the blame is anyone's, it's clearly mine.'

The details of how Abela had got to Orlov didn't matter to Merlin. The fact was that a major opening in the defences of the gang chiefs had been plugged. He would have to wait a long time for another potential songbird like Orlov. Meanwhile he had nothing further to say. There were other battles to fight.

Johnson set out the artist's drawings, which covered three sheets of paper, on Merlin's desk, ready for Joan Ryman. He had the office to himself. Cole had hurried off after receiving a call from Mary Walker's neighbour informing him that she had reappeared. Johnson had suggested Cole wait until he'd seen the secretary as then he could take the drawings with him, but Cole was too anxious Mrs Walker would disappear again.

Miss Ryman arrived dead on eleven as arranged. Johnson could see she was very nervous. 'I've never been to a police station before, Inspector, let alone Scotland Yard. Being here makes me feel like I've done something wrong.'

'Can I get you a calming cup of tea? No? There's nothing to worry about. All you have to do is look at these pictures and then you can be off.'

'I thought I only had to look at one picture?' She sat tentatively at the desk and looked down at the sketches.

'As you can see, the artist has drawn a few pencil variations of how the girl might have looked.'

'With different hair styles, it seems.'

'Yes. Wavy hair. Long hair. Short hair. Curly hair and so on. We know the colour of her hair was brown.'

'Yes, alright. Let me just look for a while, then.'

She approached her task diligently and spent a quarter of an hour considering the artist's work. Eventually she took a deep breath and put her finger on one of the drawings on the second page. It showed the girl front profile with medium length wavy hair. 'This version looks possible. Could I please have a little more light?'

Johnson turned Merlin's desk lamp on. He felt a little buzz of excitement.

She bent down for a closer look, then held the sketch out to view it from afar. She took another deep breath. 'This looks a lot like one of his girlfriends. Cowan's, I mean. The girl I mentioned. The one who helped me with a little office work.'

'Are you sure?'

She had another careful look, then nodded. 'Pretty certain. Not one hundred per cent. Perhaps seventy-five to eighty per cent.'

'Do you remember her name?'

'Cowan never mentioned names. It was always "sweetie" or "sweetie-pie" or something like that.'

'Is there anything in particular you remember about her?'

'If it's the girl I think she is, she came to the office three or four times. Always together with other girls. She was pretty but then, all his girls were pretty. Quite chatty. About normal day to day things. The weather, music she liked – stuff like that I think.'

'She was young?'

'One of the younger ones.'

'Age?'

'Very difficult to say. All the girls Cowan brought went rather heavy on the make-up, as I said before. If I had to guess I'd say about sixteen but she could have been younger.'

Johnson put a small pencil tick under the chosen sketch. 'Thank you very much indeed, Miss Ryman.'

'What will happen now?'

'I'll need to talk to my boss. I'm sure he'll want to show the drawing to Mr Cowan and see what he can tell us. You're not working a notice period for him are you?'

'Goodness, no. We both agreed I'd leave straightaway.'

'Good.'

After the disaster of Wormwood Scrubs, Merlin was determined to plough on immediately with his work and allow as little time as possible for brooding on Orlov's death. He and Bridges headed straight for South London where they hoped to find Jim Toshack's source.

Zion Baptist Chapel was at the end of a street in between the Walworth Road and The Elephant and Castle. This was an area of London which had suffered badly in the Blitz but the chapel and nearby houses appeared to have escaped unscathed. The building was little more than a large wooden hut with a corrugated metal roof. The main door was open, so in they went. They found themselves in a simple meeting room furnished with several rows of wooden chairs. It was empty save for a man in a dust coat sweeping the floor at the far end next to a lectern.

'Mr Madeley?' Merlin shouted.

'Who wants him?'

'Jim Toshack gave us your name.'

'Oh, he did, did he? May I suggest you keep your voice down?'

Madeley set down the brush and walked towards them. He was a tall, spare man, with at least a couple of inches on Merlin. He ignored the extended hands of the policemen and went to the door. He looked out and carefully scanned the street. Returning inside he said 'Seems you haven't brought any scum in your wake. Please follow me.'

He led them through a door on the right. Madeley and Merlin had to bend their heads to enter. There was a cramped dark room with a table, chairs, and a few shelves of bibles and hymn books. 'This is the minister's room. Luckily he's out of London today.'

Madeley turned on a light and now they could all see each other properly. The most striking feature of Madeley's face was a huge broken nose. He had an army issue haircut, heavy-lidded eyes and a prominent double chin. Merlin made his introductions and they sat down at the table.

'Admiring the old hooter are you, Chief Inspector? I used to do a little boxing when I was young. I was in fact London amateur heavyweight champion one year. I carried a little more weight in those days. Was going to turn pro but me old mum wouldn't have it. Broke my dad's heart it did, but she ruled the roost and we did as we were told.'

'I did a little boxing in my youth. Keener on football, though.' said Merlin.

'Yeah, I like football too. Millwall fan, me. Hardly missed a game at the Den before the war.' Madeley leaned forward. 'So how's Sergeant Toshack? I haven't heard from him in a while. I heard he got the boot from the Vice Squad. Stepped on someone's toes. I hope they weren't yours.'

'He did unfortunately get transferred but that was nothing to do with us. We are not from Vice.'

'Good. Bastards all, according to Toshack.' He tried to stretch out a leg which was not so easy in the confined space. 'So, what do you do?'

'We investigate serious crimes.'

'And what do you want with me?'

'We're investigating the case of a strangled young girl in Victoria.'

'Are you now?'

'There's a possibility the girl might have been on the game. Sergeant Toshack said you knew a few things about the prostitution rackets in London and might be willing to help the police out.'

Madeley scratched his large chin thoughtfully. 'I had told Toshack that, yes, but that was because I trusted him. How do I know I can trust you?'

'Because Toshack sent us.'

'Hmm. Tell me more about this girl. How old?

'Fifteen or thereabouts.'

'What makes you think she was on the game?'

'Don't know for certain. We've been looking into the missing girl files to try and come up with a match. One possible was a girl put out on the streets by the bombs. That led us to wonder how a girl might survive in such circumstances.'

'There are other ways of surviving on the streets than prostitution. Thieving, for example.'

'Yes we may well be barking up the wrong tree. However, we haven't got much to go on, and as we heard you had some specialist knowledge we thought we should tap it. Toshack said you were with the Abela gang?'

Madeley chewed his lips thoughtfully but said nothing. Eventually he muttered something to himself and seemed to come to a decision. 'I can help you, I suppose, as it's in a good cause. Yeah, I used to work for Abela and I know plenty.'

'You worked as muscle?'

Madeley smiled. 'No. I understand why you say that, but no. Doubtless you'll find it surprising, but I am a qualified accountant. I kept some of Abela's books for a while.'

'How did that happen?'

Madeley sought again to stretch out his legs and this time had more success by twisting to his right. 'Though I gave up boxing, I was still a keen fan. I used to go to all the East End meets. At one of them in Bethnal Green, I was introduced as a former champion to Abela. He took one look at me and thought I might be handy. I was earning a pittance as an accounts clerk in Bermondsey Council at the time. Didn't take much money from him to turn my head. At the beginning he used me for my brawn but he soon realised I had a brain as well. He got me doing some accounts, in a small way to start, but I ended up keeping the books for all of his vice businesses, and for a few other capers as well.'

'When did you break with him?'

'Four months ago.'

'What prompted you to speak to Toshack?'

'Somehow or other he got my name, heard I'd left the business and came sniffing around. I decided to talk.'

'Why?'

'Same reasons I had for packing it in. The main one being I'd had it with Abela and his whole filthy business.' He looked hard at Merlin. 'Look, I know I'm no angel. Maybe I could have stuck with him a little longer if he was only involved in normal criminal stuff like robbing and thieving. But the things that went on in his whoring business turned my stomach and I reached the point where I'd had enough.'

'And what about all this?' Merlin pointed at the bibles on the shelves.

Madeley shrugged. 'What can I say? You'll think it funny, I suppose, but I found God. The missus thinks I've gone bonkers, but there it is. Before I parted company with Abela, I happened to meet the minister here. I won't bore you with the details. Let's just say he's an impressive man and he became a powerful influence on me. Converted me if you like. Properly, I mean. Not just the occasional visit to church on Sunday type of thing. Persuaded me to try and live the Christian life. And I realised if I wanted to lead that life, I couldn't just ignore the things my employers got up to. So I packed it in and when Toshack wanted to talk, I was happy to do so.'

'Wasn't that a very dangerous thing for you to do?'

'Yes, but it was the right thing to do.'

'Does Abela know you're a stool-pigeon?'

Madeley made a face. 'Now that's not a very nice word to use, is it? If he did know, do you think I'd be here before you? I wouldn't be surprised if they're keeping tabs on me, though.'

'We must hope they don't keep tabs on this place.'

'They don't know about the chapel, I'm sure. Once in a while I've seen people near my flat and if I come here from there I am extremely cautious. That said, I was a small fish. They wouldn't think of putting much resource on me.'

'I hope you're right. How do you make a living now?'

'Stashed away enough to keep me and the family alright until long after I'm gone.'

'Ill-gotten gains, then? How does that tally with your new Christian beliefs?'

'We all have our moral dilemmas to resolve, Chief Inspector. I've given some money to the church here and am doing my best to repent my ways. Practically, though, I have to make sure the missus and kids are alright.'

'Alright. I'm interested in your help not banging you up for past crimes.'

'Glad to hear it.'

'Going back to Abela's business. You say there were things that turned your stomach. What things in particular?'

Madeley's eyes narrowed. 'It was the child prostitution that did it. That's what really got to me.'

'Abela ran young girls?'

'And boys. Youth has become an Abela speciality over the past few years.'

'How young exactly?' asked Bridges.

'Mostly the age of your girl, Sergeant. I suppose there's always been a demand for that sort of thing but it seems to have been particularly strong recently. I don't know if the war has anything to do with it. Some of the other gangs don't like doing this sort of business, but Abela has no qualms. When I was there he had a designated crew for pulling young girls off the street. There are plenty of desperate girls around these days what with the bombing and everything.

'And the clients for these special services . . . ?' asked Merlin

'From all walks of life. Some names would surprise you.'

'You kept records of the clients?'

'The bigger ones, yes. The ones who were allowed to run accounts.'

'People ran accounts, did they? Do you still have the records?'

'I kept some copies. Thought it would be useful protection.'

'May we have a look?'

Madeley looked down. 'Can I really trust you and your sergeant? Toshack used to tell me there was a lot of corruption at the Yard. Not just in Vice.'

'I promise you on my son's life you can trust us, Mr Madeley.'

'Hmm. Well I've trusted you so far. In for a penny, in for a pound I suppose. Do you have a number I can call? We can have another meet but I think somewhere different.'

Merlin gave him his Scotland Yard number.

Madeley shook his head. 'I'd prefer your private number, if you please.'

Merlin borrowed Bridges's pencil and scribbled the Chelsea details on a piece of paper.

'Be home around half six, Chief Inspector. I'll try then. And keep tonight free.'

Cowan had risen late. He had packed off the young companions with whom he had passed an enjoyable but exhausting night, and now lay back in the giant bath of his Dorchester penthouse contemplating the day, or what remained of it. There were two appointments scheduled. First, tea downstairs with two other film producers – Michael Powell and Emeric Pressburger – to discuss a possible collaboration. They were increasingly successful mavericks like him. After that he had a dinner arranged with the Crazy Gang stalwarts, Flanagan and Allen, to see if he could entice them into doing a film for him.

Cowan wasn't feeling very energetic and he wondered if he was in the right frame of mind for these meetings. There was still time to put them off. Perhaps he should just have a quiet, relaxing day in his suite for once. He decided to resolve the matter after he'd eaten some breakfast. His mind never functioned properly on an empty stomach.

Friday had been an extremely annoying day. He had never particularly liked the Ryman woman but he'd got used to her and there was no doubt she was extremely efficient. She knew the ropes and was, he'd thought, fully accustomed to his many foibles. Cowan had never succeeded in exercising his 'droit de seigneur' on her but had the magnanimity to forgive her refusal. He'd never found her that attractive anyway. A little too old for his taste.

He grunted as he strained to lever his two hundred and thirty pounds out of the bath. The secretarial agency would have to be his first call on Monday morning. Meanwhile that pretty but dim girl on the front desk would have to fill in.

An hour later, after a hearty brunch of scrambled eggs and smoked salmon, washed down by a glass of 1925 Krug, he was feeling revived and decided to go through with his meetings. In the dressing room he exchanged his grey silk robe and pyjamas for a grey silk suit. As he was placing a handkerchief in the top pocket of the suit jacket he felt something inside. The cards the two policemen had given him. Both clever guys, no doubt, although the second fellow, Merlin, had struck him as particularly sharp. A serious man with a serious brain. Still, no one had as sharp and serious a brain as Gus Cowan. If they came back he'd handle them carefully and knew he'd outsmart them. He outsmarted everyone in the end.

He splashed a little oil on his thinning pate and some cologne on his cheeks. He bared his teeth at himself in the mirror. Gus Cowan, genius of the movies, was ready to face the world for another day.

Cole asked the taxi driver to keep the meter ticking before he ran into the Yard and up to Merlin's office. Johnson was still there, as he'd hoped. 'Finished with the drawings, sir?'

'I have. Success?'

'Yes, I spoke to her. She was very anxious and not particularly talkative but she confirmed she had a daughter who would have turned fifteen in the summer. Said she had another older daughter too. Both girls ran away and she's seen neither of them for years.'

'Did she say why they ran away?'

'Didn't get on with their father. No more detail than that.'

'She's made no attempt to track down her children?'

'She said she tried a long while back without success.'

'Is she still going to be there when you get back?'

'She promised she would. Seemed an honest sort.'

Johnson handed the drawings to Cole. 'I got somewhere with Cowan's secretary by the way. She went through the sketches and picked one out. Said it looked like a girlfriend of Cowan's who visited his Victoria office. I put a small tick against it, so you know which one.'

'Very good, sir.'

Archie Tate had decided on a shopping spree. He needed some new suits. His tailor had recently made three for him but they were not to his liking. His rich friends and colleagues had encouraged him to use a Savile Row bespoke tailor. The fact was he preferred cheaper shop suits. Long drawn-out fitting sessions in Savile Row never seemed to produce as good a fit as he got off the peg at places like Burtons, Reid's and Harrods. Today he'd come to Harrods which usually had a wide range of suits to his taste. His preference was for loud checks. Not only did he like them but he felt they were appropriate to his chosen profession.

He felt a little peckish and decided to visit the Harrods café before going to the menswear department. He ordered buttered scones and tea and was enjoying his second scone when he noticed Jean Parker sitting alone at a table on the other side of the room. Their eyes met and he waved. She returned the gesture unenthusiastically, but he decided to take her acknowledgement as an invitation anyway. He collared a waiter and asked him to transfer the remains of his tea and scones to Miss Parker's table.

'Well, well! The beautiful Jean Parker. How nice to see you. Don't mind if I join you?'

'No . . . no, not at all, Archie. How . . . how lovely to see you.'

Tate sat down as the waiter rearranged the table. 'You must 'ave one of these scones, Jean. Talk about melting in the mouth! Mind, at these prices they bloody well should, if you'll pardon my French.'

'No thank you, Archie. I have to watch my figure.'

'You've got nothing to worry about in that direction. Nice buxom lass like you.'

A little boy approached with mother in tow and asked Tate for his autograph. The comic patted the boy's head condescendingly. 'Don't you want Miss Parker's too? She's a big film star as well, you know.' The boy stared blankly at the actress for a moment then shook his head as Tate scribbled his signature. 'There you are.' The boy took his book and squeaked an awkward thank you before hurrying off.

'Hard cheese, love. Can't win 'em all, eh? I bet if he were twelve or thirteen years older he'd have jumped at the chance.' Tate gobbled one of the last two scones then leaned closer to the actress. 'But what are you doing here all alone, Jean? Michael gone and deserted you 'as he?'

'He's not much of a one for shopping. He's having a bit of rest at home.'

'Still moping is he? Poor Michael. She was a damned fine little filly, that Laura but . . .'

Tate paused as he saw Jean stiffen. She opened her mouth to say something but bit her lip and stopped herself.

'Oops! I can see I've upset you. Wrong word to use I know. Please forgive my rough and rude Northern ways. Some like 'em of course. My ways that is. Like the millions who queue up to see my films.' He winked at Miss Parker and poured some more tea. 'I knew Laura quite well, you know. She had one of her early successes in my film *Postman's Holiday*. That was in 1935, I think, or was it the year after? Whichever, we filmed it in the spring and it came out at the end of the summer. She was very good. Played my girlfriend. We had some nice kissing scenes as I recall. Lovely pouting rosy lips she 'ad. Oh aye.' He smirked unattractively. 'They often say the best way to a girl's heart is to make her laugh. I 'ope it's not too boastful to say I'm pretty good at that!' He slurped his drink. 'Mind, I'm pretty good at other things too . . . if you know what I mean.'

Jean Parker bit her lip again. Odious as the man was, she knew it wasn't wise to make an enemy of him. He was a powerful man in the British film world.

'Laura, poor Laura. Pity about her disaster in Hollywood.'

'Was it really such a disaster?'

'Oh yes. Momentum is very important in this business. She 'ad it. Now she don't. Or rather didn't. I could have helped her re-invigorate her career, of course. Reinvigorate her in other ways too, maybe.'

'What a pity you didn't get the chance.'

'Oh aye, chance would have been a fine thing.' Tate's eyes suddenly bored into Jean Parker. 'But what about you, love? You're trundling along nicely in your career but a little boost wouldn't do you any harm. I've got a spot for a female lead in my next film but one. How about it?'

'Well . . . Archie . . . I rely on my agent in such things. Why don't you have a word with him?'

Tate banged his hand on the table. An elderly couple nearby turned to look and made disapproving noises. Tate ignored them. 'You're agent's rubbish, love. You should get another. And anyway, there's really no reason we can't discuss this man to man. So to speak.'

'Look, Archie . . .'

'You'd do well to consider my offer carefully, Jean dear. And there's another piece of advice I can give you for nothing. Adair. Have you moved in with him yet?'

'That's really no business of yours.'

'Last I heard he was shacked up somewhere in Mayfair while you've got your own place here in Knightsbridge. Keep it that way and drop 'im is my advice to you. He'll do you no good at all. His career is on a downward turn. The only reason he's in your current potboiler is that Victor has a soft spot for him. Yes, Adair's contracted to do more films for Silver Screen but I know that Victor's getting cold feet. You know how terribly Adair's been behaving on set recently, and it's not the first time. Handsome and charismatic as he may be, he's a bagful of trouble and you should get away from him.'

Jean squirmed in her chair. She felt she must say something on

227

Adair's behalf but could only remark limply 'Naturally, Laura's death has affected him.'

'Come off it, lass. Things run much deeper than that. He's got all sorts of problems, money problems not the least of them. You should be careful about what you're getting into.'

Jean had had more than enough and rose abruptly to her feet. 'Look, I'm sorry, Mr Tate, I don't want to be rude but I really can't sit here and put up with this . . . this . . . sort of talk anymore.' She looked at her watch. 'And I'm late. I must go.'

Tate pouted for a moment then threw his arms wide. 'Jean, dear. I've upset you again. I'm so sorry. Old Archie can be a silly bugger sometimes and too blunt by far. I'm only trying to 'elp, though. Silly as I may be, I've been around the block a few times. It's a cruel, vicious world out there. You need to take care of yourself and remember, I'm a powerful man. Perhaps about to become even more powerful yet.' He tapped his nose with a finger and gave the actress a knowing look.

Jean Parker replied curtly as she put on her gloves. 'I'll be sure to bear that in mind.'

To Cole's surprise, Mary Walker was reluctant to allow him entry again and tried to hold him at the threshold. He persisted, however, and eventually she gave way. He followed her into the living room where he discovered she had a guest. A wiry unshaven little man with oily jet black hair was occupying one of her armchairs. He was wearing grubby grey overalls and smoking a roll your own cigarette.

'My husband, Constable. Sid Walker.'

The man gave Cole a surly look. 'I gather you've been harassing the wife about some dead girl.'

'Not harassing, no. I'm sorry if your wife saw it that way. I'm trying to identify the body of a young girl. We came across some evidence which suggested there was a chance the girl might be your daughter, Ida. It's a slim chance but we are obliged to investigate.

Of course I understand it's distressing for you both to have to consider this as a possibility.'

'Mary says you were going to bring some drawings with you.'

Cole took the envelope from his pocket. 'I have them here. May I?' Sid Walker agreed begrudgingly and Cole laid out the three sheets on the dining table in the middle of the room.

Walker got to his feet, pushed his wife out of the way and went to take the first look. After a cursory viewing, he said a loud 'No' before making way for Mary. Her hands trembled as she picked up the drawings. She spent longer on them but the response was the same. 'That's not our Ida. None of the pictures. Now, I'd be grateful if you'd leave us in peace.'

'Are you sure, Mrs Walker? What about this one?' Cole pointed at the sketch ticked by Johnson.

She didn't bother to look. 'Not our Ida. Now please go.'

'It may be the drawings are not so accurate and it is a while, I understand, since you last saw your daughter? Perhaps you'd consider coming to the mortuary to see the body itself?'

Walker bristled. 'Look, copper, it's not our girl, see. We've both told you. Now leave it at that and clear off.'

As he reluctantly put the sketches back in their envelope Cole asked Walker: 'You don't live here, sir, do you? I understood you and your wife were separated.'

'We are. I've got a gaff south of the river, not that it's any of your business.'

'You work?'

'Of course. How else would I live?'

'Can I ask where you work?'

'None of your business.'

'And your daughters, sir? They ran away from home when they were both quite young, didn't they. Why was that?'

Walker's face reddened. 'Again, none of your bloody business!'

'I heard tell you were a bit of a disciplinarian.'

'And what's wrong with that? A father's right and duty.'

'And you enforced discipline . . . physically?'

'What if I did?'

Mary Walker, who'd been listening to this exchange anxiously, began to sob. Walker growled 'Happy now, copper? That's enough. Get out!'

Walker was bristling with violence and Cole decided it was best not to push it. He left them. As he hurried off down the stairs, the disappointment began to sink in. Long shot as it might have been, he'd really begun to believe Ida Walker was their girl. Now he just had another dead end to report to his bosses.

Merlin had taken Johnson and Bridges to The Red Lion for a quick pub lunch. Cole was waiting for them on their return.

'How'd you get on then?' asked Merlin.

'Not well, sir. Mrs Walker said none of the drawings resembled her daughter. Her ex-husband was visiting, and he said the same.'

'Damn it.'

'I didn't particularly take to Mr Walker. Aggressive little man. Mrs Walker seemed nervous of him. Under his thumb.'

'Did he influence her at all, d'you think? About the drawings?'

'I don't think so. As a last throw of the dice, however, I'd like her to look at the body itself. Maybe there'll be something about it she recognises. She said no when I asked her but I might have a better chance of persuading her without her husband around.'

'Alright, Constable, you do that. Meanwhile . . .' Merlin reached for pencil, paper and reading glasses. 'As there have been developments, I think we should go over everything one more time. If you just bear with me a minute or two.'

When he'd finished writing and had reviewed the note he'd made, he began to read it out:

'"The Victoria Case – Point One. A step forward. The identification by Cowan's secretary means we must see Cowan again and ask him about the girl. Visit to be arranged."'

Merlin looked at Johnson. 'I'm going to be tied up tonight,

Inspector. I suggest you and I go tomorrow morning. Which hotel does he live in again?'

'The Dorchester, sir.'

'We'll go there at eight thirty.'

'Sir.'

'"Point Two. One step back – Cole's news is disappointing. He will, though, have one more crack at Mrs Walker on her own as just discussed."'

Merlin broke off. 'Is Robinson back today?'

'I think she's on tonight's sleeper from Edinburgh, sir,' said Bridges.

'Good. When you revisit Mrs Walker, Cole, take Robinson with you. If the woman is the nervy type, a bit of feminine sensitivity might be useful.'

The constable nodded.

'"Point Three. Another step forward perhaps – We have a new contact, Vincent Madeley, formerly an Abela accountant. He seems willing to inform on his old boss. A meeting is to be arranged tonight, during which records of vice operations and customers may be acquired. Could be of help if our girl was involved in prostitution."' Merlin looked up. 'Any questions? No?' He cleared his throat.

'"Curzon Case – Point One. David Hilton, Miss Curzon's agent. His revelation about the joint life insurance policy suggests a motive for murder on Adair's part. Urgent need to follow this up with the couple's lawyer."'

Merlin turned to Bridges. 'That's one for you, Sergeant.'

'Fine, sir.'

Merlin continued. '"Hilton's comments about the bad treatment of Miss Curzon in America raise more questions as to her state of mind. That said, Hilton still doesn't think she was the type to kill herself."' He stroked his chin thoughtfully.

'"Point Two. The junior porter at Seymour Mansions, Baxter, appears to have done a bunk. Does he have something to hide? Does he know something he doesn't want to tell us? Did he see

231

someone? Was he involved in her death? Clearly he needs to be tracked down. Sergeant Bridges to handle."'

'I'll get onto it tomorrow, sir.'

Merlin looked at Bridges thoughtfully. 'You know, Sam, given your domestic difficulties, it might be wise for you take tomorrow off and be with Iris. Baxter can wait until Monday.'

'No, sir, we need to get on. Iris will be alright.'

'Sorry, Sergeant. She sounds to me like she's at the end of her tether. You owe her a day at home.'

Bridges sighed. 'If you insist, sir.'

Merlin returned to his note. His face darkened as he read out the last line. ' "Orlov Case – Now closed." '

As soon as Merlin and Bridges were in the flat, the telephone began to ring. Merlin hurried over expecting it to be Madeley, but it was Sonia.

'Are you alright, Frank, darling. Why haven't you called?'

'Sorry, Sonia. I've been busy. I know that's no excuse.'

'I know you, Mr Chief Inspector. Once you're on a case, that's all you think about. Your poor old wife might be on the moon for all you care,' she said peevishly.

'Please forgive me.'

Sonia's voice softened. 'Very well.'

'How is everyone?'

'The baby and I are fine. My parents also, though I've been finding my mother . . . oh, what's the word in English . . . ? Tiresome, that's it, I've been finding her very *tiresome*.'

'The usual?'

'What do you think?'

'Can you speak freely?'

'Yes. They've both gone to the pub. My dad has finally got round to liking your filthy English beer. And, amazingly, my mother seems to like it too. They just left. I'm going to put the baby down then sit by the fire with my book.'

'At least you don't have to put up with your mother for an hour or two.'

'She's so annoying. Criticises everything I do with the child. Lectures constantly about how to be a good mother. "Do this, do that, don't ever . . ." At the beginning I can't deny I found her advice helpful but now I know what I'm doing, and still she nags on.'

'Why don't you come home, then?'

'That's exactly what I would like, Frank. It's time for us to come back to London. I'm worried, though, that you won't be able to put up with a bawling infant and a fat wife.'

'I'm sure I'll manage.'

'So you think I'm fat?'

'How do I know? I haven't seen you for a few weeks.'

'You pig, Frank Merlin! You will pay for that.'

'You know I think you are the most desirable creature in the world, Sonia. Fat or thin.'

'Frank!'

'When do you want to travel?'

'I thought I'd come towards the end of next week. I'll need a few days to prepare my parents. Maybe Thursday?'

'That should be fine.' Merlin glanced at his watch. It was almost half past six. 'Look, darling, I'm expecting an important call here any minute. A work call. Would you mind terribly if I ring off now. I can call you first thing tomorrow to finalise the travel arrangements.'

'Always, Frank, it is the work.'

'Sorry, sweetheart.'

Sonia sighed. 'You are who you are and I knew that when I married you. Off you go, then. I'll speak to you tomorrow. And please take care.'

Within seconds of putting the telephone down, it ran again. 'Merlin?'

'Madeley?'

'I have an old uncle who lives down by the river, south side. The house is the corner house at the junction of Bermondsey Wall and Mill Street. Number fourteen. Be there at eight.'

When Jean Parker got back from Harrods to Adair's house, she found him lying comatose on a sofa. There was an empty bottle of Jameson's whisky and traces of white powder on the small table next to him. She knew exactly what the powder was and became very angry. She hated drugs. However, weary from her shopping expedition and still put out by her unpleasant conversation with Tate, her anger against Adair subsided and she decided to take a nap in the bedroom.

She slept for longer than she'd intended and it was past seven when she woke. Her stomach rumbled and she remembered that Adair had promised to take her out to Rules restaurant for dinner. She was still in the clothes she'd worn to the shops and would need to clean up and change. In the bathroom down the corridor she found Adair, razor in hand, wearing only a towel around his waist. He looked terrible, with red blotches on his cheeks and dark shadows under his eyes. His nose was bleeding.

'Are you alright, Michael?'

He grunted something unintelligible.

'I guess we're not going out for dinner, then? You don't look up to it. I might as well go home and let you sleep it off.'

Adair said nothing but stared intently at his reflection in the washbasin mirror. He put down his razor and started to wash his face with a flannel.

Jean tugged at his arm in frustration. 'Michael, please say something.' All of a sudden he turned and flicked her face with the wet flannel.

'Ow!' Her hand went to her cheek. 'That stung! What was that for?'

He dropped the flannel and suddenly embraced her, a manic look on his face. He tried to kiss her but she shrugged him off, ran back to the bedroom and slammed the door behind her. There

234

was no lock on the door and she put her back to it to try and keep Adair out. It was hopeless and he easily pushed through into the room, making odd growling sounds. The towel had fallen off and he stood in front of her stark naked and clearly aroused.

Before she could scream, he clamped a hand over her mouth. With his free hand he began to tear at her clothes. She kicked out ineffectually and he then swung her onto the bed where he pushed her head into the sheets. He sat astride her and continued to pull at her clothes. When she was almost naked he turned her on her front and held a pillow against her face. She felt she was going to suffocate. By the time he removed the pillow, she'd lost the strength to do anything but whimper. She looked up into his eyes. Their normal cheery twinkle had been replaced by an eerie intensity. She did not know this person on the bed with her. Adair's lips curled and he spoke for the first time since her return to the flat. 'Come on Laura, you know you like it like this.'

Merlin and Bridges got a taxi to Tower Bridge then walked the last mile or so of their journey. A thick and freezing fog lingered over the pitch dark old dockland streets.

They had a torch with them but even so it was difficult to find the way. They made a couple of wrong turns but knew they were back on track when they saw the street sign for Mill Street. All was silence save for the faint hum of noise from the pub they'd passed thirty yards back. As they turned into Mill Street, they suddenly heard footsteps.

'Ahead of us? Madeley?' whispered Merlin.

'No I think it's two. And they're running.'

Bridges raised the torch and shone its beam directly ahead of them into the swirling fog. They could see nothing but then, like a stage curtain, the fog lifted.

Merlin squeezed Bridges's arm. 'There's the junction at the end of Mill Street, and . . . that must be the corner house. Hang on. Look, there's someone. Come on.' They had fifty yards to run and they ran it hard. The fog was still holding off as they closed in on

235

the corner house, and Bridges's torch picked out two shadowy figures in the road. When they got to them, they found one man kneeling next to another spreadeagled on the road.

The kneeling man turned a petrified white-bearded face to them. 'Don't kill me! I ain't got nothing.'

'Police. Just stay where you are and don't move.'

Bridges shone the torch down at the other man. The policemen groaned in unison. Madeley's lifeless eyes stared up at them. There was blood everywhere. The sergeant bent down to examine the body more closely. Beneath the man's shirt he found a gaping wound. 'He's been knifed, sir.'

'Poor fellow. Looks like his confidence about not being watched was unfounded.'

The old man spoke again, his voice choking with emotion. 'That's my nephew Vince there. Said someone was after 'im. Soon as he came through the door. "They're following me, Albert," he said. Seconds later there was banging on the door and they barged in. Two big louts.' Bridges turned his torch on the house and they saw the door, broken and loose on its hinges. 'They did for Vince then scarpered.'

Merlin walked around the corner and looked up Bermondsey Wall. The fog was thickening again and there was nothing to be seen or heard. He returned to help the old man to his feet. 'Come on into the house.' The old man resisted and reached out a hand to Madeley's body. 'Please come, sir. I'm sorry but there's nothing to be done for your nephew now. Have you got a telephone?'

'No, but there's a box around the corner.'

'I'll make the call, Sergeant. You take care of the gentleman. Albert, was it? I'll be back as quick as I can.'

Bridges helped Uncle Albert through the broken door and settled him on an ancient settee in the front room. 'Got a blanket I can cover you with?'

The old man looked up and fixed his rheumy eyes on Bridges. 'Do you?'

'Do I what, sir?'

236

'Do you want it?'

'Want what?'

'The thing Vince gave me.'

'What's that, then?'

The man reached under one of the settee cushions. 'This.' He handed Bridges a small paper bag. 'Vince stuffed it here as soon as he came through the door. Then those bastards came and did him in. Looked like they wanted something from him. Maybe this?'

Bridges opened the bag. There was a black notebook inside, about the size of a paperback.

In a lock-up garage off the North Circular Road, Joseph Abela was happily tinkering with his 1922 Hispano Suiza. As rich crooks go, Abela was a man of modest tastes. He liked women, of course, and he was in the right business to ensure a steady supply of those. He wasn't a gambler, but he liked to drink, though not to excess. He loved his wife and kids, provided they didn't make too many demands on him. His biggest indulgence was his classic car collection. He had an eclectic range of models, kept safe in a variety of secure garages scattered around North London. Of all his collection, this Hispano Suiza was his favourite. Unfortunately, the heavy demands of business gave him little time to enjoy it. This was the first evening in months he'd been able to spend with the car. He was, accordingly, extremely annoyed to have this precious time interrupted.

'You've got visitors, boss' said Harry Gough as Abela was adjusting a screw on the engine.

Abela reluctantly pulled his head from under the bonnet. 'Who the bloody hell is it?' There were two men with Gough. 'Oh it's you, is it?'

The towering young Garrett cousins generally feared no one, but Abela could tell they were jittery about something tonight. He soon found out they had grounds to be.

'So what are you two doing here?'

Jem, the older of the men, replied 'We thought there was some-thing you ought to know. Your Betty said we'd find you 'ere.'

'Black mark against her then. What's up?'

Robbie, the bigger of the two, stuttered 'It's like this, see, boss. It's Madeley. You remember you wanted us to ch . . . check him out this weekend? After you got a call from one of the c . . . coppers at Vice on Friday warning you that he might be up to no good?'

'Yeah. What about him?'

'Well, w . . . we followed him today. He went from his flat in The Elephant to a d . . . dingy little church off the Walworth Road. He was there most of the day. Had t . . . two interesting visitors.'

'Who?'

'Merlin and his sergeant.'

'That *is* interesting. What happened next?'

'The coppers spent an hour or two in the ch . . . church then cleared off. After a while, Madeley went back to his gaff. Popped out briefly e . . . early evening to make a call, and then after a little more time at home, headed out on foot.'

'Alright. Get to the point. You followed him presumably. What then?'

The cousins looked nervously at each other and Jem took up the story. 'We thought 'e might be off to another meet. Followed him a few miles, keeping our distance. Weren't easy in the dark, I can tell you. He headed towards Bermondsey, down by the river. Then . . .' he exchanged another nervous glance with Robbie 'then he must 'ave realised he was being followed and started to run.'

'Not surprising with you two big lumps doing the following. What happened then? Don't tell me. You started to run too?'

Jem nodded. 'We did, yeah.'

'If you're tailing people it's usually a good idea to avoid getting spotted and if you are, it's best to break off the tail. There would have been another time.' Abela looked at Gough. 'I have a terrible feeling I'm not going to like the way this story ends.'

'So 'e disappears into a house on Bermondsey Wall. As our cover was broken we couldn't see no reason not to have a little chat with 'im. See if he'd spill the beans about what he was doing. See if he had anything . . . what's the word . . . incriminating on 'im, like. So we banged on the door. 'E told us to piss off. Well, we weren't gonna take that so Robbie here knocked the door down. Then . . .'

Abela sighed. 'Yes?'

'Madeley came at us with a shiv. He's a pretty big bloke.'

'Champion boxer in his day.'

'Yeah, well, he knocked Robbie to the floor and 'ad the knife to his throat. Obviously I needed to do something. I kicked 'im and caught his arm. He jumped up and pushed me out the door. The kick had knocked the shiv out of 'is hand, so he put 'is hands around my throat and tried to strangle me.'

'Then I came at 'im.' said Robbie. 'I pushed him off Jem. I hadn't been c . . . carrying but I grabbed his own knife. As the b . . . bloke was trying to get up I stuck 'im. Stuck 'im good.'

Abela closed his eyes and groaned. 'So you're telling me you did him in?'

The two men looked miserably at the ground without saying anything.

'I see. And did you find anything of interest on him? Apart from the shiv that is.'

'No, boss. We had a quick rummage through 'is pockets, but nothing. Then the fog suddenly lifted and we could see a torch heading our way. 'Eard footsteps. Maybe Merlin we thought and did a runner.'

Abela sat down on the running board of his exquisite old car and ran an oily hand through his hair. 'You fucking morons. You killed a man unnecessarily right under Merlin's nose and you've got bugger all to show for it. We know nothing about why he'd been meeting Merlin. We don't know if he'd passed important stuff on. We don't know if he'd fingered anyone. We don't know diddly-squat, do we? Except that Madeley knew plenty of our secrets and was talking to the most dangerous detective in the Yard. We had to off Orlov because he was about to spill his guts and was out of our control. Madeley was not yet out of our control. You should have waited for the right moment to pull him in quietly. Then we could have found out what he was up to before chucking him in the river.' He got wearily to his feet. 'Harry, get someone round to his place and give it a thorough search. Warn his family to keep their mouths shut or they'll be dead too. And make sure they check out the church as well. Maybe Madeley used that as a place to stash things.' Abela looked sorrowfully at the two cousins. 'And Harry, I don't want that someone to be either of these two idiots. You'd best keep 'em out of my sight for a while. A long while.'

Archie Tate called out to the waiter. 'Get us glasses of your best brandy and leave the bottle here. We have some celebrating to do, eh, Victor?'

The two men had eaten a hearty dinner at The Dorchester. Over two years into the war and it was still surprisingly easy to eat at some London hotels and restaurants as if rationing didn't exist. Tate had chosen the beef, Goldsmith the venison, and the meat had been washed down by a fine claret. Goldsmith had already consumed more alcohol than he liked, but didn't want to be a killjoy and dampen Tate's high spirits. 'Of course, Archie. The Remy Martin is excellent.' The waiter hurried back with the drinks.

Tate filled the glasses to the brim. 'Here's to us, partner!'

'Yes, indeed, Archie. Partner!'

Tate, of course, would be a partner in name only. Silver Screen Productions was a one-man dictatorship and that's how things would continue. Goldsmith would brook no interference in management. He didn't think, however, it would take long to put Tate in his place. Apart from anything else, Tate was going to be kept too busy churning out his films to have time for anything else. Now, however, was not the time to discuss the running of the business.

'Is there any reason, Archie, why we can't get the lawyers to process the paperwork rapidly next week? I should think everything could get wrapped up by Wednesday at the latest. Then you could send the funds in by Friday.'

Tate studiously swirled the brandy in his glass. 'Hold your horses there, Victor. I'm happy to get the contracts done as soon as possible, but regarding the money, one hundred and fifty thousand pounds is a very substantial sum. I haven't got that sort of cash sitting idly by in a current account. Nearly all of my liquid assets are in stocks and shares or term deposits. I'll need a few weeks for timely liquidation to raise the necessary money. Some stockholdings are significant and I'll have to unload them carefully if I'm to get the right price.'

'How long do you think that'll take?' Goldsmith tried hard not to give any hint of concern in his voice.

'I'll have to speak to my broker, but my guess is five or six weeks for the stocks. In regards to the term deposits, I think I have around sixty-five thousand in six-month certificates of deposit maturing in early March.'

'You're saying we'll have to structure the deal to allow for money coming in stages over a three-month period, with the majority coming at the end?'

'Not a problem, surely? It's not like you're hard up for money is it?'

'No, no, of course not!' Goldsmith thought of suggesting that Tate borrow against the certificates of deposit to accelerate payment, with Silver Screen covering the interest. A moment's reflection told him this would look desperate. He had his bird in the hand and couldn't take the risk of scaring him away. 'That will be fine. We'll instruct the solicitors to draft it that way.'

Goldsmith sipped some brandy then pursed his lips. He'd had enough drink and he'd had enough of Archie Tate for one day. He yawned ostentatiously. 'I'm sorry, my old friend. I know you'd like to continue the celebration but it's been a long week and I'm pooped. If I drink any more I'll be asleep at the table. Will you forgive me if I head home?'

Tate looked disappointed for a moment then brightened. 'If you must, partner. But you'll have to make it up to me next week. We'll make a proper night of it when we sign the papers, eh? Perhaps we can arrange a little female companionship. What'd you think?'

Chapter Ten

Sunday December 14ᵗʰ 1941

Merlin had finally got home in the early hours of the morning. The forensic team had been slow coming and, once at the scene, the Bermondsey fog had hampered their investigations. They'd found nothing, but Dennis Armstrong had promised to repeat the search on Sunday morning in hopefully clearer conditions. The police doctor had examined Madeley's body and determined that a stab wound to the heart was the cause of death. When the two detectives had finally left the scene, Armstrong had retained the notebook but promised to return it to Merlin in the morning.

Before leaving for the Yard, Merlin called Johnson to cancel the planned visit to Cowan. The notebook had now become Merlin's priority. Then he made two further calls. The first was to Sonia as arranged. They agreed she would catch a morning train on Thursday the eighteenth which would get her and the baby into Euston at six in the evening. Merlin assured her he'd be there, come hell or high water. The second call was to Sergeant Bridges:

'I'm just calling, Sam, to check that you're going to be obeying my order today.'

'What order, sir?'

'My order to stay home and be with your wife.'

'Did you really mean it, sir? There's so much to do, particularly after last night. Iris . . .'

'Of course, I meant it. Take Iris out for lunch or something. Take her mind off the Far East. I can survive without you for a day.'

'If you insist, sir.'

'I do, Sam.'

'Can you . . . can you give me a call if there are any significant developments?'

'I'll try but I'm not making any promises.'

'Alright, sir.'

When Jean Parker came too, sunlight was poking through a chink in the curtains. For the briefest of moments, she thought the events of the previous night must have been a nightmare. Then she saw the bloody sheets and felt the pain kick in. It had all been too real. A male arm was draped over her shoulder. Adair looked to be fast asleep.

She carefully removed the arm, slipped out of bed, grabbed a dressing gown and crept to the bathroom. She examined herself in the mirror. There were purple bruises on both cheeks and her left eye had been blackened. There were several dried cuts on her face, one of which started bleeding again when she touched it. To her relief, her teeth were intact and her nose looked unbroken. She found a comb in the cabinet above the sink and attempted to do something with the tangled mess of her hair. After a few splashes of cold water to the face, she returned to the bedroom to get dressed. Her clothes of the day before were unwearable but she had a couple of other outfits in Adair's wardrobe. She was as quiet as possible and was just about to go out of the door when she heard his voice behind her.

'What are you doing, darling?'

'What the hell do you think I'm doing? I'm going!'

Adair levered himself up onto his elbows. She forced herself to turn and look at him. He was regarding her with bemusement. 'Was I snoring?' Then he rubbed the sleep from his eyes and saw her properly. 'Goodness, what on earth's happened to you? Did you walk into a door or something?' He reached out to touch her but she drew away in disgust. Despite her best efforts to hold herself together, she began to cry.

'I say, dear thing, whatever is the matter?'

'Don't pretend you don't remember.'

'Remember what? I can tell from my thumping headache that I must have had a little too much to drink. Presumably I crashed out?'

Jean's seething anger helped staunch the tears. 'You are a bastard, Michael. You drank too much. You indulged in your foul drug habit. Then went into some sort of delirious, manic fit, beat and battered me and violently forced yourself on me. You raped me. All these cuts and bruises you see were caused by you. I'm lucky not to be dead.'

Adair's expression shifted from bemusement to astonishment. 'Jean, darling, please. Look, I'm sorry if I drank too much and if the sex got a little out of hand. Some girls like it a bit rough, you know. Laura did. Perhaps I misunderstood and thought . . .'

Jean slapped him hard on the face. 'Look at me, Michael. These are not the marks of a bit of rough and tumble. These are the signs of violent assault. How dare you try to excuse yourself! Look at my clothes over there. They are ripped to shreds. You were worse than a wild animal. I am going home now. I should really be going to a police station.'

Adair got up. He approached her, naked, his arms spread wide and tried, unsuccessfully, to embrace her. She slapped him again and pushed him away. He fell back on the bed. 'Look, darling, if I behaved as you say, I'm most tremendously sorry. The booze and dope must have somehow got the better of me.'

'You can say that again.' The actress turned to the bedroom mirror and tried once more to untangle her hair with the comb. 'But you can't just put your behaviour down to drink and drugs. I think you ought to go and see a doctor, Michael. There is something seriously wrong with you.'

He sat on the edge of the bed looking pathetic. 'Please, Jean.

Don't go. It's true I am in a bit of a mess though I'm not really sure it's the sort a doctor can sort out. And then there's Laura . . . I've been so upset about the poor girl.'

'Don't try and blame this on Laura's death,' Jean snapped.

'No, of course not, but . . . but there's other stuff getting me down as well. There's . . . well, the fact is, I need money.'

'Come off it Michael. You're an established film star. A screen idol. Earning money beyond most people's wildest dreams. Don't dredge up such pathetic reasons for your behaviour. Get yourself off to Harley Street. Meanwhile . . .' She picked up her handbag and shopping bag from the previous day and turned to the door. 'Goodbye. I hope I never see you again!'

'What about the film?'

'What about it? Thanks to you, I doubt I'll be able to go in front of a camera for weeks.'

'But we have to finish the film, Jean. We can't let Victor down and I need to keep in with him. There are the other films, the fees . . . I really will be in dire straits if he and I fall out.'

Jean could bear the sound of Adair's voice no longer. She turned and left.

Cigar smoke, as usual, accompanied the illustrious passenger who entered the wardroom of HMS *Duke of York*, a destroyer ploughing its way through the towering winter waves of the North Atlantic. Captain Harcourt was not a smoker and sorely wished to tell his guest to put the damned thing out, but wisely decided that discretion was the better part of valour.

The Prime Minister acknowledge him with a wave of the hand as he sat down. 'While I sip my morning coffee, Captain, perhaps you'd show me our current position and future course on the map you have laid out on the table.'

The Captain leaned over Churchill's shoulder and put a finger on his charts. 'We are there, sir. Approximately two hundred and twenty miles directly south of the Faroe Islands and one hundred and sixty miles west of the Irish coast.'

'Still pretty close to Europe. Let's hope there are no Nazi U-boats or aircraft lurking nearby. We are still on schedule to arrive in Virginia as planned a week tomorrow?'

The Captain waved away another cloud of smoke. 'I can't say with certainty, sir. The weather conditions are challenging. We shall, of course, do our best. God willing we shall arrive there on December twenty-second.'

'God willing? Why would God not be willing? He is an Englishman, is he not?'

Humour was not one of Captain Harcourt's strong points. He stared back in confusion at the Prime Minister.

'A joke, Captain. A rather weak one so you are forgiven for not laughing. If God were in fact an Englishman, I doubt we'd all be in this dreadful mess in the first place. Perhaps he's American? Either way I'm covered. My mother was American.'

Winston Churchill had boarded the *Duke of York* two days before, after a period of intensive preparation, and in defiance of the White House, whose occupant thought it foolhardy of the PM to risk the appalling Atlantic seasonal weather and patrolling enemy vessels to cross the ocean. He had a large party with him, including Lord Beaverbrook, Averell Harriman, and the First Sea Lord, although everyone appeared to be elsewhere in the vessel this morning. His only attendant was his loyal and long-suffering personal doctor.

'Would you care for some breakfast, sir, or, as it's a little late, an early lunch?'

'They call it brunch, Captain. I believe the word originated in England, but the meal itself is more prevalent now in the United States. In any event, I am a late riser and thus used to a late breakfast, or brunch, or whatever you want to call it. However, this morning I thank you but must decline your kind offer. I don't seem to have much appetite.'

'I understand, sir. There is a pretty strong swell on.'

Churchill bristled. 'I can assure you, Captain, that any loss of appetite on my part bears no relation at all to the motion of the sea. Despite being a very senior officer, you seem to forget that here sits a former First Sea Lord. Indeed, a First Sea Lord twice over. I had the privilege of holding that august position between 1911 and 1915, and then again just prior to taking up my current job. I can assure you that a First Sea Lord lacking sea legs would be a creature abhorrent to nature. I do not require food for the simplest of reasons. I am not hungry. However, a little liquid refreshment would not go amiss. I'll take a mild whisky and water. Doctor Moran, who is lurking over there by the door, will have the same.'

The Captain disappeared and while he was away a radio operator came to deliver a cable to Churchill. The Prime Minister read the first page then summarised it to his principal medical advisor.

'Reports from the Far East suggest that the survivor list from the *Prince of Wales* and *Repulse* may be longer than initially expected. The current view is that over fifteen hundred may have been saved. That means around eight hundred dead. A terrible loss but . . .' he sighed 'we shall have to hope that our army commanders in Malaya are more effective against the Japs than were poor Tom Phillips and the navy.'

'Hear, hear to that.' said Moran.

The Prime Minister carried on: 'News from Hong Kong is not good. All troops and Imperial personnel on the Kowloon side have now completed their evacuation to Hong Kong island under heavy fire. The Japanese are massing their forces on the mainland prior to what will, no doubt, be a thunderous attack on our people. Spirits are still high, according to the commanders there, but they find it hard to remain confident of a successful outcome.'

Churchill removed his spectacles and set the report aside. He was deep in thought when a rating appeared with the whiskies. 'Put them down there, my lad.'

The ship took a sudden dip and Moran reached out to steady the whisky glasses.

Churchill was oblivious. 'Of course, while it's excellent that we now have American partners in arms, any meaningful intervention

248

on their part in the Pacific theatre of war must be months away. Much too late for our forces out there.'

'But don't we have substantial manpower in Malaya?'

'We have over eighty thousand men operating out of Singapore under Arthur Percival. He's not a bad soldier. Maybe he'll be able to take the fight to the Japs. And we have plenty of Aussies. They're damned good fighters. Perhaps I'm being too pessimistic.' He was thoughtful for a moment. Then he took a sip of whisky and picked up the second page of the wire. 'Let's see what else is in here.'

Merlin and Johnson had spent a frustrating morning waiting for Armstrong to turn up. Finally, just before midday, he arrived, puffing heavily after hurrying up the stairs. He handed Madeley's notebook to Merlin.

'Sorry, Frank. A busy morning repeating our search and then I got detained on something else. Regarding the book, I only got one print from it in the end and unfortunately that was the victim's.'

'Did you look at the contents?'

'Bunch of numbers and names. All gobbledegook to me but no doubt you'll make something of it.' He took a couple of deep breaths. 'Those stairs will be the death of me. I'm afraid our second outing in Bermondsey produced nothing of note. Now, if you'll forgive me I've got to get off. My name will be dirt if I miss a third family Sunday lunch in a row.'

'Off you go then. I'm envious. Having something nice?'

'Rabbit again, but done a different way to usual, I think. The missus can be quite inventive when she puts her mind to it.'

After Armstrong had left, Johnson went to stand beside Merlin so they could look at the notebook together. They went through the book carefully. Most of the pages had long lists of numbers with the odd word or letter occasionally inserted.

'An accounts book, Peter. I'm guessing these are some or all of the Abela business records he told us he'd retained.'

'For the prostitution racket, do you think, sir?'

'I presume so.' They gradually worked their way through the book and when they got to the last few pages, found they were laid out differently.

Merlin looked hard several times at each of these pages then said: 'I think these might be summaries of what has gone before.'

'I think you're right, sir.'

'Let's see what we can make of them.'

There were six of these pages in total, four set up one way, and the last two a little differently. Each of the first four pages had initials at the top, which Merlin and Johnson decided were probably page headings referencing the items beneath. The first page heading was 'CL', the second 'B(L)', the third 'S' and the fourth 'Y'. Beneath each heading were columns of letters and figures. The letters on the left led off with 'J', 'F' and 'M' and obviously had to refer to the months of the year.

'Sixteen letters, sixteen months, Peter. Ending in April.'

'What if the initials at the top refer to a criminal activity and the columns depict the takings from that activity over the period.'

'Sounds feasible. Some pretty big takings if you're right. Against April on the first page we have "5,200". Presumably five thousand two hundred pounds. That's a lot of money and there are plenty of other significant amounts on all the pages. Let's have a go at guessing the headings. Page one has "CL" at the top. I can't, off the top of my head, think of a criminal activity beginning "CL". Can you?'

The two men struggled away for several minutes. They flipped back and forth between the other pages seeking inspiration until Merlin tapped the desk and said 'I think I've got it. Perhaps the headings aren't specific activities but locations. Locations where business is done. So "CL" could stand for "Clubs". The Abelas have plenty of those.'

'So on the next page we have "B(L)". "B" for "Brothels"?'

'Maybe . . . but then what's the "L"?'

'The Abelas aren't just active in London. They have operations in places like Bristol and Southampton. So perhaps the "L" qualifies the location of the business. "B(L)" equals "Brothels(London)".'

'Good, Peter. Let's assume that's right. The next page has "S" as a heading. What do you reckon to that?'

'"Sex" is too general, I suppose.'

Merlin agreed and they got stuck on this for a while. Eventually Johnson asked 'What about "Streetwalkers"?'

'Or maybe "Street"? As opposed to clubs or brothels?'

'Prostitutes on the street corners? Yes that sounds more like it, sir.'

'So we have Abela vice activities in clubs, London brothels, and on the street. Then on the fourth page we have "Y". Now what the heck is "Y"? What location begins with "Y"?'

They couldn't think of a plausible answer to that question and after some time batting ideas around, Johnson said 'Maybe this one isn't a location. Madeley wasn't bound to be consistent in the way he categorised things, was he? Perhaps it's another form of descriptive word.'

Then Merlin had an idea. 'How about "Young" or "Youth"? That's the Abela activity Madeley got upset about and which supposedly drove him out of the gang. Maybe he decided to keep a specific record of activity involving youngsters?'

'Maybe, sir.'

'Perhaps Abela somehow ran it as a separate category of prostitution? In the absence of any other reasonable suggestion, let's go with that.' Merlin flipped back to the beginning of the notebook. 'So, if we're right, the pages at the back contain a summary financial record of these various subsections of criminal activity over a sixteen-month period. These pages which go before must give the underlying detail going into the summary. In terms of timing Madeley said he left Abela three or four months ago. Given that, I think it's fair to assume we're looking at summaries for the period before he left in 1940 and the first four months of this year.'

'He probably hadn't got the figures in for May and June by the time he left.'

'Sounds about right. There's always a lag of a few months finalising records in proper businesses, so why not criminal ones?'

Merlin flipped through the pages again and came to the last two. 'And what are we to make of these?' Here there were no figures, but the four categories they had identified were listed again. Beneath each were what appeared to be sub-categories and then a mix of names and addresses. Under the heading for clubs 'CL', was a sub-category 'CL-BP', under 'B(L) was 'B(L)-BP', and so on. Under 'CL-BP', were listed the names and addresses of four well-known clip-joints in Soho and Seven Dials. Under 'B(L)-BP' were four addresses, two in Mayfair and two in Knightsbridge. Under the last two categories, names rather than addresses were listed. Under 'S-BP' were the Christian names of four girls, and under 'Y-BP' were listed nine names, initial and surname, in two columns of six and three. The column of six had a couple of lines through it, while the names in the column of three were underlined.

Again the two policemen took their time over the pages. Then Merlin said: '"BP" has to be "Best Performers", don't you think? This is a list of the best performing clubs, brothels, street girls over the period.'

'I'd agree sir, except that doesn't account for the final "Y-BP" sub-category. If the names are those of girls, why not just show them as girls' Christian names as under "S-BP"? Why initials and surnames?'

Merlin grunted with frustration and disappointment. 'Perhaps we've got it all completely wrong, then.' He stared hard again at the list of names. An idea came to him. 'Peter. What if, in this case, Madeley has listed not the best performing young prostitutes but the best performing customers? The most prolific users of young prostitutes. Madeley said he kept a record of the bigger clients for young girls. Maybe this is it?' He looked at the page more carefully. 'Since he put lines through this column on the left, let's ignore those names for now.'

'These other three names on the right have been underlined.

Seems reasonable to assume they're the ones to look at,' added Johnson.

'Alright, agreed. We can always revisit the left column later, if need be.'

The three names had been entered in quite small print and weren't easy to read. Merlin bent closer to the book. The first name listed meant nothing to him. Nor did the second. When he saw the third, however, he got excited. 'Look Peter, last in the list. "G. Cowan". Is that our Gus, do you think?'

'Could be . . . and the second rings a bell too. "A. Tate." Perhaps that's that the film star. You know. Archie Tate.'

'That awful comedian.'

'He's not awful, sir. I quite like him.'

'Taste is a funny thing, Inspector, and I won't blame you for yours. But he makes my flesh crawl, and I wouldn't be surprised in the least if he turned out to have a taste for young girls.'

Johnson returned to his side of the desk and sat down. 'What shall we do then?'

'We were going to see Cowan anyway so that's something else to discuss with him. No doubt there'll be other listings with that name, as there will be of "A. Tate".'

'And of the first name, "M. Waring". I'll get onto it, sir.'

'First things first, though. To the Dorchester.'

Merlin hadn't called Bridges as he'd half promised, and when Bridges took the initiative and telephoned the Yard he was told that his boss and Johnson had just hurried out of the building. 'Forgotten me, he has,' he muttered to himself grumpily.

He'd spent the morning with Iris and thought he'd done some good. She seemed a little calmer at least. A friend of hers who also had a baby suggested a walk in Battersea Park with the prams. He'd managed to get Iris to agree and she'd just left. He would have an hour or two to himself and should really try to relax but he knew it was going to be impossible. It had been a terrible few days. The sinking of Dan's ship, Orlov's death, Madeley's stabbing. Then there was Iris's anxiety, the baby's demands, lack of sleep. Little wonder his nerves were taut.

In the front room there was a small desk where Bridges occasionally worked. He sat at it and opened his police notebook. The two specific tasks he had for Monday had already been entered. 'See lawyer re: insurance. Chase down Baxter.' He read over the notes he'd made of the Saturday meeting at the Yard. He had a feeling something was wrong. What was it? He read over the notes again. Something important was missing. Something important in the Curzon case. Then he realised. There had been no mention at all of the outstanding forensic matters. There had been nothing on the loose thread, the handkerchief, the perfume et cetera. As far as he was aware, they'd received no further reports and forensics should have been chased. Someone had dropped the ball and Bridges had the uncomfortable feeling it was him. He got a pencil and added the words 'Curzon forensics' to his list of To-Dos for Monday.

Cowan was nowhere to be found at his hotel, and reception had no information as to when he might be back. The two officers hung around for forty minutes then gave up and returned to the Yard.

There were messages awaiting them at the duty officer's desk. Cole had left one apologising for his absence. His mother had been taken ill and he'd had to accompany her to the hospital. There was also a message from Robinson informing them her train had been cancelled and she would now be on the Sunday night sleeper. Lastly there was a message that Bridges had called.

Back at his desk, Merlin thought for a minute before telling Inspector Johnson 'I'm not going to call Bridges back. He'll only argue about coming in. His wife deserves to have him to herself for at least one day at a very difficult time.'

'Of course, sir.'

'I hope Cole's mother isn't too seriously ill. He's very close to her, I believe.'

'That he is, sir. I believe he's been a rock for her ever since she was widowed.'

Merlin gave Johnson a solicitous look. 'I'm sure you're missing your wife, Peter.'

'Very much, sir.'

'Any prospect of an early return?'

'Not at the moment. My parents-in-law continue to be very poorly. Work allowing, I'm hoping to get up to Tyneside for Christmas.'

'You must do that, and to make sure, we'd better get on and solve these cases hadn't we? Can you go and see what you can dig up on the other two names?'

Johnson returned to his own office, and Merlin wandered over to the window thinking about Gus Cowan. Assuming the man on Madeley's list and the film producer were one and the same, what did all this information they now had on the man actually mean? That the man used prostitutes, young or old, did not mean he was a murderer. Nor did Miss Ryman's evidence that he'd consorted with someone looking very much like their dead Victoria girl. All circumstantial evidence but it was really piling up. It was likely, he thought, that Cowan would have some sort of answer to all his questions. He was a type who'd be hard to pin down.

He returned to his desk and considered for a while how best to tackle Cowan. Then his thoughts passed to the Curzon case. Although he was still trying to keep an open mind, he felt sure her death was neither suicide nor accident. There had to be something more to it. Maybe Baxter would be able to shed more light on things? They had further to delve on the drugs angle. There was Adair and the insurance. And, he suddenly remembered there were the outstanding forensic matters to resolve.

Over an hour and a half had passed when Johnson returned to interrupt Merlin's thoughts. He had a magazine in his hand.

'Progress, Peter?'

'I think so. I started with M. Waring. Surprisingly there was only one person with that name listed in the London phone book.

He has an address in a particularly rough part of the East End. I've noted the details but my first instinct was that our man wouldn't live somewhere like that. I think you'd have to be wealthy to be a big client of Abela's.'

'And have a nice house in a good area.'

'Yes. So, I made the assumption that our Waring was ex-directory. I wondered how best to track him down on that basis. I took a little punt. A wealthy man might have an active social life. A wealthy man with an active social life might find himself mentioned in gossip columns. I remembered there was a collection of *Tatler* magazine back copies in the police library. I got a key from the duty desk downstairs and went to have a look. Six issues in, I believe I struck gold. There was a photograph of a man called Marcus Waring at a war bond fundraising party in a Mayfair hotel. The party was in September. Look.'

Johnson passed the magazine to Merlin. A slender man with slicked back hair, a small moustache and saturnine good looks was smiling at the camera, champagne glass in hand.

'Smooth looking fellow.'

'The magazine describes him as a City financier and industrialist, a Kensington resident and a generous supporter of the war effort.'

'Pillar of the community but secret paedophile, eh? We shall see. Got an address?'

'Not yet. I'm going back to the Library now to see if I can find it.'

'Good work, Peter. I'd like to know a little more about him before arranging an interview. If and when you get the address we should take a look, get the lay of the land.'

It took a while for Johnson to get what he was looking for. He eventually found Waring's address in a copy of the 1939 Kensington and Chelsea Electoral Register which was at the bottom of a pile of miscellaneous documents on one of the top shelves. He hurried back up to Merlin and they grabbed a car and headed for Kensington.

The road was one of several to the north of Kensington High Street and close to Holland Park. They parked their car a distance away from Waring's house. It was dark now and they had not brought a torch. The blackout meant there were no street lamps and they only had the moon to light their way. When they reached Waring's place, they stopped on the pavement opposite. From what they could see, the house was quite a grand affair. Merlin counted five floors. At the top was a strange dome-like structure which was not replicated in any of the neighbouring houses so far as he could see. He nudged Johnson and whispered. 'Looks a bit like a mosque up there.'

'An observatory, perhaps, sir?'

Merlin shrugged and looked at his watch. It was six thirty-five. He could see the outline of a tree a little further along the pavement. 'We're too much in the open here in the moonlight. Let's get cover over there. I'd just like to hang around for twenty minutes or so. I know we're not likely to see anything, but you never know. When we're done, there's a nice little pub nearby where I'll buy you a drink.'

They'd been behind the tree for close to the allotted twenty minutes when a van pulled up outside Waring's house. It looked like a grocer's van but in the dark they couldn't see if there was any lettering on the side. Someone got out from the passenger's side, and seconds later someone from the driver's side. Merlin heard subdued male voices and then silence. The men didn't move and Merlin thought for a moment they might have somehow registered the policemen's presence. Then they turned and went to the rear of the vehicle. There was the rattle of doors opening, then more voices. Female this time, and they sounded anxious. Merlin's heartbeat began to accelerate.

One of the men said 'Shut the fuck up, girls. I'll thump the next one who speaks. Follow George to the front door.'

The moon dipped behind some clouds and the policemen couldn't see anything. They heard the rap of a knocker, the opening of a door, a brief muffled conversation, the sound of feet shuffling, and finally the door slamming. Then the moon suddenly reappeared and they were able to watch the men get back into the van and drive away.

'What do you think of that, Peter?'

'Perhaps they were waitresses being delivered to work at a party?'

'Would a man speak to waitresses like that? "Shut the fuck up or I'll thump you." I think not. This was something more sinister. A delivery of young prostitutes more likely. Right in front of our eyes. The question is, what to do? We have to do something, that's for certain.' He looked down in thought. 'That pub I mentioned is only a ten-minute walk away. Come on. We can discuss things properly there.'

When they got to The Windsor Castle, Merlin ordered a couple of shandies and found a quiet corner. 'Nice place this. Used to come here with Alice before we were married. She liked going out to pubs, unlike most women of my acquaintance. Anyway. To the matter in hand. I'm thinking we should get a warrant.'

'On what grounds, sir?'

'On the grounds that we have reason to believe an abuse of minors is about to take place. I'm going to assume that this Waring is the man in Madeley's book.'

'A bold assumption, sir?'

'If I'm wrong we'll soon find out. I know we weren't able to see the girls but if he's our man, chances are some or all of them are under-age. And if he's our man, what do we think he's going to do with them? Give them elocution lessons? I think not. If we believe he's going to have some kind of sexual relations with the girls, we are entitled to a warrant. We could also justify a warrant, at a stretch, on the basis that we anticipate a breach of the peace.'

'It's a bit of a stretch and I don't believe it will be that easy to justify a warrant, sir. If we're wrong, there'll be hell to pay.'

'I know, Peter. But we must take our chances.'

'Remember, it's a Sunday night. It's not going to be so easy to track any judge or magistrate down, let alone a compliant one.'

258

'We can but try. We'll need to get some more men too. Come on. Knock back your drink. Let's get back to the Yard.'

Waring had spent an absorbing afternoon supervising the preparation of the observatory for the evening ceremony. The circle, the pentagram, the runic symbols, the animals, the knives, the swords, the table, the receptacles, the sheets, the gowns – all had been laid out or prepared in accordance with the Black Book of Gilgagoth, and all that had been done or was to be done reflected the authentic revisions newly recommended by Crowley. The sliding section of the observatory roof had been opened to admit the lunar light.

It was half past eight and he was entertaining his twelve male guests with drinks and canapés in the library, prior to the main business of the evening. Conversation had begun to flow freely after a slightly stilted start. Crowley, ever the iconoclast, was wearing a striped red and white blazer and blue-spotted bow tie. He was holding court with two powerful-looking men, one of whom Waring knew to be a successful publisher, and the other an eminent economist. The two men were listening with rapt attention. It never ceased to amaze Waring how many respected figures of authority in London society had a secret interest in the dark side of the universe.

An elderly, monocled dilettante whom Waring had met in Monte Carlo before the war sidled over to him. 'Aleister Crowley, eh, Waring? That adds a little zip to the evening.'

'I hope it does, Torode. He is a fascinating man.'

'Indeed he is. You have done well in getting him to attend. When I was in California in '38, I was friends with Aldous Huxley. I presume you've read some of his books?'

'*Brave New World*. Very thought provoking.'

'Quite so. In any event, I spent a lot of time with Huxley. He was a great admirer of Crowley. Thought he had a magnificent intellect. He also . . . er . . . had some rather wild stories to tell about him.'

Waring's eyes skipped to the nearby bookshelf where several of Crowley's works were shelved. 'He has certainly lived an adventurous life. A supremely original thinker in so many spheres – philosophy, the creative arts, the occult, sexuality . . .'

Torode put a hand on Waring's arm and gave him a sly look. 'Speaking of which, dear fellow, are the Handmaids of the Dark Lord already in place?'

'Yes, they are being prepared upstairs.'

'Good, good. As comely as always?'

'Of course.'

'And when is the ceremony to commence?'

'In an hour or so. Give or take. Luckily we have a reasonably clear night. '

'Excellent. That gives me plenty of time to go and speak to the man himself.' Torode melted away in Crowley's direction. Soon after, Waring could hear 'The Beast' lecturing him excitedly on the subject of his latest literary undertaking, *The Book of Thoth*.

'Look, Joe. I've been thinking. I definitely do want to proceed with our arrangement as originally discussed.' Goldsmith leaned back in his chair, telephone receiver in hand. He was at the studio where he'd spent most of Sunday secluded with Seltzer running over the figures of the three films currently in production and the two planned to commence in the first half of the New Year. His after-dinner discussion with Tate had given him yet another disturbed night. Did the man really have the money? His flannelling about when the cash would become available was worrying. He'd had plenty of experience over the years of people pretending to have greater wealth than they had. For God's sake he'd been guilty of it himself on many occasions. Goldsmith's contacts in the City, however, had given Tate a clean bill of health, so perhaps he was only telling the truth? Or perhaps he was introducing the delay as a bargaining ploy so that he could start chiselling at the terms on Monday? 'Improve the deal, Victor, and I'll make sure the money comes in quicker.' Whatever the truth, it clearly wasn't wise to rely totally on Tate. He needed certainty and that he could only get from Joe Abela.

The gangster took a long time to reply. Eventually, he said: 'I'm not a man who likes to chop and change you know, Victor. After our last conversation, when you suggested you didn't need the money, I put some thought into the reallocation of the funds set aside for you.'

Goldsmith sighed. He knew where this was going. 'So what are you saying, Joe. You don't want to do the business now?'

'No, Victor. I'm just saying that fairness demands that there be a rearrangement fee, if I have to adjust my plans again.'

Goldsmith tried to remain calm. 'That would be instead of the cancellation fee?'

'Oh no. In addition. There would be a cancellation fee and a rearrangement fee.'

Goldsmith sighed again. 'You know, Victor, I hate doing business over the telephone. Why don't we discuss this in person? Come round to my place. I'll break out one of my vintage malts and we can resolve everything over a civilised drink. What do you say to that?'

Abela took a moment to think before he agreed. 'Alright, Victor, I don't mind doing that. But if you think I'll be more easy-going face to face, I wouldn't get your hopes up.'

'Half six tomorrow night good for you? You know where I am?'

'Of course. I make it a rule of my business to know where all my important clients live.'

'Of course you do. Until tomorrow night.' He put the phone down. He'd need to have the house to himself. Valerie would have to go out. It might be a good idea to have Ted near at hand, though. Abela was one of the biggest crooks in London after all. It would be wise to have some security.

In the flickering candlelight, Waring held the long ceremonial dagger high above his head then lowered it. In one smooth

261

movement he slit the throat of the first sacrificial victim. There was a gargling noise after which the only sound in the room was that of the victim's blood hitting the marble floor.

The second sedated victim was swiftly brought forward. Waring intoned the prescribed Latin words then repeated the procedure with equal efficiency. After the sound of spurting blood had subsided, the circle of masked celebrants linked hands and began to sway and chant a litany, the words an ancient mixture of Latin, Greek and medieval French. All the circle were in red robes while Waring wore blue. The moon began to edge into view in the open space above them and its beams mixed with the candlelight to produce an eerie blue-green light. When the moon was fully visible to all in the circle, the chanting stopped and Waring stepped up onto the black-draped table behind him. He spread his arms and bowed his head three times. At this signal, some of the robed men broke the circle and disappeared through a door at the back of the room. When they returned, they led four white-robed girls up to Waring. The girls appeared to be in a trance, with eyes only half open. Their robes were removed and they were lifted, naked, onto the table. The men positioned them on their backs with their feet facing towards the circle. There was a communal sigh as Waring held up a large silver goblet filled with blood from the two sacrificial victims. The deep crimson of the liquid shimmered in the moonlight as Waring slowly trickled the blood over the pale skin of the first girl and then the second, third and fourth. The chanting resumed, becoming louder and more insistent until Waring raised the dagger high above him again, his eyes fixed on the waxing moon. The voices picked up again and with everyone rapt in attention, no one heard the sound of heavy boots tramping up the stairs towards them.

Merlin was first into the room, followed by Johnson and three of the uniformed officers who'd been dragooned into Merlin's search party. The scene he saw was hideous. Before a masked audience, an unmasked man in robes stood on a table, dagger in hand, with four naked female bodies drenched in blood beneath him.

262

The scene got worse when Johnson shone his torch in front of the table to reveal a tangle of bloodied limbs glistening in the moonlight.

Merlin eventually found his voice. 'Hand your weapon over.' Without complaint, Waring did as he was asked. 'Can you check if those poor girls are alive, Inspector?'

Johnson moved forward and bent over the nearest girl. 'This one's breathing, sir.' He carefully went down the line. 'All alive, sir. I don't think this blood is theirs.'

'Thank God for that. So what is that disgusting mess?' Johnson pointed the torch down again and Merlin knelt to examine it. When he realised what he was looking at he got back to his feet with an odd mixture of revulsion and relief. 'Goats or sheep, Peter. Goats I think. They've had their throats cut.'

Johnson picked up the goblet which Waring had set down on the table and sniffed it. There was still an inch or two of blood at the bottom. 'Looks like the goats' blood was put in here, then poured over the girls for whatever reason.'

'Hmm.' Merlin turned to the uniformed constables. 'Can two of you get these girls cleaned up and find something for them to wear.' He looked up at Waring. 'Are there any women in the house who can help my men in this task?'

'There are female servants below.' Waring sounded strangely calm, as if Merlin and his men had just invaded a tea party.

'Presumably the girls were wearing something earlier?'

Waring inclined his head to his right and Johnson's torch picked out the girls' discarded robes on the floor.

'And we could do with some light in here, Inspector.'

Johnson found the light switch. 'Could you all move back to the wall please.' The men in the circle did as they were told, allowing Merlin a clear view of the various odd symbols set in the floor. The largest was a circle enclosing a five point star.

'A pentagram, Inspector. Put together with the sacrificed goats and everything else, we appear to have interrupted a Satanic mass.' He surveyed the celebrants. 'Anyone care to explain what's going on here?' Silence. He turned to the man on the table. 'Mr Waring, I presume? Anything to say?'

Waring spoke calmly again, but now there was an edge in his voice. 'Yes, officer. I'd like to know by what authority you have invaded my private residence and halted a perfectly legal gathering.'

'By virtue of the search warrant I have in my pocket, the details of which I suggest we discuss back at the Yard.' He turned back to the others. 'Please remove your masks.'

This request prompted a minor stampede as several of the men made a burst for freedom. Two of the three constables at the door were occupied helping the girls. The third free officer struggled but was overwhelmed and pushed to the ground. Johnson jumped across and managed to grab hold of two of the fleeing men but three got through. Merlin had left two other constables on the ground floor. He shouted down a warning.

Chapter Eleven

Monday December 15th 1941

It was half past six and Merlin had only just got into bed when the telephone rang. He hauled himself out to take the call. It was the AC. He didn't sound happy.

'For God's sake, Chief Inspector, what on earth have you been up to now? The Commissioner just rang me to say he'd been called in the middle of the night by the senior partners from two of London's biggest solicitors firms. One complained that an eminent colleague had just been arrested, and the other ditto regarding one of his best clients. In both instances you were apparently the arresting officer. You'd better have a good explanation for this.'

'I do, sir.'

'Then be so good as to be in my office at eight to give it to me.'

There was clearly no point in trying to grab some sleep. He had a quick bath, dressed and headed to the Tube station. On the train he considered the night's events.

It had taken two hours to find a magistrate willing to issue a search warrant. Once that had been done, men were needed. Luckily there were a large number of officers on night duty, and he managed to corral five of them into his search party. Then they'd set off in two cars and arrived at Waring's house just after ten.

Merlin had asked the servant at the door for Waring. The man had lifted his eyes upwards by way of response. Leaving two constables in the hallway, Merlin had raced up the stairs with Johnson and the rest of the men, checking each floor on the way, until they reached the top and came upon Waring's ceremony. Over the next hour Black Marias were organised and the host, his guests, the girls and the servants transported to the Yard. Of the three men who'd escaped down the stairs, one had somehow managed to get away. The constables he'd evaded described him as a fat bald fellow with a surprising turn of speed.

Back at the Yard, Merlin had interviewed Waring while Johnson had taken responsibility for coordinating the interviews of all the others. Waring had been exact and polite in his responses. It was not against the law to hold Black Masses, morally repugnant as some may find it; it was not illegal to slit a goat's throat; there had not been any physical or sexual assault on the girls who were, in any event, willing participants in the ceremony; the girls had confirmed to him that they were all of age; he had given tranquillisers and liquor to them at their request. In cricketing terms, Merlin thought, Waring had played an immaculately straight bat. At some time in the early hours of the morning, he'd decided to break off and let Waring stew while he saw what he could get from the girls, who'd not yet been questioned by anyone. However, they'd all still been too out of it for any sensible discussion.

He'd then seen Johnson to find out how the other interviews had gone. A couple of Waring's guests had provided nothing more than names and addresses. The rest had been reasonably compliant. All were men of substance. Lawyers, accountants, academics. They admitted interest in the occult and that was why they were at the house. Like Waring, they'd asserted the legality of their actions. None had admitted to any involvement in recruiting the girls. Waring had been responsible for all the arrangements. No one had seen, let alone participated in, any assaults on the girls.

Waring's servants had revealed little of interest, saving the fact that the ceremonies were a regular occurrence in the house. After due consideration, Merlin had agreed with Johnson that everyone be released with the exception of Waring and the girls. Johnson had everyone's personal details. All lived in London and could be contacted easily, if required. He doubted anyone would try to disappear.

He thought it unlikely, in any event, that he'd want to pursue Waring's guests through the courts. They'd have access to good lawyers and it would be a major undertaking. Better, he thought, as the train pulled into Westminster, to concentrate his enquiries on Waring alone, while also hoping that the girls would be able to shed important light on Abela's prostitution racket and perhaps even the Victoria girl.

'So, Chief Inspector.' The AC looked sternly across his desk, chin jutting out. It was an expression Merlin had seen many times before. He was not fazed. Calmly and assuredly, he provided the AC with a full description of the night's events and the actions taken. By the time he'd finished, Gatehouse's features had relaxed.

'What I don't understand is why you didn't call me at the outset, Frank? Before you went off looking for a magistrate. I could have made the process smoother and quicker.'

'Well, sir, I did think about it but it was a Sunday night and I didn't want to disturb you.'

'Poppycock, Frank!'

Merlin paused to search for the right words. 'I'll admit, it did occur to me, given Waring's high profile, that you might have felt obliged . . . um . . . to inform the Commissioner of the situation.'

The AC's mouth turned down. 'I can't be trusted, is that it?'

'I wouldn't put it like that, sir.'

'So how would you put it?'

'I always place the greatest confidence in your support and judgement, sir. As to the Commissioner, however . . .' Merlin shrugged.

'I think it's probably best not to go down that path.' The AC fiddled with his collar stud. 'Just make sure you confide in me promptly the next time something like this happens. What are your plans now?'

'As I mentioned in my summary, I'm going to go after Waring

alone. We haven't the time or resources to consider something on a grander scale.'

'I suppose we must be thankful for small mercies.'

Merlin ignored this remark. 'The potential crime in issue here is abuse of minors. If I can get the girls to talk then maybe I'll have something with which to nail Waring.'

'And estimable as it would be if you succeeded in doing that, how exactly does it advance your Victoria case?'

'I'm hoping the girls will be able to give us something on Abela's trafficking of young girls.'

'But at present, you don't know for certain it was Abela who sent these girls. You said Waring wouldn't say where the girls came from.'

'It's a reasonable inference, I think, from the presence of Waring's name in Madeley's notebook. But of course the girls can confirm whether we're right and they haven't done so yet. However, even if the girls had nothing to do with Abela or the Victoria girl, surely it's valuable and important to glean whatever information they have? It might help us eliminate this type of crime? This child prostitution.'

'Hmm.' The AC grimaced and flashed his gums. 'But, Frank as we still don't know exactly who this girl is, this is all highly speculative. As to bringing an end to any type of prostitution, you should bear in mind King Canute and his attempt to halt the waves.'

'There is a chance, of course, small though it may be, that the Victoria girl was known to one of the girls downstairs. Perhaps she was on the menu at another of Waring's events? Who knows?'

'Alright, Frank. I won't detain you any longer. You've a lot to be getting on with. I suppose I'll have to call the Commissioner. He was waiting on our talk.'

Merlin struggled to his feet. Lack of sleep was beginning to tell.

'And Frank, after ranting at me about the arrests, the Commissioner still remembered to ask about the Curzon case. Any more progress on that?'

'Bridges is following up some important leads today.'

The AC's eyebrows rose. 'Much as I admire the good Sergeant, don't you think it should be you following up these leads, with his assistance?'

Merlin was already halfway out of the door. 'If you'd like to get a saw, sir, and cut me in two . . .'

Victor Goldsmith was down on the studio floor later than he'd intended after another restless night. Kaplan was filming a scene set in a police station. It featured a cameo appearance by an old music hall comedian Goldsmith had known years before. As soon as the director shouted 'Cut', the old man hurried over to greet the producer.

'Victor, old boy. You're looking good, dressed to the nines in your Savile Row finery. You've done very well for yourself since last we met, haven't you?' There was a hint of the West Country in his accent.

'Billy, my friend.' The men shook hands. 'I've missed you. Glasgow Empire 1933, I think, was the last time. You're looking good too. Remembered all your lines, I hope?'

Billy Walters made a bow. 'Once a pro, always a pro, Victor. Word perfect wasn't I, Emil?'

'Indeed you were, Billy. Now I hope you don't mind, but I need a few private words with Victor.'

'Of course. Catch you later, Victor. See you for lunch in the canteen at one? Chew over old times?'

'That would be lovely, Billy.'

'And, Victor . . .'

'Yes?'

'Thanks for thinking of me.'

Goldsmith patted Walters on the shoulder then turned to follow Kaplan to a distant corner of the studio.

'Jean Parker called me at seven this morning, Victor. Said she wasn't feeling well. I asked her what was wrong and she burst into tears then slammed the phone down. Shortly after, Adair called.

Despite the hour he was plastered. The gist of what he had to say was that if Jean said anything bad about him I should know it was rubbish. Fact was, she'd fallen down some stairs. Entirely her own fault. Nothing to do with him.'

Goldsmith threw his hands in the air. 'My God! That's all we need. The bastard must have beaten Jean up.'

'Sounds very much like it and now we are short two stars, not just one.' Kaplan started wringing his hands. 'But what am I to do? I had planned to do Jean's few remaining scenes without Michael in the first part of the week, and then catch up with Michael on Thursday and Friday. All being well, I could have made the final wrap just in time before Christmas. But now . . .'

Goldsmith asked a passing electrician to get him a chair. 'I need to sit and think for a moment.' If Jean Parker was in a bad way, he had no choice but to halt the whole production immediately with a view to finishing it in January at the earliest. The release date would have to be put back, money would be lost and there would be a knock-on impact on other productions. Before committing to such a drastic course of action, however, he needed a reliable report on Jean Parker's condition.

'Emil, I'm going to ask Valerie to go round to Jean's place and assess the damage. Perhaps we'll be lucky and find all that's needed is a good make-up job. If so we have the best people. Meanwhile you carry on with whatever you can today. We'll talk again when I've heard from Valerie.'

Merlin was cheered by the welcome sight of WPC Clare Robinson smiling at him through the half-open door of his office. 'Come in and sit down, Constable. You've been sorely missed.'

Robinson took a seat at the desk.

'I'm going to put a ban on any of my team going away on these stupid courses from now on.'

'It was very educational, sir.'

'I'm sure it was. Criminology?'

'Yes, sir.'

'I hope they've moved on from those mad theories that you could tell criminals by the shape of their skulls. Anyway, I'm glad you're back. Someone filled you in have they?'

'DI Johnson just gave me a quick run-down.'

'Well, bully for him if he was able to condense everything into "a quick run-down". Originally I had planned for you to join Cole on his next visit to Mrs Mary Walker. However, I'm not sure he's in this morning. Did Johnson tell you about his mother?'

'That she'd been taken to hospital, yesterday? Yes, sir. But I was with the Inspector when Cole called a quarter of an hour ago. Apparently it wasn't as bad as they thought. Some sort of minor seizure. She's been kept in for today but all seems well so Tommy, I mean Cole, is on his way in.'

'That's good to know, but I've changed my mind. There's something else I'd like you to do and Cole can deal with Mrs Walker on his own. I presume Johnson has told you about the young girls downstairs?'

'Yes, sir.'

'I think you're the best person to interview them. We need to know how they ended up at Waring's house, what really happened there, what their real ages are, who they work for and what they know about that organisation's set up. I shall be surprised if they're not working for Joe Abela. Oh and . . .' Merlin picked up the envelope containing the artist's drawings. 'Cole will need these again later for Mrs Walker, but as he's not here you get first use today. See if any of the girls recognise our Victoria girl.'

'Have they been questioned at all?'

'I tried last night but they were in no fit state. I'm told they're in better shape this morning but pretty unhappy. Off you go then.'

An excited Cole arrived before Robinson could get through the door. 'Sorry to interrupt, sir, but the second I got in I got a call from Mrs Walker's neighbour to say she'd been attacked this morning and was in a bad way.'

'*Madre de Dios*! Well, don't hang about. You'd better get round there now.'

Cole looked awkwardly at Robinson. 'You said I should take Constable Robinson with me when I went to the hospital next.'

'I did, but now I've given her something else to do. You can continue on your own.'

'Righto, sir.'

'And Cole.'

'Sir?'

'Glad to hear your mother's alright.'

At the studio, Goldsmith was receiving bad news over the telephone. His wife was with Jean Parker. 'She's in a dreadful state, Victor. The police have been called. You have to sack Michael Adair. The man is a monster. Jean has told me everything.'

'Valerie, Valerie. He may be a monster but he is *my* monster. I can't just sack him. I have a ton of money in this latest film. He has to complete it for me and how is he going to do that if he's in jail?'

'Well, I'm sorry about that, Victor, but the man almost killed her. Jean's face is a complete mess, she's got bruises all over and he sexually assaulted her.'

'How the hell can he have sexually assaulted her? They've been lovers for months.'

'It is possible, Victor, you know, to rape your own wife. Apparently Michael went on a huge drink and drugs binge and became demented. He beat her up, ripped off her clothes and took her against her will. That is rape!'

'God help us! When did she call the police?'

'She didn't. She was too overwrought to think straight. I called them.'

'Jesus Christ, Valerie. What the . . .' Goldsmith managed to stop himself before saying something he'd regret. It was pointless losing his temper with his wife. In normal circumstances he'd probably have applauded her action. These were not normal circumstances, however. His studio was on the precipice of ruin and he had an important film to complete. He closed his eyes and kneaded his forehead. 'Yes, well, I'm sure you did the right thing, darling. It just . . . well, it just makes life a little complicated.'

'Will you be staying at the studio tonight, Victor?'

'No. I'm coming back into town. I have a meeting at the house. I hope you don't mind but it would be best if you went out for the evening.'

'Are you saying that because you're angry with me?'

'No, darling, no. It's just that I have some important business which I don't . . . I don't want to mix up with . . . with my family. If you are there, I have to introduce you and I'd prefer . . .'

'Alright, Victor, I get it. Don't worry. I'll call the Duchess. I'm sure she'll be up for dinner at Scott's.'

'Thank you, my darling. I appreciate it.' He had calmed down a little and when he'd put the phone down was able to think more clearly. If Adair went to jail he'd have to junk the entire production of *Murder at Midnight*. Either that or reshoot all Adair's scenes with a new actor. The delay and expense would be disastrous even if everything else was rosy, as it was not. He had to try and pull a string or two to keep the actor out of police hands. He considered the possibilities then called out to his secretary. 'Gloria, see if you can get me Mr Korda on the line.' Vincent Korda's close relationship with the Metropolitan Police Commissioner might be a good string to pull.

Mary Walker had already been hospitalised by the time Cole got to her Holborn flat. McAllister had made it perfectly clear over the phone that she'd been badly hurt, so Cole wasn't surprised. There were two officers from Holborn police station with the Scot in the flat and Cole quickly explained why he was there. McAllister was just going over his statement with the officers. When the officers were satisfied, the senior one, Sergeant Harley, turned to Cole and began to summarise what had happened.

'Mr McAllister here heard a racket at about eight fifteen this morning. Shouting, screaming, pots and pans being thrown around and so on. Apparently this was not a unique occurrence.'

McAllister intervened. 'I told these officers what I told ye before, Constable. About the rows.'

'Mr McAllister didn't actually see the person arguing with Mrs Walker but is certain it was her estranged husband.'

'Och, it had to have been him. I could hear a man shouting abuse. I've never actually exchanged words with Walker but he was the only male visitor she ever had. Apart from him, her only visitors were lady customers.'

'Why don't you carry on and tell Constable Cole exactly what happened yourself, sir?' Harley suggested.

'Alright, Sergeant. First of all, when the racket began, I turned the volume of the radio up to drown the noise of them going at it. As ye know Constable, when I'd tried to intervene in their rows before I'd been sent packing so I sat tight. But it kept on going and I banged on the wall a few times. Soon after it went quiet. I usually go to buy a newspaper around that time in the morning, so I went out the door. As I passed I thought I'd better try and check if she was alright. I knocked several times but nae answer. Naturally I got worried. As ye know, I have a spare key from her for emergencies and the like. I went back into my place to get it and came in to find her sprawled unconscious on the living room floor over there.' He inclined his head to the fireplace. 'Just to the right of the mantelpiece. Her face was bloodied and bruised and it looked like she might have broken her nose. Her breathing was very shallow.'

The sergeant added: 'The medics had a quick look at her before they took her away. She was as Mr McAllister described but they also found red marks on her neck.'

'He tried to strangle her?'

'Someone certainly put his hands around her neck and exerted pressure. Whether there was intent to kill, that remains to be seen.'

'So I ran straight away to the telephone box and called 999. Then ye, Constable.'

'For which, many thanks Mr McAllister.' Cole walked over to the fireplace and bent down to examine the bloodstains Mary

Walker had left on the carpet. 'Quite a lot of blood. Which hospital, Sergeant?'

'The London in Whitechapel.'

'And what do you plan next, if you don't mind my asking?'

Harley, a tall man with thinning grey hair and a hawk-like nose patted the shoulder of his powerfully built young colleague. 'I'm going to ask Dooley here to spend an hour or two canvassing the neighbours, and then get off to the hospital to monitor Mrs Walker. As for me, I'm going to Holborn nick to pick up a couple of men and go in search of Mr Walker.'

'You have an address for him?'

'I've an idea where he lives, Constable', said McAllister. 'Mary and I were chatting one day about the Oval cricket ground. I'd seen a story in the paper. The Government had announced they'd taken the place over as a reception area for Prisoners of War, though none had gone there yet. Mary remarked in passing that her Sid lived near the ground. In Magee Street, if I remember rightly. She didn't mention a number, though.'

'We'll just have to knock on every door then, won't we?' said the sergeant. 'It's a while since I was round that neck of the woods. Last time was in '38 when I was on crowd duty. The match Hutton got his 364 against the Aussies.' The sergeant savoured the memory briefly. 'You're welcome to join our search party, Constable.'

'I would love to, Sergeant, but I'd better report back to my boss in the Yard. There's a lot going on at the moment.'

'And who is your boss, Constable?'

'DCI Merlin.'

The sergeant was impressed. 'Merlin, eh? I've heard plenty about him. A fine copper, everyone says. Perhaps you could introduce me one day?'

'A pleasure, Sergeant. Meanwhile you'll keep me posted on developments?'

Osbert Pringle, solicitor to Michael Adair and Laura Curzon, had his offices in a courtyard off Fleet Street, a few yards from the Old

Cheshire Cheese pub on one side and Doctor Samuel Johnson's House on the other. Pringle was a round little man with bouffant brown hair and a purple birthmark the size of an egg beneath one eye. He had been droning on for some time to Bridges in tedious legalese about the law's position regarding suicide and life insurance when Bridges suddenly realised with a jolt that the solicitor might have said something interesting.

'Beg your pardon, sir, but could you say that again?'

'What I said, Sergeant, was I appreciate this is all legal mumbo jumbo to you, but in any event none of it really matters.'

'It doesn't, sir? Why doesn't it matter?'

'Because, as I told Michael, the premiums had been in abeyance for some time.'

'You mean the premiums hadn't been paid?'

Pringle gave Bridges a superior look. 'Yes, Sergeant. That's what "in abeyance" means, you know. Mr Adair believed that a regular transfer from one of the couple's joint accounts had been mandated. Naturally a mandate can only be effected if the account in question has sufficient funds. For whatever reason, the account had not had sufficient funds for several months and thus numerous premiums had been missed. I have noticed before that Mr Adair has a rather slapdash approach to money and business. Surprising in such a successful man, but there it is.'

'How did Mr Adair take this news?'

'He was not happy.'

After he'd finished with Pringle, the sergeant drove to Terry Baxter's former address in Bethnal Green. On his previous visit to the grimy four-storey house on Roman Road, the landlady had not been in residence and it was one of the other lodgers who'd informed him about Baxter's moonlight flit. Today the landlady was at home. Adele Hill greeted Bridges with a cold stare and grudgingly invited him into her dark and damp-smelling ground floor parlour. Grotesquely fat, she sat on a heavily cushioned settee which Bridges reckoned must have been reinforced with steel to hold her weight. 'T'ain't good for business having coppers round, so I'd be obliged if you'd state your business quickly then clear off.'

'You had a lodger name of Baxter until very recently.'

'What of it?'

'He left in something of a hurry, I understand?'

'Hurry? You could say that. Enough of a hurry not to pay me two weeks of rent owing.'

'We're investigating a death at his place of work. A young woman fell from a balcony in the block of flats where Baxter worked as a porter.'

The woman mountain shifted her buttocks and the sofa springs squealed as if in pain. 'Yeah, heard about that. Don't tell me you think he pushed her over? He's a weaselly little squirt but I doubt he'd have the balls to do something like that.'

'We don't consider him a suspect at present, but we'd like to speak to him. It seems very odd to us that he quit his job and lodgings so quickly after the woman's death.'

'Yeah. Very fishy. I can see that.'

'I was wondering whether you have any idea where he might have gone?'

'If I knew that, I'd 'a been round there like a shot for my money wouldn't I?'

The unlikely idea of Miss Hill travelling anywhere like a shot distracted Bridges momentarily. He continued. 'Do you know of any family or friends?'

Her jowls undulated as she shook her head. 'Nah. He's an East Ender is as much as I know. No idea which part.' She picked her nose thoughtfully. 'You might try Ralph upstairs. Lodges on the second floor. He and the boy used to play dominos together once in a while. Go to the stairs and shout his name. Tell him Miss Hill wants him. He's pushing eighty but very spry. He'll come running.'

Bridges called out and, as predicted, an elderly little man quickly appeared. 'You wanted me, Dellie girl?'

'Copper here wants to know about Baxter. You used to pass the time o'day with him, didn't you?'

'Him who slung his hook last week? Yeah. Played the odd board game with him. Why?'

Bridges asked: 'Did Baxter ever talk about where he came from? Mention family or friends?'

Ralph's heavily creased brow creased some more as he considered Bridges's question. 'Didn't say much about his family 'cept to say he'd had a rough time growing up with his dad but now they were getting on better. He fancied himself a bit. Reckoned he was going to get on in the world. Said some teacher had told him he was very bright. A lady teacher.'

'Did he mention the name of the school?' asked Bridges.

'Some saint's name. Saint Michael, Saint Mary . . . ? Something beginning with an "M". Ah!' He looked pleased with himself. 'Got it. Saint Magnus. I remember 'cos he was very proud of knowing a little Latin. "Magnus" means "big", or so he said. The Latin has never been one of my strong points.' He grinned broadly and revealed a completely toothless mouth.

'I don't suppose you know where the school was?'

The brow creased again. 'Now I think about it, I think he once told me his dad was a docker. If that's the case I suppose the school was somewhere down by the docks.'

'Which docks, Ralph?'

The old man looked down at the floor. 'I have a feeling it was the East India. Yeah. That was it. The East India Docks.'

The sofa springs suffered agonies again as the landlady heaved herself forward. She reached out to pat Bridges's hand. 'As and when you find him copper, don't forget to get my rent off him.'

The first three girls Robinson interviewed had stuck to the same unlikely story and refused to be shaken from it. They all had identity cards showing they were sixteen or over. They'd been invited through a friend to a party at Waring's. Two older friends had given them a lift in their van. They'd had no problem agreeing to participate in the strange ceremony Waring had described. It had sounded a bit of fun and Waring had promised he'd make it worth

278

their while. What seemed to them like a large sum of money had been mentioned. There'd been no talk of exchanging sex for money. Waring had offered them drinks and some funny pills which had made them feel good. As for the ceremony itself, none of them could remember much but they were sure they hadn't been harmed. When Robinson had showed the drawings of the Victoria girl, no one had recognised her. All in all, she'd got nowhere. Thus, when the fourth and last girl, very pretty with a bob of jet black hair, was brought into the room, she wasn't optimistic.

The girl sat down and looked warily across the table at Robinson. 'Letting me go, now, are you?'

'Soon. I need to ask you a few questions first.'

'Oh, yeah?' She slouched back in her chair and crossed her legs. Robinson saw the painted outlines of a nylon stocking on each leg. This was common practise now as real nylons were like gold dust in wartime Britain. The girl or whoever'd done it for her had done a good job.

'What's your name, dear?'

'Shirley.'

'Is that your real name?'

The girl shrugged.

'Surname?'

'How about Smith.'

Robinson sighed. 'Age?'

'Nineteen'

'Thank you. So, Shirley, would you like to tell me the story of how you and your friends ended up last night at a black magic ceremony in Kensington?'

'Seen the others, have you? What did they say?'

'I'm only interested in what you have to say.'

Shirley assumed an air of indifference and carefully scrutinised her fingernails. 'If I answer your questions, does that get me out of here?'

'If you tell the truth, you'll get to leave quicker.'

The girl sighed, uncrossed her legs and moved closer to the table. 'We got invited to a party, didn't we? By a friend.'

'Name of the friend?'

'He was really a friend of the other girls. Billy, Johnny, Davy. Something like that. I haven't got much of a memory for names.'

'And who took you there?'

'Some friends. In their van. Freddy, Mike. I really don't . . .'

'. . . have much of a memory for names. No.' Here we go again, Robinson thought to herself. She asked the same additional questions and got the same replies as she'd had from the other girls. She thought for a moment. She'd been hard-nosed with Shirley's friends. Perhaps a softer approach would yield better results.

'Look, dear. You're not in any real trouble, you know. We are interested in your welfare. We're not going to book you for anything. We know there was something bad going on and we'd like to go after the people responsible. If you can help us identify them it . . .'

The girl didn't let her finish. 'Look, I ain't going to be a snitch, if that's what you're thinking. Even if I knew anything, which I don't, there's no point pretending my "welfare" would benefit by getting other people into trouble. D'you know what happens to snitches? Nasty things. I . . .' She left the sentence hanging as a frustrated Robinson suddenly slammed the sketches down in front of her. Shirley couldn't resist looking. 'Who's 'at then?'

'Maybe you can tell me. Just over a week ago, the body of a teenage girl was found on a bomb site in Victoria.'

'So what? Plenty of festering bodies on bomb sites thanks to the Germans.'

'This girl had been strangled.'

'Yeah?'

'Chances are she was in the same sort of racket as you. If so, we thought you might recognise her.'

'I ain't involved in any racket as I've told you. I'm . . .'

'Just have a proper look, please. Can't do you any harm.'

280

With a sigh of irritation, the girl picked up the drawings and proceeded to examine them more closely than had her friends. Watching carefully, Robinson thought she saw a reaction when Shirley focussed on the portrait recognised by Miss Ryman. A flicker of the eyelid, a slight change in breathing. Something. The girl lingered a moment before moving on to the other drawings. When she reached the last one she looked away. Then she returned to the ticked sketch and pointed at it. A couple of tears trickled down her cheek.

'You know her?'

'She's really dead?'

'I'm afraid so.'

Shirley wiped her face with a sleeve. 'She went by the name of Marion but she told me once her real name was Ida. We were friends for a few months. Hit it off for some reason. Similar sense of humour, I suppose. Then one day she wasn't around and I never saw her again.'

'When would that have been? The last time you saw her.'

'In the spring. Flowers were out in bloom. She loved flowers. Roses, daffodils, lilies.'

'So you met her when?'

'Around Christmas time. She'd run away from some bombed out children's home down by the river. Been on the streets for a few weeks before she was picked up.'

'Picked up by who?'

The girl stiffened. 'Look, Miss, I already said I ain't going to be no snitch.'

'But, Shirley . . .'

'I'm not stupid, you know. You might know plenty but you've got no hard evidence. You need someone like me but there's no way I'm gonna be the one to give you names and details. I'm not going to get up in the witness box and risk being bumped off for my pains. Come to think of it, that's probably what happened to poor Marion. Snitched to someone then got found out and given the chop.' She held herself tight in her arms and began to tremble.

281

'We wouldn't allow anything like that to happen to you.'

'Ha! Big talk.' Shirley stood up abruptly. 'I'm very sorry about Marion . . . or Ida . . . or whatever her name was but I can't tell you no more. I've got to look after myself. Now let me out of here.'

Robinson got to her feet as well. 'One last thing, Shirley. Did Ida ever say anything out of the ordinary to you before she disappeared? Something unusual. Can you remember?'

Shirley's eyes flared, and she gave the constable a furious look. Robinson assumed she was going to be uncooperative but the girl's anger subsided as swiftly as it had arisen. She considered the question and eventually replied. 'I remember her saying there was some rich bloke who treated her nice. A regular who seemed dead keen on her. I suppose it's possible she might have gone off with him. Maybe . . . maybe it was him who strangled her?'

'What do you . . . ?'

'No. I'm sorry, Miss. That's you're lot. I'd like to leave now.'

Robinson gave her a rueful look. 'I'm sorry but I can't just let you walk back out onto the streets. It's dangerous for a girl like you out there. Also, you're a minor and . . .'

'I'm nineteen. Says so on my ID card!'

'You and I know that all your ID cards are fake. You and your three friends are minors who have somehow been lured or forced into prostitution. We can't just allow you back on the streets for the pimps to put you back to work. You seem a bright girl.' Robinson reached out a hand to the girl's shoulder but was shrugged off. 'There are organisations which can help you, you know. Wouldn't you like to get back to living a normal life?'

'Normal life?' she shouted angrily. 'You mean being forever hungry? Being fiddled with all the time by my disgusting uncle and his friends? Being bashed and battered every day? At least with Joe . . .' She blushed. 'At least with my new friends I get three square meals a day and a decent bed to sleep in.'

Robinson reached out again and this time she was not rebuffed as she put an arm around Shirley's shoulder. 'I'm sorry, dear, but we are going to have to keep you here until my superiors decide what's to be done with you. We'll try to make you as comfortable as we can. Come, sit back down at the table.'

The girl did as she was asked then started to sob.

Robinson raced up the stairs. In Merlin's office, she found her boss waving a piece of paper angrily in the air and shouting at Johnson and Cole. He paused and pointed her to a chair.

'I'll say it again for your benefit, Constable. I'd just nipped out-side for fifteen minutes to clear my head before my next go round with Waring. When I got back, I found this note on the desk. Sent by the AC who's tied up in some meeting in the Houses of Parlia-ment.' He read it out. ' "Chief Inspector. I was just pulled out of my meeting so the Commissioner could tell me over the phone that he'd ordered Waring's release. Said the man was an important businessman who, for various reasons, was valuable to the war effort. Took the view his embarrassing hobby should be over-looked and scandal avoided. He insisted we put a lid on everything. Sorry. Gatehouse." '

Merlin thumped the desk with his fist. ' "His embarrassing hobby"! Corrupting young girls in orgiastic devil worship. That's just an embarrassing hobby?' He looked up to the ceiling in disbe-lief. 'I immediately hurried off to the cells but was too late. The Commissioner can act like lightning when it suits him. The bird had already flown the coop.' Merlin leaned back, swung his legs up onto the desk and closed his eyes. The brooding silence which ensued was a silence none of his team dared to break. Eventually, the Chief Inspector opened his eyes, looked at Robinson, and spoke.

'So, young lady. You looked pretty keen to say something when you came through the door. You can spit it out now. I just hope to God it's good news.'

'It is, sir. One of the girls downstairs recognised the girl in the drawings. Specifically the version identified by Cowan's secre-tary.' Robinson went on to give full details of the interview.

The constable's news brought an improvement in the atmosphere. When she'd finished, Merlin was surprised to find himself chuckling. 'It's a funny world. God giveth and God taketh away, except this was the other way round. Well done, Clare.' He turned to Cole. 'And well done to you, too, Tommy, for setting us on the track to Ida Walker in the first place.'

Cole blushed.

'Any more news on her mother?'

'There's a Holborn officer keeping an eye out at the hospital. He called a short while ago. There's been some improvement so the outlook is not as bleak as it seemed earlier. That said, she's still not fit enough to see us.'

'And the husband?'

'Nothing as yet.'

Merlin swung his legs back down to the floor. 'Alright, let's go over what we now know about Ida Walker. You said Shirley made a slip of the tongue and mentioned someone called "Joe". I think we can take that as our final firm confirmation that she and the girls worked for the Abelas. She was obviously picked up from the streets by an Abela man in December or thereabouts last year, a few weeks after the bombing of the orphanage, and forced into prostitution. She must have worked for and been housed by the gang until around this April when she disappeared, as far as Shirley was concerned. Perhaps she ran off with this rich man who treated her nicely. Perhaps this man bought her from the Abelas? In any event, she was dead soon after. Had she become a snitch, as Shirley speculated? Had she fallen foul of a client, either the rich man mentioned or someone else? A lot of new questions to answer. Yes, Inspector?'

'If the girl was snitching to the police, wouldn't Sergeant Bridges's friend have known?'

'Not necessarily. The Vice department has a lot of officers and people can be very proprietary about their sources. Obviously we can ask Sergeant Toshack, though.' Merlin reached into a drawer and took out an Everton mint. 'You know, interesting as the idea is, I would be surprised if that's what lay behind her death. If we're right about everything, she was just a simple new recruit to a prostitution gang. What special knowledge would she have to sell or give? A more likely reason for Abela's people to punish her would be if she'd gone away without permission, or withheld earnings.'

'Well you say that about snitching, sir, but aren't we very interested in what Shirley and her friends have to tell us?'

Merlin sucked thoughtfully on his sweet for a minute or two. 'You know that's quite true, Constable Robinson. Very well, let's say that the Abelas are definitely in the frame as suspects in Ida's death, for motives as yet unknown. But as well as them, don't forget, we have others to consider. We've got Cowan who knew the girl according to Miss Ryman. Is he the "rich man" Shirley referred to? We also have the possibility of a random client.'

Merlin got up and went to the window. It was a bleak, overcast day outside. For some reason the river traffic was very thin today. Perhaps they were still running light on qualified boatmen to pilot the vessels. He turned round and asked 'Anyone heard from Sergeant Bridges?' No one had, and then the telephone rang. Merlin went to answer it.

'Good day, Inspector. Oh yes. I see. You don't say? And you're off there now? Well thanks for calling. Please keep me posted.' Merlin replaced the receiver. 'That was Inspector Jay from Gerald Road police station. They responded to a 999 call this morning. A woman had been beaten up and sexually assaulted. The name of that woman was Jean Parker.'

'Adair's girlfriend?'

'Yes. And Adair is the alleged culprit.' Merlin resumed his seat and folded his hands in front of him. 'Michael Adair a man of extreme violence. I have to admit I'm a little surprised but this certainly puts a new perspective on the Curzon case, does it not?'

Bridges was in Wapping, standing outside an end-of-terrace house a stone's throw from the Shadwell Entrance to London Docks. The efficient young woman secretary of St Magnus's Church of

285

England Primary School had provided this address as the last they'd had for Terry Baxter as a pupil. The sergeant had with him a young fit-looking constable called Amiss, whom he'd picked up at the nearby Wapping station. The secretary had warned that Baxter's father had a reputation as a bit of a bruiser, so Bridges had decided to take some back-up.

Amiss gave the door a couple of hard thumps. A dour-looking heavy set man came to the door and growled. 'No need to break the door down. What d'you want?'

'Mr Baxter?'

'George Baxter, yes.'

'Is your son at home?'

'Nah. My kid don't live here no more. Even if he did, he'd be at work this hour.'

'Our information is that he's given up his job.'

'Has he now? I'm sorry to hear that.'

'When was the last time you saw him?'

'Couple of weeks back.'

'Do you mind if we come in and have a look?'

Baxter folded his bulging arms. 'Well, yes I do as it happens. Got a warrant, 'ave you?'

Bridges stuck a foot in the door. 'No, but it would be helpful if you could . . .'

A door slammed somewhere above and the policemen could hear footsteps hurrying down some stairs.

'If you want to avoid trouble, Mr Baxter, you'll let us in now.'

The man swore and stood his ground, but Bridges could sense his heart wasn't in it. Another door slammed and at a nod from Bridges, Amiss barged George Baxter aside and ran ahead of the sergeant towards the back of the house.

The policemen found themselves in a small kitchen overlooking a grubby vegetable patch. They arrived in time to see someone disappearing over the garden wall. Amiss hurried out and vaulted the wall with ease. Bridges followed with a little less grace. Behind the wall was a lane bisecting the rears of two parallel streets of housing. A deep pile of bricks and other debris closed off the near exit on the left so the only way out was to the right. When Bridges landed in the lane Baxter was some forty yards off, close to the turning into the next road. Amiss was some twenty yards behind. As he set off in pursuit, Bridges saw Baxter halt momentarily as he dithered about which direction to take. This hesitation proved costly as by the time he'd decided to go left, Amiss was nearly on him. Both men disappeared from the sergeant's sight but when he rounded the corner he found that Amiss had got his man. Baxter was pinioned to the ground, his head face forward in a puddle, spluttering.

Bridges reached down to help the boy up as Amiss kept a tight hold. 'Nice to see you again, Mr Baxter. We've been looking for you. I'd appreciate a word.'

Baxter wiped his muddy face with the arm of his jacket. 'This big idiot of yours almost drowned me, Sergeant. What the hell are you playing at?'

'Why did you run away?'

Baxter bent to brush his filthy trousers and said nothing. Bridges moved closer. 'You could be in big trouble, sonny boy. You quit your job immediately after Miss Curzon's death. You quit your lodgings in a hurry without paying your rent. You came to hide in the family home and scarpered at first sight of a policeman. Clearly something's wrong. You'd better tell me everything.'

The boy struggled uselessly against Amiss's rock-solid grip. 'I quit the job because it was a lousy one. It had nothing to do with the Curzon lady. I left the lodging house because it was a shithole. That old cow should have paid me to stay there.'

'So if that's the case why did you do a runner just now?' Bridges tried to look Baxter straight in the eye but the boy turned away. 'Yes. I thought so. The real explanation for your behaviour is that you had something to do with Miss Curzon's death, isn't it? That's why you decided to go into hiding. Perhaps you were up there on the terrace when . . .'

'No!' Baxter shouted. He'd gone deathly pale beneath the

smudges of dirt still left on his face. His eyes darted around nervously. 'I didn't have nothing to do with her death. I've never been up in her flat.'

'So you say.' Bridges turned to Amiss. 'I'll need to get the boy back to the Yard to get to the bottom of things. Are you alright to drive me there?'

'Pleasure, sir. Never been to Scotland Yard.'

'I don't think Baxter has either. It'll be a nice little outing for you both!'

Inevitably, Cowan kept the two policemen waiting in his office reception area. Merlin was about to lose his temper when the receptionist finally came to get them.

Cowan welcomed the policemen into his office with a look of amusement and guided them to a suite of enormous black armchairs to the right of his desk. Flyers for Cowan's latest productions littered the marble coffee table in front of them. The producer took a few contented puffs on the cigar he was smoking.

'A cigar always tastes better after lunch I find. I don't know if it's a general thing or something specific to my own palate.' He noticed Johnson's eye on one of the flyers. '*Montezuma's Daughter*. A loose adaptation of a Rider Haggard story. Filming starts in June. I hope to God we have a decent summer. Sussex is to stand in for Mexico and that's a bit of a stretch I have to admit. Stewart Granger and Phyllis Calvert are lined up to star. We haven't cast Montezuma yet. I was hoping for authenticity's sake to get a Mexican for the part. Someone like Cesar Romero would be great but that's nigh impossible with the war and everything. D'you know . . .'

Merlin raised a hand to halt the flow. 'I'd appreciate it, sir, if we could get to the business in hand.'

Cowan showed no sign of being put out by Merlin's abrupt interruption. 'Sure, Mr Merlin. And what is the business in hand?'

'There is some new information we need to discuss.'

'New information, eh? Well, well. I have a feeling this interview is going to be extremely boring, so if you'll just excuse me.' He got up and reached over to the intercom on his desk. 'Honey, bring me a scotch and water will you? A large one.' Back in his chair he leaned back and spread his arms wide. 'And so. Lead on, Macduff, as they say in that play you're not allowed to name.'

Merlin passed the artist's sketches across the coffee table. 'We now have these drawings of the girl found dead in the rubble of your old office building. As you can see, the artist has produced alternative versions of the same girl. We now know her name to have been Ida Walker. Do you recognise her?'

The whisky arrived and Cowan was distracted by the rear view of the departing receptionist. 'Nice curves, don't you think?' The policemen made no reply. Cowan checked his watch, contemplated his glass, swirled the whisky and drank. Then he repeated the procedure. Finally he picked up the drawings. After a cursory glance, he looked up and took another puff of his cigar. 'You know, Merlin, I've been around the block a few times. I'm sensing you feel you have me in some kind of difficult position here. I'm thinking maybe you've got some sort of evidence which puts me together with this girl.' He put the drawings back down on the table. 'And you're wetting your pants about it. Am I right?'

'Do you know her, Mr Cowan?'

Cowan drank more whisky. 'I am a Jew from one of the poorest and roughest parts of Europe. I have encountered many difficulties and hardships on the path to success. There have been many tight corners to escape but I have got out of them all. This, although you probably think otherwise, does not feel like a tight corner to me.' He looked back at the drawings. 'Yes, I do believe one of these resembles a girl I've met.'

'You do?'

Cowan winked. 'Now, let me take a guess. You've seen Miss Ryman, right? And shown her these pictures? I bet she had a good time trying to dish the dirt on me. But there is no real dirt. None that should interest a policeman anyway. This girl you say was Ida Walker I knew as Marion. I had a little fun with her. I took her a few times to the office where Ryman no doubt had a good look at her. So what? You say she's dead. I'm very sorry to hear that. She was a sweet little thing but I didn't kill her. And I'll bet you don't have any evidence that I did.' He looked Merlin straight in the eye. 'You don't do you? And please don't embarrass yourself by alluding to that sweet wrapper. She could have got that from any number of people.'

Merlin took the drawings back from Cowan. He pointed at the ticked sketch. 'This is the girl as you remember her?'

'Yes.'

'This is Ida Walker. Did you pay for her company?'

'What if I did? It's not illegal. I don't have any problems with paying for a woman. One always pays, whatever the circumstances. My two ex-wives cost me a lot more and gave me a lot less pleasure than most of my professional liaisons.'

'It's illegal to have sex with under-age girls.'

'I always ask for identity cards. Marion's said she was of age.'

'A fake.'

Cowan shrugged. 'How was I to know that?'

'We have some further new evidence about you. It suggests you have a particular interest in young girls.'

'What red-blooded male doesn't have an interest in pretty young girls? A little birdie told me you have your own pretty young girl, Merlin.'

Merlin was surprised and disturbed that Cowan knew about Sonia but managed not to show it. He looked at Johnson who took Madeley's notebook from his pocket.

'That book in the Inspector's hand names you as one of the Abela gang's biggest customers for under-age prostitutes.'

Cowan's smiling expression remained unchanged. 'Does it now? And who is the author of your little book, Inspector Johnson?'

'A former employee of the Abela gang.'

'I see. A "former" employee. And where is this fellow now, if I may ask? Is he prepared to give direct evidence to support the contents of his book?'

Johnson hesitated before admitting: 'Unfortunately, he's dead.'

Cowan's shoulders shook with silent mirth. 'That's a good one. Do you really think you're going to nail me with the scribblings of a dead gangster? I thought you were meant to be the cream of the Yard, Merlin? This is pretty flimsy stuff. Please.' He sighed. 'Look, I've told you I recognised the girl. I've admitted knowing her. But I most fervently deny knowingly having sex with a minor and I absolutely deny killing her. She was a cute little thing. Why would I kill her? I'm an admirer of women, not a twisted misogynist. And I'm not a violent man. Ask around if you like. People will tell you, like me or not, that I have no reputation for physical violence. I get a thrill out of loving women, not strangling them.' He took another puff of his cigar before stubbing it out. 'Now, gentlemen,' he got to his feet, 'if that's really all you've got, I suggest you take your leave.'

The two officers reluctantly got to their feet. 'You can expect to see us again, Mr Cowan.'

'I very much hope not, Mr Merlin, but if there is to be a next time, I'll make sure to have my lawyer with me.'

Outside on the pavement, the disappointed policemen paused under a shop awning. 'As I expected, Peter. A formidable fellow.'

'He's certainly a tough nut, sir.'

'We'll stick at him, though. Despite all that guff about being a peaceable lover of women, I bet a man with his sort of drive has a hell of a temper on him when pushed. Perhaps Ida did something to provoke his anger and he lost it for a moment?' Merlin rubbed his forehead. His head was beginning to ache. 'But we'll need hard and fast evidence to nail this fellow, if he's our man.'

Back at the Yard, the policemen saw Cole hurrying down the stairs towards them. They managed to catch three of the words shouted as he raced past. 'Hospital. Walker. Conscious.'

There was a note from Bridges on the desk. The sergeant had Baxter in interview room three on the first floor. Merlin and Johnson turned straight round and went back down the stairs.

They found Bridges and Baxter facing each other over a battered wooden table in the interview room at the end of the corridor. There was an officer they didn't know near the door.

'This is Amiss, sir. Helped me bring Baxter to heel. Alright, you can leg it now, Constable. And thank you.'

'Pleasure, Sergeant. Any time.' Amiss disappeared through the door and Merlin and Johnson joined the sergeant and Baxter at the table. The porter was scowling at them but something about his posture and demeanour suggested to Merlin he was going to be cooperative.

'You've cautioned him?'

'Of course.'

'You carry on, then, Sergeant. We'll intervene as necessary.'

'So what can you tell us about the night of Miss Curzon's death, Baxter? And the truth would be preferable.'

The young man muttered something under his breath.

'Sorry. Didn't quite catch that.'

'You mean the Monday night?'

'I suppose if we're splitting hairs it's the evening of Monday eighth and the morning of Tuesday the ninth.'

Baxter leaned his elbows on the table and clasped his hands tightly together in front of him. Merlin guessed his hands would be shaking if left free. 'It was like this. As you know, the porter's desk wasn't being manned at nights. Jackson and I both normally knocked off at half past six. That evening he had to get off half an hour early 'cause he had a darts match. As it happens, I'd planned to hang around longer than usual as a couple of mates of mine with army leave were coming up west for a drink and I'd told them to meet me at work. They said they'd try and get to me by eight so I had quite a wait. Luckily I had a Zane Grey to keep me going.'

Johnson said: 'Who?'

'Cowboy books, sir,' said Bridges. 'They're very good. You should try them.'

Baxter continued. 'Around quarter to seven, Miss Curzon

comes in through the front door. Says she's got a delivery arriving during the evening. Courier apparently wanted to make the delivery through the back way. She had a bad sore throat so she wasn't so easy to understand but I heard her say something about "prying eyes". Anyway, tipped me half a crown and I said yes. I'd have agreed without the tip. Beautiful woman she was. Hard to refuse.'

'You mean she wanted you to wait for the delivery at the back door?'

'Well, no.' Baxter's eyes went down to the table. 'She knew I'd be knocking off shortly. She just wanted me to leave the back door on the latch so the courier could get in and take whatever it was up the back stairs directly to her floor.'

'And that's what you did?'

'Yeah.'

'Thus compromising the night time security of the building.'

'I suppose. Look, nothing ever happened in the place anyway. Jackson said they'd never had an incident in the five years he'd been there. Didn't seem like there was much risk.'

'You left the back door open on the night that a resident died for as yet unknown reasons. I'd say you chose a bad night to take the risk.'

Baxter flushed. 'L . . . look I . . . did . . . I tried . . .'

Merlin intervened. 'Just keep on with your story, Terry. Let's not worry about the risks of opening the door for now.'

'Alright. So, after I'd opened the back door, I comes back to the lobby just in time to see Mr Adair getting in the lift.'

'What time was that?'

'Some time between seven and seven thirty. Nearer seven, I'd say.'

'You knew him?'

'I knew him to recognise. He weren't living in the flat but he visited once or twice after I started. Had his own key. Jackson pointed him out to me but I'd have known him anyway. Seen a few of his films. Not much cop, in my opinion. I like westerns best.'

'Did he see you?'

'I don't think so. The lift was opening when I entered the lobby. He looked behind him but away from me. To be honest, he seemed a little unsteady on his pins. Like he'd had a drink or two.'

'Did you see him leave later?'

'No.'

'Alright. Carry on.'

'So he went up in the lift and I returned to my book. Time passed. Eight o'clock came and went and it was clear my mates were running late. You might not believe it, but I had started worrying a bit about the back door. I rang through to Miss Curzon's flat to see if the delivery had been made. No answer. I decided to go out back and check things for myself. See if I could tell if someone had been in and out. At the same time I was worried about my mates arriving when I was away from the lobby so I put the front door on the latch for them. Then I went back, turned on the lights and was looking around when I hears steps coming down the stairs. I thinks to myself that if the courier is meant to be secret, I'm not meant to see him and I went behind some packing boxes to keep out of sight. I was too slow, though, and he saw me. Big lump of a man. Black coat. Collar up and trilby on top. Couldn't see his face very well although I think I did see some sort of a mark on it. He reaches out a long arm and grabs me by the throat. "You ain't seen me, right?" he growls.' Baxter paused. The policemen could see the fear in his eyes as he recalled the encounter. 'Then he says "If I hear you've breathed a word about me to anyone, you're a dead man, pal." Then he turns to the door. As he's going out, he says one more thing. "Leave the door open. I may have to come back." Then he clears off.'

There was silence for a moment before Merlin asked: 'And this is why you quit and did a bunk from your lodgings? Fear of this man?'

'Yeah. When Miss Curzon died I couldn't help thinking this bloke might have had something to do with it. His threat was scary enough without thinking he might be a murderer.' Baxter unclasped his hands. They were trembling as Merlin had expected. 'And there's another thing you should know. When I got back to the lobby my mates were there. Obviously I was shaken but I couldn't tell them why. I made up something about falling down the stairs and they thought that was funny. One of them said the best medicine was a pint so off we went to the pub.'

'That's it?'

'No, Sergeant. The thing is, in all the commotion when I met my friends, I forgot.'

'Forgot what?'

'About locking the front door.'

'You mean the main door was on the latch all night as well?'

'Yeah.' Baxter shrank into his chair. 'But I . . . I remembered, didn't I? Even though I'd had a skinful with my mates, the following morning I woke early and remembered the doors straightaway. I knew I'd be in trouble if Jackson found out so I got up immediately and cycled into work. When I arrived I . . . I saw the body. I must've been the first to see her. Poor Miss Curzon.' He started tearing up.

'Come on, Terry. Keep going.'

'Well, despite having to deal with that, I still remembered to cover my tracks and lock both sets of doors before Jackson arrived.' Baxter looked down at his feet. 'So I was naturally in a bit of a state that Tuesday. Worrying about what happened to Miss Curzon, about the doors and about the courier. I managed to avoid a detailed interview with you and when I got home that night, I decided the best thing would be to sling my hook.' Baxter looked anxiously at Merlin. 'That's it. The truth. I swear.'

'Quite a story, Baxter.' Bridges turned to Merlin. 'What do you think, sir?'

Merlin looked hard at the young man. 'I don't know that it doesn't have a ring of authenticity about it. You know Terry, things would have been much smoother for you if you'd told the truth from the beginning.'

The porter burst into tears. Between sobs he managed to ask 'Am I going to . . . to prison?'

Merlin took his time to reply. 'Your actions were foolish in the extreme. Some might say criminal. I can't make any promises. However, if you continue to cooperate and help us solve the case, I might be prepared to put in a word for you. You can forget the job, obviously.'

'Don't care about that. What about the courier? If he knows I'm talking to you, he might come after me.'

'You'd better take care then. The fellow might be a murderer.'

There was a message from Gerald Road Police Station waiting for Merlin back in the office. Adair had been taken into custody. Would DCI Merlin care to handle the interview himself? He would and called to say he'd be round there straight away.

'I don't think it's necessary for us all to go.'

'I'll stay here, sir,' said Bridges. 'You go with the Inspector. I can write up the report on Baxter while it's fresh in my mind and there are one or two other things I can be getting on with.'

'Alright, Sergeant. Before I go, you'd better let me know how you got on with the solicitor this morning. I presume you saw him?'

'I did, sir. In quick summary, it's not quite clear what the legal position is but it doesn't matter from a practical viewpoint. The premiums weren't kept up on the policy, so it's effectively null and void. There can be no payout regardless of the exact legal status.'

'Did Adair know that?'

'Not until he saw the lawyer.'

'So an unpleasant shock for him. It still stands as a possible motive though if he wasn't aware it wasn't paid up. I'll raise it when we see him. Now we know where Cole is, but what about Robinson? Either of you know?'

'I think she's been dragged into a meeting about the girls,' said Bridges. 'She wants to make sure they aren't just turfed back out onto the street. Some people from Westminster Council have become involved, along with some juvenile delinquency officers.'

'God help us. We've got better things for her to do than that.

She's got a kind heart I know but we haven't the time to be social workers as well as coppers. If she doesn't appear soon, go and extricate her, Sergeant.'

Gerald Road Police Station was twenty minutes by car from the Yard. On the way there Merlin and Johnson discussed the Baxter interview. They now knew Laura Curzon had had at least two visitors. Adair himself, and the man who came through the back entrance, presumably a drugs courier. It was possible the courier had visited twice, as he'd indicated he might to Baxter. They also now knew the apartment building had been wide open all night, front and back. Merlin's suspicions that foul play had been involved continued to deepen.

The Chief Inspector had always thought Gerald Road an unlikely place to put a police station. It was located in a very rich and exclusive part of London. Merlin had it on the good authority of Jack Stewart that the famous playwright and actor Noel Coward lived in a house close by. His Scottish friend had had an interesting chance encounter with Coward before the war. They had met in a hotel bar off Piccadilly and, after several drinks, Coward had suggested a night cap at his home. Stewart had innocently agreed. Once over the threshold the Scotsman, to his great surprise and embarrassment, had found himself fending off Coward's amorous advances. The rebuff had been taken in good spirits by the writer who had then proceeded to entertain him with an impromptu concert at the piano. The men parted on friendly terms and Stewart's passable imitation of Coward singing 'Mad Dogs and Englishmen' had thereafter become one of his favourite party tricks.

The station had as elegant a frontage as the other houses in the street, but the interior had the usual drab and utilitarian décor of the average nick. The officer in charge, Inspector Jay, a pinkish man with a shock of salt and pepper hair, swiftly briefed them on Jean Parker's injuries, her statement, and the state in which they'd found Adair's bedroom. He confirmed Adair had been cautioned then led them down a corridor to the overheated and windowless room where Adair was waiting at a table and, with a nod, left them to it.

The policemen sat down and Adair grunted a greeting. The actor's face was pale and blotchy, his hair unruly and his tie askew. The immaculately turned out matinée idol was nowhere to be seen.

'Anything to say, Mr Adair?'

Adair stared down at the table and shrugged. 'What do you want me to say?'

'Why you attacked Miss Parker, would be a good start.'

'I didn't.'

'Hard to explain the mess in your bedroom, isn't it? The bloodied sheets. The ripped and blood soaked clothing. You know as well as I do that when we get the blood analysis back it will prove to be Miss Parker's.'

There was a flash of defiance in the actor's eyes. 'I have friends in high places, you know. Someone will . . .'

'If you want to make sure I throw the book at you, that's the sort of talk to do it.'

Adair shrunk back into his chair. He remained stubbornly silent for a while before bursting out: 'It was just an accident I tell you. *An accident.*'

'Drunk, weren't you?'

'I'd had one or two.'

'Or six or seven. And there were traces of cocaine everywhere, I'm told.'

Adair replied grudgingly: 'I admit I'd been on a bit of a bender during the day on Saturday. Then I had a nap and slept most of it off in the afternoon.'

'You passed out.'

'Yes alright. But I woke up eventually. I was still a bit squiffy so I can't remember everything but I do remember her coming into the bathroom and not being . . . not being nice to me.'

'How so?'

'She hit me.'

'She probably had good cause, given the state you were in. What happened then?'

'Next thing I remember is finding myself in bed with her. She was asleep.'

'You don't remember battering her? Ripping her clothes off?'

'Look, I can't have done that. It's not in my nature. Now sometimes, I admit, sex can get a bit rough, intentionally, I mean. Some women like it that way. I guess we might have engaged in . . . in that sort of thing.'

'You are aware that she had cuts and bruises all over and it's a miracle she hasn't broken any bones. Yet you say this all came about in some kind of consensual sex romp?'

Adair looked down again. His fingers began nervously thrumming on the table. 'Yes.'

'And what happened when you both woke up? Was Miss Parker jolly and cheerful after your night of passion?'

'No. Not really.'

'She accused you of assaulting her, didn't she?'

'Yes.'

Merlin turned away in disgust. 'This is really rather pathetic. Come on, man. You haven't got a leg to stand on. If Miss Parker presses charges, which I understand she intends to do, you're going to jail. Inspector?'

'Did you ever behave like this with Laura Curzon, Mr Adair?'

'What do you mean?'

'Miss Parker told Inspector Jay you called her Laura several times during your attack?'

'Look it wasn't an attack, I tell you. I . . .'

'Just answer please. Did you ever assault Miss Curzon in this way? Did you imagine yourself with her when you were with Miss Parker on Saturday night?'

'Look, I might have used Laura's name by mistake. I was a bit tight. But no I never assaulted Laura.' Adair's fingers stopped thrumming. He took out a handkerchief and wiped the perspiration from his face. 'Perhaps it's fair to say that what happened in my lovemaking with Jean was a little over the top but I can tell you with all sincerity that I never did anything over the top with Laura. I was always . . . always very sweet with her. We used to play . . . you know . . . games but no one ever got hurt.'

'What sort of games?'

'Games . . . you know.'

'Not really. So you're claiming you were never violent in any way with Miss Curzon?'

'I was never . . . no.'

'The night of Monday, December the eighth. You told us you paid a short visit of some forty-five minutes duration to Miss Curzon's flat.'

'That's right. We had a short friendly chat and a drink and then I went home.'

'What time was it you said you arrived?'

'Around seven. Maybe quarter past. I didn't look at my watch.'

'The junior porter was still on duty and saw you at the lift around then so that tallies. That would mean you left around eight, or quarter to. You agree?'

'Yes.'

'However, the porter, who didn't leave until well after eight, says he never saw you leave.'

Adair waved a hand in irritation. 'Those porters aren't the sharpest pencils in the box, now are they? Maybe he was in the lavatory when I left. Maybe I was a few minutes later than eight. What does it matter? You're making something out of nothing there.'

'It matters because if you tell us a lie, that undermines everything else you tell us.'

Adair opened his mouth to respond but thought better of it.

'When you were in the flat with Miss Curzon, did she have any visitors?'

'No.'

'Are you sure? No deliveries?'

'Not that I . . . I'm sorry. I forgot. There were a few minutes when I was in the bedroom. I felt a little unwell when we were having our drink and Laura suggested I lie down.'

'You were drunk?'

'Certainly not. Why do you say that?'

'Because the porter said he thought you were unsteady on your feet when he saw you.'

'Pure bollocks. I'd had a quick cocktail at home before leaving for Laura's and that's all. I felt faint because I felt faint. We work long hours in the film business you know. Sometimes it has an effect. Also I have occasional difficulties with my blood pressure. Anyway, if I may continue, I lay down for five or ten minutes. It's possible a delivery might have happened then without my knowing. Laura never mentioned anything though.'

'Did Miss Curzon have a rest at the same time? With you?' Merlin asked.

'Hell no. You're barking up the wrong tree there.'

'You didn't stay the night and indulge in some rough sex for old times sake?' Merlin's voice became more insistent.'

'Certainly not!'

'And you didn't chase Miss Curzon around the flat as you had Miss Parker?'

'No! No!'

'And Miss Curzon didn't run out onto the terrace and fall escaping from you?'

'No!'

'Or maybe you remembered the insurance money and pushed her over?'

'No! No! None of that!' Adair's eyes almost bulged from their sockets. 'For God's sake, Merlin. You have to believe me. I had nothing to do with Laura's death.' His head slumped to the table.

The room itself had no windows but there was a small observation panel in the door. Adair was getting on Merlin's nerves and he got up and wandered over to look out. There was a large window in the corridor outside which opened onto Gerald Road and he could see some of the houses opposite. Perhaps one of them was Noel Coward's? Was that the distant tinkling of a piano he could hear? Was a new comical hit song being composed? No. He realised there was a radio on somewhere in the station. He returned to the table.

'Look Adair. Call it copper's instinct but I just know you're not telling us everything. The only way things are going to improve for you is if you tell us the full truth of what happened that night. I'm going to give you one more chance. If you hold anything back or tell lies this time, Inspector Johnson and I will do our level best to ensure that you are finished. Now. Begin again.'

The river traffic had picked up since earlier. Bridges always thought there was something strangely compelling about the steady flow of barges trundling up and down the water and he took a moment to watch. Before he turned away he noticed a couple of men in air warden uniforms taking in the view, like he was, but from the lower angle of the Embankment pavement. Back at his desk, he opened his notebook and was about to make a new entry when a thought came to him. In the Curzon investigation, he realised, they had made no attempt to canvass the local wardens in Mayfair for evidence. It was always possible that one or more might have seen something around Seymour Mansions. The failure to do so must be counted a mistake. A mistake that must be swiftly remedied.

After Merlin and Johnson had gone off to Gerald Road, Bridges had written up the Baxter interview and then chased up the outstanding forensic items. The news wasn't great. Little real progress had been made. Nothing had been gleaned from Miss Curzon's night clothes, although it was thought likely the tear in her pyjama jacket had preceded her fall. The team had managed to identify that the piece of thread discovered on the fencing had not come from any of the clothes in Miss Curzon's cupboards. They now wanted to see if there was a match to Adair's clothes. A positive match wouldn't be conclusive of anything against the actor. As a former flat resident, he could have snagged a suit or a coat on the railing months before. However, if there was no match, they would know the thread came from an unknown third party and that line of enquiry would remain open. They had nothing further on the perfumed handkerchief. The person Bridges spoke to had said he was out of the loop on that, but didn't believe they'd got any further.

Bridges now began to run through all of his Curzon notes again. He came to his reference to Miss Curzon's desk and the correspondence and documents therein. There was no report on this, as far as he knew. Another item which had slipped through the net. Had forensics discovered anything of interest in the desk? He needed to know and was about to pick up the phone to the junior forensic officer again when Denis Armstrong himself appeared at the door.

'Hello, Sergeant. Frank out?'

'Yes, sir, he's interviewing Mr Adair again.'

'Is he now? Well that's the case I wanted to discuss. The Curzon case.'

'I was just told by one of your people that things were going slowly.'

'Well, yes, I'm afraid they are. As I was just passing I was going to bring Frank up to date. And you, of course, Sergeant.'

'I know about the thread, sir.'

'Yes. We need to rule out Adair next. In terms of material and design, some type of checked worsted. Good quality. Probably from a man's suit.'

'And the handkerchief?'

'Unfortunately we haven't been able to lift any prints from it. Normally I'd expect to get something. I suppose the conditions weren't conducive. Early morning frost. Anyway, nothing.'

'The perfume?'

'We checked it against the stuff in Miss Curzon's bathroom and on her dressing table but nothing doing. So it doesn't look like it's hers. I was planning to send someone on a fishing trip around the

London shops, but haven't had anyone free. In the overall scheme of things it seems a little tangential but I'm hoping to get someone on it tomorrow.'

'What about Miss Curzon's correspondence, sir? We've heard nothing about that.

'You didn't receive the package I sent over?'

'No, sir. When was that?'

'I asked one of my lads to drop it off a couple of days ago. There was a note explaining that her correspondence was pretty useless. Bills and routine mail, mainly. There was one thing, though, I thought you'd want to see. We found a diary. Not a "tell all" type of diary but a diary of appointments and engagements. I enclosed the diary with the note. If you've not seen it, maybe Frank kept it to himself?'

'I doubt it, sir. If he's not mentioned it, that's because he hasn't seen it.' Bridges looked at Merlin's desk. As usual, within a few days of its last clear up, it had descended into chaos. He rummaged through the pile and eventually found Armstrong's unopened package hidden away under a couple of old files and a boring and probably unread memo from the AC. He tore off the brown wrapping paper. The small pocket diary was bound in pink leather and engraved 'LC'.

'There it is, Sergeant. That's the one.'

Adair had asked if he could light a cigarette before starting and Merlin had allowed him. He took a couple of puffs and the tension in his drawn face eased slightly. 'Very well. This is what happened.'

'Truly?'

'Truly.' He blew a stream of smoke through his nostrils then took a breath. 'As a preliminary, you ought to know that I'm in the devil of a financial mess.'

Adair saw the disbelief in the policemen's eyes.

'I know. I know. How can the big shot film star be hard up? Well it can happen. A few poor decisions here and there and hey presto.' Adair ran a hand through his hair. 'I tried to maintain a ridiculously extravagant lifestyle, I made a few unwise business investments and borrowed money from the wrong people. In consequence I am pretty much broke. Well, actually, it's worse than just being broke. I owe a lot of money I haven't got to the wrong sort of people.'

'Have drugs anything to do with this?'

Adair nodded. 'Bingo, Chief Inspector. Drugs have a good deal to do with this. With my financial troubles, that is.'

'Do they have anything to do with what happened on the night of your wife's death?'

'What do you mean?'

'Were you, Miss Curzon, or both of you high on drugs?'

'No.'

'What about that row your neighbour says she heard and which you deny?'

Adair looked away briefly. 'It is true that we had an argument, or rather a slightly heated exchange of words. Laura had a sore throat as you may recall and couldn't do much more than whisper. Anyway it was nothing serious and there was no question of violence, regardless of our having had a drink or two. And no drugs had been taken.'

'What did you argue . . . or, rather, exchange words about?'

'I wanted to borrow money. She didn't want to lend it to me.'

'Had you borrowed from her before?'

'Yes.'

'You wanted money from her to pay off your debts.'

'Some of them, at least.'

'Who is it that you owe money to?'

'I'm overdrawn at a couple of banks but that's not the problem. The problem debts are to drug suppliers. I've run up rather a large bill on credit.'

'At extortionate rates of interest, no doubt.'

'Indeed.'

Johnson said dismissively. 'I'm sorry, Mr Adair, but I just

can't believe this. You're a movie star. You're earnings must be huge.'

'Not huge enough, sadly. If expenditure outstrips income, however large the income, you have a problem. Remember Micawber in David Copperfield? I thought WC Fields was excellent in the film. How does it go? "Annual income twenty pounds, annual expenditure nineteen nineteen and six, result happiness. Annual income twenty pounds, annual expenditure twenty pounds and six pence, result misery." That's my position, except it's much, much worse than sixpence. The fact is, also, that my star is beginning to fade. Some of my recent films haven't done very well. My bargaining power is less than it was. Victor Goldsmith has helped and remained a good friend until now, but I . . . I might have tried his patience a little too far.'

'Were drink and drugs a contributory factor to the split with Miss Curzon?' Merlin asked.

'Not really. She's . . . she was pretty keen on them both herself. It was the adultery which did for us. I always had a wandering eye and there's so much opportunity in an actor's life, as I told you before. She played around in retaliation. Once that becomes a pattern the relationship is obviously never the same.'

Merlin examined Adair carefully. 'Mr Adair. You're broke. You're an addict. You're an adulterer and you can be violent. You're a mess. Sometimes people with their backs to the wall, like you, lash out. Did you lash out at Laura Curzon and kill her?'

'No. I did not.'

'Very well. We seem to have gone off the intended track. You were going to tell us exactly what happened when you visited the flat that night. In chronological order, please.'

Adair put down his cigarette. 'I got there just after seven. The meeting, as I've said, was purely social. A quick drink and catch up. I have to admit, I did think beforehand I might try and tap her for a loan but we'd not discussed it in advance. After we'd had a drink or two, I tried my luck. She wasn't that over the moon at my request, hence the exchange of words, but agreed to give me something in the end.'

'Why wasn't she happy to discuss a loan?'

'Because she'd lent me something before she went away and that hadn't yet been repaid. Also she'd found out while she was away that I'd drained all the money remaining in our joint accounts. So I was already substantially in the red with her.'

'Were the insurance premiums payable from one or other of those accounts?'

He shifted awkwardly in his seat. 'Well, yes, I'd forgotten about those.'

'You hurried off to your solicitor pretty sharpish after Laura's death. Subject to some finer points of law, I gather you could have been in line for a very big pay out. All your problems would have been solved.'

Adair looked down at his hands and said nothing.

'Not a bad motive for murder. And, you weren't aware of the premium problem before you saw the solicitor, according to him.'

Adair replied through gritted teeth. 'Do I have to say it again? I didn't murder her. Not for the insurance or any other reason. I had loved the woman. I could never have harmed her.'

'Who are the people you owe?' asked Johnson

'The people I deal with work for the Abelas.'

'How come they haven't broken your legs yet?'

'I've always managed to come up with the money in the end. They know I'm contracted or being lined up for other films so they're looking to those fees for payment. Trouble is I've already taken significant advances against those fees.'

'And if you're in jail, you're not going to get any more fees are you?' added the Inspector.

Merlin drew in his breath. 'Alright. Let's get back to Miss Curzon's flat. She agreed to lend you money. What next? According to the original story, you left at this point.'

Adair shook his head. 'No that wasn't true. I stayed. We made up after our few harsh words. Agreed we shouldn't fall out for old times' sake. She asked if I'd like some cocaine. There had been no mention of drugs until that point. Said she was having a delivery any minute. Sure enough, moments later there was a knock at the door. She got her drugs from the same people as me, so, for obvious reasons, I made myself scarce in the bedroom. When the coast was clear she told me she'd arranged another delivery so that I could take some supplies away with me. The courier had agreed to go to the trouble of a second run that night.'

'What then?'

'A couple more drinks, a few snorts, more chat. A couple of hours passed pleasantly. There was no sign of the second delivery. Then she said she was feeling sleepy. Said I could take most of what she'd received in the first delivery, and she'd keep the second. Then she sent me on my way.'

'What time would that have been?'

'Twenty to eleven. On that occasion I did look at my watch.'

'How did you get home?'

'I walked. It's only twenty minutes or so to my place.'

'Did you see anyone on your way out or in the vicinity of the building?'

'No.'

'Was Miss Parker waiting for you at home?'

'No. She had stayed overnight at the studio as we all sometimes do when we have an early morning call.'

'Is that it, then? The full story?'

'Yes. Christ, yes!'

Merlin looked at Johnson. 'Anything else, Inspector?'

'No, sir. Obviously it would have been much better if Mr Adair had come clean at the outset.'

'Look, I'm sorry, I panicked. I thought I'd be in trouble if I told you what happened. I was at the flat until late. I was perhaps the last person to see her alive. There was our argument, the drugs . . . It would all look bad, so I thought it would be best if I . . .'

'Lied,' said Merlin.

Adair picked up his half-smoked cigarette. It had gone out and he relit it. He looked cowed and pathetic. 'What happens now?'

'You'll have to stay here until we know what Miss Parker wants to do about the assault. If she wants to lay charges . . .'

Adair put his head in his hands and started to cry.

In the end, Robinson hadn't needed Bridges's help to get out of her meeting. It had broken up after a couple of hours with no decision reached pending a further report from the council on available accommodation. Her final contribution had been to make it clear that whatever was decided with regard to the other three girls, Shirley could not be allowed back on the streets. The girl had provided valuable evidence and might yet provide more.

She found Bridges on the telephone in Merlin's office, scribbling something down on a piece of paper.

'Yes. Good. Where? Thank you very much.' He put the receiver down and looked up at Robinson. 'You got away then.' He stood up. 'On the move, Constable. Things are on the move. That was the ARP. I've just got the name of the air warden who was patrolling the area around Seymour Mansions on the night of Miss Curzon's death. He works in Piccadilly and I'm off to see him. You can come with me.'

'Has something happened?'

'You've missed a few developments while you've been dealing with those girls. I finally got hold of the junior porter, Baxter, and he gave us a lot of new information. That included the fact that both front and back doors of Seymour Mansions were open throughout the night of Laura Curzon's death. There's always a chance the warden on duty might have seen something. We really should have spoken to him before, but better late than never. I'm off to see him now. Are you free to join me?'

'Of course, sir.'

'I'll bring you up to date with other developments on the way there.'

★

Mary Walker had been placed in a private room at the insistence of Constable Dooley, the officer Sergeant Harley had despatched to the hospital to keep an eye on her. Dooley now sat in the corridor outside, and watched Constable Cole pace back and forth like a nervous expectant father. It had been almost two hours since he'd received Dooley's urgent call at the Yard. A few more minutes passed and Dooley got up to apologise to Cole for the fifth or sixth time. Minutes after his call, Mrs Walker had suffered a relapse. When he'd called the Yard to tell Cole, the constable had already left for the hospital.

'Really, Constable Dooley, don't worry. It's just one of those things. I could have returned to the Yard. It's my lookout I decided to wait. I . . .'

A frazzled-looking young doctor suddenly came out of the room and interrupted him. To the great relief of both officers, he gave them the go-ahead. 'She's still extremely frail but insists she wants to speak to you. Fifteen minutes and no more, mind.'

Cole and Dooley sat down either side of the bed. Strands of Mrs Walker's greying hair had arranged themselves like a halo on her pillow. She looked to be fast asleep but as the spindly hospital chairs creaked under the policemen's weight, one eye opened and fell on Cole.

'Constable?' she croaked.

'Yes, ma'am, and I've got another officer with me. Constable Dooley.'

Her second eye joined the first in the search for Dooley and when they'd found him, she managed a half-smile of acknowledgement. Then her eyes closed again and she stuttered 'P . . . p . . . pain and . . . s . . . suffering from cradle to grave, the p . . . poor thing.' A tear trickled down her cheek. 'It was . . . 'er . . . 'er. In the drawing. Our Ida.'

'You knew from the outset?'

'Of course.' Another pause. Her eyes cracked open again

A grimace of pain distorted her face. 'Your artist . . . 'e did a

310

good job. It's three or four years since I seen 'er but a mother can always tell.'

'Why didn't you tell us before?'

Mary Walker coughed violently then waved a hand at a jug of water on the bedside table. Dooley poured out a glass and helped her to drink it. When she'd finished, she whispered 'Why do you think?'

'Your husband?'

The woman's eyes rolled. 'Yeah. 'E didn't want me to tell you. I knew I'd get beaten up if I did. So I didn't. Then 'e beat me up anyway.'

'But why?'

'Can't help himself. Likes it, don't 'e? Likes the sound of flesh and bones crunching under 'is fist. Likes fighting down the pub. Likes 'itting me, even though we're not together no more. Liked 'itting his two girls when he had the chance. Violence is in his blood.'

Cole glanced at Dooley. 'Are you able to tell us the story of your two daughters, Mrs Walker? Why they left home?'

Her eyes closed and Cole thought she'd drifted off but then they were open again and she began to speak. 'Quite a few years between them there was. Ten or eleven was it? You know I can't remember. Anyway the eldest, Bessie, was a teenager when she cleared off. Ida was just a toddler then. She was a tough one, Bessie. He made her tough. Sid. She left when she was fourteen or fifteen, I think. Never seen her since. I had one letter several years after she'd left and after I'd been in touch with the local council to try and track her down. Said she was 'appy and I should forget all about her. Course I couldn't forget. Never. Nor Ida. I tried but . . .' She started coughing again and this time seemed unable to stop. Dooley helped her to more water but that didn't work. A doctor and nurse hurried in and they were briskly excluded from the room.

Merlin and Johnson got back from Jean Parker's flat just after two. The actress had been in a shocking state, and Merlin's heart had been hardened against Adair. The victim had, however, been insistent that no charges be brought. She'd said that Valerie Goldsmith had acted against her wishes in calling 999. She didn't want to ruin Adair's life and career over an isolated incident, and was acutely conscious that the publicity of a lurid court case would do her own career no good at all. When they'd parted, Merlin had made no commitment to Miss Parker, but on the way back in the car had reluctantly agreed with Johnson that they ought to go along with her wishes. This decision gave Merlin cause for some sour amusement when the AC telephoned soon after he'd sat down at his desk.

'Sorry, Frank, but I'm afraid to say I've had another intervention from the Commissioner.'

'Have you, sir? What now?'

'He had a call from Vincent Korda about the actor Michael Adair. He's in some sort of trouble, I understand?'

'Yes, sir. He viciously beat up and raped a young woman.'

'Ah. Mm. Yes. That sounds pretty . . . um . . .' The AC struggled but failed to find an appropriate word. 'The thing is, Frank, the Kordas are powerful and influential men.'

'As you have already made clear to me regarding the Curzon case, sir.'

'Yes . . . um . . . the Commissioner made much of the fact that they are important to the war effort.'

'Ah, yes, the war effort. Like Waring.'

'Quite so. Apparently Alexander Korda is involved in some secret . . . ah, but I better not go into that.'

Merlin took his time before speaking again. 'Do I understand you to be asking me on the Commissioner's behalf to drop the case against Adair, sir?'

'If you could, Frank. I think . . .'

Merlin allowed another long pause. 'Consider it done, sir. Now if you don't mind, we are very busy down here.'

'Oh. Um. Yes. Of course you are, Frank. Carry on and . . . er . . . thank you.'

Merlin put the receiver down. 'Did you get the gist of that, Peter?'

'I think so. I liked the way you made him sweat.'

'I should have strung him out a bit longer. This Commissioner fellow is becoming a real menace. I'll be glad when he pushes off. With luck, Gatehouse will get the job. He's not perfect but he's more of a copper than the current chap.'

'I suppose I'd better call Gerald Road then and tell them to let Adair go.'

'There's no hurry, but when you do, ask Inspector Jay to warn him off Miss Parker. I'd also like Adair to keep us apprised of his whereabouts on a daily basis. I'm still not fully convinced we have the whole truth about what happened that night.'

'Will do, sir. Now if you don't need me, I'll get back to my office and see what's what.'

Once Johnson had gone, Merlin relaxed back in his chair and contemplated his desk. It was looking very tidy. Good old Bridges had obviously done one of his clear ups. There were only a few items on the desk. The ever present Eiffel Tower replica, his preferred stationery, a cup with pencils, and then, he saw, one unfamiliar thing. A pink leather notebook. He leaned forward and picked it up.

Cole and Dooley had been told there was no point in them hanging around the hospital any more that day. Mary Walker needed to be left in peace for at least twenty-four hours. Dooley rang his station to be told that Sergeant Harley and his men were still looking for Walker south of the river. The two constables decided to join them.

Magee Street was a shabby cul de sac of Victorian tenement buildings sitting in the shadow of the famous Oval gas holder. As they got out of the car, Cole caught sight of a flash of blue uniform disappearing into one of the buildings. He led Dooley over to the doorway, and they went through. They found themselves in a shabby central stairwell with stairs leading off left and right to the several floors above. There were open walkways leading from the stairs on each floor to the flats. Dooley saw one of his fellow officers up above and shouted out.

'Oy, Foxy!'

His Holborn colleague, Constable Fox, turned and looked down. 'Keep it quiet, Dooley. We're in Number Thirty-Four waiting for Walker to show.' He beckoned them up.

When they got to the flat they found Harley, Fox, and another constable. They had a quick look round. The place was a tip. Dirty clothes and bedding, empty food cans and bottles were scattered everywhere. There was a powerful stink of sweat, rancid food and worse. In a corridor to the left Cole saw two sullen scrawny men in nightshirts. Harley explained that the flat was a cheap doss house for labourers. He'd been directed there by the landlord of a pub at the end of the road who knew where Walker lived.

'These two work nights,' said Harley. 'Walker works days. He's been living here as long as them, which is about a year. There was no sign of him when they got in at half seven this morning.' Harley inclined his head to a door behind him. 'That's where he sleeps. It's a mess like the rest of the place. I presume these rooms cost peanuts. Anyway, we decided to sit it out for a while and see if he returns. We just heard a loud noise in the street and I sent Fox here to check it out. It was just a car exhaust. I think we . . .' The sergeant broke off abruptly and put a finger to his lips. They could hear footsteps on the walkway.

They watched as the doorknob turned and Sid Walker came in. After the briefest of looks at the policemen, he turned sharply on his heels and hared off. It was Cole who set off first in pursuit, with Dooley and the others hard on his heels. Cole was almost on Walker when he started down the stairs, but one of the constable's shoes caught in a crack on a broken step and he fell, bringing Dooley down on top of him, and blocking the staircase for Harley and the others. Thirty seconds were lost during which Walker made it to the bottom of the stairs. When Cole finally got to the street, their quarry was fifty yards down the street. He was almost at the exit of the cul de sac when a lorry appeared from somewhere and blocked his way. Panicked, he turned to his right and ran through an archway. When the policemen reached the archway and went through, they found themselves in a crowded coal merchant's yard. Cole looked everywhere but couldn't see their man. Then he heard someone shout.

'Don't go in there!'

He looked in the direction of the voice and saw someone looking very much like Walker slipping into a doorway at the far end of the yard. He led the others across to the doorway and was about to go through when he heard a loud noise from inside. He waited a moment then opened the door. The room behind, he could see, was a coal storage facility and the noise was that of rivers of coal pouring onto the floor from chutes in the wall. A large mound of coal was piling up rapidly and was already quite deep. A trousered leg was sticking out of the mound on the nearest side.

'We'd better hurry,' said Cole. Luckily, the flow of coal began to slow, then stopped. The swirling clouds of coal dust made breathing difficult and Cole put a handkerchief to his mouth as he bent down for Walker's leg. He and Dooley gave it a tug as the other three officers began clearing coal away from Walker's body. It didn't take very long to pull him out but he looked in a pretty bad way. They carried him carefully out into to the yard.

'Keep back please,' said Sergeant Harley as the coalmen crowded around. 'The man needs air! He's been suffocated.' They couldn't hear any breathing and Cole initially feared the worst. Then, suddenly, Walker came to life. He began to cough violently then started spewing out a torrent of black vomit. Unfortunately for Harley, he caught much of this. He stood away, furious and disgusted. 'Jesus bloody Christ. I'm covered in the stuff. Get me some water someone. The little bugger!'

A bucket was brought and Harley sluiced off as much of the mess as he could. As he was doing this he asked Cole 'Can you try and find a telephone in this bloody place and call for an ambulance. The man's clearly alive but God knows what his lungs are like after breathing in all that dust. We'd better get him to hospital as quick as we can.'

Bridges and Robinson found Daniel Myers, the air warden, at the ground floor counter in Hatchards Bookshop as the man in the ARP office had said they would. Myers was a distinguished looking man in his sixties with a military bearing and close cut silvery grey hair. He was dealing with an elderly female customer and they waited patiently for him to finish.

'I have read it, indeed, madam.'

'I didn't really enjoy her last one. *Castle* . . . something wasn't it?'

'*Castle Dor.* A rather unusual enterprise, in that Miss Du Maurier was completing a novel started by someone else, Arthur Quiller-Couch. I quite liked it though.'

'Not a patch on *Rebecca*.'

'Well, that was a great story to be sure. And the reviews of this one have been very good.'

'Very well. I'll take it, then.'

The woman paid for her copy of *Frenchman's Creek* and Bridges moved forward to display his warrant card.

'Good afternoon, Sergeant. We don't often get visited by the police here. How can I help?'

'We have a few questions concerning your ARP duties, Mr Myers. Can you spare us a few minutes?'

'Of course.' Myers called over a colleague to take his place at the counter, then led Bridges and Robinson through the busy bookshop to a door at the back. Through the door was a cramped office in the centre of which was a large desk piled high with books. Robinson examined the book titles with interest.

'Sit down, please,' said Myers. 'Sorry for the clutter. I have all these newly published books to sort out after the shop closes.'

'No warden duties tonight then, sir?' asked Bridges.

'No, this is normally one of my nights but a colleague wanted to swap so I'm on tomorrow night instead.'

'We understand you were on duty on the night of December eighth to ninth?'

'December eighth? Last Monday? Yes I was. Why?'

'We gather your patch covers part of Mayfair. We are interested in an apartment block called Seymour Mansions.'

'I know it. Many Mayfair residents think they are too grand to have to comply with the blackout. Smart blocks of flats like Seymour Mansions are among the worst culprits, so I make a point of checking it most nights when I'm on duty.'

'There was a terrible incident that night. A film actress, Laura Curzon, fell to her death from the roof terrace of her flat.'

'I read about that, although I hadn't realised it was that particular night. Terrible indeed. I saw nothing of it, otherwise I'd have contacted you. It must have happened after my patrol.'

'Can you remember at what time you passed the building?'

'Relatively early, I think. Around eleven. I usually vary my route, sometimes I start near Berkeley Square, sometimes near the Park, sometimes by Oxford Circus. That night, I started at Marble Arch so Seymour Mansions was near the beginning of my tour.'

'Do you remember anything particular about that night? Anything unusual involving Seymour Mansions?'

'I don't believe so. Let me have a think.' He looked down and started absent-mindedly stroking the cover of one of the many books on his desk. Robinson saw it was Mrs Christie's latest, *Evil Under The Sun*. 'Of course, Monday is always one of the quieter nights. Apart from one or two drunken soldiers and the usual scattering of ladies of the night, I don't think I saw anyone. But let me think.' Myers's absent-minded hand moved on to the new Patrick Hamilton.

'Did you see anything around the apartment block, perhaps? Any visitors going in or coming out?'

'Well now you make me think about it, I remember I did. As I said, Seymour Mansions is a frequent transgressor as regards the blackout. So it wasn't so unusual but there was a breach that night. Someone had entered the building and left the front door open.

Light was consequently spilling out onto the street. I hurried over to close the door. When I got there, I looked in and saw the presumed culprit standing by the lift. I called out to him to complain about his thoughtlessness but he ignored me and stepped into the lift.'

'Can you describe him for us?'

'I didn't see his face properly. He turned my way briefly when I called out but he was heavily wrapped up. Heavy winter over-coat, hat, scarf and so on. It's sometimes difficult to gauge size and build when people are dressed like that but he seemed a pretty substantial fellow. Medium or just above medium height.'

'Anything distinctive about the coat?'

'Black. Hint of a check, maybe. And a similar hat. Maybe it was matching. I'm not sure.'

'Scarf?'

'Black again, I think. Plain black.

'Colour of hair?'

'Sorry. Can't help you there.'

'Age, sir?' asked Robinson.

'Middle-aged at a guess, young lady, but I couldn't swear to it.'

'Was that the last you saw of him?'

'Yes. I made sure the glass in the front door was properly covered by the black drape inside, pulled the door to and carried on with my patrol. I do remember thinking it odd that the door was on the latch but decided that was the building management's business, not mine.'

Bridges asked a few more routine questions but the bookseller had nothing more of interest to tell them. The sergeant gave Myers his card and everyone got to their feet.

'I wish you luck in your endeavours, Sergeant, young lady.' Myers looked with interest at Robinson. 'I couldn't help noticing, Constable, that you seemed to take an interest in my new stock. Are you a keen reader?'

'I am, sir.'

'I don't know if you're allowed to shop on duty but if you are, is there anything you'd care to buy?'

318

Robinson turned to Bridges who shrugged. 'Go ahead, Constable, if you want. It's no skin off my nose. But be quick about it.'

'I shall, Sergeant. I know exactly what to buy. Could I have a copy of *Hangover Square*?'

'A good choice, Constable. The critics are saying it's Hamilton's masterpiece. I can even sell it to you for a small discount, as long as I'm not going to be accused of bribing a policewoman!'

Abela got Harry Gough to drive him to Goldsmith's house in the Hispano Suiza as it hadn't had a run out in a while. He was pleased to see it draw approving attention from several bystanders when they parked in Charles Street. It still felt good for the once impoverished boy from Malta to make an impression on the nobs of Mayfair. He told Gough to get out of the car and wait for him in the house. Goldsmith was a straight guy, but Abela never liked to go anywhere these days without having protective muscle close to hand.

Goldsmith, likewise, had Ted Morris nearby. He was stationed in a little store room off Goldsmith's study. 'There's a nice old armchair, Ted. You make yourself comfy in here while I deal with Abela. I'm not expecting any funny business but you can never be certain with people like that. If you hear anything going on in the study which sounds dodgy, you come on in, right?'

Valerie, as promised, had gone out for dinner with the Duchess and the other staff, with the exception of one maid, had been given the night off.

On the dot of half past six, the doorbell rang and the maid let Abela in. 'Thank you, dear. My associate, Mr Gough, will wait for me here in the lobby. I'm sure he wouldn't say no to a nice cup of tea.' The maid bobbed her head then guided Gough towards a chair by the staircase before escorting Abela into the study.

'Joe! There you are.' Goldsmith bustled across the room to shake Abela's hand. 'You're looking well. Can I get you a whisky? There's a wide choice.'

'What are you having, Victor?'

Goldsmith went to the drinks cabinet and picked up a bottle. 'I thought this twenty-five-year Talisker.'

'I'll have the same with just the tiniest bit of water. No ice.'

Goldsmith poured out the drinks and led his guest over to a blazing fire and two comfy old red armchairs. The men sat down, sipped their drinks, and eyed each other carefully. Goldsmith broke the awkward silence. 'Business good, Joe?'

'Can't grumble. The war, as you know, has been pretty good to us.'

'Indeed. Rationing, the black market, the blackout, an under-manned police force, booming prostitution. You are, no doubt, making hay while the sun shines.'

'Yes, and it looks like the sun is going to keep shining for a while yet, touch wood. With the Americans now in the war, Churchill's odds must have improved a little, but the end is still a very long way off. Or that's what we think.'

'I agree. Another three or four years at least. It will take a hell of an effort to get shot of Hitler.'

Abela gave Goldsmith a sharp look. 'I suppose I don't need to ask you the same question.'

'How do you mean?'

'Well, your business can't be going that well, can it, if you're having to resort to me?'

'As a matter of fact, Joe, business is booming. I'm just having a temporary short term cash flow issue. I . . .'

'Pull the other one, Victor.' Abela snorted. 'Just because I'm a crook, doesn't mean I'm without good contacts in the City. As soon as you phoned me I made a few calls to check your situation out. I know it's not widely known but I found out about that pon-cey insurance company of yours leaving you in the lurch. In consequence you have a big hole in your finances to plug while you're out finding new suckers to invest in your company.'

Goldsmith's face clouded over as he flicked a piece of lint from his trouser-leg. 'I commend you on your sources of intelligence, Joe, but your words are a little harsh, don't you think. "Suckers"?

I've done pretty well for my shareholders, you know. "Shrewd investors" would be a more appropriate description.'

'Apologies, Victor. I overstepped the mark there. You do indeed have an excellent track record as a film producer. If you didn't, I wouldn't be here. I have little doubt you'll ride out this difficult patch as you have before and be good for the money when due.' He took a gulp of whisky and smacked his lips appreciatively. 'A very fine scotch indeed, Victor. Thank you. Now, as my colleague Billy Hill likes to say, let's get down to brass tacks. As I've said before, I'm not a one for chopping and changing. You ask. I arrange the money. Then you say you don't want it. Then you say you do. And so on. That's not the type of business I like to do. So, this is your last bite of the cherry, Victor. No more dilly dallying. What's it to be?'

'It's my turn to apologise, Joe. I'm sorry I've been so indecisive, but there's been a lot going on.'

'That's all very well but as I said before there's a price for mucking me around. "Contractual Penalty Clauses" as the lawyers would have it.'

Goldsmith looked thoughtfully into the fire. 'I've been a good customer to you over the years, Joe. Our business relationship goes back what . . . eight, nine years now? You helped me out when I came over from America and none of the legitimate sources of money would touch me. I remember and appreciate that. I understand, of course, that you only lend on a high interest basis. The terms originally agreed between us provided for such interest. When I make repayment, you will receive a spectacular return. In such circumstances, and given that I am an old customer, is there really any need for exorbitant "penalty clauses"? This seems unduly harsh for old acquaintances who've done good business before.'

'Hmm. "Unduly harsh", you say. I think not, Victor. Business is business, even between old friends.'

Goldsmith got up to poke the fire, then sat back down and spoke calmly. 'Look, Joe. There is no more dilly dallying. I definitively wish to borrow the full amount as originally discussed. There is, though, one small change I'd like to make. I'd prefer the term, if possible, to be for nine months instead of six.'

'Things getting worse then, are they?'

'No, I am just being prudent and conservative. I already have a few interested "suckers" as you put it. I want to be able to reel them in carefully and it's easier to do that if I take my time. The stronger my cash position, the better I can negotiate. Now we are here together as friends and I don't want to fall out. I propose we forget these so called penalty clauses but I am prepared to pay extra for the three month extension.'

Abela examined his whisky glass thoughtfully. 'How much?'

'I'll pay additional interest of ten per cent for the three months.

'Twenty.'

'Twelve and a half.'

'Fifteen.'

'Done. Let's shake on it.' He put his whisky glass down on a side-table, and stood up to shake hands. Abela did the same but before their hands could meet Goldsmith took a couple of jerky steps to his right. His face became white and his hand went to his throat. He started choking and struggled desperately to loosen his collar. He was unsuccessful, his eyes bulged and he fell heavily to the floor, taking the side-table and the glass with him. A shocked Abela knelt down and quickly started tugging at Goldsmith's tie and collar.

It was then that Ted Morris, alerted by the sound of smashing glass, entered the room. What Morris saw was Goldsmith prostrate on the carpet and Abela's hands at his boss's throat. There was no time to think. He felt bound to launch himself at the murdering gangster. Abela had heard the door open but not yet seen Morris. Somehow, though, he sensed danger, let Goldsmith go, and got to his feet. As he looked up, he saw Morris charging towards him. The first punch caught him on the chin, the second on the nose. It was now Abela's turn to collapse to the ground, and his head landed with a sickening thud on the fireplace's marble surround. Then

Harry Gough joined the party. Responding to the various loud and unusual noises from the study, he barged into the room. The sight which immediately met him was that of his boss flat out on the floor and a wild-looking Morris standing over him. He took out his gun and pointed it.

'Don't move an inch. What have you done to the boss?'

Again, Morris didn't take time to think but automatically charged headlong at the gunman. Gough was slow to react and failed to get a shot off before being grappled to the floor. The men rolled and wrestled back and forth. Morris managed to land a few punches on Gough's head and was clearly gaining the upper hand when the gun went off. The men fell apart for a moment, dazed, and Morris realised he was hit. He managed to get to his feet first and saw a growing red stain on the right side of his shirt. As he tried to staunch the flow with a handkerchief, he saw Gough stirring. With a grimace of pain, he struggled to the fireplace and grabbed the poker. Gough had just got back on his feet when the poker caught him hard on the back of the head. He toppled back to the floor. He looked like he was out cold but Morris bent down to make sure he wasn't feigning. Satisfied, he then went to check on Goldsmith. His boss was still alive but breathing with difficulty. Morris tore his collar and tie away, then fell back heavily into one of the armchairs, polished off Abela's whisky and, coughing and spluttering, calmly surveyed the scene of mayhem before him.

It was Johnson who took the call from the Mayfair station. He immediately recognised the address as the Goldsmith residence. His boss was out. To Merlin's extreme annoyance, the AC had strong-armed him into attending a supposedly urgent Government meeting about the soaring London crime rate. Johnson immediately rang to see if Merlin could be got out of the meeting, but was told it was impossible. So he hurried off with Bridges to Charles Street, leaving a message for Merlin at the downstairs desk.

It was past nine when Merlin finally joined them. A young

constable waiting in the hallway indicated a door behind him. 'They're in the study, sir.'

Merlin's men were hovering in a corner at the back of the room as Armstrong's forensics team got to work. 'I think we should go elsewhere, sir,' said Johnson, 'we're in the way.'

He led them back out of the study and into the drawing room where he'd interviewed Mrs Goldsmith the previous Thursday. They sat down on one of the creamy sofas and Johnson summarised what was known so far.

When the Inspector had finished, Merlin asked 'Where's Goldsmith's wife? Has she been informed?'

'She was out dining with a friend but she's been told. She's at the hospital now,' said Bridges.

'And you saw the dead body before it was taken off in the ambulance with the others? The victim was definitely Joe Abela?'

'We did see the body. I've never seen the man in the flesh, but he looked like his mugshots, and Abela was the name given to the maid on arrival.'

Merlin sank back into the chair. 'This is a turn-up, isn't it? I'm not a particularly religious man, but the words that come most immediately to mind are "God moves in mysterious ways".' He shook his head. 'Why on earth was Goldsmith seeing a crook like Abela? Goldsmith has a pretty clean reputation, doesn't he? I thought he was a straight businessman.'

'Is there really such a thing as "a straight businessman", sir?'

'Ever the cynic, eh Sergeant? Well, unlikely as it seems, the fact is these two people were having a meeting. Correct me if I've got anything wrong, Peter. Their meeting started at six thirty. They were alone in the study together but there were apparently two other people in the house, Goldsmith's driver, Ted Morris, and Abela's driver, name unknown. The maid was in the kitchen when she heard a loud disturbance and then a gunshot. She was naturally petrified but, to her credit, got up enough courage to enter the room, where she found three men out on the floor and one bleeding profusely in a chair. The initial medical assessment is that one man, Abela, died from hitting his head on the marble floor. A second, Goldsmith, suffered a stroke but lives. The third man, Abela's driver, also lives but went off in the ambulance unconscious from a heavy blow to the head. A handgun was found underneath him. Finally, the fourth man, Ted Morris, has a nasty gun wound to the right side of his belly. You were able to talk to both Goldsmith and Morris when you got here, although both were obviously not in the best of condition. From what they say, the events of the evening appear to have been a tragic comedy of errors. Goldsmith and Abela are having some sort of business meeting over a drink by the fire. Goldsmith suddenly collapses to the floor with the onset of what we now know to be a stroke. Morris hears the noise of glass smashing and rushes in from an adjacent room. He sees Abela with his hands on Goldsmith's throat. Morris thinks, correctly or incorrectly, that Abela is trying to strangle Goldsmith. Morris strikes Abela who falls, his head crashing fatally against the marble. Abela's driver hears a racket and piles into the room, gun in hand. Despite being struck by a bullet, Morris manages to knock the driver out. The maid arrives and then rushes off to call 999. Have I got it all right, Peter?'

'You have, sir. Except, from what Goldsmith said, I think Abela was trying to help loosen his collar rather than trying to strangle him.'

'Yes, well, as I said, a comedy of errors. Have we heard anything from the hospital?'

'I spoke to a doctor there just before you arrived,' said Bridges. 'They don't think Morris's wound is life-threatening. Abela's man is still unconscious. They can't say anything at present.'

'I see. And Goldsmith's stroke?'

'Too early to say what will happen.'

'Which hospital are they in?'

'The Westminster.'

'We'll get round there tomorrow morning.'

'Charges, sir?'

'Morris's position could be quite complicated. I think the fellow should get a medal, of course, but a court might not see it that way. In regards to Abela's man, at the very least, there'll be a gun charge.'

'Goldsmith and Morris will be at risk of revenge from Abela's men,' said Bridges.

'Let's worry about that later.' Merlin was weary and had sunk so deeply into the plush cushions of the sofa that he had a job getting up. When he'd managed it he grunted with relief and said: 'Give me Scotland Yard standard issue chairs any time. Let's go and see if forensics have discovered anything worthwhile.'

Chapter Twelve

The team gathered early in Merlin's office. Much had happened. Merlin asked Cole to go first.

'So, Mrs Walker has now acknowledged that the Victoria girl was her youngest daughter, Ida Walker. I haven't yet been able to get more detail as the poor woman suffered a relapse shortly after she'd told me this. As for the husband who'd left her in such a bad state, we managed to track him down later in the day. Unfortunately, while trying to escape he had an accident with a ton or two of coal and is now himself in hospital. He almost suffocated from breathing in coal dust. The doctors think he'll recover but he's not fit for interview yet.'

'Where is he?' Merlin asked.

'The London Hospital.'

'Same as the wife. That's handy for you, then. You'll be off there after this?'

'Yes, sir.'

Bridges raised a hand. 'I was just wondering what value the Walker family have for us now. We've identified Ida. Isn't that all we needed from them? Clearly the husband is a brutish thug but what relevance does he have to our case going forward? Shouldn't Constable Cole be redeployed now?'

Merlin folded his arms and looked at the sergeant. 'That's a fair point, Sam. We could certainly use the constable's talents elsewhere.

However, I think he should carry out a last interview with Ida's parents to dot the Is and cross the Ts. There is always a chance they'll reveal something else which helps our investigation. Alright, Cole?'

'Sir.'

'Inspector.'

Johnson proceeded to bring everyone up to date with the violent happenings at Goldsmith's house. He'd also had the morning news from the hospital. 'Goldsmith isn't doing too badly after his stroke. He has some paralysis on the left side but seems mentally unimpaired.'

'I'm glad his mind is unimpaired but what sort of state is it in?'

'Agitated. Agitated and frightened, according to the doctor. He's arranged for a couple of security men from his studio to stand guard.'

'I'm not surprised. And the two drivers?'

'The bullet was removed from Morris's stomach overnight and he's comfortable. Abela's man has regained consciousness. He's got a cracking headache, but they think he'll be alright.'

'Do we know who he is yet?'

'No. He won't answer any questions. I've asked for a photograph to be taken and sent here as soon as possible so we can try and find a match in our records.'

'He's bound to be in there somewhere.' He turned to Bridges. 'Your turn, Sergeant. Or perhaps we'll get the constable to do it? I hear enough of your voice as it is.'

Bridges smiled. 'Fine by me, sir.'

'Off you go, Constable.'

Robinson cleared her throat. 'We went to Piccadilly to see Mr Meyer, the ARP warden who was covering Miss Curzon's patch of Mayfair on the night of her death. He remembered seeing a man in the lobby of Seymour Mansions at around eleven at night. We haven't got a great description as his face was obscured, but we know he was a well-set man of medium height wearing a black coat, scarf and hat. As you may recall, none of the tenants

328

interviewed admitted to having had visitors that night and Jackson the porter couldn't think of a resident fitting that description.'

'So a good chance it was a visitor for Miss Curzon?' said Merlin.

'Yes, sir.'

'Could have been the drugs courier on his return visit, I suppose?'

'If it was, sir,' said Bridges, 'why'd he use the front entrance after all that palaver about leaving the back door open?'

'It was late. Perhaps he was in a hurry? Perhaps he tried the front door for luck and found he could save himself the journey round the back? Perhaps, because it was late, he wasn't worried about bumping into anyone? Remind me, Sergeant. How did Baxter describe the man who threatened him?'

'"Big lump of a man in a black coat and trilby" if my memory serves me correctly, sir.'

'So it could have been him. Better have another word with Baxter.'

'Sir.'

'Good work both of you. Now, the sergeant has also been making progress on some of the outstanding Curzon forensic matters, haven't you?'

'I've told everyone about the thread and the handkerchief, sir. The other development is that we have Miss Curzon's appointments diary.'

'Over what period?' asked Johnson.

'The book goes back a year or so but includes appointments arranged after her return from America. The Chief Inspector and I have only had a brief look so far. We're going to look at it again today.'

Merlin clapped his hands. 'Right, let's get back to work. Good. We've all got plenty to be getting on with. And Cole, this time you can take Robinson with you to the hospital.'

The photograph sent to Johnson from the hospital pictured a man with a thickly bandaged head. This obviously made his task of identification more difficult. The two-inch scar clearly visible beneath the right eye was, however, helpful. He focussed on that as he ploughed through the Yard mugshots and after a couple of hours finally found what looked like a match. The picture showed a younger man but the mugshot was dated February 1936. It was attached to a charge sheet for a minor assault in Camberwell. According to the file notes, Harry Gough was a known member of the Abela gang at that time. An addendum entered in 1940 noted that Gough had risen high in the organisation and become influential in the Abela drugs business. The man was apparently much more than a driver and bodyguard and Johnson realised his knowledge of Abela operations must be extensive.

First things first, though. They knew from Adair that an Abela man had delivered the drugs to Laura Curzon on the night of her death. Could it have been Gough himself? Johnson thought Terry Baxter might be able to tell from the photograph. He rummaged in his jacket pockets. Baxter's parents had no telephone, but Baxter had written down the number of their next door neighbour on a piece of paper. Now where was the damned thing . . . ?

It would have been great, of course, if the diary was a detailed personal one, Merlin thought. They might thus know exactly how she was thinking and feeling in the run up to her death. But there was nothing in it except telephone numbers, addresses, and appointments. There still might be something of interest in the appointment records, although they were not that easy to decipher. This was because the names attached to dates and times were in initials only. Some initials were easily identifiable. They knew Laura Curzon had gone to Gus Cowan's party on the Saturday night and this was duly recorded by an entry of 'GC 8.30'. There were two other listings for 'GC', one for lunch on the day after her death and the other for a dinner engagement on the Friday of the same week. The entries for 'MA' clearly referred to her husband. One was for the cancelled lunch originally agreed, according to

Adair, for the Sunday after Cowan's party. This had two lines through it. The second was for drinks at seven on the night of her death. The identity of other entries was not so clear.

'How about these two evening engagements for last week, "PL" and "LO"? Come on, Sam. You're the film expert.'

Bridges thought hard. He and Iris were keen cinema goers. '"LO" . . . Laurence Olivier?'

'Hmm. There was a photograph of Laura Curzon with him on her wall. But isn't he in Hollywood these days? Wasn't that last Nelson picture filmed over there?'

Bridges shrugged. 'I don't know. The only "PL" I can think of is Peter Lorre. He's definitely in California.'

'Luckily for him. He's Jewish isn't he? He did well to get out of Germany in good time.'

'The one for last Wednesday, "OP", must be Osbert Pringle, the solicitor.'

'What about this one for the Thursday after her death. "SS". Any ideas? No Nazi jokes please.'

'Isn't Victor Goldsmith's film company called Silver Screen?'

'You're right! That must be it. If you put it together with the Cowan meetings the pattern is one of an actress seeking to re-establish herself back home with some of the leading film producers. I bet you "LO" and "PL" are other producers.' Merlin turned a page of the diary. 'Then we have "C" a couple of times. On the afternoon of Friday the fifth and then the following Thursday. Cowan again?'

'Overdoing it a little, don't you think, sir, along with the party and the two other meetings?

'Perhaps they were about to do a deal?' Merlin looked at the entries again. 'She's put an exclamation mark after each "C". What's the significance of that, d'you think?'

'Surprised to be seeing whoever it was? Happy to see them?'

'Or unhappy?'

Inspector Armstrong appeared at the door. 'May I?'

'Of course, Denis. Take a pew. Any news for us?'

Armstrong sat down looking pleased with himself. 'We have identified the scent on the handkerchief.'

'That's excellent. And?'

'It's a product called "Zizonia". A perfume used by both women and men, apparently. It's made by a perfume house, Penhaligon's. They have a shop in Bury Street.'

'Well done, Denis!'

'Thanks, Frank, but much as I'd like to claim the credit, it's due to one of our younger chaps. He recognised it as a scent his father uses as an aftershave.'

'You still get the credit, Denis. It's your outfit.'

Armstrong touched a finger to his forehead in gratitude.

'That's your cue for a shopping trip, Sergeant. Better get off to Bury Street and see what you can learn.'

Armstrong continued. 'Before you go, Sergeant, you should also know about the thread. We managed to get hold of a microscope more powerful than our own. We have the exact pattern. The material would be black with a faint grey check.'

'Hmm. Now that's interesting, isn't it, Sergeant?'

Baxter eventually responded to Johnson's call and turned up at the Yard in the afternoon. His cowed demeanour of the previous day had gone and his first words were of complaint. 'I'd arranged some job interviews today. Thanks to you, I'm going to miss them.'

Johnson sighed. 'After what you told us yesterday, you're lucky to be able to seek employment at all. Now sit down and listen. I need your help.'

Baxter grumbled but did as he was told.

'Look at this, please.' The Inspector put the hospital photograph of Gough down on his desk.

'Recognise him?'

Baxter picked up the photo. 'That bloody huge bandage over the bloke's head doesn't help.' He considered for a moment then shook his head. 'No. I can't say.'

'What about this one?' Johnson passed him the six-year-old

mugshot. 'This was taken a while ago. The man's face has filled out a little since then.'

Baxter gave it his close attention. When he looked up he said: 'I'm guessing you think this might be the drug courier on the night of Miss Curzon's death?'

'You guess correctly.'

'Why's the man wearing a bandage in the first picture?'

'He was involved in a serious fight last night. A gunfight.'

'He's in trouble?'

'Yes.'

'Is he going to be put away?'

'Yes.'

'For a long time?'

'Yes.'

'And I'll be safe from him?'

'You will.'

Baxter looked thoughtful. 'You'll remember, I said I saw a mark on his face.' He considered further. There was a nervous catch in his throat when he said 'Y . . . yeah. That's him, I think. I think that scar is the mark I saw when he grabbed my throat.' He shuddered and put the photograph down. 'Nasty piece of work. I . . . I hope he's banged away for a long, long time. I don't want no more sleepless nights because of him.'

'Thanks, Terry. One more thing. Do you remember anything about his clothes? His coat for example?'

'His coat? What does that matter now I've identified his face?'

'Humour me, Terry. Do you remember the coat?'

'It was black, I think. Look, I wasn't really concentrating on his clothes when he had me by the gizzards. And it was quite dark in there. Yeah I'd turned the lights on but they're pretty dim back there and if you remember I was hiding behind some boxes when he caught me. I'd say a thick dark winter coat. Probably black . . . maybe navy.'

'Might it have been a black, grey mix?'

'I really can't say,' Baxter said irritably. 'Look, I've told you as

333

much as I can. If I get off now, there's still a chance I could make the last of those interviews.'

'What's the job?'

'Something down the docks. My old man spoke to someone.'

'Alright you can go. Good luck!'

Merlin had just got off the telephone when Johnson came in. 'Cole's still having no luck at the hospital. They won't let him see either patient.' Merlin noted the excitement on the Inspector's face. 'Progress?'

'Abela's man is called Harold Gough. It says in the file that he's a big fish in Abela's drugs business. And that's not all. I got Terry Baxter in and showed him Gough's picture. He's pretty certain Gough was the drugs courier at Seymour Mansions on the night of the eighth.'

Merlin jumped to his feet. 'What are we waiting for then, Peter? Let's go and talk to him.'

Before they could get to the door, the telephone rang again. 'Yes, Sergeant? You've got somewhere at the perfume shop? Excellent! Look, the DI and I are off to see Abela's driver. We'll see you back here soon and you can tell me your news then.'

Gough's bandage had been removed. He was sitting up in bed, and greeted the arrival of the policemen with an icy glare. His face was swollen, and the left side of his skull had been shaved. As his visitors sat down he winced as he turned his head to face them 'So whad'you plonkers want?' he asked in a gravelly voice.

'Mr Harold Gough?'

Gough did a slow hand clap. 'You discovered my name, coppers. Congratulations. It's "Harry" by the way. Can't stand "Harold".'

'Nice scar you have there. How'd you get it?'

'Argument with a colleague many years back.'

'I'd guess you're the kind of man who often gets into arguments like that.'

'Hazards of the trade.'

'Quite an argument last night, wasn't it?'

Gough turned his head to the window and shrugged but made no reply.

'It's certainly got you into a lot of trouble. Attempted murder, assault, unlawful discharging and possession of an unlicensed gun. No doubt I'll be able to think up a few more charges, if I put my mind to it.'

Gough sighed. 'Got the wrong end of the stick, ain't ya, copper? I was rescuing my boss from a maniac's attack. And defending myself from same. Self-defence pal. My brief will make mincemeat of your charges.'

'However good your brief is, you know as well as I do he's not going to save you from a long stretch. Her Majesty's Judiciary aren't that keen on scenes like the OK Corral being played out in the heart of London.'

Gough muttered something under his breath.

'And as if you weren't in enough trouble, your involvement in another serious matter has now come to our attention. You were acquainted with the recently deceased actress, Miss Laura Curzon, I believe?'

Gough was taken aback. He started to say something but then appeared to think better of it.

'We have a witness who saw you at Miss Curzon's apartment building on the night of her death. On a drug delivery run.'

'I . . . I 'ad nothing to do at all with that woman's death.'

'You admit you were in the building?'

'I admit nothing.'

'Inspector Johnson, perhaps you'd care to tell Harold here a few facts of life.'

'With pleasure, sir. You see, Mr Gough, we have solid evidence that you visited Miss Curzon's flat on the night of her death. If you say nothing, given that you are a known gangster, we would be bound to conclude that you were instrumental in her death, and a conviction would surely follow. However, if you are innocent of her death, you'd best tell us everything. If you cooperate, it may

335

be that we are able to treat these other charges you face with a degree of leniency.'

'Very articulately put, Inspector. A simple choice for you. If you didn't in fact murder Miss Curzon, help us and you'll benefit. Spin us a yarn and we'll throw the book at you. We've probably got enough already to put you away for twenty years.'

For the first time, Gough's face began to register doubt. He examined his gnarled hands as he wrestled with his thoughts. Eventually he looked up. 'Of course I don't trust a word you say, copper, but I take your point. I didn't kill the girl so where's the harm in telling you the truth of what happened that night. She was a belter of a woman and I'd be perfectly happy to see her killer swing. The thing is, will you believe me?'

'Try us.'

Gough reached out to his bedside table and poured himself a glass of water. He drank all of it down before he began.

' 'Ere goes, then. I'd been called on the Sunday by Miss Curzon requesting a Monday evening delivery. I don't do deliveries myself much but I sometimes make exceptions with special customers. You can't get more special than a film star, can you? This was the first time she'd been in touch since 'er return from America and I fancied saying hello.'

'Her husband was a customer of yours too, I believe.'

'Yeah but 'e's in our bad books. Laura Curzon was a good customer. Always money on the nail. So I agreed to personally drop off what she wanted. Said I'd be there around eight.'

'And you asked to come in through the back entrance?'

'I did. On some previous delivery runs in the summer, before she went away, there was a busybody old bag who challenged me in the front lobby and complained to the night porter because she didn't like the look of me. I don't need people drawing attention to me like that in my line of business. I knew there was some sort of tradesman's entrance in the back with easy access up the stairs. Told her to fix it so I could come in that way.'

'And you made your delivery.'

336

'Yeah. Got there just after eight. Miss Curzon paid up but said she needed more. Asked if I'd mind making another delivery the same night. Well, it was a bit of a pain in the neck, to be honest, but when she turned those baby blue eyes on me, it was hard to say no. She was a sight for sore eyes, no mistake, God rest her soul. So off I goes. On my way out, I bumped into that little squirt of a porter who I presume is your witness. Put the fear of God up him and told him to make sure the door was on the latch when I returned. Then I left.'

'Did you see anyone with Miss Curzon when you made the first delivery?'

'Nah, though I did notice a couple o' empty fizz glasses and a bottle of something good on one of the tables.'

'When did you make your second run?'

'It was somewhere around half eleven or quarter to midnight. Back door was open but I didn't see the porter this time.'

'You didn't come through the front door?'

'Why would I do that? Back door was on the latch, weren't it? I went up the back stairs as before, got to the flat and just as I was about to ring the bell, this geezer came out the door, knocked me to the ground and ran off towards the lift. I was a little slow getting up as I'd been taken completely by surprise, and 'e was lucky to find the lift waiting for 'im. I thought about chasing down the stairs after him but decided I was too old for that sort of stuff. So I went into the flat. Called out for Miss Curzon but there was no answer. I looked everywhere but there was no sign of 'er. Then I noticed a curtain flapping behind one of the sofas. The French door was open and I went out onto the terrace. Same story. Nobody there. Then I went back inside and 'ad a final look round. By that point, I'd begun to feel something was seriously wrong and decided to scarper.'

'You were careful not to leave prints?'

'What do you take me for? I'm a pro. I near as much sleep in my gloves.'

'What happened then?'

'This is the worst part. On the way there, the taxi dropped me right by the back door. I didn't go past the front door. Now I had to find a taxi home and it was late. I thought I'd have a better chance of finding one in Berkeley Square. To walk there I had to go round the front of the building. So I saw 'er. There were no street lights on of course but the moon was out. There was this . . . this awful mess on the pavement. Weren't sure what it was to begin with but then I recognised the blue dressing gown she'd been wearing earlier. I've seen a lot of nasty things in my time and it takes a lot to shock me but . . . well, I ran the hell out of there. Didn't see another soul and found a taxi in Mount Street.'

'And you went home which is where?'

'Clerkenwell.'

'I see.'

There was silence in the room until Gough sighed and said: 'As God is my witness, copper, that's the truth. Whether the poor thing jumped or the chap who barged into me did for 'er, or someone else, I don't know. I do know, though, that I 'ad nothing to do with it.'

Merlin started hard at Gough. 'What colour is your overcoat?'

'That's a funny question. Black if you must know. I have two black overcoats.'

'Pure black or is there a check in either of them?'

'No checks.'

'Matching hat?'

'I've got a couple of trilbies. One black, one brown.'

'You wore the black one that night?'

'I did.'

'What about a scarf? Were you wearing one?'

'No. Can't abide scarfs. They make my neck itch. Don't own one.'

'This man you say barged into you. Can you tell us more?'

The doctors had finally given the officers clearance to interview Sid Walker. They decided it might be best to split up. Robinson would continue to wait on Mary Walker who they'd been told would be available very shortly, while Cole would see the husband.

'I'm not well enough to talk to the likes of you,' croaked Walker as Cole entered the room.

'You look alright now they've cleaned you up.'

Walker grunted unintelligibly.

'So tell me, Walker. Why did you run?'

'Never been much of a fan of coppers, 'ave I? Just seeing you all there made me panic.'

'You must have a very guilty conscience.'

'Yeah. Well. Life's hard, ain't it? I always expect the worst. You might have been aiming to fit me up for something I never done.'

'Like attempting to kill your wife?'

Walker made a disgusting sound as he brought up a large gobbet of black phlegm and spat it into the metal bowl on his lap.

Cole looked away and waited until Walker had settled down before asking his next question. 'Why did you beat up your wife?'

'Beat her up? I just gave her a little slap is all. Wouldn't do what I asked. Nothing out of the ordinary. Thing is actually she was trying to 'it me and lost her balance. Serves 'er right. Fell awkwardly she did, that's why she's in a state.'

'She's black and blue all over and has strangulation marks on her neck. All that from an awkward fall?'

'Always bruised easy, she has. She's as tough as old boots though. She'll be fine. And I never tried to strangle 'er. Why would I do that? It was just a little domestic. No need for you rozzers to get involved. She won't want to go to law when she gets her senses back, mark my words.' Walker began to retch again and more black phlegm hit the bowl. After an interval of a minute or two, he said 'By the way. I 'eard the nurses talking. She's in this hospital, ain't she? I'd like to see 'er. Can you fix it?'

'Of course not.'

'Why's that, then? We have our ups and downs, sure, but she's still my wife, y'know.'

Cole sat down at the end of the bed. 'You should know,

she's confirmed that the dead teenager we found in Victoria is your girl.'

Walker responded with an odd crooked grin. ' 'As she now?'

'You don't seem particularly upset.'

'Maybe I don't believe it? Mary ain't seen 'er for a while. Don't see as 'ow she can tell from a stupid drawing.'

'Someone else recognised the drawing as a girl she knew to have been called Ida. I'd say it's all pretty certain.'

'If it is, so be it. Don't mean much to me. Ain't seen the girl for years, 'ave I? Cleared off and never once tried to look up her old dad, did she? Always a disobedient little bitch, same as the other one. Two peas in a pod. I . . .'

Walker paused as Robinson's head poked through the door. 'We can see her in fifteen minutes.'

'Alright. I think I'll come with you now. I'd prefer to continue with this gentleman once we know what his wife has to say.' He turned back to Walker. 'I'll return shortly.'

'Whatever, copper. I like your girlfriend. Cracking little piece ain't she? Neat little figure, pretty face. You're a lucky boy, eh?' He leered unpleasantly at Cole until he was obliged to use the metal bowl again.

Out in the corridor, Robinson suggested a quick trip to the canteen. 'We've got time for a quick cuppa. Dooley's back now and keeping an eye out for her.'

'Alright. Maybe it'll help me get rid of the nasty taste in the mouth that bloke's just given me.'

Bridges was waiting in the office when Merlin got back from the hospital.

'Inspector not with you, sir?'

'There was a message for him downstairs. He's gone off to deal with it.'

Merlin sat down and told Bridges about Harry Gough.

'Did you believe his story, sir?'

'He was surprisingly convincing, I have to say. If he's telling the truth, perhaps the man who flew out of Miss Curzon's flat and the fellow seen by the air warden are one and the same? But come on. Tell me how you got on at the perfume shop.'

Bridges blew on his fingers. It was cold in the office. The radiators were no more than lukewarm this morning for some reason. Perhaps the Yard was running out of fuel. 'So. Penhaligon's in Bury Street. A pretty swish place. There were two men serving in the shop. Initially they were reluctant to provide customer information but they came round in the end. However, they were limited in what paperwork they could show me as their annual audit was in process. Most of the sales ledgers were at the office of their accountants. They only had the records for the past month which was after the audit cut-off date. I was allowed to look through those. Most were cash purchases which told me nothing, and none of the names on cheque payments rang any bells. Then I tried a different tack and asked the shop assistants whether they had any film people as customers. The younger of the two perked up and reeled off a string of well-known names, though none with any known links to our case. Then the older fellow chipped in. "What about that film producer fellow? The loud American chap? What's his name again?" The other assistant came back straight-away "Mr Cowan". Gus Cowan is a regular customer apparently. He holds an account so didn't feature in the day to day records I'd seen. And it turns out this Zizonia is a favourite scent of his.'

Merlin whistled. '*Madre de Dios*. Murkier and murkier. We have evidence of Cowan having appointments with Miss Curzon. We have broad descriptions of a man at Seymour Mansions from the air warden and Gough which could easily fit Cowan. And now we have Cowan's favourite perfume all over our handkerchief with the "C" monogram. Perhaps we've been chasing him for the wrong murder?'

'Or perhaps he's guilty of both?'

Merlin began to feel optimistic. Things suddenly seemed to be coming together. 'Call his office, Sam. Another interview is required.'

341

Merlin went over to the window as Bridges made the call. A klaxon blasted out as two barges had a near miss.

'Sir?'

'Yes, Sam.'

'They say he's in Scotland today. He went up on the train last night. He's somewhere in the countryside scouting locations for a new film.'

'Damn it. This is a funny time of year to look out locations, I'd have thought. In Scotland, too. He must be working on something dark and gloomy. *Macbeth* maybe? Do we know where he's staying?'

'He was booked into The Balmoral Hotel in Edinburgh for the night but a message was sent saying that had been changed. Cowan's apparently been invited to stay over at someone's country estate tonight. The girl at the office doesn't have the details.'

'D'you think we should get the Edinburgh Constabulary involved? Ask them to try and track him down. Perhaps . . .'

Johnson came through the door. Merlin told him about Cowan, the perfume, and Scotland. 'What do you think, Peter? I don't really like involving other forces if I don't have to.'

'Neither do I, sir. I'd recommend patience. Cowan can have no inkling of what we've discovered. Let him complete his business in Scotland. Don't involve another force. Let's get a return time from his office and pick him up at the station.'

'I agree. Best deal with it ourselves.' Merlin sat back in his chair. 'What was the urgent message, Peter?'

'Yet more on the subject of Hess from MI5. The investigation goes on and on.'

'Is the man still telling the same story?'

'The same. He still maintains his claim that he flew to Scotland to negotiate peace with the Duke of Hamilton.'

'Why the Duke of Hamilton, of all people?'

Johnson shrugged. 'Months have passed and they still can't fathom it. The consensus seems to be building to a conclusion that Hess is mad.'

Merlin allowed Johnson and Bridges to go and deal with other duties. He opened his desk drawer in search of an Everton mint. Instead he found Madeley's notebook. He hadn't looked at it for a day or two and flipped idly through the pages. He came to the page which listed Waring, Cowan and Tate. Cowan was a work in progress but Merlin had been thwarted in regards to Waring. After his improper release, Merlin had asked the Kensington station to keep a watch on his home. The story so far was that Waring had remained indoors and seen no one. As he considered the man, he became angry again about what had happened. He was very sorely tempted to forget the Commissioner's orders and have another crack at him. They'd hardly scratched the surface of what went on at Waring's house. Merlin remembered the Penny Dreadful horror stories he'd read as a teenager. Tales calculated to titillate an impressionable teenager's mind. Satanic orgies, lustful vampires, human sacrifices, the raising of demons. He'd quickly outgrown them but some men obviously never did. Waring had struck him as someone more interested in young, naked flesh than quasi-religious mumbo jumbo. But maybe he was wrong. Perhaps the man was truly evil and Ida Rogers had fallen victim to him, somehow. He'd like to dig deeper but to go and see the man would be a direct declaration of war against the Commissioner. Was that wise? He turned the matter over in his mind and ultimately decided to shelve the issue for the moment. He'd wait to see how things developed.

As for Tate, the last name on the list, they'd done absolutely nothing so far. Johnson hadn't yet been able to confirm whether the Tate of the list and the comedian were the same man. There were several other 'A. Tates' in London. However, Johnson had established that Archie Tate the comedian was a very wealthy man, with a substantial property in a very smart part of Chelsea. He was certainly a man wealthy enough to indulge expensive tastes. Merlin decided it was time to pay him a visit.

The canteen tea was very strong. It wasn't to Robinson's taste and she'd left most of hers in the cup. Cole liked tea you could stand a spoon in and had already drunk his. After the events of the summer, their conversation had become awkward and stilted. They discussed what Sid Walker had said, the weather, then got stuck. The subject of the broken relationship had been taboo since Cole's return from Portsmouth. Thus it was a considerable surprise to both of them when Robinson suddenly blurted out 'I'm sorry I hurt you, Tommy' as they were rising from the table.

Cole was too stunned to speak for a moment but he eventually replied 'Hurt? How do you mean?'

'You know. I . . .'

Cole flushed. 'You didn't anyway.'

'Didn't what?'

'Hurt me. It was obvious things weren't going to work. With our different backgrounds. Posh girl, poor East End boy.'

'I thought we got on well regardless of our different backgrounds.'

Cole shrugged. 'The fact is your uncle's the big boss and he wasn't having it, was he? As soon as he knew about us, he had me shipped off to Portsmouth and the coast was clear for your snooty barrister friend.'

Robinson blushed. 'Look Tommy, it wasn't . . . that's not . . . it's just that you were no longer around. I had no idea if you'd be back, whether you'd got another girlfriend . . . everything just sort of happened without my really thinking about it.'

'Well, no, I didn't get another girlfriend. I thought you'd wait. I wrote . . . look, what's the point of all this? Why are you mentioning it now? It's all water under the bridge.' He rummaged around for spare change in his trousers. 'I'll get this.' He walked off abruptly to the cashier by the door.

Robinson hurried after him and tugged on his jacket. 'Look, Tommy, I want us to be friends. We can be friends, can't we?'

Cole looked her straight in the face. She was a beautiful girl and he missed having her on his arm. He tried to smile but couldn't. Instead he reached out to squeeze her hand. 'Friends? Yes we can

344

be friends. It will be difficult working together if we're not.' He finally eked out the smile. 'Now, come on, there's important work to be done.'

They were surprised not to find Dooley in the corridor outside Mary Walker's room. A passing nurse said he'd been asked to give his station a call and gone to the phone box on the floor below. The nurse also told them she thought Mrs Walker was ready for them but they still required a final doctor's clearance before they could go in. They decided that Robinson would go and search out the doctor while Cole remained on the chair outside.

When Cole had sat there before, he'd always been able to hear Mrs Walker's laboured breathing from within. He quickly realised he couldn't hear anything now. He wondered whether, as she was improving, her breathing had become more regular and quiet. But even so, to hear nothing at all was strange. Strange and worrying. Then there was a sudden sound. Not of breathing but of movement. Bedsprings creaking? Footsteps? Had he misunderstood and a doctor or nurse was in there with her? He decided it wouldn't do any harm to put his head through the door to check. He did so and got the shock of his life. A man wearing a hospital gown and face mask was bending over the bed holding a pillow over Mary Walker's face. The constable knew he had to act immediately. He launched himself at the man and tore his hands away from the pillow before reaching his arms around the man's upper body and hauling him from the bed. With a shriek of thwarted outrage, the man wriggled from Cole's grasp and found the space to throw a punch. His fist thudded powerfully into Cole's cheek and the constable reeled back towards the door. The man saw his moment and tried to push past him and out into the corridor. Cole was dazed but he managed to grab the man's gown and pull him back into the room. Then he swung his arm and connected a blow of his own. Cole heard the crunch of cartilage. The man swore and fell to his knees. Cole caught hold of the door knob and pulled it sharply towards him, slamming it hard against the man's bowed head. With a scream the man slumped to the floor in a pool of blood. As he did so the face mask slipped. Cole should have guessed. It was Sid Walker.

Robinson arrived, followed by a doctor and two nurses. Then Dooley.

'Everyone other than medics out of the room,' shouted the doctor as he tried to find Mary Walker's pulse. Cole and Dooley lifted Walker up, took him out and dumped him unceremoniously on the corridor floor.

'What the hell happened in there, Tommy?' asked Robinson.

Cole's cheek had started bleeding and he dabbed it with his handkerchief. 'I heard a noise, looked in and found this maniac trying to suffocate his wife.'

Dooley was looking distraught. 'Christ, I'm so sorry. I shouldn't have gone to make that call. If the poor lady dies, I'll never forgive myself.'

'Don't take it so hard. No one could have foreseen something like this. What was he thinking trying to bump off his wife in broad daylight?' Cole gave Walker's leg a kick.

'Oy! Watch it, copper.' Walker levered himself onto his elbows. 'You've got the wrong end of the stick as usual, ain't ya? I was just about to have a nice private chat with the missus. I was trying to make her comfortable, rearranging the pillow as she's always had a dodgy neck. Then you flew at me like a maniac. It's you who'll be in trouble. Common assault they call it.'

Cole was struck dumb for a moment by the audacity of Walker's lie. 'I'm the maniac, am I? You've got a nerve.' Cole went to kick him again but thought better of it as Walker retched up more black sludge.

'Why don't I take him off and put him in the cells at Holborn?' offered Dooley. 'You can move him on to the Yard later if that's what you want.'

'Good idea, Constable,' said Robinson.

Dooley hauled Walker to his feet and dragged him off down the corridor. His wheezing and whining could be heard for some time.

346

Ten minutes later, the doctors came out to speak to them. 'It's a miracle. She'll live. If you'd been delayed another twenty seconds, Constable Cole, I think it would have been too late.'

'Thank God, Tommy,' said Robinson.

'You'll want to speak to her, but obviously you'll have to wait a while. I'd like her to rest for at least three hours. Then we'll see how she is.'

Archie Tate lived in a mews off the King's Road, about a fifteen minute walk from Merlin's flat. He had a large property, made up of two houses converted into one. Johnson was impressed. 'Very nice,' he said as they got out of the car.

'Very nice indeed, Inspector. And if he's a drinking man, there's a very good pub just round the corner.'

'A lot of good pubs in Chelsea, sir.'

'Yes, and I'm afraid to say I think I know them all. Come on. Let's go and find out if our funny man will admit to a taste for young girls.'

Tate opened the door to them himself. He looked surprised but not concerned as Merlin introduced himself and Johnson.

'This is a turn up for the book, isn't it? What the 'eck do the police want with little old me, eh? Whatever it is, you'd better come in.' He ushered them through to a brightly lit hallway, its walls plastered with framed posters of Tate films. *The Cheeky Maid, Blackpool Tower, One Over The Eight, The Cat's Cream,* and many more. The officers couldn't help but look.

'Aye, have a good look, lads. Some of the most profitable and popular films in British movie history. You see I put the word "profitable" first. That's the important thing. No point in being popular but losing money. Or worse, being unpopular and losing money! A point a lot of the other film-makers in this country don't get. The artsy-fartsy ones. Art my arse! The masses don't give a fig for art. They want a few good belly-laughs and a bit of saucy fun to take them out of their dreary lives. And that's exactly what Archie Tate gives 'em.' He stroked the arm of his red silk smoking jacket looking very pleased with himself. 'Now, I'm a very busy man. I'm guessing you're collecting for some police charity or other. Just provide the details, I'll sign a cheque and you can be off.'

A harsh female voice boomed down from above. 'Who is it, chuck?'

Tate turned towards the staircase on their left, looked up and shouted, 'It's nothing, mother dear. You can get back to your radio programme now.'

'But who is it? What do they want?'

'It's people collecting for a police charity.'

'Oh is it? You be sure to make a good contribution, chuck. Remember, it's Christmas!' A door slammed shut.

'As it happens, Mr Tate, we aren't collecting for charity. We have a few questions for you. Your name has come up in one of our criminal investigations. As you'll understand, it's necessary for us to follow up in such circumstances as a matter of routine.'

Tate was momentarily taken aback. 'One of your criminal investigations, you say . . .' Tate looked again towards the stairs. 'You'd better come to my study. Follow me.'

He led them down a corridor leading off the hall. After passing through several doors they came to a high-ceilinged room at the far end of which stood an almost cinema-size film screen on wheels. There were several rows of standard cinema seating in the room and nearest the screen, several comfortable-looking armchairs. Merlin looked around half-expecting to see an usherette with a tray of ice-creams strolling the aisles.

'We always have a fine old time here when I've got a new film out,' said Tate. 'My "domestic première" I call it. I've had some very grand bottoms gracing these seats but I'd best not name names. Play your cards right gentlemen, and I'll invite you to the next one in the New Year.' He carried on down the room past the screen and led them through another door.

They entered a cosy wood-panelled den. Books lined every wall and a large mahogany partner's desk dominated the room.

What looked to Merlin like a film manuscript lay open on the desk. Tate picked it up as he manoeuvred himself into his desk chair. 'The second draft of my next masterpiece but one. The script of the next film is finished and ready to go. I like to be organised and plan ahead. I'm not a man for last-minute rushes.' He signalled the policemen into the seats opposite. 'Let's hear it, then. What's this all about?'

'As I said, your name came up in one of our cases. A teenage girl was found murdered in the rubble of a bombed building in Victoria. She was a runaway and, we believe, fell into prostitution. In the course of our investigation we've learned there is a thriving London trade in under-age girls. Child prostitution in other words.'

The study lighting was subdued and, from where Merlin was sitting, Tate's face was in shadow. It was impossible to gauge what effect his words were having. He continued. 'We came across your name in some paperwork uncovered in this investigation.'

'What paperwork?' There was no hint of strain or anxiety in Tate's voice.

'We gained access to a set of accounts relating to gang business. The vice business. You were listed as . . . as a major customer of that business.'

Tate's voice rose. 'By 'eck, this is bloody preposterous. I'll 'ave you know I'm a deeply religious man. I would never 'ave truck with stuff like this. On what basis 'ave you identified the name as mine?'

'There's a listing of "A Tate".'

Tate snorted. 'Is that all? There must be scores of people in England with that name. This is ridiculous. I suggest you stop wasting my time and clear the 'ell off.'

'You deny using prostitutes?'

'Of course I bloody do!'

'The gang we are talking about was run by a man called Joseph Abela. Ever come across him or his associates?'

'Never 'eard of the man.'

'It so happens that Mr Abela died yesterday and we have one

349

of his key lieutenants in custody. A man called Harry Gough. He is compromised and we expect him to cooperate fully with us. He is bound to know a good deal about the Abela vice business and its biggest customers. You should bear that in mind if you are lying to us.'

Tate slammed his hand down on the desk. 'That's bloody enough, Merlin. I've never heard of Abela nor this Gough fella. And how dare you accuse me of lying!'

'Please think carefully, Mr Tate. If you've strayed a little here or there with the ladies, we can understand. We are only concerned here with finding this girl's killer. Abela's customers interest us only in that context. If you can help us out, and provided you had nothing to do with the girl's death, we can be . . . discreet.'

Tate made no reply and for a while the only sound in the room was the ticking of a large, square antique clock on one of the bookcase shelves. Eventually Tate asked in a moderate tone 'It's not against the law for men to use prostitutes, is it?'

Johnson answered. 'Provided the girls aren't under-age.'

'That's under sixteen, right?'

'Yes.'

'And if the man is unaware a girl is under sixteen?'

Merlin stroked his cheek thoughtfully. 'That may depend on the particular circumstances. Look, as I said, we're only interested in finding our killer. We can turn a blind eye to lesser transgressions.'

Tate looked away briefly then jumped to his feet. 'Nice try, Merlin. Scare tactics, threats and enticements. But Archie Tate is no mug. I know absolutely nothing about your gangsters or this girl. I'm saying no more. If you want to ask me any more stupid questions, you'll have to do so another time and in the presence of my solicitors.'

'If that's how you want it, sir.'

'It is.' Tate moved past the policemen and led them back to the front hallway. There they found a tall and fierce-looking elderly woman. 'I thought I never heard the front door shut. These your policemen, then, chuck?' She turned to Merlin. 'Archie's been entertaining you nicely, I hope.'

'Yes, madam.'

'And I hope he's made a nice donation. He's a wealthy man, you know. He can afford it!'

'Mother, please.'

'Well you are, aren't you chuck? How much was it then? A tenner? No I bet it was twenty. That's more the mark, I'd say. That's a decent gift for the poor and hungry at this time of year. And he don't just pay out at Christmas, you know, officers. Gives a lot to the church and the orphanages, don't you chuck?' She cast a loving look at her portly offspring. 'Oh, I forgot to tell you, Archie, I did a little shopping for you earlier today. I . . .'

'Tell me later, Mother, after I've shown the policemen out.'

'No. If I don't tell you now, I'll forget about it. Forgive me officers, but I'm such a scatterbrain.' Mrs Tate picked up the wicker shopping bag at her feet. 'I noticed you'd run out so I got another dozen for you at Barkers. And while you've been busy with these gentlemen I've been doing the necessary sewing so they're as you like them.'

'Leave them in the bag, Mother. I'll see them later.' She ignored him and reached in. Tate angrily grabbed her arm and there was an awkward little tussle for the bag during which some of its contents fell out onto the floor.

Mrs Tate shook her head. 'You silly boy, Archie.' She bent down and picked up some coins and a postcard. 'Oh and look. One of my presents. I hope it's not dirty.' She stood up and held it out. 'A nice bit of sewing, if I say so myself.'

'May I have a closer look at your workmanship, Mrs Tate?' asked Merlin. 'My mother loved to sew.'

Tate's mother flushed with pleasure. 'Of course, Officer. Here it is. A big monogrammed "C" for my darling "Chucky" here. It's a Northern term of endearment, you know. Always been my little chuck, haven't you, Archie?' Mrs Tate tweaked her son's ear affectionately. Tate had gone very pale.

Merlin held the handkerchief to his nose and muttered. 'No perfume . . . yet.'

Mrs Tate heard him. 'Oh, thanks for reminding me, love.' She turned to her son. 'I noticed, Chucky, that you'd run out of that scent you like. Zizzy something isn't it? I looked in the department stores but they didn't have it. I thought you'd said you could get it in a shop in Mayfair but I couldn't remember the name. Remind me now and I'll go there tomorrow.'

'Can you speak up, Mrs Walker?' Her eyes closed again. Cole hoped to God she wasn't going to die on them. Her eyes reopened and this time the voice was clear. 'Can you pass me some water, love. My throat is sore.' She saw Robinson for the first time as she poured out a glass and seemed to become a little more alert. 'Who's this young lady then, Constable Cole?'

'WPC Robinson.'

'Pretty little thing, ain't you darling? Too pretty for the police force. Treat you alright, do they?'

'They treat me fine, thanks Mrs Walker. How are you feeling?'

'I'm feeling alive, that's the main thing isn't it? Taken 'im off, have they? My old fella?'

'Yes.'

'Brain of a maggot he's got. When you put stupidity like that together with . . . oh what is it . . . what's that fancy word begins mend . . . mend something.'

'"Mendacity"?' suggested Robinson.

'That's it. Stupidity and mendacity. That's Sid Walker.' She frowned. 'No, sorry. There's another word should be added. "Lechery". "Stupidity, mendacity and lechery". That's my 'usband for you!' She smiled. Cole didn't think he'd ever seen her smile before.

'Why did he want to kill you?' he asked.

The smile quickly faded. She took a deep breath. ' 'E was afraid I was going to tell you something. Afraid of it for months, 'e was. Stupid bastard needn't have worried. I'd have kept quiet. What

352

would have been the point? You can't . . .' She caught a frog in her throat. Robinson gave her more water and patted her hand.

'Take your time, Mrs Walker. There's no rush.'

The woman took another deep breath. 'Lovely little thing, my Ida was. Both of my girls were. Nice-natured I mean. And pretty. I weren't so bad myself before the endless struggles of a miserable life made their mark. Sid, though, was never up to much. He started as a scrawny sour-faced young man and now he's a scrawny sour-faced old man. Course, I never wanted to marry him. It was a put-up job by our dads. They were betting and boozing cronies. My old man ended up owing a lot of dough to Sid's dad. Marrying me off to Sid was a sort of debt settlement. I tried to get out of it but my dad took his fists to me. My ma was no help, so that was that. Pretty soon I realised that settlement of debt was only one part of the deal as far as Sid's dad was concerned, if you get my meaning. Excuse my French, dear, but he was a dirty filthy bastard.' She looked down at her hands which were worrying away at the bed cover. 'After we got married, Sid managed to make a living with his hands and I was able to contribute with my dressmaking. Eventually we got our own place, then the first girl came along, then quite a bit after, the second. As time passed it became clear the son took after the father. All it took was a tipple or two and 'e was off. Started fiddling with the eldest when she was about eight. I tried to protect her but I was busy and didn't have eyes in the back of my head. That's my excuse anyway. I was weak and . . . well, eventually she decided she'd 'ad enough and ran away. I tried to find . . .' Mary Walker had been on the brink of tears from the outset and now they began to flow. Robinson offered her a handkerchief and the woman wiped her eyes. ' 'Course it 'appened all over again with Ida and once she'd scarpered I was like a dead woman. I stuck it a little longer with 'im, but we were finished.'

'You left him?'

'Yes dear. Just over a year ago now. I needed a little help, though. One of my fancier dressmaking clients knew how Sid was treating me and asked me to stay with 'er. A bolt hole, she said. Miss Spring. Nice big house in Tottenham. Of course, Sid tracked me down, but for once 'e surprised me. Said he'd rather be on his own too and he wouldn't bother me provided I carried on giving 'im a healthy chunk of my earnings. I was doing quite well in the dressmaking, so I agreed for the sake of a peaceful life. I 'ad to put up with his visits to pick up the money, of course. Half the time he'd turn up drunk so they weren't very pleasant. I see now I'd have been better off getting out of London. I could 'ave lived near my sister in the country perhaps. But I'm a London girl and I still thought there was some chance my girls would try and find me, and if that 'appened I didn't want to be stuck far away in the sticks.' She looked away. 'Bloody stupid, really. They could have gone to Timbuctoo for all I knew. Anyway, after a while at Miss Spring's I found the place in Holborn and got on with my life there.'

She pointed at the water glass again and Robinson obliged. 'In April this year, I think it was, or was it May? Anyway in one of 'em months Sid turned up for one of his handouts. This time he'd 'ad more than a skinful. I couldn't understand much of what 'e was saying, but at one point he picked up an old toy I'd kept as a . . . a memento. A toy donkey Ida had loved. He sat down and started talking to it. 'E was speaking slowly and for once I could understand his drunken drivel. 'E was saying something like "You were a naughty girl, weren't you, leaving me like that. It was a pity, eh? A real pity" but over and over again. After a few minutes of this I told him to shut up and took the donkey off him. 'Is face got all screwed up as if he was about to explode. Then he suddenly blurted out "Ida! I've found the little bitch. Our Ida!" Naturally I was shocked and excited and disbelieving all at the same time. I was all, "you can't have, where, when, why, 'ow?" 'E didn't say nothing. Just stared back blankly at me as I rattled on like an idiot. Then, eventually, I shut up and 'e comes over to me. Bends down and whispers in my ear. "I found Ida, then I killed 'er".'

Cole and Robinson both caught their breath. Mary Walker's tears started again. Through the sobs she cried 'Killed my little baby! The bastard killed Ida! 'Is own daughter!' Robinson tried to put an arm around Mary's shoulders but was shrugged off.

It took a while but Mary Walker's sobbing eventually subsided. When she seemed a little calmer, Robinson asked, 'Why did he kill her?'

'That's the first thing I asked 'im, wasn't it? After I'd got over the immediate shock. For once in his life he gave me a straight answer. Said 'e'd been having a drink with some mates in a pub in Victoria. When time was called, 'e finished his drink and left, drunk no doubt. There were some girls out in the street. It was the blackout of course, and he couldn't see very clearly, but 'e knew they must be on the game. He'd be able to tell that sort of thing, naturally. For once he'd won a little money at cards and decided to spend it on one of the girls. 'E walked up to one and started chatting. After a few words, the girl burst out giggling. "God, Dad, is that you?" Well, naturally he's taken aback. 'E lights up a match to get a better look at her and, a few years older and made up to the nines though she is, recognises his daughter. Ida tells one of her mates and they're both giggling now. Then she says . . . excuse me, dear . . . that she's seen more than enough of his cock for one lifetime and tells 'im to piss off. Being the idiot he is, he goes berserk. Throws a punch and clouts 'er. She spits at him and runs off into the dark. 'E follows. They're on some sort of bomb site. He can't see much and loses 'er but then he hears the sound of crunching rubble and a small cry from a few yards off. 'E goes in the direction of the sound and lights another match. Finds she's fallen and caught 'er foot in something. They're in the ruins of a collapsed building. He goes to help her out but she starts swearing at 'im again. Calls him some things he wouldn't repeat but I can guess. 'E tells her to shut up, she doesn't, and he loses it.' She looked down at her hands. They were trembling. 'Puts his hands on her neck and squeezes. "I didn't mean to, Mary. I didn't realise my own strength." That's what he said. Then she died.'

Robinson reached for one of Mary Walker's shaking hands and held it tight. The woman's eyes darted anxiously from Robinson to Cole and back. Then a strange calm seemed to come over her. 'Thank God, I don't 'ave to keep that bastard's terrible secret anymore.'

'Did he say anymore?' asked Cole.

'Yes, but not that first time. When he'd got that off 'is chest, I turfed him out. I was afraid I might commit murder myself and stick a knife into him. I told 'im to never return. The bastard did of course.'

'And?'

'Came round looking for money a few weeks later. That's when 'e told me about the body. What 'e'd done with Ida. Said he dragged her further into the ruins. There were other bodies, killed in the raids, and the building was creaking and smoking so it had only just been bombed. He realised there would be firemen and wardens and the like crawling all over the place for the next few days. Knew there was a good chance Ida would be found and written off as a casualty of the raid. But Sid thought 'e'd be clever. Saw a bucket marked lime and thought he could mix things up more. 'E said to me that everyone knew lime would speed up . . . what's that word . . . deco . . . decomp . . . ?'

'Decomposition.'

'That's it, dear. Anyway so 'e gets the lime and covers poor Ida's neck and face with it, thinking no one would ever be able to tell she was strangled. But obviously the idiot did it wrong or something as you police could tell she was strangled.'

'He used the wrong lime. Builders' lime. That preserves. It's quicklime which destroys.'

Mary Walker looked up to the ceiling. 'Idiot. Trust Sid to get that wrong too.'

'Did he tell you anything else?'

'About Ida's death? No. But he kept on turning up for the hand-outs. Naturally 'e disgusted me beyond words but if I tried to close the door on him 'e'd get violent. Thing was, the fact he'd told me what he'd done was clearly playing on 'is mind more and more as time went on. He was getting more and more scared I'd go to the police and rat him out. Then you turns up, Constable Cole, with your news of the body's discovery. I knew straightaway it was Ida, given the location and cause of death, but I couldn't 'elp for fear of what Sid would do. When you came back with the drawings and we were both there, I kept mum. After you went, 'e was almost mad with fear I'd spill the beans.'

'So when he came round yesterday morning, do you think it was his firm intent to make sure you'd never be able to speak to anyone ever again?' asked Cole.

'To kill me you mean?' She shook her head. 'I don't think 'is puny brain is that well organised. 'E must have been stewing over things since leaving my place after you on the Saturday. He would have had a drink or ten on Sunday then come to see me first thing on Monday, hungover or still drunk maybe. The moment 'e saw me he just lost it and went for me. But if 'e'd decided to top me for certain all 'e had to do was pull a knife from the kitchen drawer. 'E'd beaten me for no real reason many times before. I think this was just another nastier version of that. Thankfully, McAllister's banging on the wall or something brought him to his senses.'

'You can have no doubt about his murderous intent today, though?' said Robinson.

Mary Walker looked away towards the window. 'No. Nothing can save him now. I suppose after you caught Sid and brought 'im here, he must've been stewing some more, getting more desperate. 'E'd beaten me badly and put me in hospital. He knew you were going to question me thoroughly. Must have decided there was no way I wouldn't tell you about Ida. Why wouldn't I now? Probably thought 'is luck was in that we were both in the same 'ospital. It was a mad, lunatic thing to do to try and kill me here but it was the only option 'e had left.' Her eyes began to flicker with weariness. 'That's it now. It's enough, isn't it?' The eyes kept on flickering. Robinson signalled to Cole and they stood up. By the time they were at the door, Mary Walker was asleep, snoring gently.

*

357

Franklin Delano Roosevelt, the thirty-second President of the United States, had enjoyed a light lunch and now sat back in his wheelchair behind the Oval Office desk. In front of him lay a list of his engagements for the remainder of the day. Shortly, he had a meeting scheduled with the Secretary of War, Henry Stimson. Later he would be seeing the Under Secretary for the Navy and then the Soviet Ambassador. His evening engagement was a dinner with the Crown Princess of Norway. Charming as the Princess was, it would be hard to enjoy the dinner against the background of the disasters currently taking place in the Far East.

There was a knock at the door and Henry Stimson was ushered in by the one of the Presidential staff.

'Mr President.'

'Mr Secretary.'

Henry Stimson was a distinguished looking man with sad eyes, a large patrician nose and a bushy moustache. An energetic seventy-four, he was now serving his second period as Secretary of War, having held the same office under President Taft almost thirty years before, just prior to the outbreak of the last World War. A brilliant lawyer, he weighed every word with painstaking care.

'Sit down, Henry. What news?'

'The Japanese are making rapid headway on the Malaysian peninsula. I am not confident the British will be able to handle them.'

'Me neither. And Hong Kong is as good as gone. What about our positions?'

'The Japanese landings on the Philippines are continuing. Their air attacks, as you know, are continuing to cause havoc to our planes on the ground. Our boys are fighting hard but we are hopelessly undermanned and underarmed.'

The President had his habitual cigarette perched precariously on his favourite ivory cigarette holder. He took a few puffs. 'Pretty bleak, then?'

'Seemingly, sir.'

Roosevelt picked up the progress report he'd received from the British Embassy that morning. 'And while all this is going on, Winston Churchill is battling his way across the ocean to join us.'

'Yes, sir. A most foolhardy undertaking in my opinion.'

'I'm with you there, Henry. As I've said a hundred times, the Atlantic chop will be horrific at this time of year, and the chances of his flotilla being spotted by a U-boat are pretty high, according to what the US Navy tells me. I tried to get him to hold off but you know what he's like when he gets the bit between his teeth. He's a little . . .' The President tapped his forehead with one of the fingers of his free hand.

'I know, sir. We must trust to God's providence to give him a safe and speedy journey.'

Roosevelt set down his cigarette in an ashtray burnished with the Presidential seal. 'I keep asking myself, Henry, why we allowed the Pearl Harbour attack to take place. The pressure was building on the Japs all the time. We had good intelligence and . . . I don't know. Maybe we should have taken the initiative and attacked them first.'

Stimson stroked his moustache. 'No point second-guessing, sir. We are where we are and must deal with the cards as they are dealt.'

'Hmm. Speaking of cards, Mr Secretary, I was hoping to put together a little poker game after tonight's dinner. Are you up for it?'

'You can certainly count me in, sir.'

Roosevelt looked again at the British cable. 'This tells me where Churchill is now, but can you remind me again of when he's scheduled to arrive?'

'December the twenty-second, sir.'

'We must hope he makes it. God knows what would happen to Britain without him.'

In his office at the end of a long and eventful day, Merlin dug the bottle of Johnnie Walker out of its hiding place in the cupboard under the cuckoo clock and poured glasses for himself and Johnson.

359

A few hours earlier, having discovered along the way that Mrs Tate had an unexpectedly inventive range of swear words to deploy when she chose, they had managed to extract Tate from his house and transport him to the Yard. The comedian had been unco-operative and refused to answer any questions without his solicitor being present. While waiting for the lawyer to turn up, Merlin and Johnson had had the opportunity to join Bridges and listen in amazement to Cole and Robinson's report on the astonishing events in the hospital.

Tate's solicitor had eventually arrived and spent some time consulting with his client. When the interrogation resumed, Tate had seemed a little more compliant. Merlin assumed the lawyer had drawn Tate's attention to the compelling evidence the police now had of his presence on Laura Curzon's terrace. When they were only a few minutes into the questioning, a note was delivered to Merlin. In it, forensics confirmed that the thread on the fence matched a black check coat in Tate's house. Merlin had put this immediately to Tate, and also informed him that an air warden had seen a man matching his description, and wearing such a coat, entering Seymour Mansions on the night of Miss Curzon's death. It had not taken long thereafter for Tate to buckle and admit he'd visited Laura late that night.

The comedian had proceeded to give a long and halting explan-ation of what had happened, contradicting himself frequently before settling on a final relatively fixed version in which he claimed complete innocence of any wrongdoing. At that point he'd complained of severe chest pains. The solicitor had insisted on a doctor being called. The medic had not identified anything serious but erring on the side of caution had advised that further questioning be postponed to the following day.

So there the two policemen were in Merlin's room, whiskies in hand. The team had had a draining day. Everyone was exhausted and Bridges, Cole and Robinson had been allowed home. Merlin was not quite ready yet, however, to put work aside. 'Peter, I know it's late, and we're tired, but this is the first chance we've had to discuss Tate and his story on our own together. We ought to go over it now.'

'Right you are.'

'Let's take a sip first. Cheers.'

'Down the hatch, sir.'

Merlin relaxed a little as the alcohol entered his body. He leaned back in his chair and swung his legs up on the desk. 'So. First of all we have Mrs Tate's nickname "Chuck" or "Chucky". I didn't have a chance to tell you before, but I called Adair when you went down ahead of me to the interview room. He told me the nickname was well known in the studio and some people used it behind Tate's back. Laura Curzon was one. That's why the meetings arranged with Tate were listed under the initial "C".'

'I'd worked that out for myself, sir.'

'Of course you had. But Adair then told me something else. Something interesting about Tate's reputation with the ladies.'

'Go on, sir.'

'Tate was notorious for his lecherous behaviour, apparently. He used his power and authority to get his way with many young actresses and studio workers. He didn't always get what he wanted, though. Some managed to escape his clutches or refused to pander to him. Laura Curzon was one such. When she was younger and less famous, she rebuffed Tate in what Adair says was quite a public and humiliating way.'

'So he could well have harboured a grudge against Miss Curzon.'

'He certainly could. Now, consider recent events. Miss Curzon returns from America with her career in the doldrums. She's anxious to re-establish herself. Tate's career, on the other hand, is booming. Hit film after hit film. Might Tate be able to help revive Miss Curzon's career?'

'Wouldn't it have been a bit of a come-down for her to be in a Tate film?'

'Maybe a few months ago, yes, but things had changed. She'd suffered a debacle in America. She still had to worry about what that vengeful American producer Max Flack might say or do to hurt her. Whatever one thinks about Tate's films, there's no denying they're immensely popular. It might have been worth her while to take a chance.'

'And so?'

'We know Laura Curzon had meetings with "Chucky" Tate. If they were discussing a part for her in one of his films, Tate would obviously have had the upper hand. He would have been in a position of power over her. Power which, according to Adair, he's known for abusing where women are concerned. So, imagine Tate in Miss Curzon's flat late that night. Knowing what we know about him and his history with her. Knowing that Laura Curzon was an extremely beautiful woman dressed only in her nightwear. A vulnerable woman who was under the influence of drink and drugs. What do we think Tate would have done?'

'He'd have made advances to her.'

'Dead right he would. Now, let's consider the story he finally settled on in our interview. On that Monday night he was having a nightcap in the Dorchester Hotel. Previously at dinner in the hotel restaurant, a screenwriter friend had given him a film script to consider. Over his solitary drink, Tate had a look at the script. He realised it had potential and, what's more, contained a part which would be perfect for Laura. It occurred to him that Seymour Mansions was nearby. Knowing that Laura was a bit of a night bird, he decided to drop in and show her the script. He found the front door of the apartment block conveniently on the latch and headed straight up to her flat, after a brief encounter with a warden. Miss Curzon was naturally surprised to see him but invited him in. He quickly realised she was half-cut and in no position to discuss any script. She poured him a large drink and started to prattle on nostalgically about the film they did all those years ago. She remembered a dance in the film and jumped up intending to recreate it. Flailing unsteadily around, she knocked over some furniture, then went out onto the terrace. She threw her shoes off, attempted the dance again, tripped and tragically went headlong over the low railing. He panicked, considered the potential bad publicity, and decided to quit the scene without reporting the accident. He hurried out, barging past a man we know to have been Harry Gough and went home to Chelsea.'

'His story fits in with the scene we found. The overturned chairs, the scattered shoes, and so on.'

'It does. It's certainly credible. The thing is I don't believe it. He's not telling us the whole truth. There's something missing. His advances to her.'

'What do you think really happened, then?'

'So it's late Monday night. Tate has had a good dinner with someone. He ends up in the Dorchester bar. He's had a few drinks. He's seen Laura only a couple of days before and his mind is full of her. He remembers she lives only a few minutes away. Maybe he has a script to show her, maybe not, but that's not what's really on his mind. What's on his mind is sex. He's about to do the actress the big favour of boosting her career and he thinks she should do him a favour back. He goes to the flat and she lets him in. She's tipsy or worse. Perhaps there are some preliminaries. Drinks, some film talk. I don't believe the stuff about the dance. At some point Tate makes his move. She resists, he persists and tries to impose himself. She tries to escape him. Some chairs are knocked over. So is a glass. She runs out onto the terrace. He chases. Another chair is knocked over. There's a struggle. She tries to scream, but she has a sore throat and nothing comes out. Tate loses his handkerchief. She loses her slippers. They end up by the low fencing where Tate's coat snags. He refuses to take no for an answer. He tugs at her pyjama top and tears the fabric – remember that tear forensics believe happened before the fall? She loses her footing as she tries to fend him off, and over she goes.'

Johnson took a long sip of his whisky. 'Very compelling and persuasive, sir. But how on earth do we prove that's what happened and that he was criminally responsible?'

'That is the question, isn't it?'

'He might confess.'

'An outside chance, I suppose. We'll need to work away at undermining his story. One weakness is the failure to report the fall. It's hard for him to justify not calling 999. Makes more sense that he didn't call it in because he was responsible.'

'Perhaps he just didn't call it in because he's a shit, sir.' Johnson stifled a yawn. Merlin looked at the clock. It was gone eleven. 'Alright, Peter. Off you go. You need your bed and so do I. We can carry on this discussion tomorrow morning.'

After Johnson had gone, Merlin, against his better judgement, poured himself a second glass of whisky. As he brought the drink to his lips, his eye was caught by a flash of pink on his desk. Laura Curzon's diary was there hidden under some papers. He put down his drink, found his reading glasses and flipped through the pages to see if there was anything he'd missed. He hadn't and was about to put the diary away when for the first time he noticed a slight bulge in the rear cover. He ran a finger over it and then over the inside. He found a small slit at the bottom. The opening was too small for a finger but he managed to get a pencil head in. He wiggled it around and encountered some resistance. There was definitely something there. After a couple of minutes of man-oeuvring, he managed to winkle out a tightly folded piece of paper. On opening it up, he found a letter written on flimsy cheap stationery. The ink had faded but he could just make out the words.

July 30th, 1936

My dearest Bessie. It's been a long time. Bill and I are so proud of you. My daughter the film star! How wonderful! I hope you don't mind if I still call you "daughter". I know we were only foster parents but you were and remain a real daughter in our hearts. We don't have a current address for you but I saw in one of the papers that you were working on location in the West Country and stay-ing in a particular Plymouth hotel so I thought I'd try my luck and send a letter to you there. I very much hope this reaches you. (I've addressed it to you using your stage name, of course!)

I'm so sorry you don't feel like keeping in touch with us any-more. We both miss you terribly. We have lots of family news if you are ever interested in hearing it, but I know you must be very busy so I'll keep this short. We are still where we have always been, but have a telephone now if you want to call. The number is EAL4831.

Wishing you well and sending lots of love
Peggy and Bill xx

PS I wasn't sure if I should tell you this but have decided you ought to know. A month ago a man from the local council called to say someone had been enquiring after Bessie Walker. Had the council any information on whether Bessie had been adopted or fostered? He told her nothing for reasons of confidentiality. How-ever he called me to ask whether we were in touch with you and whether you'd like to be put in contact with the woman who claimed to be your mother. I put him off but he insisted on giving me the woman's address. If you want it, please let me know.

The letter took Merlin's breath away. He paused then read the let-ter again. When he'd finished, he stared fixedly at his whisky before downing it in one.

Chapter Thirteen

'There you are, Frank.' The winter sun was shining into the AC's office from a low angle and Merlin had to squint to make out his boss's face. Gatehouse's mood seemed as sunny as his room. 'Come on in, my good fellow. Sonia and the boy got back to town alright?'

'Yes, sir. They had a delayed journey but got here in the end just after ten.'

'Oh, dear. I hope the little boy wasn't too put out?'

'Slept all the way, apparently.'

'And you? Did you sleep well with your household fully restored?'

'Not really, but I can't blame Sonia or the boy. It's been quite a week and my head was buzzing.'

'Success should be no cause for sleeplessness.'

'I'm not so sure about success. Our investigations were far from perfectly carried out.'

'You are being over hard on yourself, Frank. As usual.'

'We made several mistakes and wasted time on a number of false leads, particularly on the Ida Walker case.'

'The path you followed may have been a little tortuous but you found the culprit in the end. The chocolate wrapper, Gus Cowan, Waring, the Abelas. All contributed, one way or another, to the identification of the girl and the sad way of life into which she'd

366

fallen. Without identifying the girl you'd never have got to the father. And in the Curzon case you got to the culprit with, if I may say so, a fine piece of detective work. Textbook stuff, indeed. I'm proud of you and your team.' The AC's broad smile was suddenly replaced by a frown. 'And how is poor Mrs Walker?'

'The doctors are encouraging. Say she's making steady improvement.'

'Good. Good. And her vile husband?'

'Charged with attempted murder and on remand in the Scrubs. Murder charges pending.'

'Do you think he'll admit to what he told his wife?'

Merlin shrugged. 'It will make our lives easier if he does.'

'If ever a man deserved to swing . . .' The AC shook his head. 'Has Mrs Walker been told about Miss Curzon? Bessie Walker as was.'

'Not yet. The doctors don't want to prejudice her chances of recovery.'

'Quite understandable. Perhaps it would be best not to tell her at all? Such a terrible story. Two pretty sisters. One a film star, the other down in the gutter. Both cruelly killed within months of each other in the centre of London. Ida by her own father. Poor things.'

'Poor mother.'

'Indeed, Frank.' The AC looked down at his shoes and contemplated them gloomily for a while. Eventually, he looked up. 'And what about Waring? I know we're meant to leave him alone, but a little birdie told me you have the Kensington station keeping tabs on him.'

'That's . . . er . . . true, sir. I'm sorry . . .'

'No need to apologise, Frank. As long as you don't bang the man up again. What is your intelligence on him?'

'He's spent all the time since his release holed up in his house, except for one excursion to the West End for lunch. His table companion was a man whom the restaurant *maitre d'* identified to us as Aleister Crowley.'

'Crowley? Goodness! A notorious bounder and Devil worshipper.'

'From the description I was given, he sounds like the fellow who escaped from Waring's house on the night of the raid. The two men lunched at Quaglino's. I know the management there. Not a very amicable meal, apparently. At one point Crowley threw a glass of water in Waring's face.'

'You don't say? Probably unhappy Waring almost got him arrested.'

'If you'll allow me, sir, I think I have enough to go after Waring on an under-age sex charge. Constable Robinson got quite a lot more out of the girl Shirley, and one of the other girls decided to cooperate as well.'

The AC gave an embarrassed cough. 'I'll mention it to the Commissioner, but . . . er . . . I wouldn't hold out too much hope. Feel free to keep an eye on him, though. Who knows? One day we might have a different Commissioner.'

Merlin sighed. 'Very well, sir.'

'And what about our big fish, Archie Tate? Last time we spoke you said things were looking promising.'

'Things moved on after we allowed a visit by Tate's mother yesterday. She's quite a formidable woman. The solicitor had told her Tate's story and she didn't seem convinced. Cross-examined her son quite vigorously it seems. To cut a long story short, Tate conceded that what had happened was much nearer to what I'd suspected. Nearer, albeit still not exactly how I see it. Mrs Tate relayed her son's revised story to the solicitor, and he in turn advised his client to tell it to us. In this new version Tate acknowledged the dancing story was a lie. He admitted to "making a pass", to use his words, at Miss Curzon in the drawing room. When she, in his words again, "played hard to get", he followed her around the flat and out onto the terrace. He says they eventually ended up by the fence where he leaned over to kiss her. As his lips approached hers she unaccountably slipped and fell to her death.'

'I see.' The AC pondered for a moment. 'But, Frank, if that's really how it was, where's your case? It's not murder and man-slaughter looks a bit of a stretch. You need to show gross negligence don't you?'

'We do, or assault, and if it all happened like he says, we're on a losing wicket. I'd bet my pension, though, that there's more to the story. A different slant to the events he described. I think its even worse than I originally thought.'

'How do you see it, then?'

'When Tate got Laura out by the fence on the terrace, he says he leaned over to kiss her. Sounds fairly innocent, doesn't it? In his detailed admission to us, he even categorised his behaviour as "romantic".' Merlin snorted with disgust. 'From my reading of the man, he hasn't a romantic bone in his body. I know the man's character now and I've thought a lot about him. He's a nasty vindictive piece of work. I'm convinced what happened is this. Tate tried it on in the drawing room and Laura ran from him. There was no question of her "playing hard to get". She wasn't interested. He chased her out onto the terrace and cornered her by the fence intent on getting his way. He lunged and tried to force himself on her. Terrified, she resisted and tried to fight him off. He grabbed her and ripped her pyjama top as they struggled. At some point he pushed her forcefully away and over the fence.'

'Are you saying he pushed her with intent?'

Merlin nodded. 'That's my belief. He was furious at her refusal of him. He lost his temper and his self-control. He is a murderer and we should charge him accordingly.'

'My God, Frank. If he really did that the man . . . the man's a complete fiend! But how on earth do we prove it?'

'It won't be easy. We'll be able to adduce evidence of his prior offensive behaviour to women and we have the ripped pyjama top. Then we must hope he performs badly in the box. Arrogant big-heads often make poor witnesses. If we get an excellent QC like Geoffrey Fuller to prosecute, he might be able to make mince-meat of Tate on the stand.'

'If the man goes into the witness box.'

'Tate is a showman and an egotist. He won't be able to resist giving direct evidence.'

The AC looked up at the ceiling, then nodded. 'Very well, Chief Inspector. We'll do as you suggest and have manslaughter in the alternative.'

'There may also be scope for a third charge. Engaging in under-age sex. Robinson's two girls are both sure they had encounters with Tate. I'm arranging an identification parade today. If they're prepared to give evidence, he'll be up against it.'

The AC stroked his chin. 'So in summary then, Frank, and being realistic, would you say we have an outside chance of a murder conviction, a slightly better chance of a manslaughter finding, and a decent chance with an unlawful sex charge?'

'That's about it, I'd say.'

The AC looked down at the desk thoughtfully. 'In the unhappy event that none of the charges stick, we should be able to take comfort from the likely collapse of Tate's career. I'd be surprised if it survives the inevitable bad publicity. He is meant to be a family entertainer, is he not? Do you remember the Fatty Arbuckle case in Hollywood?'

'Vaguely, sir. Please remind me.'

'He was a very popular fat comic like Tate. A girl died at some sort of orgy he was holding in a hotel room in San Francisco. He was charged with murder but acquitted. The case nevertheless killed his career.'

'Tate will be convicted on one charge at least. I'm sure of that.'

'You're usually right on these things, Frank.' The AC brushed a fly off his jacket. 'And what about your other lead characters? Gough, for instance?'

'Singing for all he's worth. He's given us more than we expected on Abela's operations and useful intelligence on Billy Hill. Abela's death will create a natural vacuum which someone will try to fill. Inter-gang tensions are bound to arise and Gough's given us useful insights into what might happen.'

'Good. And the film people?'

'As you are aware, no charges are being preferred against Michael Adair. I'm not sure what's going to happen to him. The film he's making for Goldsmith has been put on hold. Even if Jean Parker is prepared to act with Adair again, she won't be able to go in front of a camera for a while. And Abela's death won't solve Adair's debt and money problems.'

'So things are looking bleak for him. What about Goldsmith? Is he still in hospital?'

'They're allowing him home on Monday.'

'Do you think he's in danger?'

'I've been thinking about it and on balance, I doubt it. Billy Hill is a sensible man. He knows Goldsmith is well connected and a hit wouldn't be worth the fuss it would cause. It would be bad for business, which is always Hill's principal concern. I'm sure he'll keep the Abela people in line. I wouldn't care to be in Morris's shoes, though.'

'No, I doubt there'd be much fallout if someone made an attempt on him. Let's hope they show restraint. And Gus Cowan?'

'It's amazing when you think about it. Only a few days ago he was a prime suspect in both cases. Now, the tables have turned and he's completely in the clear. I suppose I could consider going after him on a child sex charge, like Tate, but I don't think we've got enough. Robinson showed Shirley and her friend his photo but they didn't recognise him. In terms of third party evidence, all we really have is Miss Ryman's circumstantial evidence about the girls in the office, and that's not really enough. I think we'll have to leave him be.'

The AC gave a smug smile. 'I have a little news of my own on your film people.'

'Oh yes?'

'I had dinner with a couple of big shot City friends last night. They got a little squiffy and became indiscreet. One of the friends does a lot of business with the London Providential Insurance Company. The other manages money for a tycoon called Addleshaw. Apparently, a couple of weeks ago, Victor Goldsmith was confronted with financial disaster. The insurance company, which had been his principal backer for several years, abruptly pulled the rug on him and asked for the return of its investment. His company wasn't in a position to do that and therefore he required new backers, investors or loan capital urgently. He approached two men. Addleshaw and Archie Tate. It seems reasonable to presume, knowing this, that Goldsmith was also in touch with Abela for the same reason, although I imagine Abela would have been very much a lender of last resort.' The AC paused for dramatic effect. 'Now consider Goldsmith's position as of yesterday. Of his three options, the first, Addleshaw, had decided he wasn't interested, the second, Tate, was in custody, and the third, Abela, was dead. Meanwhile he himself was recovering from a stroke. Who or what would save him now?'

'No idea, sir.'

'You've got security for Mr Goldsmith at the hospital of course?'

'Naturally.'

'Do you know who has visited him recently?'

'A record has been kept but I haven't seen it.'

'I bet I know one of the names on the list.'

'You do?'

'One of my friends overheard a man talking loudly in the Dorchester bar last night. He was bragging to someone that he was about to become Goldsmith's partner in Silver Screen Productions. In consequence, he claimed he was going to be the most powerful man in the British film industry. Can you guess who that man was?'

'The Commissioner's friend . . . Korda?'

'No. It was your pal Gus Cowan. Turns out he's agreed to bail out Goldsmith and merge his company with Silver Screen.'

After the initial surprise of hearing this, Merlin couldn't restrain a smile. The man had balls, that was for sure. 'Good for Cowan. Good for Goldsmith too but he'd better watch out. I wouldn't trust Cowan as far as I could throw him.'

'And how far is that? He's rather a big chap isn't he?'

Merlin chuckled.

'It's good to see you laugh, Frank. Now you've got these cases solved, you can start to relax. Christmas is coming after all. Your first with a child.'

'He's not going to appreciate it much, is he, at just over a month old?'

'But you and Sonia will. Family togetherness. That's what the season is all about.'

'You're right, sir. I should make the most of it. I'm lucky. One only has to think of all the families in the country torn apart by the war.'

'Indeed. Speaking of families, I understand the sergeant had some good news about his nephew?'

'He did. His wife got a telegram confirming the lad was rescued and is in reasonable shape. He's back in barracks in Singapore.'

The AC became pensive. 'Not out of the woods yet though, with the Japs storming down the Malayan peninsula towards him. Let's hope our boys can handle them.'

'Let's hope. It'll be a hell of a battle. Do you still think it was a good thing Japan declared war?'

'I do, Frank. We could never win the war without the Americans on our side. We had blind hope before. Now we have some justification for our hope. But make no mistake. It's going to be a long haul and thousands are going to die.'

'More like hundreds of thousands, I should think. Or millions. Makes our own battles on the home front seem pretty small.'

'No. Without us fighting and winning our battles against crime, there would be chaos. And you know what I say about that.'

'Of course, sir. "And chaos, Chief Inspector, is worth a hundred divisions to Herr Hitler."'

'That it is, Frank. Care for a sherry?'

THE END

I am very grateful to my poetic Liverpudlian friend Geoffrey Barclay for his many insightful suggestions regarding this, the fourth Frank Merlin book. I'd also like to thank my family Victoria, Kate, Claudia and Alexander as always for their advice, support and encouragement during the writing process. Kate Ellis's legal knowledge proved particularly invaluable. Many thanks are due to everyone involved with the book at Midas PR for their great efforts on my behalf. Finally, huge gratitude is owed to my wonderful publishing team.